Life at the Coffin Joint

A tall woman stood at the bar, sparks shooting from her eyes. Broad-shouldered under her gray wool coat, she wore men's pants over a pair of long legs. As Boone watched, the bartender pointed toward the table next to him. The woman turned, her gaze narrowing into a squint upon finding her mark. She strode toward the neighboring table. The closer she came, the more Boone's chin lifted. Holy hell, she was tall! She had to be over six foot, for sure. Maybe as tall as him even.

"Hello, Finnigan." Her voice was like aged whiskey, smooth on the surface with an underlying rough-and-tumble edge to it. "Have yourself any exciting pokes lately?"

A chubby lump of a man smoking a stubby cigar while playing cards snorted. "Who's asking?" he asked out of the side of his mouth.

She answered with her hands, hauling him from his chair. Finnigan squawked and flailed, knocking his grease-stained derby to the floor. She drew him up to her level, her height forcing the card player onto his toes.

Boone had not seen a woman in men's britches before, let alone watched one lift a grown man from a chair with such little effort. She was as strong as any man. Hell, probably stronger than many, for that matter.

"Clementine Johanssen," the geezer next to him said. "Best not mess with that wildcat. She'd jus' soon put ya in the ground as look at ya." He scratched at his chin under foot-long whiskers. "Clem Clem Clemytine," he sang in a high voice. "She'll clean up the towny-town-town mighty fine."

"Yeah, but *what* is she?" Boone whispered.

"Corpse hugger. Undertaker. Death dealer. Put ya down and then put ya away."

She's an undertaker? In all of his travels, Boone hadn't come across a female undertaker. Not once. Not until now.

"Clem Clem Clemytine," crooned the geezer. "She's gonna clean up them whangdoodles mighty fine."

Dear Reader,

Once upon a time there was a story about Violet Parker, a single mom with fraternal twins who'd recently moved to Deadwood, South Dakota, and started a job as a real estate agent only to learn that little girls were being kidnapped in town and her daughter was at risk.

Over the years, readers have asked a lot of questions about what happened in Deadwood prior to Violet's arrival. After all, if you've read that series, you know that Violet has basically stumbled into a hornet's nest of paranormal creatures, beings, and struggles for power.

And so was born the Deadwood Undertaker series.

This first book, LIFE AT THE COFFIN JOINT, starts in late 1876, back when Deadwood was a new town full of miners, gamblers, businessmen, and a few other non-human beings who were all vying for money and control in a landscape full of gold and greed. After all of our research (and a lengthy discussion), we decided to weave non-fiction threads throughout the story. For example, the town of Gayville, named after town founder Bill Gay, was a real mining camp between Deadwood and Central City (near the intersection of Maitland Road and State Route 14). Incidentally, even though there is some dispute as to his guilt, Mr. Gay was later hanged for killing a deputy in Montana.

Co-writing a book is no easy feat, but we figured that after almost 20 years of marriage, a house remodel, two children, and a few cats we could handle this new joint project without killing each other. The good news is that after seven months we are still breathing today and our marriage isn't a hot mess or smoldering ruins. The bad news is our two children are being driven slowly insane by our constant talk about characters, plot, setting, what-ifs, and cover ideas.

For those of you unfamiliar with Old West vernacular, we've included a glossary near the end of the book.

We hope you enjoy this version of Deadwood's past.

Happy reading!
Ann and Sam

Life at the Coffin Joint

Book 1

Ann Charles
Sam Lucky

COPYRIGHT 2019 ANN CHARLES & SAM LUCKY

Thank you to the fans of the Deadwood Mystery Series. You wanted more Deadwood. You got it!

We hope you enjoy this trip to the past!

Life at the Coffin Joint

Copyright © 2019 by Ann Charles & Sam Lucky
Prescott AZ, USA

All rights reserved. Except as permitted under the U.S. Copyright Act of 1976, no part of this publication may be reproduced, distributed, or transmitted in any form or by any means now known or hereafter invented, or stored in a database or retrieval system, without the prior written permission of the author, Ann Charles.

This book is a work of fiction. Names, characters, places, and incidents are the product of the author's imagination or are used fictitiously. Any resemblance to actual persons, living or dead, business establishments, events, or locales is coincidental.

Cover Art by C.S. Kunkle
Cover Design by B Biddles
Editing by Eilis Flynn
Formatting by B Biddles

Library of Congress: 2019901568
E-book ISBN-13: 978-1-940364-61-2
Print ISBN-13: 978-1-940364-62-9

Acknowledgments

This first book in the Deadwood Undertaker series came to life with the help of several people. We want to thank:

Our kids, Beaker and Chicken Noodle, for encouraging us to stop and play during the work day.

Our First Draft team: Margo Taylor, Mary Ida Kunkle, Kristy McCaffrey, Jacquie Rogers, Marcia Britton, Paul Franklin, Diane Garland, Vicki Huskey, Lucinda Nelson, Bob Dickerson Marguerite Phipps, Stephanie Kunkle, and Wendy Gildersleeve. Your feedback was encouraging and helpful.

Our editor, Eilis Flynn, for your promptness and attention to detail.

Diane Garland, our Worldkeeper, for keeping track of the characters, settings, and more.

Our Beta Team for finding those goldurn last few errors.

C.S. Kunkle for helping readers to visualize our story.

Our readers for giving this book a try. You were the motivation behind the creation of the Deadwood Undertaker series.

Authors Bill Markley, Jacquie Rogers, and Kristy McCaffrey for your great quotes.

And our old cat Bamboo for sitting on our keyboards and demanding milk with crotchety meows.

Also by Ann Charles

Deadwood Mystery Series
Nearly Departed in Deadwood (Book 1)
Optical Delusions in Deadwood (Book 2)
Dead Case in Deadwood (Book 3)
Better Off Dead in Deadwood (Book 4)
An Ex to Grind in Deadwood (Book 5)
Meanwhile, Back in Deadwood (Book 6)
Wild Fright in Deadwood (Book 7)
Rattling the Heat in Deadwood (Book 8)
Gone Haunting in Deadwood (Book 9)
Don't Let It Snow in Deadwood (Book 10)
Deadwood Shorts: Seeing Trouble (Book 1.5)
Deadwood Shorts: Boot Points (Book 4.5)
Deadwood Shorts: Cold Flame (Book 6.5)
Deadwood Shorts: Tequila & Time (Book 8.5)

Jackrabbit Junction Mystery Series
Dance of the Winnebagos (Book 1)
Jackrabbit Junction Jitters (Book 2)
The Great Jackalope Stampede (Book 3)
The Rowdy Coyote Rumble (Book 4)
Jackrabbit Junction Short: The Wild Turkey Tango (Book 4.5)

Dig Site Mystery Series
Look What the Wind Blew In (Book 1)
Make No Bones About It (Book 2)

AC Silly Circus Mystery Series
Feral-LY Funny Freakshow (Novella 1)
A Bunch of Monkey Malarkey (Novella 2)

Goldwash Mystery Series (a future series)
The Old Man's Back in Town (Short Story)

Coming Next from Ann and Sam
Deadwood Undertaker Series
A Long Way from Ordinary (Book 2)

"Full of characters, both human and animal, you'll come to love and never forget!"
~**Bill Markley**, Author of Deadwood Dead Men

"Saddle up. You've never seen a Deadwood this spooky. Don't miss this full-flavored western with unforgettable characters."
~**Kristy McCaffrey**, Author of the Wings of the West series

"For a good dose of page-turning Old West grit and edgy humor, the Deadwood Undertaker series can't be beat!"
~**Jacquie Rogers**, Author of the Award-winning Honey Beaulieu – Man Hunter Series

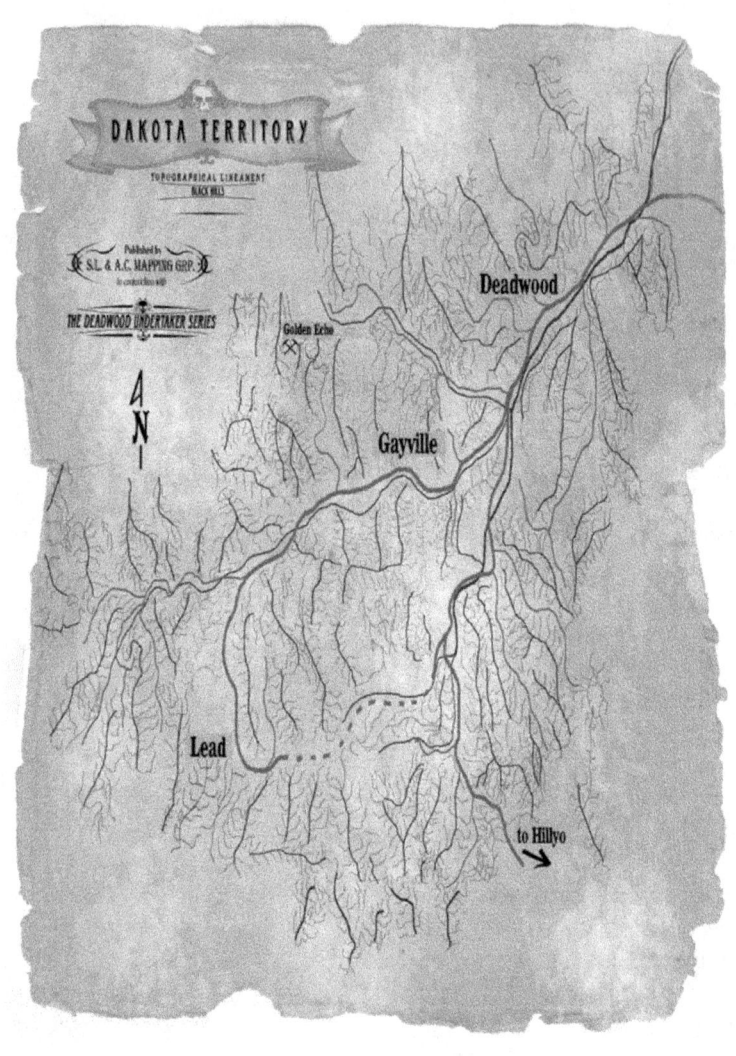

"It's not the size of the dog in the fight, it's the size of the fight in the dog."
~Mark Twain

ONE

Late Fall 1876
Deadwood, Dakota Territory

"I'm starting to see why you call this town the last lawless frontier," Clementine said, bending over the naked bear-sized dead man laid out on her examination table. After a quick search for obvious signs of death, she stood upright, wincing. "I tell you, Hank," she said to her assistant. "This business of bending over one corpse after another all day is hell on my back."

Hank agreed with a grunt. " 'Specially for someone with pockets as high off the ground as yours." He squatted in his preferred spot next to her wood stove, rubbing his hands together.

She frowned at the second corpse he had carried in moments before, this time without her help, and placed on her other table. The body looked about half the size of the first. She unbuttoned his wool shirt, spreading the fabric wide to bare his torso. Half as furry, too.

"What's the tally so far today?" She linked her hands behind her and stretched her aching muscles. Too much dallying with what Hank periodically called "buzzard bait" was going to turn her into a crookback before she turned thirty, like so many others in her newfound profession. "Five?"

"Yes, ma'am." Hank opened the stove door and poked at the embers in the firebox. "Forgot to mention we have one more keepin' cold outside in a snow bank."

One more? She already had two wrapped in waxed canvases in the storage shed behind her place, waiting to be hauled to the cemetery. Clementine was accustomed to corpses showing up at her establishment weekly thanks to the unruly streets of Deadwood, but The Pyre's business was booming lately.

It appeared she'd hit the mother lode of traveling souls on their journey to Valhalla. She frowned at the hairy giant. Or maybe the dishonorable that were passing through the gates into the goddess Hel's realm.

"I swear, Hank. Wildfires burn slower in dry brush than the dead move through my hands these days."

She hadn't dealt with this many bodies all at once since the smallpox epidemic that marked her arrival in camp several months ago. Just thinking about those gruesome days made her shudder. There'd been so many deaths, and in the August heat, to make matters worse. When she signed on to help clean up the Black Hills, she hadn't bargained on her job as undertaker demanding so much of her time, especially considering the fact that it was meant to be a front for her actual duties.

"Want me to fetch the last one, Miss Johanssen?" Hank continued to poke at the small fire, which kept frost at bay in the room, but did little to thaw Clementine's freezing fingers. "Last one fer now, anyways."

Her building was one of the few clapboards thrown up in the last couple of months as the town prepared for autumn snowstorms in the gulch. Cold air seeped in between seams in the rough-cut pine boards, but she didn't complain. Well, not out loud, anyway. Several local businesses were still operating inside of tents prone to collapsing under the weight of what some days seemed like never-ending snowfall.

"Not yet, Hank." She crossed her arms. "What have I told you about using my first name?"

His cheeks darkened under his scruffy gray beard. "My

apologies, Miss Clementine."

"Just 'Clem' is fine," she reminded him as she had periodically since she hired him.

After a small nod, he glanced toward the dead bodies on the tables and grimaced, pulling the brim of his hat lower. Clementine had seen him shield his eyes that way before around the dead.

Over the last few months, Clementine had learned that Hank Varney was not a man to be measured as average. He'd come to the Black Hills months before the smallpox epidemic to load very large bags with free gold and to conquer the new frontier. Or possibly just for the gold. But the gold had proved difficult to procure and the touch of Midas had eluded him. Hour after hour of picking, shoveling, and sluicing demonstrated both his ineptitude for mining and the pure bust his claim turned out to be. With a little luck, a day's work might result in a small bag of dust and the occasional picker, which he would promptly deposit at Belle Grande Theatre or Yellow Strike Saloon, Hank's preferred gambling and drinking establishments in Deadwood, leaving not quite enough coins to silence his often-grumbling belly.

Clementine had watched Hank for some time until she'd felt comfortable with her idea to take him on as her assistant. From what she'd witnessed, he had no real vices to speak of other than drinking and gambling. On top of that, he went out of his way to help a stranger when he could. He was the trustworthy sort, she was fairly sure.

She walked around the hairy feet of the big corpse, patting Hank on the back as she passed. "Not too much fire. We don't want to help these poor buggers along any quicker than is natural."

Clementine did what she could to control the stench of decomposing flesh in The Pyre. The cold weather helped, but the unpleasantness of her task had soaked into the clapboard walls and anything else in the room that was semi-permeable. On warm days, Hank would say, "Skunk cabbage is bloomin' again," plug his nose, and pretend to gag.

"Lucky it's freezin' outside." Hank stood. He made a point of keeping his chin and gaze lifted, probably to avoid the bodies on her tables. He looked toward the front window, which she'd draped with thin white curtains that blocked the view into the room while still allowing plenty of light to enter. "Snowin' so's can't hardly see across the street. It's a pain in my backside. I gotta get Fred the mule and that wagon moved before I can't find 'em."

"There's an apple in the bowl on the sideboard for your sidekick."

Clementine was fond of "Fred the mule," as Hank liked to call him. He had more personality than most of the scrubby miners and slick gamblers she'd met, along with a belligerent streak that served him well. Nowadays, the mule lugged more bodies than mining equipment. His job pulling Hank's wagon took him all around Deadwood, south to Lead, and clear out to Slagton when necessary.

"Let me take a closer look at this big fellow and then we can move him to the shed. Maybe stack him on top of the other beefy one." Rubbing her hands together, she tried to warm her palms and fingers. Not that her customers ever complained about her cold touch. The lack of protests in her establishment was one of the benefits in working with the non-living.

"Yes, ma'am," Hank said, his gaze still focused on the falling snow. "We're gettin' full up out there."

"I'll talk to Ling and Gart about gathering the deceased from the shed, but I doubt they'll be willing to brave this storm."

Waiting on the pair of gravediggers had become a pastime for Clementine. She paid them decently enough, but they weren't what could be considered reliable. From what she'd witnessed, most of their money went to liquor, women, and opiates.

However, in her line of work, beggars couldn't be choosers. Most folks were too superstitious to touch the dead, let alone spend days and nights digging graves in the bone orchard.

Hank was a golden nugget on that score. He didn't like watching her work on the bodies, but he had no trouble with moving them from here to there, especially when they were wrapped in canvas.

With her hands as warm as they were going to be for the moment, Clementine opened the dead man's large maw.

She made no attempt to hold her breath. Her history of dealing in death had rendered her desensitized to the unpleasantness of unwashed bodies, coagulated blood, and decayed flesh.

Mostly.

Other than a hint of tooth rot and a putrid ripeness that Clementine associated with the early stages of death, the body smelled better than most that landed on her table. Maybe the man had recently visited a bathhouse prior to dying.

She peeled back the rubbery lips. The sight of a ragged, gaping hole in the gingiva up front on the right made her pause.

"I think we have a problem," she said more to herself than to Hank, noting the condition of the flesh around the hole in the man's gums.

"We do?"

She stood upright. "This body makes two."

"Two what?"

Hank moved next to her, looking down at the dead guy for a second before cringing and averting his eyes. He grabbed a pair of surgical forceps from the small stand next to the worktable and tapped them on the porcelain washbowl.

"You're going to break my washbowl again, Hank." She stepped away from the corpse, her thoughts swirling like the snow outside the window.

"Sorry, Miss Clem." He slid the forceps back into place

alongside the other instruments. "Dead people cause me some discomfort, 'specially when they're disrobed."

"I know." She frowned at the corpse. "This is the second decedent whose maxillary cuspid on the right side has been removed post-mortem."

The first corpse missing that particular tooth had come through The Pyre the week prior. Clementine had scratched her head about it at the time, curious why someone would remove a tooth from a dead body, but she hadn't dwelled on it for long. After all, having a mouthful of healthy teeth was rare out West. For all she knew, the tooth had been hanging on by root strings and had gotten knocked loose when Hank hefted him into the wagon.

But now there were two bodies within a week that had the same tooth removed post-mortem. What at first seemed odd was now suspect.

"What's a max... maxlrary cus ... shit." Hank gave up.

"Maxillary cuspid. Eyetooth. Canine." She pulled the big man's lips back again and pointed at the hole in the gum left by the missing tooth.

"Oh, ya mean dog tooth." Hank wrinkled his upper lip, exposing his own not quite complete set of yellowed ivory surrounded on all sides by scraggly whiskers. "Lotsa folks 'round here are missin' choppers. I know a card sharp, Whistlin' Wilbur, had so much trouble with his teeth he had 'em all pulled when he hit thirty-three years, says he ain't had no toothaches since. Wears clappers. Says they wiggle some and sometimes fall out if he bends down to pick somethin' up, but ya look at him and it's apparent he eats good. He took a week's pannin' and pickers off me two nights back with a streak of luck. Started with a pair of tens."

Clementine knew all about Whistling Wilbur and his games. He'd bought her a whiskey the last time she'd stopped by Yellow Strike Saloon to pick up some raw alcohol for cleaning her instruments. His mistake was thinking that gave him permission to get grabby—first a fistful of her braid to hold her still and then a handful of her breast.

She'd gotten "handsy" right back, using her knuckles to show him how much he'd overstepped. A quick, well-placed jab had sent him yowling to Doc Wahl with a broken nose and lacerated upper lip. The touchy bastard was lucky she'd been feeling charitable that day. Next time she wouldn't stop at his face.

Whistling Wilbur, like many of the scoundrels in Deadwood, preferred to take liberties and forgo permission altogether. Unfortunately for them, Clementine was no shrinking violet, standing at least as tall—if not taller—than most men and wielding big fists with forearms strong enough to break bones.

Her size was no genetic anomaly according to her grandparents who'd raised her. Ancestors from her family line had been sizable and powerful since the time of their Viking reign. While she'd grown comfortable with her height and strength over the years, some males tended to see her as a challenge to their manhood.

Others aimed to bed her but only a handful had ever wooed her out of her clothes. Of those, two ended up taking dirt naps not long after she'd left their beds because of the shadows that followed on her heels from contract to contract. She'd learned early in life that attachments of any kind, especially those of the heart, were dangerous to all involved. Even worse, they made her vulnerable.

Out of necessity, these days she kept her pleasures private and her affairs brief. Her work allowed nothing more.

She walked around Hank and grabbed the canvas measure from the stand. "I need you to hold this on his big toe," she said, handing Hank one end of the measure.

He followed her instructions with a grimace aimed at the man's face. "Sure is a strange-lookin' fella. Never saw a jaw and nose that big. Kinda like an animal. A wolf or bear or somethin'.

Bet this 'Big Joe' could really swing a sledge. Bet he broke more'n one on a rock or two."

Big Joe? Not having found a proper name for the corpse since it had come to them without a stitch of clothing on it, Clementine supposed Hank's nickname was as good as any. More than a few of Deadwood's inhabitants had ended up in unmarked graves in Ingleside, nameless and forgotten.

Hank's gaze drifted down over Big Joe only to come to an abrupt stop at the large protrusion south of his belly button. He focused on his finger holding the measure. "Uh, Miss Clem?"

She tried to hide her smile at his blush. "Yes, Hank?"

"Do you really need 'em unshucked?" His voice sounded slightly higher than normal.

"You're the one who brought him to me without clothes, remember? My britches may be big for a girl, but they're not big enough to fit Joe here."

"Yeah, but I had him covered up good with canvas."

She focused her attention on the measuring rule she had pressed to the top of Big Joe's slanted forehead. "Seven feet, three inches."

Damnation. This one had been a giant among men.

She tugged the canvas rule from beneath Hank's finger, staring down at the dead man as she rolled up the measuring rule. Where had he come from? How long had he been in this part of the country? She would've remembered seeing him around Deadwood, so it couldn't have been long.

She set the rule down on her instrument table and returned to Big Joe's corpse. She lifted and examined both his massive arms, checking for anything out of the ordinary, but found nothing to explain the cause of his demise. The post-mortem tooth removal and chew marks on his thigh obviously weren't fatal. In fact, she found no sign of major trauma at all excepting a round, slightly swollen, purplish bruise on his upper abdomen that measured about three inches in diameter with a hole in the center the size a small-caliber bullet or slender knife would make.

She took another look at the hole in the middle of the bruise. How could such a small wound take down a giant like Big Joe?

She didn't think it could. There was only one way to know for sure, and that meant slicing him open to see what was going on under the surface.

"Great Odin's sow," she muttered, using her grandfather's favorite curse at the mess that would surely follow her carving into Big Joe.

"Can we move the large fella to the shed now, Miss Clem?" Hank was back at the stove, warming his hands.

"Not yet. I need your help turning him over. Grab above the ankles, will you?"

"Oh, Miss Clem." His forehead wrinkled. "He's in his altogether."

And he looked to be even hairier on his backside, a sight Clementine didn't relish witnessing. Some grisly sights took longer to clear from her mind, and she had a feeling this one would haunt her for a good length of time due to Big Joe's size and girth. However, her job as a caretaker of the dead—and the other work for which she'd been contracted—left her no other option.

"Hank, I thought we'd already established the fact that this man was without clothing."

"Yeah, but ..."

"Close your eyes then, but grab above his ankles first."

"When I ... couldn't we ... okay." He straightened his shoulders, appearing to bolster his resolve, and took hold of Big Joe's ankles. "But if this pilgrim sets off any more vapors—"

"Turn!"

She grunted as she pushed on Big Joe's stiff shoulder while Hank twisted on the dead man's thick legs. The corpse rolled over, almost sliding off the pine slab before Clementine could catch it.

As soon as Big Joe was stable, Hank returned to the stove and stabbed at the embers inside the firebox again. "That man ain't right."

Clementine suspected Hank was more spot-on with that assessment than he realized. Steeling herself, she continued to search for any signs of trauma on Big Joe's backside, crevices and all. She looked for something besides that odd wound on his upper abdomen, for anything else that could be the cause of death.

After several moments she cursed again and stepped away from the body. Nothing. Her gaze traveled down Big Joe's corpse. Make that nothing besides a remarkably muscled build under an even more impressive crop of body hair. Seriously, this man probably didn't need a coat even in the snow and wind. In that matter, she envied him. He had a natural fur pelt.

"It appears this man was shot or possibly stabbed. It doesn't seem likely he died from such a small wound. But ..." She trailed off, her thoughts moving faster than her lips.

"But what?"

Miners often died in accidents that involved asphyxiation, falls, or cave-ins. Most of the men she'd dealt with who were victims of mining accidents displayed more widespread or apparent bodily damage. Crushed torsos and skulls were more common on her worktable than gunshot wounds some weeks.

"Never mind," she said to Hank. "Help me turn him over onto his back again."

She knew her take on a client's cause of death didn't usually hold much interest for Hank. He was more concerned with fetching and moving corpses, or running errands for her. Occasionally, he worried out loud about some of the corpses waking up on his watch and demanding he take them back to where he found them.

Hank helped without comment this time, his gaze holding steady on the dead man's feet while they repositioned the body.

After they had Big Joe belly-up again, Clementine turned to the smaller, leaner body on the other table. She did a swift search from top to bottom, removing his raggedy clothing as she progressed. In the process, she discovered a knife wound below and in front of the left armpit and a slashed Achilles tendon.

The wounds told a fairly clear story. First the victim had been disabled by the severing of his tendon. Then, a skillful thrust with a slender blade straight into the left thoracic cavity had finished the job.

The knife wound was much cleaner than most others she'd seen since coming to Deadwood. Usually, there were multiple, jagged stab wounds and knife tears placed randomly during the heat of a battle. But this blade had been adeptly guided between ribs to pierce the left lung and probably the heart.

In other words, the murderer knew his way around knives and swords. An ex-member of the military, maybe? Deadwood certainly had plenty of Civil War veterans roaming the gulch, playing bounty hunter, miner, or gun for hire. Some were trying to shake off the horrors of war and build a new future. Others were bored and looking for trouble wherever it could be found ... especially in this unruly frontier.

Upon a second closer inspection, Clementine noticed the dead man's scuffed palms and knees. She suspected he'd groveled or attempted a crawling escape before the blade penetrated his lung and heart. He'd bled to death as his heart pumped blood into his chest cavity.

A miserable way to die, certainly. Not that there were many good ways to make peace with the ground, but the quicker the better in Clementine's experience.

This corpse still had all of its teeth, although several molars smelled of rot. Judging by the layer of dirt behind the dead man's ears and between his toes, not to mention the rank odor from his armpits and nether regions, he hadn't seen the wet side of a washrag in weeks.

She moved to the feet, grabbing the dead man's legs. "Let's move this one out to the shed, Hank, and then you can bring in the last one."

"What about Big Joe?"

"I'm going to need to look him over a little more first."

They made fast work of carting the knife victim to the shed. Clementine palmed the few coins Hank had found in the dead man's pockets, extracting enough for her time and pine-box services before dropping the remaining pieces into a "collection" bowl she kept tucked away in her work desk in the exam room. This spare money was used to pay for those who passed through The Pyre without any money to cover the cost of their burial.

"Would you like help bringing in the last body?" she asked, following Hank to the front door.

"No, Miss Clem. This one's even lighter than the last." He closed the door behind him.

While she waited, Clementine wiped down the empty examination table with raw alcohol.

The cold wind blew snow inside with Hank when he returned, the body draped over his shoulder. He kicked the door closed behind him and carried the corpse through the parlor and into the exam room, lowering it onto the table with more care than most others he handled.

She unwrapped the waxed canvas. One look into the empty eyes of the dead explained his tender touch. It was a female with extensive bruising on her face.

An ache tightened Clementine's gut as recognition washed over her. "Oh, Ginny," she whispered.

Ginny was one of the working girls from Yellow Strike Saloon. An innocent, simple spirit who'd been tricked into coming to this land of greed and wickedness.

Clementine didn't bother stripping off the young prostitute's clothes. There was no need. Judging from the swollen contusions on her head and the bloodstains on her bloomers, she could guess the cause of death. The girl had been bludgeoned to death by one of the many vile miscreants in town who roughed up whores to get their peckers hard.

Whether Ginny had been raped before or after she'd died, Clementine wasn't sure she wanted to know. But if she found out who was responsible for the girl's demise, there'd be hell to pay, and Clementine was going to relish collecting the toll.

She motioned for Hank to take Ginny out back with the others, adding, "When you're finished, wash up and head on out for the night."

"So we're just leavin' Big Joe where he is?"

What she had planned for Big Joe was going to be messy. She'd have to lock the doors and close the shutters Hank had built for her privacy. Thankfully, her oil lamps were full with plenty of wick left to take her deep into the night.

"Don't worry about him for now."

"You sure, Miss Clem?"

She nodded, untying the bag filled with coins someone had left tied to Ginny's dress. She had no doubt that the money was sent to cover the girl's funeral costs. This wasn't the first time Clementine had taken care of a dead prostitute, nor would it be her last in this godforsaken place.

She handed the bag to Hank. "Here. Go and enjoy something that smells better than Big Joe."

After Hank carried the dead girl out the back door, Clementine strolled over to the window, peeking out through a part in the thin curtains. It seemed so peaceful out there in the growing darkness.

The snow was too deep now for wagons, and few folks were willing to brave the way on foot. She glanced down the street toward Yellow Strike Saloon. Most likely, the saloons and brothels lining Deadwood's rowdy streets were bursting at the seams with lonely, rough sorts who were busy drinking, gambling, and whoring to pass the time.

Clementine rubbed her arms, trying to warm them through her wool shirt. She doubted anyone suspected that a killer with a fetish for collecting canine teeth was hiding somewhere in the midst of it all … anyone except for her.

TWO

If there was one thing Jack "Rabbit" Fields had learned from riding trails for years it was to keep his pistols handy. This morning was no exception, but trudging through knee-deep snow on the steep side of a hill had put a crook in his usual style. He unbuckled his gun belt, brushed the snow from the leather holsters, and draped his two-gun rig over the saddle on his buckskin, Dime.

"What are you doing, Rabbit?" Boone McCreery asked from behind him.

Boone had been Rabbit's best friend since they were two young whelps no taller than the tops of a coyote's ears. It was Boone's bright idea to bring up the rear this morning, keeping an eye out for trouble from behind while Rabbit broke trail. "You need to keep your cannons on your hips. I'm dead certain that cat is still ghosting us."

"Ain't no cat." Rabbit didn't look up from the harrowing slope they were halfway across, stepping carefully. One misstep and he might slide right down over the edge of the cliff and into the canyon below, trading in his banjo for a harp before the sun even peaked in the sky. "Not so stealthy as a cat. Peculiar it ain't spookin' the horses."

"You should lay up for a little while at the top of the next hill and wait for it to poke its head over that ridge again," advised Boone, who liked to think he was the boss of their operations being he was a hiccup older than Rabbit. "The taste of your lead might discourage it from thinking we're its next meal."

Boone was quick with his pistol, but Rabbit was quicker and they both knew it. He was white lightning on the draw with a dead-on aim to follow it through.

Unlike many practiced gunmen, Rabbit came by his skill naturally, which was partly how he'd landed his nickname. In his greenhorn years, he'd enjoyed putting on a show and wowing folks with his slick pistol work and marksmanship with a rifle. These days, he'd grown more wary after dealing with one too many up-and-coming hotshots with more guts than brains who were determined to show the world they were the next Wild Bill or Johnny Hardin. "Deep with guts but shallow with brains" was his assessment.

Quick as Rabbit was, most folks would be hard pressed to choose which of the men was more dangerous, him or Boone. Only the fools too ignorant or drunk to know better tangled with either one. Time and plenty of trail dust had earned them the moniker "The Santa Fe Sidewinders," which made Boone cringe and bellyache every time he heard it. Rabbit, on the other hand, grinned wide.

"Don't think I need to shoot it," Rabbit told Boone. He squinted at the group of trees on the ridgeline Boone kept eyeing. He rested one hand on the Sharps rifle stowed in its scabbard, just in case. "More than fifty yards between us. He's only watchin'. Too big to be a cat, though. Maybe some kind of bear. But it can't be."

"Well, just the same, let's keep moving."

"I'm doin' my best, considerin' all this goldurn snow in my way."

"And be ready with that cannon," Boone added. "I'd hate for you to have to down a big cat, but if it comes, it'll be quick."

If it came, it'd end up dead.

Rabbit pushed onward, reaching the more sure-footed safety of the trees again. The snow wasn't as deep here, but still hindered.

Last night's storm had amounted to two feet of windblown powder before petering out mid-morning. Sleeping had been almost impossible with the whistling wind and stinging cold nipping at them all night. They'd broke camp soon after the sky cleared and continued on their way, spending part of the time in the saddle and part on foot to rest the horses. Another hour or two should see them into Deadwood shortly after noon, if all went right.

Every bit of the trail from Cheyenne on northward had been some kind of grief. Blistering winter storms, knee-deep mud, snow and frigid water crossings. The snow-covered ice was the worst. Rabbit had landed on his ass more than once with a good dose of cussing each time. Same with Boone. The last thing they needed was one of their horses breaking a leg in the middle of nowhere.

Then there was the band of road agents bent on taking what didn't belong to them. They were easy enough to deal with compared to the weather, though. Rabbit and Boone had plenty of experience with big mouths, slow wits, and even slower guns.

Rabbit crested the top of yet another hill, pausing to catch his breath, huffing steam like a locomotive as he stared out over the treetops. In the distance, he saw a column of smoke. He glanced back at Boone. "Told you."

"You told me what, exactly?" Boone asked when he'd closed the gap between them.

"We coulda' pushed in last night. Slept in warm beds with good grub in our bellies, maybe a wom—"

"Seal up your lips." He joined Rabbit overlooking the hills and surrounding gulches. "In case you didn't notice, it's dark at night. You'd have taken a bad step and tumbled down that cliff back there. No question. And," Boone raised his pointer finger for emphasis, "maybe it escaped your attention, but it was snowing a wee bit last night."

A gust of wind swept up a cloud of icy particles and swirled it into their faces. Both men paused to dip their broad-brimmed hats into the wind. The horses had no such luxury as hats and took the freezing blasts head-on.

"Wind sure has some winter in it," Boone muttered.

"We could've at least stayed back at Hillyo." Rabbit closed the lapels of his coat over the lower part of his face, knocking loose the frost that had accumulated on the hairs of his moustache. It was a good bet their horses would have voted for a night in Hillyo as well.

"It would have been dark tonight before we reached Deadwood if we'd done that," Boone shot back.

Maybe so, but they might have missed the damned storm. Rabbit started down the hill, digging his heels in and taking it at an angle. "Another hour or so and we should be in town."

They slogged on, stepping once again through knee-deep powder in the clearings with the horses following, their heads hung low.

Life at the Coffin Joint

Rabbit and Boone's introduction to life on the trail had begun on a wagon train headed for California. Five-year-old, towheaded Rabbit had ridden on a heavy buckboard wagon next to his ma while his pa walked alongside to save pulling weight for the horses. They'd sold about everything they owned in Virginia to "build the biggest ranch west of the Mississippi," his father had boasted to those who'd asked, or didn't.

Those big plans were long gone now, same as his parents.

Boone's story was similar, but he was half a year older than Rabbit and his family was from Youngstown, Ohio. Rabbit quickly found a friend and fellow troublemaker in the young dark-haired boy as they bounced along the Santa Fe Trail. If it hadn't been for the move west, Rabbit would have been wearing gray and Boone wearing blue during the war, sworn enemies. Funny how things worked sometimes. That didn't keep them from barking and snarling back and forth some days.

The pines grew thick again, limiting their view to trees, sky, and the next turn in the trail. It wasn't long before they'd walked themselves into a rhythm of crunching snow, labored breathing, and the occasional nicker from an unhappy horse. The fresh snow was keeping trail traffic non-existent, excepting the two fools from New Mexico.

Rabbit stopped to catch his breath again, gazing out over another steep slope and drop off on the right. The blue sky set against the dark pines and pure white snow made for a mighty fine sight of Mother Nature's beauty, but he was ready to peer into the bottom of a shot glass and enjoy the fire of whiskey in his belly and a warm woman in his bed. He turned back to Boone. "I swear, if Uncle Mort ain't in Deadwood and we gotta drag our sorry asses through more snow, I'm gonna—"

Boone caught the tip of his boot on a snag of tree root hidden under the snow. He stumbled forward, winding his arms wildly to regain his balance, but his momentum carried him to the ground chest first. He slid down the steep slope, heading straight for the edge of the drop-off, clawing at the snow and small saplings as he went.

"Raaabiiiit!" His howl echoed down into the canyon below.

Quicker than the snap of a bullwhip, Rabbit leapt through the snow, racing to head off Boone at the cliff's edge. He dove head first as Boone neared the rim. He flew across the snow with enough speed to catch the ankle of Boone's boot as his upper half disappeared over the edge.

"Gotcha, ol' man!" Rabbit dug the toes of his boots into the snow and rocks, holding onto Boone's ankle with both hands. As he worked his way up onto his knees, an icy gust lifted Boone's hat from his head and swirled it slowly down, depositing it in the trees far below.

Grunting and tugging, Rabbit hauled Boone back onto solid ground. They both stilled for several seconds, huffing steam in the cold, pine-scented air.

"Sonofabitch! That was too dang close, Booney." Rabbit got up and shook himself. He peered over the edge of the cliff. "You ain't gettin' that hat back. Might as well floated off the edge of the world."

Boone rolled over and sat up, snow packed into every nook and cranny of his front side, turning his black hair and beard almost white. He blew a tiny snowball from each nostril and shook his head. "I do believe I have a firm understanding of the geological—"

Nickel grunted and tore at the snow with his front hooves. Rabbit looked up toward the horses in time to see Nickel rear up, kicking his front legs at the air.

Rabbit scrambled up the slope to the trail. Before he could grab Dime's reins, both horses spun around, dug trenches in the white fluff with their back hooves, and bolted back down the trail the way they'd come, leaving rooster tails of snow in their wake.

"Shit! Git back here with my guns!" Rabbit glared after the

horses. There was no use chasing, he'd never catch them. He turned to Boone. "What in tarnation sent Nickel runnin' for the—"

A heavy *thwump* on the snow behind him had him reaching for his pistol as he spun around.

Unfortunately, his guns had galloped back down the trail.

"What the hell is that?" Boone asked.

Not ten feet away crouched a white-haired creature big as a grizzly with a mouth overflowing with long, pointy teeth.

"This here critter is what's been stalkin' us for the last ten miles, waitin' for the opportunity to ambush."

Boone cursed. "I told you to shoot it back there."

The creature's chest rumbled with a growl. It sized them up with its milky eyes, Rabbit on the left, Boone on the right. Then it lowered its head, eyes steady on Boone. It opened its jaws and clacked its sharp spiky teeth together several times.

Rabbit pulled out his Bowie knife a split second before Boone grabbed his. "*And* I told you it wasn't no cat." He stepped farther away from his friend, attempting to flank the beast. "If one of us can get behind the thi—"

It lunged at Boone.

"Look out!" Rabbit shouted, but Boone was ready. While the toothy bastard was still in the air, Boone stepped right and spun left, lifting the knife high. He dug his boot in and stopped his spin square with the beast's side and brought the blade down hard, tip first, sinking it deep into its hindquarter. As he pulled his blade free, the creature twisted around, extending a thick paw bristling with dagger-like claws. It swiped at Boone, connecting with his backside, and sent him flying into a rocky bank.

The creature turned, but Rabbit was one step ahead of the milky-eyed hunter. He sidestepped its lunge and twisted around to position himself at the beast's side as it landed. He raised his knife with both hands and with a grunt buried the blade to the hilt between its ribs.

It roared, clawing at the air where Rabbit had been a second prior. Before it could get its bearings, Rabbit rammed into the beast's side, sending it slipping and sliding down the slope. With one last snarl, the white beast disappeared over the edge of the cliff. The sound of tree limbs cracking and breaking below ripped through the air, followed by a muffled thump.

Rabbit rushed to Boone, who was sitting upright with a grimace on his face, holding his shoulder. "Fucker took my pig sticker with it, Booney!" He moved Boone's hand away from his shoulder to examine the damage. "Your sheepskin is ripped up some, but the beastie didn't draw no blood." He sat back on his haunches and blew out a breath of relief. "You gotta be quicker, ol' man. How's your head?"

Boone touched the side of his head then looked at his palm. He must have been expecting blood, or worse, but Rabbit had seen the whole thing. Boone's shoulder had borne the brunt of the impact against the rocks.

Boone rotated his arm and winced. "That's going to slow me up a little. Least it's not my gun arm."

Rabbit chuckled. "Don't think it'll make no difference no how. Pure blackstrap molasses with that pistol."

"Stuff a carrot in it, bunny rabbit. And quit calling me 'old man.' I'm just enough older to know more than you do." Boone pushed to his feet and gave a loud, low-to-high whistle. Holding his shoulder, he eased down the slope to the edge of the cliff. "It isn't down there," he said, peering into the canyon below. "Looks like it left a trail of broken tree limbs and sprigs where it ran off, though."

Rabbit joined him. "Didn't leave much blood. We both stuck it pretty good, but it still vamoosed like a sidewinder in hot sand." He turned back to the trail. "I hope Nickel and Dime are headed back. Don't really wanna go after them."

"If Nickel heard me, he'll be along shortly."

It was no secret that Boone trusted his piebald almost as

much as he trusted Rabbit. He'd found Nickel as a foal nearly dead from dehydration on a freight run near Camp Nichols along the Cimarron Cut to Fort Dodge. Boone nursed little Nickel back to health, and with Uncle Mort's experience had him bridlewise by the age of three. The two had been together long enough now that a nudge, tongue click, or nod from Boone was direction enough for the horse.

Rabbit glanced back down into the canyon below. "Weren't no puma or bear." He rubbed the back of his neck. "Weren't no wolf either. What the hell was that thing? Are there animals up this way we don't know? I mean, we seen some things in our travels, but that thing was just plumb *loco*."

Boone frowned at Rabbit, shaking his head slowly. "What are we getting into?"

The *clomp-swish-clomp-swish* of hooves in the snow interrupted Rabbit's reply as they turned to watch the horses trot around a bend in the trail. Dime followed right behind Nickel, who was faithfully returning to his best buddy, Boone.

Rabbit scoffed, climbing up the slope to the horses. "Nice of you boys to drop in."

Nickel pulled up alongside them, ears tall and alert, turning his head this way and that. Dime snorted, nudging Rabbit in the shoulder, looking for comfort.

Rabbit checked his gear and found it all in order, including the gun belt he'd left secured over the saddle.

Boone did the same.

"I coulda used this, ya know," Rabbit told Dime as he wrapped the gun belt around his waist. The horse nickered, his unease apparent in his flared nostrils and wide eyes. "Dime says we oughta dash, Booney."

Boone climbed up on Nickel with a grunt, still holding his shoulder. He settled in. "You could have named that plug anything, but you went and chose 'Dime.'"

"Thought it fittin' since he's worth more than that plug of

yours." Rabbit got a kick out of their mounts' matching names. He suspected Boone felt the same, but the old boy was too hardheaded to admit it.

"You would, Rabbit. Let's get out of here before that white grizzly comes back for seconds." Boone gave a squeeze with his knees to start the moseying in motion.

Rabbit shot one last glance toward the cliff's edge. Just what sort of critters were they growing up here in the Hills, anyway?

He nudged Dime to follow Nickel and then pulled out his pistol, double-checking the chambers were full and ready in case their stalker returned for the kill this time.

THREE

Boone shifted in his saddle and winced. This week was going to hell in a bucket.

He'd been shot at by road agents, frozen his onions off in a godforsaken snowstorm, and then lost his favorite hat when he'd nearly slipped off the edge of that damned cliff. Being thrown into a rock wall was no Saturday dance either. Lucky for him a group of saplings helped cushion his shoulder, which throbbed plenty now, the muscles likely good and bruised. Nothing that a bottle of mescal wouldn't fix, though, so long as he could make it to Deadwood in one damned piece.

Bracing against the freezing gusts of wind blowing snow off the trees and into his face, he rode along with Rabbit trailing. It wasn't long before they reached the outskirts of Deadwood and began to see signs of life. A wisp of smoke from a chimney, a small cabin up the hillside, then another. Soon, the snow along the trail had been plowed by one horse, and then two. With the trail blazed, the landscape rolled by more quickly. Wagon tracks joined, looking like endless lines of rope to each side of the hoof prints.

The "not a cat" hadn't returned, but Boone felt no need to mention it. He could see that Rabbit was more at ease with each additional sign of civilization, too.

If Deadwood could be considered civilization.

"Heard this was a busy little burg," he said to Rabbit. "But I'm not seeing much to support that notion. Could be the snow's a deterrent." Boone stuck his hand in his coat pocket to grab a chunk of chaw and frowned. "Shit."

Rabbit chuckled but it came out a snort probably due to the frost built up on the whiskers under his nose. "Why'd ya quit, anyway?"

Rabbit had never been partial to tobacco, smoked or chewed, and had made no secret of his dislike for Boone's short-lived habit. Boone had heard countless times, "That shit's givin' you nasty brown teeth," or "Your breath smells like a dog's ass."

Hell, Boone didn't like the smell either, and he hated the gobs of chaw and spit peppered around spittoons and boardwalks. His preference was tequila, whiskey, and a bit of chocolate, when he could get it.

He glanced back at Rabbit. "Maybe I was plain tired of hearing you caterwaul about it, old biddy."

"Just watchin' out for you. Besides, you're savin' money now."

Boone's smile was one-sided. As if money was ever a concern for Rabbit.

The tents and shacks grew thicker along the creek as they wound their way down through the gulch. The occasional miner they spotted working a claim near what they were told was Gold Run Creek became two, then eight, then more than could be counted. Soon, the miners trekking to and from their claims on foot, horseback, and wagon became a nuisance to navigate around.

"Never feels right headed north down a hill," Rabbit said.

Boone nodded, wishing he had his hat to pull down low. His ears could use the protection, too. They burned in the cold gulch, almost as much as the back of his throat from the smoky air.

They rounded a bend and the young but thriving little town came into view. Cradled between two high ridgelines with not more than a half-mile between them, a name with "gulch" in it was fitting. Most of the timber had been cut, and it was obvious men were set on removing the rest. The miners' shacks and cabins had given way to one long main street lined with the businesses essential to supplying the miners and gamblers that ceaselessly poured into the growing town.

Mercantiles and barbershops, saloons and brothels bordered the street. Many were completed clapboard buildings, several yet were framed and in need of siding and a roof. Interspersed throughout and behind were canvas tents and lean-tos. Stacks of lumber and crates and trash littered the slushy street. Deep washes visible even with the snow and mud cut through the beaten path, spanned here and there by single plank bridges.

Boone took a moment to soak in all of the hustle and bustle. In spite of the almost knee-deep snow left by the storm the previous night, the place was alive with miners, horses, and wagons loaded with freight. It hadn't been long since gold was discovered in the Black Hills, or as the Lakota knew the area, *Paha Sapa*, and already Deadwood was said to be host to thousands, with more folks rolling in every day.

"I guess we found the party," Boone said under his breath.

They made a path toward the center of town, dodging and sidestepping the traffic. It reminded Boone of red ants on a mound.

Rabbit steered his horse around a stack of lumber to catch up to Boone. "They haven't come to terms with the privy situation." He wrinkled his nose. "Let's find some grub." Rabbit could always be counted on to keep food at or near the top of his list of priorities.

"The smell of shit and piss in the streets makes you think of food, does it?" Boone pointed at a nearby saloon. "Look. Nutall & Mann's. That's where Wild Bill was killed." A low *whup* from him stopped Nickel. "That place is gonna be famous, I bet," he said to Rabbit.

But Rabbit didn't appear to hear him. Something had caught his eye down an alley on the other side of the street and stopped him up, too.

"Boone," Rabbit said. "You recognize that Mitchell wagon?"

"What's that?" Boone asked, his attention still on the building that marked the demise of the best-known lawman he'd ever heard of along the trail. He'd read enough weeklies and story papers to know that Wild Bill was a man with whom to reckon. Had been, anyway, but Boone also knew there was a fair bit of storytelling in those readers.

Out of the corner of his eye, he saw Rabbit grab his hat by the brim and swing it high in the air. It *thwapped* down on Boone's sore shoulder. "Boone!"

Boone jerked his head and nailed Rabbit with a glare. "Dang it, Rabbit! That's my bad shoulder." He rubbed it to emphasize the point.

"Take a gander at that Mitchell," Rabbit said, cramming his hat back on his head and pointing toward the alley.

Down the snowy street a deep voice thundered, "That's it for you, Pigeye!"

A gunshot cracked in the air, followed by shouts and screams.

The street was crowded enough that Boone couldn't see through to the commotion. Another shot and more shouting had them both out of their saddles and making a quick play for the alley. After a shared frown, they focused on the street, pistols drawn.

A short, lean, hunched man staggered up the middle of the street into view at the end of the alley, a Colt .45 pointed back the way he'd come. Blood soaked his shirt below his ribcage. He turned, apparently intending to flee into the alley, and lit off a shot down the street.

A flurry of gunfire followed.

The little man arched, his arms flailing as if he were swimming on his back, and collapsed into the muddy snow. Not long after, a rabble of fifteen or so men surrounded him.

"Cheatin' bastard!" one scorned.

"Down fer good," another said.

Several others uttered even less friendly statements concerning the character of the dying man, their harsh words his only escort out of this world.

Then the men slowly went their separate ways, slapping backs and congratulating each other for the good work they'd done, leaving the corpse alone in the street.

A reckoning, as this appeared to be in Boone's experience, was nothing new to him or Rabbit and wasn't reason enough to show a hand.

"So that's what this town is about," Boone said, and Rabbit nodded, obviously grasping the situation as well. Under the right—or wrong—circumstances, a man might find himself dead real easy.

"I got your back, ol' Booney," Rabbit said.

Boone nodded. After all of these years, there was no need for reassurances between them, but Rabbit liked to talk.

"Looky there." Rabbit pointed at the dead man. "They left his hat behind. You think it'll fit your hard head?"

Boone stroked Nickel's muzzle to soothe out any disquiet the gunplay had caused. The horse nuzzled him in return.

"I'm not wearing a dead man's hat," he told Rabbit. "Now gather the reins of your ten-cent puddin' foot and let's make." He grabbed Nickel's reins to lead him from the alley onto the street.

Rabbit pointed at Nickel and said, "Tortoise." Then he patted Dime's shoulder. "Hare. You familiar with that Aesop fable, Mr. Reads-a-lot? Besides, the wagon?" Rabbit bobbed his head toward the Mitchell wagon behind them. Their retreat a moment earlier had ended near the pulling end of the freight wagon. "Recognize those wheels, ol' man?"

Boone could tell by the set of Rabbit's jaw under his dark blond scruff that he took some amount of satisfaction in sleuthing out this bit on his own. He waited with arms crossed as

Boone examined the wagon.

A lead weight settled in Boone's gut. "No mistaking this outfit. It's Uncle Morton's Mitchell."

He studied the iron wheel bands he'd watched his uncle painstakingly forge. This wasn't any normal freighter. The distinctive spokes made from red and black oak and the inlay on the seatback unmistakably displayed Uncle Morton's craftsmanship. But the *Morton & Sons Drayage* painted on the side panels guaranteed what it was—a unique wagon meant to impress potential clients. Such attention to detail was the sign of a diligent owner who took care of his possessions.

"Looks like our job is darn near done already," Rabbit said. "He's probably in there." He thrust his thumb at the building next to the wagon.

Boone figured the same thing. He and Rabbit had come to Deadwood for a reason different from most. They weren't here to seek their fortune in gold or cards. Instead, they were here to find a missing Morton. Uncle Morton, who'd left Santa Fe with a load of goods bound for Cheyenne. The plan was for Uncle Morton to deliver his load of freight and wait for Boone and Rabbit to join him in Cheyenne after their freight run to Laramie. Then they would all head home together.

But a snowstorm had stranded Boone and Rabbit in Laramie, so they had telegraphed to Cheyenne that they would be several days late. Uncle Morton replied via telegraph that he was taking the trail to Deadwood to scout for potential expansion of his freighting business and they were to wait for him in Cheyenne. The storm shifted and they made it in from Laramie days before they'd figured. They decided to travel by horse and catch Uncle Morton on the trail up to Deadwood. Unfortunately, they'd run into storms again along the way north, slowing them up.

"You stay with the wagon and horses," Boone told Rabbit, sparing a glance at the fresh corpse sprawled at the mouth of the alley as he rounded the front of the building. Bad egg or no, that fella went down hard.

A short time later, Boone returned to the alley to find Rabbit sitting in the wagon's custom seat with his eyes closed and his hat lowered.

"Look at you up there sleeping away, soft as a honeysuckle blossom." He nudged Rabbit's leg and found himself at the business end of a pistol in a blink.

"I told ya before, Booney. Don't sneak up on me."

"I didn't sneak up. You were sleeping, numbskull."

"I wasn't sleepin'. I was just thinkin' real hard."

"Never known you to spend too much time at that." Boone chuckled. "The man inside said the owner of this wagon is in a saloon called Yellow Strike down the street." He grabbed Nickel's reins and led him to the end of the alley, waiting for Rabbit to follow.

The dead man was gone, bloodstained snow the only eulogy left in his stead.

Together, they made their way to the entrance of Yellow Strike Saloon, pausing to stomp the muddy slush from their boots on the uneven boardwalk outside. Rabbit in his usual setting-the-woods-on-fire manner led the way.

"Swing them doors wide," Boone said as he followed Rabbit.

Rabbit paused on the threshold. "What?"

"If you don't push hard enough, the doors will swing back and hit your gun belt. Might knock that fancy hogleg out of the holster. Or maybe you'll shoot yourself in the ass."

"I know how to walk into a bar, Slim."

"Name's not Slim, smartass."

"Well, you ain't, that's sure enough."

"I'm not what?"

"Slim." Rabbit eyed him top to bottom before stepping the rest of the way inside. "Addin' another whiskey or beer to that won't be doin' neither of us no good."

Boone followed Rabbit on a crooked path through the maze

of tables and chairs, half of them occupied by odiferous, alcohol-soaked claim jumpers and wannabe card sharps. Their trail ended at the bar.

"You are overly occupied with my shape, Rabbit."

"Nah, you're just overly shaped. Sort of pumpkin-bellied."

Boone might not be whipcord lean like Rabbit, but he certainly was nowhere close to the roundness of Rabbit's description. "I'm not fat, you walkin' broomstick. This here is solid muscle." He patted his stomach.

Further down the bar a barrel-chested, hulk of a man had the open end of a whiskey bottle stuck into a thicket of hair about where a mouth should be. Two companions cheered him on until the liquid was gone.

"Pay up!" he demanded, slamming the bottle on the bar.

Yellow Strike Saloon was indistinguishable from many other saloons Boone had been in over the years as far as he could tell, serving up women, gambling, and what was probably a mixture of raw alcohol and burnt sugar as whiskey. But hell, at least the beer and liquor were warm along with the temperature, thanks to the big wood stove in the corner chugging out heat and a puff of smoke now and then.

Boone gestured to the bartender. "Whiskey."

"Same," Rabbit said, tapping the bar.

Uncle Morton wasn't present, a fact that Boone was sure Rabbit had noticed as well.

The bartender filled fingerprint-smudged glasses with not quite enough whiskey to make Boone happy. "Porter," the man behind the bar said as he handed over the drinks and stuck out his hand for a shake.

"Ho, Potbelly Porter," cackled a voice from the other end of the bar.

Boone hadn't noticed the spindly little man until now. As far as he could tell, the old guy was speaking to no one in particular.

Porter glanced at the scraggly geezer and dismissed him with a wave.

"Name's Boone," Boone said to Porter and thumbed toward Rabbit. "This here's Jack."

"Good to meet you." Rabbit tipped his hat in greeting before taking a swallow of whiskey.

"Dan'l Boone dead too soon," crooned the geezer.

Porter scowled. "Ignore him. He's got cobwebs in his attic."

The smell of phlegm, rotten tobacco, and spit made Boone cringe. He glanced down, noticing he was too close to a not-often-emptied and even less-often-cleaned spittoon. It was no wonder Rabbit had bitched and moaned about his chewing tobacco.

"We're lookin' for the owner of the wagon in an alley up the way with *Morton & Sons Drayage* on the side." Rabbit spoke loud enough for most in the bar to hear. He tipped the whiskey into his mouth, grimaced, and then clunked it back on the bar. "Another'n."

Boone leaned on the bar, focusing on his own glass of whiskey in between taking small sips. On the sly, he used the mirror behind the bar to size up the characters in the room, taking particular notice of any glances their way or other oddities when Rabbit mentioned the wagon.

To his right, the geezer went off on a whispered rant to himself about wagons and buffalo and other things not quite clear or even close to lucid.

Porter contemplated a moment before answering Rabbit. "Don't know the wagon myself, but that gentleman over yonder was just braggin' about winnin' a wagon yesterday."

Not one to waste time, Boone nodded his thanks and then moved through the tables. He shifted his whiskey glass to his left hand to free his gun hand, his injured shoulder complaining with a twinge or two.

Rabbit took his cue and edged to the end of the bar closest to the door, positioning himself for a full view of the entire room.

Boone pulled a chair and sat at a table with a short but stout man grasping a half-empty beer in his hand. "Buy you another one?" he offered the beer drinker.

The man eyed him cautiously before giving a short nod. Boone set his glass on the table and waved at the bartender, pointing at the man's beer. Drink ordered, Boone sat back and let his coat fall away from his shiny, almost new Colt.

The man studied the pistol and Boone's face before looking down at his beer. "Listen, mister," he said, shaking his head slightly.

Boone raised his eyebrows and dipped his chin. "Hmm?"

"I won that wagon, fair an' square."

"Did you now? Mind putting your other hand where I can see it?" No gun was evident, but it was best to take no chances.

"Yessir." The wagon's new owner put his non-drinking hand on the table. "I ain't lookin' for no trouble with you. Like I said, I won that wagon. It's a fine piece of machinery, to be sure. Name's Billwitty. I run freight 'tween here an' Yankton, mostly."

As Boone listened to the freighter's story, he noticed Rabbit's focus had been diverted. He swore under his breath. The damned towhead had the attention span of a gnat.

He followed Rabbit's gaze. A tall woman stood at the bar, sparks shooting from her eyes. Broad-shouldered under her gray wool coat, she wore men's pants over a pair of long legs. Her dark auburn hair was woven into a braid down the middle of her back. Her strong cheekbones and high forehead spoke of classic beauty, such as the kind he'd learned about in books on ancient Greece that Uncle Morton had used to school him long ago.

Boone glanced back at Rabbit, who couldn't seem to take his eyes off the woman, which left Boone exposed.

"Rabbit!" Boone called.

His partner hesitated before turning his way, scowling as Boone motioned him over. "What?"

Boone kicked out the chair opposite him. "How about you

join Mr. Billwitty and me."

As Rabbit settled in, the fourth chair at the table scraped back. The muttering geezer plopped down between Boone and Rabbit.

Rabbit raised an eyebrow at Boone and stuck his thumb toward the old guy. Boone shrugged back before returning to the wagon's new owner. "Now what is it you were saying, Mr. Billwitty?"

"See, I was playin' a game of jackpot over in the Badlands when …"

Out of the corner of his eye, Boone saw Rabbit's head turn. His partner was once again eyeballing the tall woman where she stood at the bar talking low to the bartender.

She held two bottles of clear liquid by the neck in one of her hands. What was that? Raw alcohol? Her hand matched her large stature, her fingers long and strong. They were nothing like the dainty mitts of so many of the *señoritas* back home with their dark eyes and flirty touches.

As Boone watched, the bartender pointed toward the table next to him. The woman turned, her gaze narrowing into a squint upon finding her mark. She set the bottles down in a basket at the end of the bar and strode toward the neighboring table.

The closer she came, the more Boone's chin lifted. Holy hell, she was tall! She had to be over six foot, for sure. Maybe as tall as him even. Certainly she'd stand nose-to-nose with Rabbit.

"Hello, Finnigan." Her voice was like aged whiskey, smooth on the surface with an underlying rough-and-tumble edge to it. "Have yourself any exciting pokes lately?"

A chubby lump of a man smoking a stubby cigar while playing cards snorted. "Who's asking?" he asked out of the side of his mouth.

She answered with her hands, hauling him from his chair. Finnigan squawked, flailing, and knocked his grease-stained derby to the floor in the process. She drew him up to her level, her height forcing the card player onto his toes.

"Sheeat," Rabbit said in the sudden quiet. Like most of the population of the bar, including Boone himself, Rabbit's jaw had gone slack, his hat tipping back as he stared up at the spectacle playing out before him.

All concerns about Uncle Morton's absence and Billwitty's rambling tale slipped from Boone's mind. He'd not seen a woman in men's britches before, let alone watched one lift a grown man from a chair with such little effort. She was as strong as any man. Hell, probably stronger than many, for that matter.

"*I'm* asking you, Finnigan. That's who." Her lips barely moved as she glared into Finnigan's round eyes. "Tell me, did you fuck Ginny before or after you beat her to death?"

"Let go of me, whore-lover." Finnigan tried to put on a brave face, but the tremble in his voice betrayed him. He struggled as she tightened her grip on his collar to near choking.

The other men at the table—even those at nearby tables—rose and backed into the fringes of the room.

Boone was so mesmerized that he didn't notice the crazy geezer reach out and steal his drink until the whiskey glass was empty. The thief reached for Rabbit's glass next.

Rabbit scooted his whiskey out of reach without looking away from the woman. "Don't even think about it, you ol' fart."

The geezer fidgeted with Boone's empty glass, muttering what sounded like, "Comin', comin', comin', comin'. They's comin', comin' ...."

"If you kill one more girl, Finnigan," the woman said, her smooth-but-deadly voice snaring Boone again. "I will hunt you down."

"Whatta ya gonna do?" Finnigan blustered, his lower lip quivering. "Tickle me with those big ugly man-hands of yers?"

"You're throwing up a lot of dust here," she returned. "Keep it up and I'm going to beat you lumpy and then do a two-step on your head when I'm finished."

"You don't scare me, woman."

Boone almost laughed aloud. The blowhard was shaking in his boots so much it was a wonder the piss hadn't leaked out of him yet.

"If one more girl ends up on my table because of you," she continued, "I'll make sure you're next. Maybe I'll stop your heart before I gut you." Her smile was hard and brittle, matching her eyes. "Then again, maybe not."

Finnigan paled. "It's none of yer damned business who and how I fuck."

"You can't seem to control your fists or your lips, can you, Finnigan?" She set the card player back down hard on his boot heels. "And here I was thinking I'd let you off with just a warning today, but I can see you're the type who needs a hands-on lesson to grasp how a dead wasp can still sting."

"Dead wasp?" Finnigan repeated, his brow wrinkling. "What in the hell is that suppos'd to—"

With lightning speed, she grabbed his left wrist and pulled his arm straight. Still holding his wrist, she shot her other arm underneath his elbow, lifting hard and fast.

The sharp *crack* of a bone breaking made Boone flinch and bump the table. Whiskey sloshed out of Rabbit's glass.

Finnigan squealed, his eyes bulging.

Rabbit jerked backward so fast his hat tumbled to the floor. He shot Boone a stunned glance before scooping it back up.

"Clementine Johanssen," the geezer said as Finnigan wailed and moaned. "Best not mess with that wildcat. She'd jus' soon put ya in the ground as look at ya." He scratched at his chin under foot-long whiskers. "Clem Clem Clemytine," the geezer sang in a high voice. "She'll clean up the towny-town-town mighty fine."

"Yeah, but *what* is she?" Boone whispered.

"Corpse hugger. Undertaker. Death dealer." The geezer

pointed at her with a gnarled finger that appeared to have been broken and smashed more than once. "Put ya down and then put ya away." He cackled again.

She's an undertaker? In all of his travels, Boone hadn't come across a female undertaker. Not once. Not until now.

"From here on out," Clementine interrupted Finnigan's whimpers. "I suggest you whistle nice and loud when you walk past a cemetery and keep your hands to yourself when it comes to your pokes."

"You … you … you whore-lovin' bitch!" Finnigan shrieked and took a wobbly swing at Clementine.

The undertaker snatched Finnigan's other wrist and twisted it halfway round, pulling his arm straight in a move so quick Boone would have missed it if he'd blinked.

"What was that you called me?"

Finnigan's eyes rolled wildly in his head. "Please, no. Stop."

Clementine held tight. "How many times did Ginny beg you to stop before you crushed her skull?"

When he stuttered in response, she shot her forearm under his other arm, bending it the wrong way.

Finnigan cried out.

"How many?" she growled, her gray eyes flashing.

"I don't 'member. Maybe twice."

She levered his arm higher. "How many, Finnigan?"

"Five times," Finnigan yelled.

"Five damned times, you limp-dick bastard." Clementine shook her head, disgust pulling down her mouth.

"Just a whore," he bellowed.

Another sickening crack filled the room.

Rabbit turned away, cringing as he looked at Boone.

Finnigan howled in pain, louder than before. The sight of both of his elbows now bent the wrong way made Boone wince. He'd seen some things in his days, but this was the first time he'd witnessed anything like this at the hands of a woman.

"That's for the poor girl you beat to death." She grabbed the injured man by the collar and leaned in close. "You're lucky I'm letting you live today."

Finnigan sobbed, drool dripping from his chin, his arms hanging limp from his shoulders.

Clementine shoved him away and started toward the bar.

"I'm g-g-gonna kill you," Finnigan called after her between wet snorts and sobs. "You think yer so high and m-m-mighty."

Boone held his breath along with everyone else in the bar, waiting to see if the undertaker was going to keep walking.

Clementine stopped and looked up at the ceiling, her shoulders lifting and falling. "What did you say, Finnigan?"

"Y-you heard me."

She turned back, closing the gap between them. "You don't know when to shut up, do you?"

He spit in her face.

Boone gasped. The fool had a death wish.

Clementine delivered a lightning-quick jab with the heel of her hand. Finnigan's nose crunched under the blow and blood poured, mixing with drool and snot. He collapsed to the floor.

She wiped the spit off her face with her coat sleeve and then glared down at the heap of Finnigan. "That should keep you from beating on any more prostitutes for a long time." She brushed her hands together over the crumpled lump of man. "Good luck holding your pecker while you're taking a piss, asshole."

A whimper was all that came from Finnigan. Bloody snot bubbles clustered around his crooked nose.

The undertaker looked around at the faces watching her. Her cheeks darkened as if she suddenly realized she was standing center stage. She lifted her chin, clearing her throat. "Take note, gentlemen, and treat the girls of the line with care. I don't like to bury my friends."

"Clem Clem Clemytine," crooned the geezer as she walked

away. "She's gonna clean up them whangdoodles mighty fine."

"Sorry about the mess, Porter," she called to the bartender, picking up her basket of bottles. "You want me to toss him in the street?"

"That's not necessary, Miss Johanssen." Porter smiled too wide. He poured several shots, spilling whiskey in the process before downing one himself.

Without a backward glance, Clementine left the bar. It took a few beats for the din of conversation to return, and when it did, Boone's ears rang from the noise and rowdy exclamations.

Rabbit swiveled to Boone, his face alight. "Did you see that?"

"Of course I did, Rabbit. I was sitting right here at the table with you."

He left his chair to grab the beer Porter had waiting for him at the bar. When he returned, Rabbit was still grinning like a jackass eating cactus. "That woman is an angel."

Boone shook his head. "That was no angel."

Angels didn't snap elbows and crack noses without breaking a sweat.

"Listen, Rabbit. We need to head down to the Badlands." He tipped his head toward the man guzzling the second beer Boone had bought him. "Mr. Billwitty here won the Mitchell from a businessman who frequents some of the saloons and opium dens down there. The description doesn't fit Uncle Morton, though."

"I ain't never seen a woman who could take a man in hand that way," Rabbit said. "She's so pretty, I'd rather look at her than eat breakfast."

Boone rolled his eyes. That was saying something, considering Rabbit's love of food.

He reached across the table and grabbed Rabbit by the shoulder, hauling him closer. "Listen, you need to concentrate for a minute."

Boone had been through this before. Rabbit had fallen ass-deep in love more times than either of them could count.

Fortunately, his affection rarely lasted long, running fast and swift like the dry washes back home. "I think Uncle Morton might be in trouble. I'm starting to get a bad feeling about this wagon."

"Yeah, I hear ya," Rabbit said, but his gaze drifted back to the doorway.

Ah, hell. Boone groaned and let go of Rabbit. *Here we go again.*

FOUR

Clementine stormed into The Pyre, kicking the door closed. The embroidered Helm of Awe cloth she'd hung over it fell to the floor. She dropped the basket of alcohol on the parlor desk, the glass bottles clanking together. She cursed under her breath and returned to pick up the cloth bearing the Viking symbol of protection and victory. Smoothing out her grandmother's embroidered stitches, she hung the well-traveled cloth back in place, where it was meant to keep trouble away.

Unfortunately, it wasn't helping to keep Clementine from finding trouble beyond her front door.

"Damned Finnigan," she grumbled, returning to the parlor desk to collect the basket with the bottles.

That addle-headed *lombungr* had tried the edge of her patience. She shouldn't have walked over to his table in the first place, but she couldn't get the image of what he'd done to poor Ginny out of her head.

When Porter had told her who'd been responsible for Ginny's death, Clementine's hands had burned to wrap around Finnigan's throat and squeeze the life out of him. The bastard was lucky she'd left him alive.

If only she hadn't made such a spectacle of herself in the midst of her outburst.

You must hide in plain sight, her grandmother would have told her had she been here.

Clementine had struggled with that lesson since childhood.

Moving into her exam room, she took one of the bottles from the basket and tucked it away in the cupboard that Hank had built last month. She grabbed a ragged piece of muslin from the stack of clean cloths on the shelf. Closing the cupboard door, she rested her forehead against it. The pine felt cool, unlike the frustration and anger still boiling under her skin.

Patience had never been her strong suit. While being raised and schooled back home by her mother's parents, Clementine had excelled at two subjects: foreign languages and hand-to-hand combat.

The former was taught by her grandmother—her amma, who'd been fluent in nine different languages, each of which she'd practiced weekly. According to her amma, being multilingual was a skill necessary to hide in plain sight. More than once in their ancestral skein tales were woven about Clementine's kind being hanged, stoned to death, or gutted upon discovery ... or worse. Amma's stories of past atrocities often haunted Clementine's childhood dreams, driving her to practice harder the next day. She wouldn't make the same mistakes as her mother.

Her grandfather had been in charge of teaching her to fight. After losing his only daughter to servants of the *jötnar*, or the "devourers" as her grandmother called them in English, her afi approached his role as trainer with grim determination. His diligence to secure the family line was evident each time he had Clementine don the battle gear he'd crafted specifically for sparring. She had suffered many, many cuts and bruises over the years to master her fighting skills.

Not that her afi would have been proud at her display of combat over in Yellow Strike Saloon. He'd have chastised her for making so much noise when she should have been drifting along in silence, avoiding being "seen" by her enemies.

However, being a large female in a land of petite women made hiding in plain sight nearly impossible most days.

She carried the other bottle of raw alcohol and muslin cloth to the empty exam table, setting them down where Ginny had lain.

The one thing neither of her grandparents had been successful at teaching her was how to control her temper. Unfortunately, this inheritance from her Viking ancestors hadn't mellowed with centuries of breeding, nor hours of lectures at her amma's table.

She curled her hand into a fist and scowled at it.

Great Odin, it would've felt so good to snap Finnigan's neck.

And Angus Monty's, too, while she was at it. The owner of Yellow Strike Saloon needed to be taught not to treat women like animals that could be owned or abused at will. Too bad Yellow Strike was the only establishment in Deadwood willing to sell her raw alcohol dirt cheap for disinfecting her equipment. This forced Clementine to set foot in that den of corruption on a regular basis. Over time, she'd found several of the working girls to be friendly, funny even. More surprising, they accepted Clementine in spite of her large frame and daily dealings with the dead.

She shrugged off her coat and hung it by the front door, frowning up at the Helm of Awe. The truth of her grandparents' words of warning weighed heavy on her. If she attracted too much attention from local residents and her true identity was revealed, she'd need to pack up and leave before she was ready, contractual obligations be damned.

She had taken a big risk with Finnigan today. If word spread about her public beating of the no-good weasel, the Helm of Awe would not be powerful enough to keep trouble from breaking down her door.

Returning to her exam room, she spared a glance at Big Joe, whose hairy feet were still dangling off the end of her table. It was time to get him out of here and sanitize the room. As she took up the muslin rag, her thoughts returned to the owner of

Yellow Strike Saloon.

Angus Monty was one of the vilest drinking, gambling, and sex proprietors in Deadwood. Luring innocent young girls to town with the promise of well-compensated, honest-to-goodness work, Angus had quite an illegal human-rustling setup. His "soiled doves" were nothing more than beasts of burden in his estimation. He'd even told her that once when Clementine had confronted him about another dead prostitute from his saloon who had come through her door. The waif had died from a working-girl disease that had started with blindness and progressed quickly to death in her already frail condition.

Porter, Angus's barman, wasn't exactly a peach either, choosing to look the other way when it came to his boss's shady deals in order to save his own hide. How Porter could work for that devil and look at himself in the mirror behind the bar was beyond her.

The barman might seem obtuse at times, but he didn't miss much. Fortunately, he was willing to keep Clementine apprised of these goings-on for a few bits of gold now and then.

The girls in the line shared information with her, too.

Clementine had few friends in town due to the fact that she handled the dead on a daily basis and the superstitions that surrounded her profession, not to mention that taking care of the dead kept her busy day and night. The ladies at Yellow Strike eased some of her loneliness. They offered unprejudiced friendship when Clementine stopped by for some raw alcohol, especially during their "slow times" when Angus wasn't around and Porter was gold-fed enough to look the other way.

Clementine yanked the cork from the bottle of raw alcohol and dumped a gulp or two onto the table where Ginny had lain, scrubbing it into the wood.

Poor Ginny. She'd been lured to Deadwood from the poverty of St. Louis's muddy streets. "Gold appears from every scratch in the ground, making kings and queens of paupers," she was told by one of Angus's scouts.

But abundance had not been in Ginny's future. Instead, a sadistic brute had caved in her skull.

Clementine wondered if the girl had family somewhere worried about her. Or was Ginny like so many in the West—lonely souls without anyone to miss them when they were gone. Destined to end up in an unmarked grave on the side of a rutted wagon trail.

She finished scrubbing and tipped a small slug of liquid fire into her mouth. The raw alcohol burned like a blacksmith's glowing forge all of the way down her throat, matching the burn in her belly caused by Angus and his loathsome cohorts.

"Before I leave this town," she told Big Joe, "I'm going to face off with Angus and teach him a thing or two."

Maybe that was the raw alcohol talking.

Maybe not.

She corked the bottle and set it on her desk, and then stood over Big Joe's corpse. Before she'd left, she'd covered the dead man with a wool blanket to save Hank from complaining about the naked corpse when he showed up for work.

"What about you, big fella?" She peeled back the blanket and studied his mottled face. "From where did you hail and who was there at the hour of your doom?"

Dead men told no tales.

She wrinkled her nose and dropped the blanket over his face again. He was reeking with more gusto now that he'd had a good, long thaw.

She'd left Big Joe on the table after slicing him open and poking around his insides since his massiveness precluded her moving him to the shed without help. That, and she hadn't finished determining his cause of death.

Normally she was happy to move the dead through her establishment as quickly as possible. However, Big Joe—and possibly the man in the shed who'd fallen victim to a professional with a blade—might be the reason she was hired to come to Deadwood in the first place. She needed to make sure, and that would take additional study.

She grabbed her journal from her desk and opened it to the page of notes she'd taken while examining the corpse. Running her finger down the page, she reviewed her scrawls for any clues she might have missed previously due to fatigue.

> *Moderate tissue damage and some tissue removal from the thigh frontal region by midsized omnivore or carnivore species evidenced by bite radius and type of damage. Post mortem.*

The body had probably been exposed to some of the scavengers roaming the hills. Possibly wolves, a mountain lion, or some other predator. She frowned at her notes, still wondering why the animal hadn't finished the job.

She'd also noted the more curious bit ...

> *Circular, slightly distended, purplish black contusion on upper left abdomen, three inches in diameter. Small hole in center of contusion. Source of hole possibly bullet or blade. External evidence of trauma seems insufficient to cause death.*

The real head scratcher had come after she'd opened him up.

She'd made the standard Y incision through the hypodermis from his outer collarbones to the upper middle of his chest and then straight down to his pubis, spreading the flesh to expose his ribs. The ribs near the abdominal contusion were intact, no fractures were visible. Then she split his ribcage with the rib shears and opened them wide with rib spreaders.

What she'd found had made her take a step back. The organs beneath the small hole in the flesh resembled soupy porridge, as if they'd been put through a meat grinder and poured back into his torso. Only portions of his heart, lungs, and intestines remained intact.

What could cause such internal damage while barely marring his skin? Even more curious, she'd found no bullet.

The front door swung open.

"Whew! Hullo, Miss Johan … Miss Clementi … uh, Miss Clem." Hank closed the door and joined her in the examination room, dumping a stack of folded waxed canvas tarpaulins in the corner on the floor. "Sun's peekin' outta the clouds, but ain't much warmth to it this mornin'." He shed his coat and hooked it on a wall peg next to hers in the parlor, returning with a warm smile. "Ling an' Gart took four of the deceased. Said they'd be back fer the rest soon as they got them four in the ground. I tell yuh …" He shook his head, his face scrunching up with a snigger. "Hee hee, them two's a hoot! Ling was carryin' a—" He broke into a hooting laugh, his words undecipherable for a moment. "Then Gart clunked Ling on the noggin' with his whip staff an' stole his—" More snickers broke up his tale. "Ooo! Pert near forgot."

He raced out of the exam room and through the front door, leaving it wide open in his wake. A gust of snow blew in, sprinkling white powder over the parlor floor.

Shivering, Clementine smiled at Hank's lighthearted nature. Having him around some days was as refreshing as the gust of cold air swirling at her feet.

Hank charged back in, bumping the door closed behind him. He carried a muslin cloth tied into a bag.

"What did you bring me, Hank? A dead cat?" she teased.

"Miss Clem! I never could! This here's a passel of sinkers. Picked 'em up for you from Grand Central since you takin' the time to feed yerself proper is a rarity. Them's good biscuits, too. Fresh. They was outta butter but there's a lump of bacon grease in there for 'em." He held the bag out to Clementine.

"That's real sweet of you, Hank." She took the bag and untied the string securing the muslin, inhaling the aroma of freshly baked biscuits, and then set the bag on the desk in the parlor.

"Before digging in, I need you to tell me something," she said, returning to Hank's side. "Where did you pick up Big Joe's body?"

"Down to the Kee Luk Laundry near the end of the street." Hank scratched at his beard. "They had him out back, wrapped up tight as a whore's pur ... well, in canvas, just like I delivered him."

Right, with a bite out of his leg. She walked over to the cupboard and grabbed another piece of muslin, pouring alcohol on it. "Is there anything else you remember?"

"They had them some sorta soup bubblin' in a big pot over a fire in the back room. Smelled like they was cookin' horse droppin's." He scrunched his face tight. "Liken to put me off my breakfast. A ways back I was visitin' with Deadpan Tom an' he cooked up a couple rats in some nettles an' bearberry. Some taters in there too I think. Made a kinda stew." He shook his head at the recollection of the concoction. "I think them rats mighta been off. Sorry I ate that. But he was hungry, and bein' his guest I was obliged to take a quantity of it. It took me the better part of a week to get past that one."

"Was it possibly the laundry?" Clementine asked as she began to wipe down the table holding her instruments.

"Huh?" Hank snapped out of his memory of stewed rats.

"The boiling pot of rank-smelling soup."

"Oh. Don't know. Mighta been."

"Anything else come to mind about the place?"

He looked toward the ceiling, closed one eye and stuck his lips out in a kiss, and then he looked back at Clementine. "Nope."

"All right then." She stopped cleaning and set down the rag. "I need your help moving Big Joe out to the shed."

"Yes, ma'am."

"Then I want you to go back to Kee Luk and find some answers for me." She walked to her work desk and tore a scrap of paper from her journal. "I'll write down the questions I want you to ask."

Hank grabbed his hat and fiddled with the brim. "Miss Clem, you think it best I'm the one that should go? I might bungle them questions yer writin' down. Might be this is somethin' you oughta take care of?"

Clementine smiled as she finished writing. "You'll do fine, Hank."

"But—"

"You remember what happened last time I went beyond the Badlands, don't you? I think it's best if I avoid that part of town whenever possible. At least for now."

"Yes, ma'am, but—"

"Besides, the Chinese don't exactly honor those in my line of work, especially women. Merely looking at me is considered bad luck, let alone speaking with me." Her tone grew frosty at the memory of the way she'd been treated each time she'd ventured into Chinatown. Her hands were *dirty* and she'd never be able to clean the death from them as far as they were concerned.

"Oh, now, Miss Clem. Don't go callin' yerself bad luck. But you surely are right about them bein' supertishus about dead people." Hank's brow furrowed, showing his unease.

"Don't fret about it, Hank. Anyhow, you know the language better than I do."

"Some. Enough, I suppose. Better at listenin' than talkin'."

It wasn't evident to most folks, but Hank had developed a number of worthwhile skills in his forty-two years. He'd told Clementine soon after starting to work for her that before coming to Deadwood he'd been a top ranch hand, a drover, and a fair roper. He'd hauled freight and ridden with mountain men. He'd even tried his hand as a trapper, but couldn't stomach the pain endured by the animals he snared in his traps.

He was most proud of being a railroad man who worked for the CPA on the Pacific Railroad. The line's name had been changed to Transcontinental Railroad, but Hank didn't cotton to that. "Worked on the Pacific Railroad and that's what I call it," he said time and again. He started as a spike driver and ended his time on the railroad as transit dog helping one of the survey crews. He loved to point out his blurry face in the photograph taken at the Last Spike ceremony in Promontory Summit, Utah. It was during that time that Hank had worked closely with the Chinese and learned a fair amount of their language.

She handed him the scrap of paper, which he tucked away in his pocket.

With considerable grunting and a bit of cursing, they carted Big Joe's corpse out through the back door to the shed. After washing their hands doubly good, they sat together in the front parlor for a small breakfast of Aunt Lou's biscuits from Grand Central Hotel. Clementine skipped the bacon grease topper, but Hank had no problem finishing it off.

As soon as they'd gobbled down the biscuits and wiped the crumbs from their faces, she sent Hank on his way. "Off you go to Kee Luk. Remember the questions."

Hank patted the scrap of paper in his front pocket. Pulling his hat down on his head, he opened the front door, but then hesitated. Before he could come up with an excuse to delay further, Clementine nudged him outside and closed the door behind him, leaning against it for a moment as she listened to the muffled rumble and racket of Deadwood outside her windows.

She'd finished cleaning her instrument table, scrubbed Big Joe's examination table thoroughly, and had started polishing what Hank called her "wall of weapons" in her private quarters by the time he lumbered back through the front door.

"Miss Clem?" he called out.

"In back, Hank."

His wide shoulders filled the doorway. "We got another'n. Shot dead in the street this mornin'. Peppered. Make a right fine strainer for coffee now. It's that no-account swindler Johnny 'Pigeye' Holley from Montana Territory. They say he got run outta Helena for sellin' fake claims. He once told me ..." Hank blinked, smiling wide as his attention snagged on her wall of weapons. "Say, you got yer weapons showin'!" He stepped closer, admiring the contents of the open cupboards, which covered the upper half of one wall.

Clementine didn't say anything about Hank standing in her private quarters. Propriety didn't apply to an undertaker, especially somewhere as rough and rowdy as Deadwood, and she'd never been a slave to social respectability. Besides, other than her cupboard full of weapons, all her room contained was a bed and her traveling trunk. She hadn't taken the time to settle in and make the place homey, figuring she wouldn't be sticking around that long.

"I was just finishing up polishing and oiling them." Her grandfather would never forgive her if she didn't keep them sharp and shiny.

Hank moved up next to her, scanning the array of blunt, pointed, and bladed weapons hanging on hooks and nails throughout. Each one had been collected and handed down through generations of her family. Her afi had adjusted several to fit her hands better. Some were made of metal, some of bone and leather, and a few incorporated stone elements like flint chips and obsidian blades. All were deadly in the right hands—namely hers.

"I know this'n. It's a knucklebuster." He pointed at it. "I seen one used before. In Kansas City, saw a man catch one right on the jaw. Knocked him on his ass ... Pardon my language, Miss Clem. Spat out three teeth and a lotta blood, he did. Course, that one was made of wood. This'n here is metal with fancy writin' on it. What's this'n here called again?" He indicated a leather glove with five ornate metal blades attached.

She smiled at the excitement lighting his eyes. The sight of her weapons often lit her up, too. "I've already told you the names of all these weapons."

"Names sometimes escape me, Miss Clem."

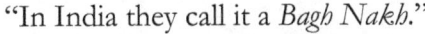

"In India they call it a *Bagh Nakh*."

Hank tilted his head and pursed his lips.

"The Chinese call it an Eagle Claw," she added.

Hank swooped his arm and snapped his fingers. "That's right! Looks awful mean. Made to open a body top to bottom, I'm thinkin'. And this'n?" He pointed at an iron ball bristling with long, sharp spikes attached to a handle with a chain.

"That's a flail."

"You've used which ones now?"

"Most of them." She touched his shoulder. "Hank?"

"Huh?" He continued to study the weapons display. "Uhh, yes, Miss Clem?"

"You remember that only you and I know about these weapons and it needs to stay that way, right?" He'd first seen them when he walked in through the back door one day and surprised her in the midst of cleaning and polishing.

"Course, Miss Clem. My lips are nailed tight."

"Good."

She closed the cupboard doors and used the chain and padlock she'd purchased from the town blacksmith to lock the doors.

One of these days she'd have to find a more discreet way to store her weapons. A chained cupboard in a town overflowing with hungry thieves desperate for anything that shined was an invitation for trouble. Maybe she'd build a bigger cupboard to fit around it—a false front like those on some of the buildings going up in the gulch.

She glanced at the small window that helped to light the room. A few bars lining the inside of the glass would be nice, too, but that might lead folks to wonder what she was protecting. So far, the rumor that she had dead bodies stored in her establishment kept the riffraff away.

She led Hank down the hall past the room she used for storage into the front parlor. "We need to talk about Kee Luk and Big Joe."

"Oh!" He snapped his fingers again and grinned at Clementine. "Right. Soo Luk said she found Big Joe when she went to slop the pigs mornin' last. Said one of the pigs was chewin' on him, but must not have taken much likin' to him because one chew was enough." Hank scrunched his face and looked at his feet. "They hauled Big Joe outta the pen and threw a couple buckets of water on him, brushing him good to scrub off the hog shit. Then they wrapped him up and sent for me."

That explained the bite marks. Soo had done a good job of cleaning up Big Joe, too. Maybe Clementine should start sending Hank there with her laundry.

"She said this'n was the first they found before the pigs finished the job."

Clementine did a double take. "This one?"

"Soo said it's happened before Big Joe came along."

A body had been dumped in with the pigs *before*? "Did Soo say *when* before?"

"Near as I could understand what she was sayin', it's happened several times recently, but the pigs just leave a few bones an' such. Parts they don't like, I s'pose."

Clementine nodded, her thoughts spinning. If this weren't the first body, then it probably wouldn't be the last. "I don't have to tell you to keep this under your hat, right?"

Her secrets were stacking up these days. By including Hank on the inside, she was putting him at risk, but she needed his help.

"Sure thing." He wrung his hands together. "These dead body dealin's makes me nervous as a pregnant mule."

As it should. Dealing in death required an iron backbone and steel ribs. "You know I really appreciate your help with the Chinese."

He nodded.

"And to show you how much, how about you take the rest of

the day off?"

"But I just got back here, Miss Clemen ... Clem."

She grabbed him by the arm and led him to the front door, pulling a handful of coins from her pocket on her way. "I know, but I didn't get much sleep last night." Nor would she tonight either, now that she knew about Big Joe and the pigs. "I'll still pay you a full day's wage."

He frowned down at the coins she placed in his hand. "This don't seem right to me."

She opened the door and bumped him out into the cold. "I'll see you tomorrow morning, Hank. Stay out of trouble."

"There ain't no fun in that." He tipped his hat and pocketed the coins, meandering down the street toward the Belle Grande.

Clementine closed the door and locked it. She returned to her quarters and the cupboard of weapons, extracting the skeleton key she wore secured around her neck by a braided strip of leather. With a twist of the key, the padlock clinked and the doors swung open silently. She kept the hinges well-oiled along with her weapons.

She stood for several moments, eyeing each piece.

Which one would do for tonight?

She followed her gut instinct and picked up the Eagle Claw. It slid on with the ease of a well-worn glove. Holding up her hand in front of the small window, she stretched her fingers wide. At the end of each finger was a shiny, long slender blade ready to slice through flesh.

"Yes," she whispered, swinging at an invisible opponent. "This should do just fine."

FIVE

Afternoon rolled along and Boone still needed a new cover. He and Rabbit had secured a place to sleep in the newly finished Custer Hotel. As luck would have it, just one room was vacant due to the shooting death of one of the patrons. Whose death, Boone didn't ask.

Their horses were taken to the livery by one of the hotel's boys. Rabbit had thrown in a generous tip to make sure Nickel and Dime were well cared for.

The beds for the new hotel's rooms were on the way, but the storm had delayed freight from Cheyenne. A clean floor for a bedroll and a roof to keep the weather away gathered no complaints from either of them. Hell, Boone was just happy not to spend another night freezing his toes off. He was going to have enough trouble sleeping with his aching shoulder.

After dropping off their gear in their room, the two of them sat for a meal in the hotel's modest dining room, which was chock-full of sophisticates and grubbers alike. Deadwood was attracting fortune seekers from every walk of life—gamblers, miners, financiers, and outlaws. All of them had one thing in mind: Money.

The hotel served up basic food at gold rush prices, but neither Boone nor Rabbit complained about that either.

"Nice to have some beans that ain't burnt or crunchy," Rabbit goaded, his mouth half full. When they sat down at the table, he'd joked that he was through with Boone's cooking, at least for now.

"Still be nice to have a meal without some saddle tramp working his jaw all the time."

"Aww, Booney. No serenades then?"

"You can't carry a tune in a bucket, Rabbit."

"You remember that Lauder's Mercantile haul all three of us did? Uncle Mort surprised us with that prickly-pear pie when we camped that night outside Las Cruces on the way back to Santa Fe?"

Boone chuckled, nodding slowly. "That javelina he cooked up was good, but not the taters. How the hell did he end up with taters burnt *and* raw?"

Rabbit grinned wide. "Could be it was the whiskey. 'Member? He was celebratin' a year's worth of freightage contracts with Lauder."

Boone nodded again. "Probably should've cooked supper for him that day."

"Uncle Mort never was much of a cook, but he sure could drive a team." Rabbit scraped his spoon across his tin plate to clean up the last of the beans.

"Probably best not to talk about him like he's gone already. We haven't really even started looking yet." Boone pushed his empty plate away and sat back, his gut heavy with more than food.

"Ah, shit. You're right. Don't know why I said it like that. Maybe we should get to searchin' for the ol' coot, though."

"First, I'm looking for a cover."

"Right, I need a new knife since that beastie took off with mine stuck in his side. Feel kinda naked without it."

"Now there's a discomforting thought," Boone said.

"What you're seein' in your mind is a *real* man. Don't be jealous."

Boone snorted.

As soon as they'd finished their coffee, Rabbit tossed some

coins on the table and Boone led the way to the front doors. They closed their coats and headed out of the hotel, pausing on the boardwalk.

"I'll head up the way," he told Rabbit. "I saw a *merceria* with some hats in the window."

"I'll find a knife someplace. Maybe poke around, see what I can learn." Rabbit looked up the street. "Meet you back here in a while."

Knowing Rabbit, he planned to do more than just *poke* around. He meant to find out about this town. Not because of an interest in the comings and goings of folks—rather an interest in survival. And he meant to find out about their uncle, too. What Boone didn't know was Rabbit's intent when it came to that woman undertaker.

Boone meant to find out some things, too.

He stood for a bit and watched Rabbit hop across a deep ditch cut into the road by runoff, wade through the mud and slush, and start up the boardwalk on the other side of the street. *Good luck, amigo.* There was no telling what kind of trouble that spitfire might get into, but Boone had no doubt that Rabbit could handle it.

The sun was showing itself now and then from behind the blue-gray clouds, but it was almost ready to say its good-byes for the day. Never sets this early in Santa Fe, he thought, and headed up the street opposite Rabbit.

Shopkeepers had pushed the snow off the boardwalks into piles that lined each side of the street, forcing foot traffic to stick to the cleared walkways. Still, Boone had no problem making his way, inquiring in this business and that with all the subtlety he could muster about wagons and uncles, undertakers, and odd creatures in the woods.

After half an hour or so, he'd gathered only a smidgeon of information, but when he added it to what he'd learned from Billwitty, it helped.

He'd never in his life run across so many different languages in one town. Not even in Santa Fe, where immigrants from all over stopped to rest before heading on to settle in new territories. Hell, San Francisco didn't have this many cultures mixed together. Of course, Boone's time in that city was consumed with securing Rabbit's release from jail, so his opportunity to scout around had been curtailed.

At the *merceria*, or the "haberdashery" as the snooty shopkeeper had called it, he'd found the perfect cover—black with a wide brim. He was hesitant to commit to a used hat, but it fit like he trained it himself. The bullet hole, and the amazing stories of survival to go with it as told by the shopkeeper, ensured that this was the cover for him. Bullet holes were good luck, Boone was pretty sure. The shopkeeper agreed that in a place as rowdy as Deadwood, Boone could use all the luck he could get.

The town was gearing up for the evening by the time Boone returned to the Custer Hotel. He stepped under the hotel's awning and leaned on a post next to Rabbit, who was sitting on a narrow bench scraping his thumb across the blade of his shiny new Bowie knife.

He grinned up at Boone and slid the knife into a new brown leather sheath strapped to his lower leg. "Got the sheath for free!"

Rabbit was particular about his rig. He had designed and tooled the custom two-gun holsters on his hips. The holster on his left hip for his sawed-off shotgun could be removed, allowing him to carry just his pistol on his right hip. This, he had explained to Boone, was so he wouldn't attract too much attention.

He squinted at Boone's new-old hat. "Kinda wide in the brim. Guess that helps even you out, top to bottom."

Boone stared impassively at Rabbit.

"Got stains on it," Rabbit added.

"Yep."

"Got a hole in 'er, too."

"Noticed."

"Looks like a bullet hole."

"The man said it was."

Rabbit pondered that for a breath, then he began picking at the dirt under his fingernails with the oversized Bowie knife. "Some folks think there's a curse on this town since this here land is sacred to the Sioux." He pointed at the ground with his knife and then resumed picking his fingernails. "And before that it was Kiowa and Arapaho and Crow. I don't recall who else they say it belonged to. Might be cursed because of that. That's what people are sayin'. Heard the name 'White Grizzly' more than once. People say it's been seen close to town at times. The beastie they described sounds to be what we attempted to dispatch back on the trail, but that wasn't like no grizzly I ever seen. Nobody knows nobody who killed a White Grizzly, or whatever it is we saw on the trail. There's talk of other things in the woods, too."

He lowered his voice. "Evil things, they say."

Boone let that set for a bit. "Well, none of us should be here, sure enough. The Fort Laramie Treaty says this belongs to the Lakota Sioux. But gold is gold, and once these poor buggers have the fever they won't stay away, even though the U.S. Army is at war with the Sioux all around these parts. After what happened to Custer, gives me pause to be here."

Rabbit stared up at him for too long.

Boone knew that look. "You should try reading once in a while, Rabbit."

"I read."

"I mean something other than those penny dreadfuls."

"It's good readin'. They got pirates sometimes. And I like the pictures."

"Pick up a newspaper. Educate yourself. Make Uncle Morton

proud."

"Just hold up one second. Uncle Mort is plenty proud. Told me so hisself."

"See, that right there. It's not *hisself*. It's *himself*. He's always wanted both of us to get a good education."

"Duuuhh, if you say so, boss. Daaar, I sure is thinkin' on gettin' me sum lernin' someday. Yuk yuk." Rabbit stood and stretched his arms over his head. "Where are we off to this evening, my good man?" he said in a passable British accent.

Boone chuckled. "A place called Belle Grande Theatre down in the Badlands, smartass." He took on a more serious tone. "From what I garnered this afternoon, it sounds like we need to watch ourselves. There's an opium den in town."

Rabbit's forehead furrowed, all humor leaving his face.

Most of the time opium knocked users on their asses, but once in a while it made them crazy in the head. It was five years past when a *loco* opium fiend in Denver went on a tear in a saloon and used a butcher's knife to carve up three prostitutes and a boozy dude. Rabbit had walked in on the bloodbath and the killer charged him. One between the eyes from Rabbit's pistol put the bastard down, but Rabbit had a front row seat to the aftermath. The sight of what was left of those girls had changed him. Easygoing Rabbit still showed at the surface, but underneath that cocky smile he now had a low tolerance and lightning-fast fuse for brutes and murderers who committed violence against the innocent. It didn't matter whether the victim was a woman, a child, or even an animal. And Rabbit could back it up.

"Let's go find Uncle Mort," he said to Boone.

Recognizing the hard look in Rabbit's eyes, Boone grimaced. If any harm had come to their uncle, there was going to be hell to pay.

He stayed on Rabbit's heels during the quick walk to Belle Grande Theatre, which sat in a line of lumber and canvas-covered buildings along Main Street in the lower Badlands part of Deadwood. An almost mirror image of the structures lined the other side of the street.

Boone stood on the boardwalk near the front entrance of the theatre. Looking anything but grand, it was much like every other building in the Badlands with timber hastily milled and assembled into a roof and walls. The tall, ornate false front suggested the grand aspirations of the owner. It was more than adequate for an establishment offering gambling, drinking, and dancing girls in a town bursting with men concerned only with gold, the price of whiskey, and a poke.

Laughter and loud voices, along with a whistle now and then, emanated from the building, adding to the din up and down the street. An occasional gunshot in the distance punctuated the gold town symphony. Business was picking up as the sky darkened fully into evening and the temperature dropped. Miners, along with those in town to take advantage of them, were heading to their favorite pastimes. Boone looked through the window to the side of the main entrance. He scanned the bar lined with drinkers and then the tables, one by one.

He glanced at Rabbit, who was slowly spinning the cylinder of his Colt, peering one-eyed at each chamber. "We're here for Uncle Morton," Boone reminded him. "No need for dustups with rough talkers."

Rabbit nodded once.

Through the window Boone's gaze landed on a man of average height and weight wearing a brown hat sitting at one of the tables. "Got him."

"You sure it's him?" Rabbit holstered his pistol and peered in the window to spy on the man Boone pointed out.

"Mostly. Brown bowler with a feather. Black hair, spaghetti moustache." He tipped his head in the direction of the man with a thick moustache curled up on the ends almost touching his nose on each side. "McDonald. Just like Billwitty described."

"We should run Billwitty outta town. He's competition, you know," Rabbit joked. "Hey, a chair just opened up at McDonald's table. I'll go see what he knows."

He was halfway through the door when Boone grabbed the sleeve of his coat and hauled him backward. "Hold up there, Jesse James."

"Sheeat, Boone. What is your problem with me walkin' through doorways today?"

"You remember what we saw earlier. If you're not careful in this town, it's likely to get you shot."

"Stop worryin', Booney." Rabbit pulled his Colt, spun it, and holstered it again in a blur. It was unlikely anyone but Boone saw it. He grinned and pointed at his face. "Ain't nobody gonna shoot somethin' pretty as this."

Boone grinned back. "Let's just try and get this done with zero bloodshed. Anyway, how many guns you think you're good for? Everybody in there's packing and we already know folks in this town don't mind using hardware."

"Enough for you not to worry your lopsided head. At least most of them probably speak English. Remember that town in *Tejas*? All German, not a one speakin' so as I could understand. They liked to point guns, too. Good food, though. Schnitzel, wasn't it?" Rabbit drifted away, probably thinking of the breaded meat and apple strudel they both filled their bellies with each time they were in that Texas town.

Boone flicked his ear. "Get your head back here. I'm taking that empty chair next to McDonald before somebody else does. You need to make sure he doesn't have any belligerent friends backing him."

Rabbit smirked. "Belligerent, right." He pushed through the door again, mumbling about Boone's inability to use the same words as everybody else.

Once inside, Rabbit turned away from the bar on the left and wandered through the tables toward the stairway on the right, studying Belle Grande's customers.

Boone headed straight to McDonald's table, excusing himself around a girl carrying a load of full beer mugs.

"Evening, gentlemen. Name's Boone McCreery. Like to join your game."

"Bill McDonald," said the man to his left, tipping his bowler hat at Boone.

"Have a seat," said the man opposite Boone. "I'm 'bout done here. McDonald's havin' himself a night."

Boone looked at McDonald's stash of two small leather bags filled with what was probably gold dust, two stacks of silver dollars—one of which had toppled over from being piled too high—and a stack of $10 gold eagles. The stranger across from Boone had two silver dollars and an empty beer mug.

Boone looked to the man on his right with his hand extended for a shake. He wore a torn, ratty ten-gallon hat and a big grin minus one tooth.

"Name's Hank Varney," he said. He took Boone's hand and shook it with gusto. "Judgin' by yer hat, yer runnin' with more than yer share of good luck. Could use a lick of it myself. Mr. McDonald here seems to think all my money's his."

Hank's stash was a small pile of two-bit and half-bit coins, barely enough to fill a palm.

Boone pulled a handful of silver dollars from his vest pocket and began stacking them on the table. He glanced at Rabbit, who had circled around to the bar and ordered a drink.

Rabbit gave Boone a fleeting nod and picked up the two shots of whiskey the bartender finished pouring, downed one of them, and waited with the other in hand.

Boone could tell by the way Rabbit was ready to spring that he'd picked up on the situation at the table and was waiting for the stranger to leave. There'd be no chance to work on McDonald before Rabbit interfered, damn it.

Hank grabbed the cards and began shuffling. "Game's

jackpot. You okay with that, Mr. McCreery?"

"Sure."

"I'm out." The stranger across from Boone grabbed his coins and shoved back his chair as he stood. "McDonald, yer a bastard!" He added a snarl before limping toward the bar.

McDonald chuckled. "No luck far tha' gimp dis' evenin'," he said in a heavy Irish accent.

As Boone attempted to translate McDonald's words, Rabbit plunked the other shot of whiskey in front of Boone and rounded the table to sit in the newly vacated seat.

"Hiya, boys! I'm lookin' to purchase a buckboard of fair quality and a fella at the bar said one of you was sellin' a wagon in here the other day." He tipped his hat at Boone. "Thought I'd buy you a drink since you're empty, mister. Get the dealin' off to a good start."

Boone understood Rabbit's game and played along. "Wasn't me." He sipped the whiskey.

McDonald looked at Rabbit and cocked one eyebrow. "A buckboard, ye say? Now why would ye be wantin' a buckboard?"

"Goin' huntin' for white bears between here and Hillyo. Need a wagon to bring 'em in. Pelts should be worth somethin' extra. You heard of any white bears around here?"

Boone stifled a cough and took another sip of whiskey.

Leaky-mouth was on a roll. Rabbit might as well come out and ask about Uncle Morton, too, while he was at it. Out of the corner of his eye, Boone noticed Hank had paused in the midst of raising his mug of beer.

"Had me a nice buckboard, I did," McDonald said. "Up until last night. Lost it in a run o' bad luck. If I dinna know better, I'd say I was cheated, but Billwitty is no cheater. Hard-workin' man, that Billwitty."

"Ain't got it to sell then?" Rabbit was on the hunt now. He'd be insufferably happy with himself for a week if this worked.

Boone settled in, waiting for the opportunity to help Rabbit if he needed it.

The piano player started in on a jumpy melody and four dancing girls jiggled onto the stage at the back of the room, lifted their ruffled petticoats, and began kicking high to a chorus of whoops and whistles from the crowd.

Boone smirked. This was the *Theatre* in Belle Grande Theatre?

"No, lad," McDonald said. "But ye might try over at Keller's livery stable. He sells equipment from time to time when his customers dunna pay him. That's where I got mine." McDonald's attention shifted to the dancing girls' flying legs, his cards lowered.

"I heard tell of some strange kinda creatures roamin' the hills out that way some time back," Hank offered, setting his mug on the table. "Ya seen any, yerself?" His gaze centered on his beer.

"Not a bear, exactly," Rabbit said, aiming a raised brow at Boone. "They *should* be hibernatin'."

Boone nodded. Hank knew something about that beast, it was obvious. "So, are you in town to hit the easy life, Mr. Varney?"

"Thought maybe I'da chance at it. Claim's a bust, tho'. Not takin' much color out. McDonald here just took two days of pannin'."

"Cards don't always favor," Boone said. "I don't know how people here find the bits just to buy a whiskey or two."

"I do okay. Work for an undertaker to earn for vittles an' such."

Rabbit perked up.

"Undertaker, huh?" Boone said, aiming a squint at Rabbit. "Dirty work, I imagine."

Hank's face wrinkled. "Miss Johanssen don't do no dirty work."

"Clementine Johanssen?" Rabbit's sights locked onto Hank.

"I know a bit about them strange creatures in the hi ..." Hank stopped abruptly, his eyes widening. "I mean them bears out ... You was talkin' about bears, wasn't ya? White bears is ...

I seen a black bear once ..." His faced contorted in a pained grimace. "I need to get goin'. Got things to take care of. Was nice meetin' you fellas." He jolted the table with his thighs as he stood, knocked his chair over, and made a beeline for the door.

Boone's slack-jawed expression mirrored Rabbit's.

"Let's go find that undertaker," Rabbit said, rapping twice on the table with his knuckles.

Boone finished his whiskey and stood. "First, we talk to Keller at the livery stable."

McDonald was so busy watching the dancing girls he didn't seem to notice them leave the table.

Outside, a stiff breeze coming from up the gulch chilled Boone's body to the bone. He pulled his coat tight around his neck.

Thankfully, they didn't have far to go. The livery was a short hop north and across the street from Belle Grande Theatre. It was a large, fully finished building with a gambrel roof and substantial upper level for hay. An adjacent lot served as quarters for stored wagons of every kind. Buckboards and farm wagons, buggies, and even a sheep wagon pushed to the back of the lot. The doors were closed against the cold, but the light shining through the windows and the steady *clang clang clang* of a hammer was invitation enough for Boone.

Toward the back of the building was a blacksmith shop, complete with a giant anvil, a forge, and a wall full of bending, pounding, and punching tools. A tall, square-shouldered man with massive forearms held a horseshoe with long tongs and struck it with the hammer. The forge kept the temperature nice and cozy on this side of the livery doors.

"Ho there!" Boone closed the distance to the blacksmith, glancing at the stalls lining each side. Inside every stall stood two horses.

The blacksmith turned, hammer in the air, and looked at Boone, then Rabbit. "We're full up."

"You Keller?" Boone asked.

The blacksmith shrugged his square shoulders. "Might be. Depends who's askin'."

"Name's Boone McCreery. Wondering if you might be able to tell us about a wagon you sold a while back."

Keller lowered his hammer and dunked the horseshoe in a pail of water. A hiss of steam billowed from the bucket. "I sell lotsa rigs, saddles, wagons, that sorta thing." He picked up a poker and shuffled the coals around in the forge, stoking it a few times.

"This one was different," Boone said. "Nice rig. Mitchell. *Morton & Sons* painted on the sides."

"Custom woodwork. Bright green paint," Rabbit added.

Keller grabbed another horseshoe from the forge with the tongs and laid it on the anvil. He struck the horseshoe and stopped. "I do remember that Mitchell. Belonged to a … what was his name … Morely … Mo …"

"Morton," Rabbit supplied.

"Yep. Think that's it." Keller struck the horseshoe again.

Rabbit crossed his arms, his eyes narrowing. "Why would you sell a man's wagon? Where's the team?"

"Sold them, too."

"You didn't answer me. Why would you sell a man's rig?"

Boone could hear the sharp edge of frustration in Rabbit's voice. He felt it in his chest, too, along with a bite of unease.

"Listen," Keller said. "I don't have room to store every wagon and feed every animal a deadbeat decides to saddle me with here. I got a business to run."

"Easy," Boone whispered to the spitfire and put his hand on his partner's shoulder.

Rabbit flexed under Boone's hand. "So, blacksmith," he said, speaking low and quiet. "Morton didn't pay his bill, you say?"

"That's right. I give three days to pay up or I sell. Them's the rules." Keller pointed his hammer at the sign on the wall stating exactly that.

"When did you sell the Mitchell?" Boone asked.

"Oh, 'bout four days ago. Yer man Morton said he was headed to Lead and would be back the next day. Well, he wasn't. Or two more days after that. Three days total." The blacksmith pointed at the sign again, and then put the horseshoe back into the forge. "But I gave him an extra day after that 'cause it was such a nice rig."

"Damn." Rabbit pushed his hat back and scratched his forehead. "Now what, Booney? He must have taken Tink and Minny with him."

"Did he have a dog and a mule when he left here?" Boone asked the blacksmith.

Keller grunted. "He had a dog and a hinny."

"That's him," Rabbit said. "We headin' to Lead at first light?"

Boone sighed. "I'm guessing so."

"If you run into the Manuels," the blacksmith said, "they got the biggest outfit up there. Can't miss it. That's probably who yer man went to see. Not sure why he would, though. They don't got much cause or use for a freighter up there. Leastways not yet. Told me before he headed out that he already got himself a contract right here in Deadwood, so I can't reason why he'd waste time goin' up there. Anyway, you boys might wanna step light in Lead."

Boone was trying to soak up Keller's news. What contract? Who with?

"Why's that?" Rabbit asked the blacksmith.

"Ain't much up there but those miners and they ain't the kind of men you wanna go messin' with. They don't take to strangers too good. You get 'em riled and it's likely to get you both killed."

SIX

It's happened several times recently, but the pigs usually just leave a few bones ...

Clementine had done her best to focus on routine business at The Pyre until the sun dipped under the horizon, but her thoughts weren't on the scrawny dead man full of bullet holes that Hank had left on her table. They were on Big Joe's cadaver and the Kee Luk pigsty.

One body found in a hog pen wasn't something to raise hackles in Deadwood. Hell, in a town where knifings and gunplay were as common as sunsets, a dead body rarely gave rise to an eyebrow or two. But multiple bodies? That gave Clementine a fair bout of indigestion.

It wasn't only where Big Joe's body had surfaced that had her frowning at nothing repeatedly throughout the afternoon, but also that odd wound on his abdomen. Had he suffered a lingering death? What could have caused that hole if not a bullet? A knife, maybe, but that didn't explain the state of his internal organs.

Clementine grabbed one of the waxed canvases Hank had left in the corner and covered the holey dead man on her table.

Big Joe's downfall wasn't natural by any means. Someone with more knowledge than she possessed should investigate his remains thoroughly. Someone who knew what to look for and why.

Her experience studying dead bodies dated back to her arrival in the Black Hills months ago—albeit they had been several grueling months filled with one body after another passing through her hands. Her days had been spent recording the *who* and *how* for each corpse, prepping what remained for Deadwood's bone orchard without discovering anything meaningful. The task for which she'd been hired eluded her as summer's green turned into autumn's gold and the snow began to pile up in the shadowed corners of the gulch.

Months of death on her hands ...

Yet she'd still received no guidance from her benefactor. Not even a note, which seemed odd.

She shook off her concern on that front, returning to her job of disposing bodies.

With her lonely routine had come a yearning for distractions, such as sharing stories with the girls at Yellow Strike Saloon and over at The Dove where she enjoyed her baths, or hunting down bastards like Finnigan—even though murderers of his ilk were not the reason she was brought here.

The roots of her purpose would lead to something much more sinister than plain old murder. At least that was what had been insinuated before she agreed to the contract.

She pulled off her leather apron and hung it on the wall peg near the back door, returning to the wash bucket warming on the stove. *Finally*, she thought as she scrubbed her hands with soap. Her blood rushed at the possibility that she was on the trail of a killer worthy of her trade.

The dead bodies found in Kee Luk's hog pen were evidence of a dark and depraved crime even by Deadwood standards. Someone was trying to hide tracks. Pigs were far better at eliminating evidence of a crime than a mineshaft, where a body might eventually be discovered, especially in these gold- and silver-laced hills.

But why go to such lengths? She held her dripping hands over the fire's warmth. The water sizzled on the hot metal.

Worse yet, how many bodies had those pigs eaten so far?

These were ponderings to which Clementine needed to find answers as soon as the world outside The Pyre quieted down and she could steal through the darkness without drawing any attention.

It was nearing midnight when she shuttered the windows and dressed for a night of sitting still under the cold stars. She could have closed her shop sooner and snuck over to Kee Luk Laundry, but she doubted anyone in the business of dumping the dead in hog pens came out to play when the living might yet be wandering up and down the streets. Plus, the moon hadn't come out from behind clouds until recently, and she needed its light to make her way through the night undetected.

She opened the front door and peeked outside, easing back as a couple of miners hurried through the cold in the direction of the saloons. As soon as they were out of earshot, Clementine slipped outside and locked the door behind her.

After a glance right, she stole left toward Chinatown, creeping from shadow to shadow. A woman alone at night on the rough streets of Deadwood garnered curiosity she'd rather avoid, even if she was capable of facing off with most men and coming out the last one standing.

Her woolen overcoat did little to block the icy gusts swirling up the street. She pulled it tighter around her, adjusting the leather-wrapped Eagle Claw that was digging into her side. She'd tied up the sides of her beaver fur hat so it kept the top of her ears warm yet didn't muffle the sounds of the night.

Unlike the Badlands with its liquor and prostitution lairs, the Chinese district's dark storefronts and tents reminded Clementine of an abandoned mining town. There was not a soul to be seen. She kept an eye out for any signs of life as she slunk along the street. At this time of night, a swaying addict might surface from one of the various opium dens in Deadwood's Hop Alley and shoot at shadows, including hers.

There was no light emanating from Kee Luk Laundry's single window or rough-hewn door. The wooden sign hanging over the entrance creaked back and forth in the frigid breeze.

Clementine eased into the dark, narrow alley dividing Kee Luk and the bakery next door, unsure what obstacles she might stumble upon as she made her way through the thick shadows. She kept a hand on the wood-slab wall for balance as she crunched through the snow and frozen mud, almost tripping twice on boards left in the alley.

A waft of hog manure greeted her when she rounded the back of the building, the smell dulled by the cold. In the moonlight she could see the sty. It butted up against the side of the gulch. A couple of shacks big enough to hold supplies or feed dotted the silver landscape.

She moved closer to the fence corralling the pen. A group of pigs huddled together for warmth under a lean-to, its roof sagging from a blanket of snow. A corn bin and what looked to be a large wooden laundry tub between the Kee Luk building and the hog pen offered good cover for her to sit and keep watch.

Sinking into a loose pile of hay in a shadow-filled gap between the bin and the tub, Clementine tried not to breathe through her nose. Whatever was in the tub reeked. A quick glance in it made her cringe. What was that? A stew of slaughtered hog offal? She pressed her wool scarf against her nose. Between that tub and the stench of hog shit, this place must be nearly uninhabitable in the summer, not to mention overrun with flies.

Worming deeper into the hay, she settled in for what was likely going to be an all-night vigil. Memories of past successes with the razor-sharp weapon secured at her hip played through her thoughts as she waited and watched in the dim moonlight.

The wind whistled through the boards in the corn bin.

A loose piece of tin on one of the shacks rattled and creaked.

A gunshot rang out farther up the gulch, followed by several loud hoots of drunken revelry.

The pigs shuffled and grunted.

Something rustled and crunched behind her, sounding like ...

She no sooner heard the footfalls than a sharp pain blasted through her head and everything faded to black.

Something was poking Clementine in the cheek.

She shifted and it tickled her nose.

Opening her eyes, she blinked a couple of times to clear her vision. What was that? A piece of hay?

She sat upright and groaned. Pain tore her thoughts into fragments, the intensity of it spurring waves of nausea for several seconds.

The stench in the air didn't help. She pulled up her scarf, breathing through the wool.

Everything flooded back at once—the shadow-filled night, the whistling wind, the reeking hog sty and offal, the sound of footfalls on the frozen ground, her throbbing skull.

She touched the left side of her head under her fur hat. Her cold fingers came out sticky and wet with blood. She must have taken a hit. Lucky for her, the thick beaver fur had helped cushion the blow. Although her afi would often say that her head was too hard to crack open with anything less than Odin's spear.

Someone must have been waiting when she arrived and watched her settle into her hiding spot. But who? Were they still spying on her?

How long was I out? Judging from the stickiness of her blood and cold but not frozen fingers and toes, it couldn't have been more than a half hour.

After listening and watching for several more breaths, Clementine struggled to her feet. The blurred edges of her vision sharpened along with her other senses while she waited. She scanned the shadows again for any movement.

Save for the scuffling pigs, the night was frozen in place.

Too bad it wasn't snowing. She could have checked for fresh footprints in the snow, but as it was there was a mess of tracks running back and forth to the laundry and shacks.

A commotion of groinks and squeals from the hog pen drew her attention. She squinted into the silvery light. Something had roused the pigs.

After one last search for a sign of whoever had hit her, Clementine crept to the pen, keeping low to the ground. She peered through the fence railings at the snorting mass huddling in the near corner. Ears and bony hooves stuck up here and there, some pigs were squeezed in so tightly they were upended.

A lone pig broke free of the crowd and waddled toward her, a muddy chunk of something gray and fleshy in its mouth. Two more pigs followed, grunting staccato protests at the escapee. All three reached the fence in front of her and began to wrestle and play tug of war with the chunk of ...

What is that?

It was too hard to see in the moonlight. She stood and leaned over the fence for a better view, making her sore head pound harder. The tug-of-war prize slipped free of the pigs' mouths and flipped into the air.

Clementine reached out and caught it by a muddy ... *finger?*

She had enough time to register that she was holding onto a human hand before one of the pigs rose up on its haunches, snatched the morsel from her, and scurried to another part of the pen. The other pigs trotted behind the first, squealing in anger.

Great Odin's beard! Clementine wiped her hand off on her trousers. She should have brought some of that alcohol from Yellow Strike Saloon with her to clean her hands.

Her focus returned to the mass of pigs undulating in the corner of the pen, each porker battling for position and a piece of the feast. She needed to know who was being served as the main course, and if any answers could be found about her attacker, before the pigs chewed up the evidence.

But that would mean joining the pigs in the sty. She groaned, her head throbbing harder at the notion. This was probably going to put her off eating pork for a good long time.

She tucked her Eagle Claw into her coat pocket for safe keeping, gearing up mentally for what she might find in the sea of pigs. They would make fast work of the pieces and parts, so there was no time for hesitation. Not to mention that her attacker might return soon to dump off more parts, and she'd rather be on this side of the fence if that happened.

She grabbed a stout herding stick as tall as she that had been left leaning against the corn bin and moved over to the corner where the pigs were wrestling for food. As she neared, more grayish chunks of human flesh became visible in the pen. Further away, at the edge of the bustle of hooves and snouts, Clementine saw what looked like a piece of a burlap bag partially buried in the mud and feces.

Mindful of her coat, she vaulted the low fence. Her boots broke through the muck on the other side, sinking up to her heels with each step toward the scuffling mob. The night was cold, but not enough to harden more than the top layer of pig shit coating the floor of the pen. The odor was even sharper up close, her scarf providing little barrier to the stench.

The horde took no notice as she picked up one of the large chunks of flesh. Her boots sank deeper into the muck where the mass's body heat had the temperature several degrees warmer. She held the piece eye-level in the silver light of the moon. There were four fingers yet on this hand. The thumb was missing, though. Bitten off, judging by the ragged skin.

She dropped the hand and waded deeper into the herd, nudging pigs aside with the end of the stick.

Another hand lay in the muck, clearly visible in the

moonlight. There were two fingers left on this one.

After a prod with the stick she found a third hand. Five digits remained, but half of the palm was bitten off.

A fourth hand was missing all but the thumb.

By the time she finished poking and jabbing her way through the crowded corner of the pen, she estimated there were around twenty hands total. However, it was difficult to know for sure. The pigs were grinding the pieces into bony hamburger, burying whatever remained with their hooves.

There were other body parts, too, mashed and driven into the muck. During her count of hands, Clementine had seen glimpses of what looked like internal organs.

She shuddered at the intensity of the hogs' snuffling and snorting and crunching of the bones. What a mess it must be under her boots. Thankfully, the moonlight dulled the colors of the gore, gracing the pen with shades of gray. But that stench! She'd have to dip her boots in raw alcohol to get them clean.

The thickest grouping of pigs shifted her way. They surrounded Clementine, bumping into her while their snouts plowed through the manure and remains. She pushed free of the huddling mass, escaping toward the fence line near the Kee Luk building.

Something glinted in the moonlight ahead in the muck. She leaned down to take a closer look. A ring! One tug and it slid free from the finger. Tossing aside the finger, she wiped the filth from the ring on her trousers and held it up to study in the silvery light.

There was something carved into the pewter. Was that a goat? Or a pig? The latter seemed appropriate given her current location. She pocketed the ring to clean and inspect later.

The mob of pigs shifted again, leaving a clear path back to where she'd first vaulted the fence. After a quick glance left and right, she headed back toward her starting point.

Several steps later, a pig snorted right behind her. She looked over her shoulder at the same time a big hog rammed into the back of her legs. The force of the shove nearly launched her into the air. She stumbled, bumping into another pig that was following the first, and then bounced off of a third. Her boots tangled together and she fell into the cold muck face-first.

Consarn it!

Before she could push upright, hooves dug into her back, shoving her deeper into the shit. The herd of pigs rushed over and around her, trailing the leader of the pack. She lifted her chin and blew the crud out of her nose.

Jävla gris! she swore mentally in Norwegian.

Another hog attempted to leap over her but didn't have the height. Its hind leg slammed into the back of Clementine's skull, knocking her face into the cold shit again.

"*Potzblitz*," she snarled, using one of her amma's favorite Old German curses. She pushed up hard, spitting, wiping her face with her coat sleeve. "I'm going to roast you all on a spit!"

Scrambling to her feet, she pulled the herding stick from the manure in time to deflect two more pigs. Her vault over the fence was not as graceful this time thanks to the slick coating of pig shit covering her from head to toe, but she managed to land on her feet on the other side with the stick still in hand.

Scooping up a handful of snow, she scrubbed it down her face, cleaning off the worst of the mess. She reached down for a second handful of snow to finish the job—and froze.

The hairs rose on the back of her neck a split second before she heard a footfall crunch in the snow behind her.

Clementine came up fast, swinging the herding stick at the same time. It slammed into her attacker's weapon with a sharp *crack!* The stick splintered into two pieces.

She dove for the second piece, rolling through the snow before springing back to her feet. She rushed her attacker, one stick at the ready in front of her face, the other held high, set to strike. This time, she would be the one doling out the pain.

The dark figure retreated a few steps, weapon raised as if to chop wood.

Was that an axe? The handle seemed longer than usual. Clementine tried to make sense of what she could see, but the shadows were deceptive.

It didn't matter. She'd be damned if the bastard would get a second chance to split open her skull. Her temper flared white-hot. She'd teach this weasel a lesson.

"You should have killed me earlier when you had the chance." She tightened her grip on the sticks. There was no time to slip on her Eagle Claw still stuffed deep in her muck-covered pocket. "Now it's my turn."

She spun the sticks between them, distracting her enemy. In a blur, she lashed out and smacked one of his raised arms at the elbow. The stick connected with a solid *THUNK!*

Her foe whimpered, his arm falling limp. The long weapon dropped into the snow at his feet.

A loud "pop" sounded from somewhere behind her.

She pitched sideways, her instincts guiding her.

A bullet hissed past her head.

The bastard wasn't alone.

"I'll send you both to Hell!" She slammed the stick into his collar. The snap of bone resonated clearly in the quiet night.

A moan leaked from him as his knees folded.

She dragged him by the scruff of his neck behind the corncrib in case more bullets flew her way. She would have liked to draw out his pain as a payback for her headache, but there was no time. Two hard blows finished him off. To be sure he was dead, she stabbed him through the chest with one of the splintered sticks.

"Odin owns you now," she whispered.

Next, the shooter ...

Across the yard, she saw a shadowy form race around the corner of the Kee Luk building and disappear into the dark narrow alley leading to the street.

Clementine grabbed the remaining stick and chased after the gunman, pain jarring the left side of her head with every footfall. Several steps into the alley, her foot snagged on something, sending her into the wall of the bakery before tumbling to the ground.

Shoving to her feet, she whirled with the stick raised. In the thick shadows, she listened for the sound of breathing or the swish of clothing.

All was silent in the alley.

Several more seconds passed and still nothing. He must have escaped.

She cursed up at the stars. Tonight was not going as planned.

Turning, she headed back toward the man she'd left with a stick jammed in his chest. She needed to check if he had anything on his person that might help her identify him—or who had sent him.

She stumbled over the snag again on her way out of the alley, catching herself this time before falling to her knees.

"What in Hades?" Clementine muttered and felt along the ground for whatever had tripped her up twice now. Her hand touched a trouser-covered leg.

The shooter?

She grabbed the body by the ankle and pulled it clear of heavy shadows. Under the moonlight, the dead man looked like every other resident of Deadwood, with his sullied woolen coat and pants, thick whiskers, and hair undoubtedly hand-trimmed with a knife. A closer examination revealed his coat collar was wet and dark.

A sniff of her fingers confirmed the coppery scent of blood. Clementine tugged away the coat collar and turned the body toward the moonlight. A wound in the man's neck located below the hinge of his jaw oozed blood when pressed.

A fresh kill.

She wiped the skin clean with a handful of snow and found a puncture wound. It'd been made with a thin blade by someone who knew right where to place the sharp steel.

Sitting back on her heels, she blew out a breath. Was this another professional kill? Clementine couldn't be sure without dragging the body back to her table, but the wound certainly reminded her of the one she'd seen on the body brought in at the same time as Big Joe. This time, however, the stab would have elicited a quick and quiet death rather than a slow and painful one.

Her search of the man's pockets brought nothing, no gun or knife or identification of any kind. But on the right hand Clementine found another ring with the image of a creature resembling a pig-like goat. She pulled the one she'd found in the pen out of her pocket, cleaned it with a handful of snow, and held both next to each other. The images carved into the rings looked the same.

Sliding the rings on her fingers, she hurried over to the attacker she'd killed with the herding stick. A search turned up a third ring. It also had an engraving of a pig-like goat creature. She slid this one onto her ring finger.

She picked up the unusual weapon he'd wielded. It looked different than the axes she'd seen sold at the mercantile, but maybe this one belonged to Kee Luk Laundry. Some sort of specialized Chinese version of an axe that had been handy for the dead man to grab and take a swing at her. She leaned it against the large tub and scooped up some snow to clean her hands of this gory business.

Her head throbbed too much to bother with moving the bodies tonight. She wanted nothing more than to return to The Pyre, wash off the hog shit, pull on a clean muslin shirt, and fall into her cot.

"I'll see you later," she told her attacker, figuring someone would probably bring him and the other body by her place tomorrow. With one last glance at the pigsty, she eased into the dark alley and headed for home.

Behind her building, Clementine stripped out of her coat and clothes, stuffing them in a bucket next to the back door. Inside the safety of her walls, she cleaned off the smell of pigs and washed her hair in the cold, breath-stealing bucket of water she'd hauled in earlier. She'd have to visit The Dove's private bathing room down the street for a full scouring tomorrow.

Even though her eyelids were drooping, she took the time to check and stow her Eagle Claw. Little had her weapon helped her tonight. Next time, she'd wear it to the dance.

Shivering, she crawled under the covers and stared at the pewter rings on her fingers in the candlelight.

Three matching rings. Something didn't add up.

The two dead men were most likely the ones who'd dumped the body parts in the pigpen. Both of them having the rings would make sense. But why was there a ring on a hand *in* the sty?

And who had killed the man hiding in the alley next to Kee Luk Laundry? Such a proficient method of murder spoke of a hunter with a deft touch and the knowledge to sink a blade for a fast, silent death.

Clementine hadn't found a gun on the knifed man in the alley, but she suspected he'd been the one who shot at her. It appeared that the bastard had gotten off only one shot before he was stabbed in the neck.

Lowering her hand, Clementine rolled onto her side to ease the pressure of the painful lump on her head. She stared at the candle on the table next to her bed, reliving the events behind Kee Luk Laundry.

She'd been sloppy tonight, and not only the shit-covered kind of sloppy. Her enemies had been one step ahead of her from the start. Next time, she'd need to take more precautions and keep her back against solid walls.

No more mucking around with the stupid pigs, either.

She blew out the candle flame, burrowing into her thick blankets. Was the assassin who'd stabbed the gunman in the alley the same killer who'd pierced the lung of the man she'd had on her table? If so, had her life been purposely spared tonight? Or was she meant to be next but someone or something intervened?

Tomorrow, she was going to find some answers. But first, she was going to take a long hot bath over at The Dove and steam the stench of hog shit out of her sinuses.

SEVEN

"Rabbit! Wake up!" A familiar voice cut through the snarls and growls, silencing the screams of pain. Rabbit groaned in the sudden quiet, his pounding heart almost as loud as his quick breaths.

"Come on, Jack," Boone said again. A warm hand tugged on Rabbit's arm, which was shielding his face. "Open your eyes."

Rabbit lowered his arm, blinking in the bright hotel room. He glanced over at the window. The sun had crested the rim of the gulch, the orange-red rays melting frost from the edges of the glass.

Boone kneeled next to him, his dark brows drawn together in a frown. "You okay, *amigo*? Sounded like you were having a real humdinger of a dream. Lots of moaning and thrashing." His gaze drifted down Rabbit's neck to his chest. "Your shirt's soaked with sweat."

Groaning again, Rabbit sat up and covered his face with shaky hands. "Uncle Mort," he said in a croaky voice, staring at Boone between his fingers. He tried to reconcile the images from his nightmare. "He was … uh …" Rabbit swallowed hard. "Fuck."

Boone studied Rabbit for several seconds, his face lined. "What about Uncle Morton?"

Rabbit's memory of the nightmare slipped away in the morning light. He tried to recall the gruesome image of the beast, wincing as visions of his uncle being ripped to pieces flashed to the forefront instead.

Lowering his hands, he met Boone's eyes. "He was ... I don't know what it was. Uncle Mort was screamin'. Gettin' ripped apart by somethin'. Then he was on the ground, his foggy dead eyes lookin' up at me." Rabbit stared out the window, trying to come up with a description of his nightmare, but the scene had been a blur of teeth and blood. "Some sorta animal ... a beast ... somethin' unnatural." His eyes watered. Watching Uncle Mort suffer like that had felt like his own heart was being ripped from his chest.

"It wasn't real, Jack." Boone spoke low and level, soothing. "Just some frustrations coming to the surface, that's all." He patted Rabbit on the shoulder and stood, holding out his hand. "This business about Uncle Morton has been rough on both of us. I'm sure he'd tell us not to fuss over him, but damn if we aren't going to track him down and tan his hide for making us come all the way up here to find him." He huffed, adding, "In the snow."

Rabbit took Boone's hand and hopped up. He wiped his eyes with his sleeve. "This is some bullshit, ain't it, Booney? If he ain't dead, I'm gonna kill him."

An hour later, after a breakfast of beans and bacon served with bitter coffee at the hotel, Rabbit had his rig packed and horse saddled. He and Boone headed for Lead. Most of the snow from the latest storm had been trodden or cleared since they arrived in Deadwood, so they were able to move at a decent pace while the cold air froze their cheeks and ears.

The horses made their way along a trail just wide enough to fit a wagon. Occasional rock outcroppings on each side of the gulch broke the tall pines and spruce stands into patches. To Rabbit's left, a creek running deep and fast enough to make a man think twice about crossing it crashed and splashed against small boulders in its path. Tents drooping under a heavy layer of snow and cabins made of hand-hewn logs hunkered along the banks, spewing smoke into the air.

Rabbit caught glimpses of miners spread along the stream, working their pans, shovels, and pickaxes. They were hearty souls to be mining in this chill. The poor bastards must be picking through ice. At least it wasn't as cold as yesterday.

Uncle Mort's dead.

He scowled, trying to force the notion from his thoughts by focusing on something else.

His gaze returned to the men searching for gold. Could he make it as a miner? He'd choose someplace a little warmer if he were going to try his hand at it. He'd heard tell they were still pulling the color in Colorado, although it got plenty chilly there, too. Maybe down in Arizona Territory would be better.

Ripped to pieces.

The image of his uncle's foggy dead eyes slammed to the front of his thoughts.

"Goldurnit!" He glanced back at Boone. "You know my dreams ain't always right, Booney."

Boone nodded, grimacing while he worked his injured shoulder back and forth. "Sometimes dreams are just dreams." But he didn't meet Rabbit's gaze. He was being his usual calm, controlled self, which Rabbit surely appreciated at the moment because the truth was his dreams were often close to spot-on.

Further on, the trees had been hacked down to stubs. The trail widened into an almost respectable main street, lined with fifteen or so canvas-covered log cabins and an equal number of tents scattered about the place. A larger building sat near the center with the look of a mercantile.

"This little settlement might soon give Deadwood a run for its money," Boone said.

Rabbit nodded, but his attention was fixed on the fact that hardly a soul occupied the street. The entire area was quiet, uncomfortably so, as if the hills surrounding him were holding their breath. Those few folks present scurried from one building to the next, glancing around and shrinking back into shadowed doorways as Boone and Rabbit passed. The windows on all of the cabins were shuttered or covered haphazardly with rough-hewn boards. The tent walls appeared to be barricaded with tall stacks of firewood.

What in tarnation was going on here? Were they trying to keep out the weather or outsiders? The sun glinted off a bear trap laid out in the snow next to a nearby cabin. Several more traps lined the sides of other cabins, set and ready to snap. Hell, could be it was something else that had these folks acting all anxious. Bears should all be hibernating, so what were the traps for? A sharp-toothed critter the likes he and Boone had run into on the way into Deadwood?

Rabbit shifted in his saddle, feeling a heavy dread pressing down on him. He couldn't tell if it was something in the air or his own imagination, but Dime sensed it too. The horse shivered, keeping his head held high and ears alert.

"This town don't feel right, Booney. People are actin' strange. It's spookin' me and Dime."

They continued up the street, keeping the horses at a steady walk. "Nickel feels it too." Boone cocked his head subtly toward a nearby building. "We're being watched."

Rabbit caught sight of a face in the window before the torn grain sack being used as a curtain fell back into place. "Hope this ain't Lead," he said under his breath.

"Let's find out." Boone cupped his hands around his mouth. "Ho there! Is this Lead?" he hollered at a brown-haired, broad-shouldered man chopping firewood between two shacks.

The man lowered his axe and stared at them long and hard.

"Maybe that one don't speak our language," Rabbit said.

"Gayville," the man answered, pointing at his feet. He raised his axe and aimed the head further up the trail. "Lead, top of the hill."

Boone tipped his hat. "Thank you kindly, sir."

The woodcutter trained his axe on the two of them. "Best you drifters be movin' along," he warned, and then nodded, agreeing with himself.

"Niceties ain't wasted in Gayville, I guess," Rabbit said.

"Apparently not." Boone gave Nickel a cluck and the two headed up the trail.

Rabbit lagged behind a moment longer, forcing Dime to stay at an even walk. He studied the buildings and the few suspicious-acting—or maybe skittish—Gayville women or children who stepped out into the sunlight for a few seconds before scuttling to the safety of another door like prairie dogs. No doubt about it, this place was cowering from someone or something. He shook his head at the lengths and trials men would go through for a handful of gold.

As soon as he reached the south edge of Gayville, Rabbit trotted Dime up alongside Boone. "Some of those people seem off kilter to you? They looked downright strange to me."

Boone didn't answer.

"Acted strange, anyway. You musta noticed that much at least, what with the big upper story you got sittin' under that bullet-holed hat."

Boone still didn't respond.

Rabbit nudged Dime closer to Nickel and kicked Boone's boot. "I say, that town is an oddity. Kinda ghosty."

"I noticed."

"Might not be a bad idea if we checked it out with more curiosity and firepower." Rabbit glanced over his shoulder at Gayville. "I got the feelin' there was somethin' besides those people that was eyeballin' us."

Boone aimed squinty eyes at Rabbit. "Like what?"

"I don't know exactly, but it felt heavy on me. Ominous like. I think those people might be in some kind of trouble."

"Well, I agree with you on that, but we have a job to do, and I don't think it's in that town."

The stream had turned west some way back, but the trail

continued to wind up through the canyon past smaller clusters of tents, lean-tos, and cabins. The sounds of clanging and booming mixed with bird shrills and the crunch of snow and twigs along the way. Rabbit sniffed, periodically warming his cold nose with his handkerchief.

"First we go north downhill," he said to Boone's back. "Now it's south goin' uphill. Disagrees with my senses." He pulled a hunk of jerky from his pocket and popped it in his mouth.

Boone glanced back at him but kept quiet, plodding along. While he normally kept to himself, the tension visible on Boone's face had Rabbit wondering if that damned dream of his wasn't making both of them sweat bullets this morning.

They made their way south through the gulch, winding slowly upward at the foot of a ridge that rose four hundred or so feet above them. Near the top, the ridge and gulch converged into an east-leaning meadow that could be considered close to flat from what Rabbit had witnessed of the Black Hills. A small cluster of shacks, more haphazardly constructed than usual for a mining camp, sat to the east. Beyond, the slope dropped out of sight into another gulch. The dull, steady booming of a stamp mill reverberated through the clear, cold air.

It appeared they'd found Lead.

Rabbit popped another piece of jerky in his mouth, thinking on what he'd learned about this part of the Black Hills so far.

Deadwood was a true frontier mining town, populated with ruffians, swindlers, and murderers determined to stuff their pockets with gold or simply to revel in the mayhem prevailing in the lawless settlement. But it did have a share of charm and a level of sophistication lent by financiers, businessmen, and socialites from the East and West coasts.

In his short time in town, he'd gotten the impression some of the folks desired a taste of law and order. If his time on the trail had taught him anything about settlements, sheriffs and jails were the start of a more civilized settlement, followed by schools, churches, and politicians.

Rabbit surveyed the grouping of shacks and tents in front of him. While Deadwood was working on pushing up sprouts of refinement, including a newspaper office to record daily events, the settlement of Lead appeared to be on a different track.

According to the front desk clerk at their hotel, Lead was founded only a few months prior, but it was easy to see that unlike Deadwood, this was a mining camp pure and simple. Niceties were inconsequential, a distraction from the business of pulling riches from the rocks. No presentable streets were evident around the shacks, maybe because of the thick covering of snow, but Rabbit suspected mud trails were all he'd find come spring thaw.

One canvas-covered clapboard building toward the edge of the cluster of hovels displayed the potential to be communal due to its size and the two raggedy-looking characters tussling to the side of the main door. Whether it was a serious dispute or a simple contest, it was hard to say.

To the south a quarter mile lay the stamp mill Rabbit had heard after cresting the rim of the gulch. The mill exhibited the same practical, sparse nature as the town. Shoddily built additions and disrepair indicated the hasty, endless expansion and overtaxing of the building.

The rugged, unrefined nature of the camp felt far more comfortable to Rabbit than Deadwood's hustle and bustle or Gayville's shrouded dread. But these shacks were a far cry from the sprawling, tranquil hacienda he and Boone shared with their uncle. From time to time Rabbit and Boone had each considered working up ranches of their own, but neither could bring themselves to leave their aging uncle to manage his spread alone, so they stayed put.

Rabbit let his head loll to the side, measuring the mining settlement from another angle. "I think I could be happy here in this rough-edged town," he jested.

Boone swiveled his head. "Where's a town? All I see are dingy tents and a few ramshackle buildings."

"Uppity, that's what you are, Booney."

"I like to think of it as refined."

Rabbit pointed to one of the less dilapidated shacks in the camp. A rusty shovel, broken-handled pickaxes, and a couple of smashed carbide lamps lay in the snow in front of it. "I'll put a garden out back of that one. You can build me a nice and 'refined' barn behind it, and we'll have a first-rate hoedown with *chicas muy bonitas* spilling out the doors."

"You're in the wrong part of the country for *chicas*." Boone smirked. "From the looks of this place, you'd have to settle for dancing with men in dresses."

Rabbit chuckled. "Since most of the fellas around here look like somethin' the cat dragged in and the dog wouldn't eat, I'll stick to livin' under Uncle Mort's roof down south."

Back ringside in front of the local watering hole, the two fighters appeared to have made amends. They slapped each other on the back and then disappeared into the building, slamming the door shut against the cold.

"That's it?" Rabbit scoffed. "Seems pretty anti-climactic after all that swingin'. They must've needed to work some kinks out of their drinkin' arms."

"You feeling anything other than homesick?" Boone asked.

"I'm not homesick." Well, that wasn't true. "Okay, maybe a li'l homesick. I'd just like to find Uncle Mort and hit the road back south to sunshine and all that cacti. I'm used to dealin' with those sorts of pricks."

"You didn't answer my question."

Rabbit sniffed the air, sitting still in the sunshine for a moment. "Only thing I'm feelin' is cold."

"We should probably start there then." Boone clucked Nickel toward the log building the brawling pair had entered.

"Spared no expense on a hitchin' rail, I see," Rabbit muttered as he dropped Dime's reins onto a rope strung between two saplings. Three other horses were hitched the same way. Along the side of the log building, racks assembled out of pine poles held furs and pelts from various animals. A few of the pelts still dripped blood, staining the snow beneath bright crimson.

Boone stared at the pelts. He walked over to one in particular—larger than the rest, chocolaty brown with a brilliant white stripe across the rear haunches.

"What?" Rabbit paused outside the door. "You see somethin' worth sniffin' out?"

Boone started to reach toward the pelt, but then pulled back, shaking his head as he came toward Rabbit. "Nothing."

"You say it's sunny, Booney, but your face says it's rainin'."

"Never mind my face. Let's go inside," Boone said, still frowning as he grabbed the door handle. "Remember what the blacksmith said."

Rabbit followed Boone into the building, cringing at the eye-burning stink of smoke mixed with the sweat of too many bodies with too few baths. As his eyes adjusted to the gloom, he kept his thumb tucked into his belt close to the hardware on his hip, prepared to brandish if the need arose.

Closing the door, he leaned toward Boone, speaking low. "Feels like we got us a rough-and-tumble bucket of blood here. Reminds me of *El Gato Loco* saloon back home. Only thing missin' are the spent casings on the floor."

"Maybe so. Or maybe it's just a plain old bodega."

Shrugging, Rabbit scanned what appeared to be Lead's version of a saloon. An unattended, rough-cut plank bar supported by stumps of wood, a keg, and a few bottles on a shelf occupied one side of the room. At the center, a potbelly stove cranked out heat and filled the drafty room with smoke. Three tables and a few chairs of hand-hewn lumber crowded the stove. More rough-cut tables and chairs were strung out along the back wall. Sunlight seeped in through two small windows, piercing the smoke to make oblong patches on the sawdust- and dirt-covered floor.

The din of animated conversations ceased as gazes swung their way. Rabbit's jaw tightened in the sudden silence. "We're wadin' into quicksand here," he whispered.

Boone cleared his throat. "Good day, gentlemen."

Hard stares were the only replies.

"These misfits must've been underground in their dens when they passed out manners 'round here," Rabbit said. He counted the potential enemies, noting the guns and other visible weapons, and gave some consideration to the likelihoods and possible outcomes if things went sour. Seven miners and mountain men types sat or stood in groups around the stove. The poorly lit back corners of the shithole left room for a few more. *Too many bad angles and ugly hombres in here.* He wished he'd strapped on his sawed-off earlier that morning.

"Is it possible," a growly voice came from the shadowed far corner, "that someone extended an invitation to you undesirables?"

The man's voice had a German accent. Rabbit could see only the silhouette of a man in that corner thanks to the shadows and smoke shrouding him.

"We're not here to waste anybody's time," Boone replied. "Just wondering if anyone has seen a businessman who may have stopped by almost two weeks ago. A freighter, probably riding a mule."

Two grubby, hard-worn men at a table beyond the potbelly stove chuckled, conversing in lowered voices.

Something in their greasy smiles made Rabbit's trigger finger itch. He took a step toward the two, intending to find out what had them so damned chatty.

Boone grabbed Rabbit's shoulder, stopping him short. He said under his breath, "Let me see if I can figure this without bloodshed, huh?"

Rabbit snorted like a bull, but eased back. "I count seven plus a handful in the corners," he whispered. "Most of them are probably slewed with booze or laudanum, but those two curs at the table are troub—"

"No one has seen anyone like that here," the stranger with a growly voice interrupted Rabbit. His tone was downright unfriendly.

"I wonder if you're speaking for everyone here," Boone replied, not wilting. "Because I believe these twittering canaries may know a thing or two we'd find interesting." He pulled up alongside the chuckling grubbers' table. Rabbit joined him, staying out of lunging or kicking range.

"How about you fellows share the subject of your humorous preoccupation?" Boone prompted.

They glanced at each other, snickered again, and then focused on the dented tin cups in their hands.

"We're waiting." There was no mistaking the lowered horns behind Boone's words.

"Just commentin' on how mules cook up," the uglier of the two said. "Rance here says not so good as elk, but not too bad in a stew. I says they's just as good, long as it ain't his wife doin' the cookin'."

The red-headed cur across the table apparently named Rance guffawed. "If she heard you say that, Barnes, she'd cut yer nuts off with a rusty sickle."

Both grubbers snickered again.

A fire sparked in Rabbit's gut. "Any particular reason why your cookin' conversation got around to mules?"

Barnes turned in his chair, glaring up at Rabbit, looking like the back end of bad luck. "Any particular reason yer thinkin' it's business concernin' you?"

Rabbit was going to feed the son of a bitch his own teeth for taking that tone with him.

"I repeat, *Mein Herr*," the shadowed man from the corner

said, his raised voice filling the room. "No one here knows anything about your businessman."

Tension rippled among the other brutes in the saloon. Several tried to pretend they were minding their own business, but kept casting glances toward the main show. Three men in ragged coats and dirt-streaked trousers tipped their cups empty and headed for the door.

"Best you open up about that mule," Boone said, his scowl downright hostile. Apparently, he was done playing nice. "And the businessman while you're at it."

"His name was Morton," Rabbit said, resting his hand on the butt of his Colt. He was done playing, too. "And if he happens to be anything but in smilin' good spirits, you muck men are gonna get unhealthy real fuckin' quick."

"If yer talkin' about the mule, it probably ain't feelin' too good." Rance snickered again.

Boone moved quick as lightning, grabbing Rance by the ear and twisting hard. "Fun's over. Cough up."

While Rance whimpered, Barnes stood. "Listen, mister. We suffer claim jumpers 'round here 'bout the same as horse thieves and businessmen. Now cut a path, or you'll end up like … what was his name?"

"Busyman Marty," Rance said, twisting free of Boone's hold and leaning back in his chair. He spat in Rabbit's direction just for spite.

Rabbit snapped. He kicked out, his heel landing square on Rance's jaw, sending him tumbling backward out of his chair. The cur landed belly-up in the dirt, knocked out cold.

"Snicker at that, asshole," Rabbit said and spit on him, repaying the compliment. When he looked around, Boone was backing toward the door with his pistol drawn while keeping an eye on the stranger in the corner.

Apparently, they were vamoosing.

Movement to Rabbit's left drew his gaze as well as his pistol.

Two mountain men with knives and one miner with a shootin' iron rose from another table, their sights on him.

"Well, hello there, boys," Rabbit taunted. "Let's don't be hasty. I can partner with each of you for a Pecos promenade if that's your pleasure."

"Huh-uh!" Boone cocked his pistol. "None of you need to die here today."

"Come on, Booney. My finger's itchy. The iron's talkin' now."

The miner took the bait. Rabbit heard the click of a hammer and cocked his Colt almost instantly. But Boone was one step ahead of him.

BOOM!

The miner with the pistol held up his bloody hand, which was now two fingers short. The gun that had been in it a second before landed in the dirt. A screech rang out and the miner crumpled to the floor, scrambling to pick up his fingers.

"I had him," Rabbit told Boone.

"I know."

Rabbit turned his pistol on Barnes, his finger kissing the trigger. "Now, what was that about a mule?"

Barnes glanced at his unconscious pal and then at the wounded miner. His nostrils flared. "We don't need nobody pokin' around here. Your businessman come along, stickin' his nose where it don't belong. He says he wants to set up a freight office. Bullshit! Hornin' in on our claims is what he was doin'."

Rabbit squinted. "Then what?"

Barnes looked at the stranger in the corner before continuing. "We roughed him up some to teach him a lesson." Barnes pointed at the man still out cold on the floor. "Rance here got excited and shot yer man's mule in the gut. Took three more shots to finish it off. Rance made him watch while he dressed and skinned the beast. Then we sent yer man on his way back to Gayville. Deadwood. Don't much matter where, so long as he wasn't here."

"It was Minny," Boone told Rabbit. "That's her pelt hanging with the others on the frames along the side of the building."

Rage burned wildfire hot in Rabbit's veins. "That wasn't a mule, you stupid sonofabitch. She was a hinny." Rabbit raised his gun, aiming square center at Barnes's forehead. "Kindest, smartest, most gentle creature you ever laid eyes on." He cocked the hammer. "My uncle Mort has a saying, 'Show compassion when you can, fight when you need, and be frugal with vengeance.' Right about now, I'm thinkin' I need—"

BOOM!

Another gunshot rang out.

"Nobody move!" Boone shouted, his pistol aimed toward the far corner.

Rabbit spun his gun around and smashed the butt upside Barnes's cheek. The cutthroat slumped to the floor.

"I said, don't move!" Boone chastised, his gun still smoking.

"Sometimes my gun has a mind of its own." Rabbit glared at Barnes, backing toward the open door while keeping everyone in sight. He didn't have time to count the barrels pointed at him, but there were enough to make him sweat.

Boone held his gun steady on the stranger in the corner. He called to Nickel with a low-to-high whistle, then waited for Rabbit on the threshold.

Rabbit's boot heel touched down in the snow as Barnes sat up, holding his jaw.

"We'll be back to finish this, you fuckin' skunks!" Rabbit looked toward the shadowed corner. "Real soon," he promised and yanked the door shut.

"Rabbit!" Boone warned from his saddle.

"Yep." He stepped to the side a second before a swarm of bullets ripped through the door.

Boone had Dime waiting for him, reins in hand. Rabbit bounced onto the horse, following Boone's lead back the way they'd ridden into town. The horses flew with little urging, spraying snow in their wake. They'd made it to the edge of the settlement before the shouts rang out behind them. Shots followed, bullets screaming into the brush and trees all around them.

They dropped over the ridge, racing down the trail for several more minutes before Boone veered Nickel off through a stand of trees and hid behind the root ball of a giant fallen spruce. Rabbit followed, springing from his saddle before Dime even stopped. He waited, ears peeled while soothing his wide-eyed horse. "You're okay, boy."

After Dime had stopped snorting and tossing his head about, Rabbit leaned over to Boone. "Those fuckers killed Minny."

"I know." Boone's cheeks were red, his brow furrowed.

A glance around the root ball came up empty. Rabbit turned back. "She used to follow us around the ranch like a pooch when she was a foal. Always wanted to bed down in the bunkhouse, like she was one of the muleskinners. Cows took to her too, like she was one of them."

Boone's jaw ticked. "Remember when she pulled that bag of oats up to the house, expecting us to cut it open for her?"

Nodding, Rabbit blew out a breath. His chest ached for the poor girl. "Gentle as a kitten and smart to boot."

Boone peered over the top of the upturned root ball, his Winchester pointed at a bend up the trail. After several beats of silence, he said, "She was one helluva hinny, Rabbit. Those bastards are in for a reckoning. I should have let you shoot Barnes but I figured it might go better without bloodshed." He nudged his chin toward Nickel. "Fill up my pistol while you're sitting there, will you?"

Rabbit grabbed Boone's Colt from the holster, replaced the spent rounds, and began checking it over. "You killed the ceiling back there."

"Yeah. That German character in the corner stood up, menacing like. Pulled out some sort of sword. Might have been a rifle, though. Couldn't tell, it was too dark and smoky. I wanted to warn him off."

"A sword, huh? And you say me readin' about pirates ain't gonna pay off." Rabbit re-holstered Boone's pistol. "I get the feelin' he was runnin' things."

"Yeah. Odd, though. Boss man pulling strings, or maybe just in their ears whispering poison to those mush-brains."

"Or maybe assholes like to congregate with other assholes," Rabbit said. "Hard to tell."

Boone relaxed, leaned his rifle against the stump and rubbed his sore shoulder. "Like I said, there's a reckoning due. Same as you, I'm not too happy how Minny came to her end."

"Bunch of no-good animals masqueradin' as men." Rabbit checked the trail again. It was still empty. He stuck his hands under his armpits for warmth.

"Right now we need to concern ourselves with Uncle Morton," Boone said. "They sent the old boy off, beat to hell most likely. On foot, even. Must be around two miles back to Gayville. Didn't see him on the way up, so we can probably assume he made it at least that far."

"Gayville. Sheeat." Rabbit scowled up at the blue sky, wishing he were back home in New Mexico, trailing his uncle around the ranch. "That's a peculiar town. Sure would like to have my smoothbore." He drew his pistol and dragged the butt through the snow, leaving a smear of Barnes's red blood behind.

"Not much sense going to get your shotgun. We have to go through Gayville on the way to Deadwood, anyway. Besides, you got your quick draw there." Boone pointed at Rabbit's nickel-plated Colt. "And your fire-breathing hell cannon." He aimed his thumb at the Sharps tucked snugly in the scabbard strapped to Dime's saddle.

"It may be that cannon will save your life sometime, Boone-dog."

"Could happen." Boone checked the trail to Lead again.

"Looks like those boys weren't up to the chase." He studied the sky. "It's only early afternoon. Sun doesn't get very high here like it does in Santa Fe. Least not in the winter, I suppose. It'll be behind that ridge again soon enough."

"Those hills surely don't help." Rabbit scanned the gulch. "Don't see no trouble. What d'ya think? Time to mosey?"

Boone grunted, climbing into the saddle.

Rabbit hopped on Dime. He stared down the trail. Gayville waited, along with its peculiarities. He nudged his horse forward.

No time to waste, not with the darkness of night creeping up on them.

EIGHT

Another dead body awaited Clementine when she finally rolled out of her bed in the early afternoon, but it wasn't either of the two she'd left behind Kee Luk Laundry last night. Maybe they'd become pig food, too.

It took several minutes of stretching to ease some of the aches and pains left over from her tussle the night before with the pigs and cutthroats. When she joined Hank in the parlor, he held out a cloth bag full of biscuits. She took a moment to eat one, waving away the chunk of pork belly he offered. With the stink of pig shit still fresh in her sinuses, it would be a while before she could stomach anything related to the swine family.

After he left her to find Doc Wahl to see if he'd be sending any more customers Clementine's way that day, she donned her leather apron and turned her attention to the latest corpse on her exam table.

The increase in the number of deaths in Deadwood was showing no sign of abating. Judging from this dead man's emaciated frame and torn, filthy clothes, the smelly bugger had apparently been residing at the lower ranks of the food chain. He'd probably not even been able to secure a mining claim, let alone one that could produce some amount of gold.

His poor health and obvious malnutrition had undoubtedly weakened his immune system, and he'd succumbed to the miserable effects of bilious fever triggered by the toxic influence of a virus. *Cause of death: L. Typhoid*, Clementine wrote in her notes. She wasn't fond of including the *L.* since she used it as code for *Likely*, but if it wasn't typhoid it was something similar.

For a name, she listed "William Smith" because he'd come to her both broke and anonymous. Considering the number of unresolved murders in Deadwood, let alone all the inhabitants who simply disappeared, Mr. William Smith was fortunate to end up in the cemetery at all, let alone with a name on a grave marker.

As Clementine prepped the body for burial her mind wandered. She'd been sloppy last night and lucky to walk away with only a headache. On top of that, not only had she made a mess of herself, but her trip to Kee Luk Laundry had left her with more questions than answers.

She started to wrap the body in muslin, pausing to say a final "farewell" to the unknown dead man in her native tongue.

Since she couldn't burn the dead on an actual funeral pyre here in Deadwood and allow the smoke to help them find their way, as was Viking tradition, she often settled for sending them off with grave goods. For this particular man, a small wooden boat Hank had carved one afternoon by her fire would do. After tucking the boat in the dead man's pocket, she secured the canvas for transport and then took off her apron.

While scrubbing her hands clean, the three rings came to mind. The fact that her attacker and the shooter both wore the same rings surely linked them, but what about the ring she found on the hand in the hog pen? How was the owner of that ring tied to her two assailants? Were three of them dumping body parts and one fell in?

No, that was too absurd. Kee Luk's pigs were not ferocious wolves hunting down prey.

She dried her hands and pulled the rings from her pocket, moving next to the window where the light was better. A study of them in the daylight confirmed last night's conclusion—the rings were nearly identical except in size. The blending of goat and pig on the crown made her frown.

She rotated her hand, letting light and shadow play over the carving. *What is the significance of a goat and a pig joined into one?*

There was only one way to find the answers to these questions. She tossed two of the rings in her desk drawer and slid the one remaining on her middle finger.

She headed to her quarters and pulled a set of clean clothes from her trunk. Hank had wrinkled his nose during their meal of biscuits earlier and declared that The Pyre was suffering from an "odiferous malady reminiscent of a dead possum" and he hadn't been too far from right. Clementine needed a thorough cleansing top to bottom at The Dove.

She bundled up her clean clothes in muslin and rope, her thoughts returning to the knifed gunman from last night. Who was his killer? The distinctive, careful method of execution—and she was almost certain it was an execution—meant that her earlier suspicion was correct. There was an assassin in town. Someone skilled at dealing death in a precise and efficient manner.

Perhaps Clementine was meant to be next, meaning the assassin had followed her to Kee Luk, but then what? Had her discovery of the ring in the hog pen somehow thwarted the assassin's plans? Or was the assassin operating by some code? One that allowed only particular victims or limited the number of possible kills per day? She'd heard of such rules from various bounty hunters in the past. Their job was too often mundane, even boring, prompting the need for a self-imposed challenge.

She slipped into her spare set of boots and carried her bundle of clean clothes to the parlor, grabbing change from her collection bowl on the way.

Whatever the answers to her questions, this must be why she was called to Deadwood. A confirmation from her benefactor would be helpful, but no matter. She was on a path now, heading in a direction her gut said was true to her purpose.

And her gut rarely failed her when it weighed in on a matter.

Sliding on the sheepskin coat she splurged on after arriving in Deadwood, Clementine stepped outside into the cold. She clutched her packaged clothes to her chest as she made her way toward The Dove, wearing the ring prominently while watching for reactions from passersby.

Unfortunately, the sight of the ring raised no eyebrows from those who bothered to look up from stepping through the slush and mud. Outside of The Dove's front doors, Clementine stopped to clean her boots on a fancy, cast-iron boot scraper.

Most of the structures lining Deadwood's streets were utilitarian, made of rough-cut lumber, stacked logs with mud and grass chinking, or threadbare canvas or oilcloth. The focus throughout the gulch revolved around picking gold from the ground—or from the pockets of those who did. Time and dollars spent otherwise were wasted. In such an unadorned setting, The Dove and its grand façade stood out like a bright yellow flower in a barren landscape.

The building's carefully assembled clapboard siding, detailed cornice, and delicate trim work that surrounded the doors and windows radiated luxury. The embroidered white curtains on the other side of the glass took on a pink hue thanks to the deep red velvet wall coverings Clementine knew lined the parlor inside. Over her head, an ornately carved shingle swayed in the cold breeze. "The Dove" had been painted on it in a flamboyant script that teased at the femininity waiting inside.

Over the threshold beyond the bright white doors awaited a miner's version of heaven—soft, willing women ready to grant the wishes of the sexually meek or libidinous alike. Along with pleasures of the flesh, The Dove offered other comforts not widely available: a hot bath and a tasty meal. In a town where the burgeoning population outstripped amenities, not to mention necessities, The Dove was beyond compare.

But luxury came at a steep price.

Initially, Clementine's much-needed services in town had garnered her a discounted rate. Now, her friendship with the madam guaranteed her a hot bath and meal whenever she was in need. And in need she surely was, judging from the sniffs and wrinkled upper lips from a handful of men skirting her on their way down the boardwalk. Her stomach growled in anticipation of what waited inside.

With her boots as free of snow and mud as she could manage, Clementine stepped into the front parlor. The heavy scent of rose water greeted her, partially masking the odor of smoke, sweat, whiskey, and sex. Various shades of red covered everything throughout the entire room, from armchairs to visiting settees to throw rugs. Even the girls wore sheer garments of pink and red.

She hung her coat on one of the hooks next to the door.

"*Guten Tag, Fräulein* Clementine!"

"Good afternoon to you," she greeted Jurgen, The Dove's doorman. The stout German was determined to learn the English language, taking lessons from anyone willing to teach him, including the ladies of the line in between pokes. "Are you well?"

"*Geht's gut.* I am fine feelings."

Jurgen's job was to refuse entrance to any wretched sort he deemed unworthy of The Dove's offerings. His large stature, including massive shoulders and a rock-hewn jaw, granted him respect from most patrons. The enormous battle-axe he kept within reach while guarding the front door left no room for argument from the rest.

However, there were a few idiots who opted to test his muscle. These simpletons would find themselves hefted by the collar and carted to the door. Clementine had witnessed this twice during her many visits, grinning as Jurgen declared "*Unwürdig!*" and tossed the troublemaker into the street headfirst.

"I am well," she corrected him with a pat on the shoulder.

"*Ja*, I am well." His smile widened.

"Is Madam Zuckerman in?" she asked.

"*Ja.*" He thumbed toward the door on the far side of the room that led to the kitchen.

"*Danke*, Jurgen."

Clementine headed toward the door, passing two girls on love seats who were in negotiations with patrons—one concerning prices, the other explaining the dos and do-nots of what was to come. As she neared the kitchen, her nose teased her stomach with the aroma of roasted meat, fresh baked bread, and hot coffee.

Through the door, the huge iron stove radiated warmth that made her glad she had shed her coat. The smell of warm bread and meat was stronger here, along with a faint smoky whiff given off by the stove. One of the working girls who went by the name of Lulu sat on a bench lining a long plank table. She picked at the piles of meat and potatoes on her plate like a persnickety raven.

"You gave me too much again, Alexey," Lulu said.

A round, bald man stirring a pot on the stove turned and shook his long wooden spoon at the girl, dripping whatever was in the pot on the floor. "You must eat, skinny Lulu." He turned back to the simmering pot.

"You'd better listen, Lulu." Clementine joined Alexey, peeking over his shoulder into the big pot. It looked like some kind of broth. Licking her chops, she stepped back out of the way of the Russian cook. "Or Alexey might spoon-feed you."

"Hello, Clem." Lulu pushed her half-empty plate toward the center of the table. "If I eat all of this, I won't have room for those delicious, crunchy sushki in the—"

"Oh!" Alexey dropped the spoon on the stove. He grabbed a singed piece of linen, opened the oven, and pulled out a metal tray, setting it next to the stove. After he closed the oven, he fanned the hot the golden brown rings of sweet bread the size of bracelets.

"Is okay, I think. Burnt only little." He glanced her way, flashing her a welcoming grin. "Clem. We miss you. Where have you been?"

"Too much killing going on around here," she explained.

He grimaced, nodding. "Is true. Too much. Need more love, yes, Lulu?"

"And sushki," Lulu agreed.

"Did dunderhead forget sushki again?" asked a voice behind Clementine.

Dmitry stood at the pantry door, holding a sack of flour on his shoulder. Alexey and Dmitry were twin brothers, identical from their bald heads and extra round bellies all the way down to their stubby legs and feet.

Clementine had struggled in past months to understand their thick Russian accent. Over time, their English was improving. Or maybe it was her understanding that was improving. Or both.

"*You* put sushki in oven, *you* take sushki out." Alexey dropped the linen and picked up his spoon. He tasted whatever was in the pot. "Broth is good."

"I ask simple thing," Dmitry said. "Take sushki out when done." He turned to Clementine, his smile almost reaching his earlobes. "Welcome, Miss Clem." He dropped the sack of flour next to the table and went to inspect the tray of hot sushki. "Aye! *Da*. Burnt. Alexey not so good cook as me. He burns pierogi, too."

Scowling, Alexey mumbled something in Russian over his shoulder at Dmitry.

"I'll eat 'em just the same, Alexey," Lulu said.

Dmitry joined his brother at the stove, tasting the broth. "Too much salt."

"I *love* Alexey's pierogi." Lulu winked at Clementine, her grin coy. "And I think he's quite fetching."

Alexey kept his back turned to Lulu and continued to stir, but his cheeks turned redder than normal, and Clementine doubted it had anything to do with the heat from the stove.

"That means you think I am ... " Dmitry started, crossing his arms. "How said you ... 'fetching'? That means I am fetching, too." He patted his twin's back. "This is good, no?"

"Firs, a li'l bite from the kitchen!" A man's slurred voice rang out from the other side of the door leading to the parlor. "Then a li'l bite from you, eh, my calico queen?" Someone must have tipped the bottle too many times before stopping by The Dove.

The door swung open and the man Clementine had seen negotiating prices lurched into the kitchen. Before the door swung shut, she caught a glimpse of Jurgen heading her way with his axe in hand.

"OUT OF KITCHEN!" Dmitry and Alexey bellowed in unison.

Dmitry snatched up a cleaver from the butcher block and held it high over his head. Alexey exchanged his spoon for a butchering knife.

The two Russian cooks might strike some as comical—hell, even cracked in the head at times with the way they could bicker about nothing for days—but Clementine had seen them in action more than once outside of the kitchen. They were the second line of defense for The Dove's safe room. From what she'd witnessed in the past few months, their training in weaponry and tandem fighting must have been extensive.

The drunk took a step back, raising his hands. "Now wait a minute," he slurred. "I was lookin' for grub, but I'm okay now so lower yer weapons and I won't get hurt." He turned to exit but the door slammed open and smacked him in the face.

Jurgen grabbed the drunk by his collar before he tumbled to the floor. "Food in dining room, *ja*?" He dragged the groaning, wounded man by the collar back through the doorway.

Alexey lowered the knife and placed two sushki on a porcelain plate, which he set in front of Lulu. "For you, sweet Lulu."

She tilted her head and blinked up at him. "You're my favorite Russian cook, Alexey." Then she winked at Dmitry and bit into the crunchy bread.

"Favorite cook, ha!" Dmitry snorted and dropped the cleaver onto the chopping block. "I cook. He burns." He grabbed the sack of flour and opened it, scooping out a small mountain worth of the white stuff onto the baking table.

"I am *Mamochka's* favorite boy," Alexey said, lifting a pitcher of water. He moved next to Dmitry, watching his brother make a crater in the center of the flour mountain.

"She tells you these things." Dmitry stood back and motioned for the water. "You are sensitive. She wishes to save your feelings."

Clementine had heard enough. Her bath was long overdue. "Boys," she said, interrupting the twins. "Save me some of that roasted meat and potatoes."

Alexey smiled at her while pouring water into the crater his brother had made in the flour. "*Da.*"

As she walked to the door at the back of the kitchen that led to the safe room, she heard him say, "Our mother tells me this because it is truth. You are hard for a mother to love, even Russian mother. I am her favorite bo...."

"*Nyet.*" Dmitry cut him off. "Hot water for Clem's bath now, Alexey."

Clementine closed the door behind her, chuckling at the twins' long-running argument about who was loved more.

She paused with her back against the door, soaking up the steamy solace of the large safe room. Divided into four bathing areas separated by curtains that could be pulled closed for privacy, each section contained a bathtub, a rack for towels and cloths, and a dressing table complete with a mirror and a chair. Further on, toward the back of the room was a cozy sitting area with regency-style furniture of chintz, brass inlay, and hand-carved mahogany.

If The Dove were a medieval castle built to protect women, then Jurgen the German stood watch over the drawbridge, the Russian twins manned the guardhouse, and the safe room beyond the kitchen was the keep. Only those who worked and lived in the building were allowed in the inner refuge, along with female associates of Madam Zuckerman, which was where Clementine fit into the bunch.

According to Lulu and the other ladies, Hildegard Zuckerman took good care of her girls, better than any other madam west of the Mississippi. Having met plenty of painted ladies in her travels and finding most to live in conditions like those over at Yellow Strike Saloon, Clementine was apt to agree.

"Good afternoon, Clementine." Hildegard walked past her and collected a stack of towels from shelves along the wall near the door. Her smooth English was only slightly accented with German, hinting at her fluency in both languages.

Clementine had heard from Alexey that Hildegard was quite capable in Spanish and French as well, but she had yet to hear the willowy white-blond madam use either beyond a fleeting instruction to a tradesman or two.

"You've been gone too long. We've missed you."

"I've been busy." It had been over a week since Clementine had last come for a bath, using melted snow to wash up in between corpses instead. "How's the business of pleasure treating you, Hildegard?" She grinned. "Screamingly well, as usual?"

The madam laughed. "Some days I envy your lack of complaints, Undertaker." She leaned closer and sniffed in Clementine's direction. "Oh my! It seems you've lately escaped a pigsty. Follow me."

Clementine frowned after the madam. Had Hildegard somehow heard about last night's events behind Kee Luk? No, surely not. How could she have? Unless ... She glanced down at the ring on her middle finger. "Why would you think I've been in a sty?"

One of Hildegard's painted eyebrows lifted. "Because there is a particular bouquet about you that reminds one of swine."

Relief trickled through Clementine, her suspicion ebbing. Right, she must stink worse than Hank's dead possum compared to the other girls at The Dove.

"I trust that beyond your need for a bath, you have fared well since I saw you last?" Hildegard pressed.

"Well enough, thank you." Outside of taking a blow to the head and dodging a bullet in the dark. Oh, and examining bodies with very perplexing wounds.

Clementine was tempted to share tidbits about her experiences last night with the madam, maybe even pick Hildegard's brain about the rings. The madam might have an idea of what it all meant, or at least be able to offer a few kernels of truth to help Clementine make forward progress. She always seemed to know what was going on all around Deadwood. It was no secret that a healthy helping of gossip mixed with truth overflowed the coffers at most brothels, thanks to lonely men and willing women with an ear available to bend.

However, while Clementine's gut told her the madam was a safe bet, she had learned the hard way that her business was better kept locked away behind closed lips. Still, she couldn't resist testing the water. "But there are some strange goings-on in Deadwood."

Hildegard looked at Clementine, her dark eyes searching. "Yes, and it is growing more dangerous every day. Are you ready?"

Clementine's gaze narrowed at the undercurrent of tension coming from her host. "For the danger?"

In a blink, Hildegard's smile returned and the unease Clementine had felt was gone. "I was referring to your bath." She led the way toward the sitting area at the other end of the room.

As they neared the bath closest to the sitting area, Clementine noticed an older woman in one of the plush chairs near the fireplace, her feet nearly touching the dancing flames.

"Before I leave you to wash away that lovely bouquet," Hildegard said, "I would like to introduce you to an old acquaintance of mine."

The older woman lowered the periodical she was reading. Her forehead lined as she looked all of the way up at Clementine.

"Clementine Johanssen, this is Miss Hundt. I don't believe you've met."

Miss Hundt set her periodical on the table next to her and rose from her chair, bowing slightly.

Clementine nodded in return. Upon taking a closer look at the visitor, she realized the woman wasn't as old as she had first thought. Miss Hundt's hair was stark white, but her face had a youthful softness to it, her skin lined only around the eyes and between her white eyebrows. Something about Miss Hundt's stature and cheekbones reminded Clementine of Hildegard. Maybe they were related—aunt and niece, or cousins. But the madam had introduced her as an "acquaintance."

"*Guten Tag*," Miss Hundt said, her voice almost scratchy beneath the guttural German dialect. "You are new here," she added in Old German. "How do you like Deadwood?"

Clementine held her tongue, wondering why Miss Hundt would assume she spoke German—and Old German at that. She supposed her last name could put her family line in North Germany rather than Scandinavia. Or maybe Miss Hundt didn't know any English.

The two women watched her, exchanging a glance or two as they waited for her reply. Prior to today, Clementine had only used German for salutations around Hildegard, not conversations. Her instincts told her they were testing her, but to what end?

"I don't understand," Clementine lied.

Hildegard's mouth tightened, but she nodded and explained,

"Miss Hundt said good afternoon and that she is pleased to meet you. She would also like to know if you like living in Deadwood."

"Ah. *Guten Tag.*" Clementine purposely mangled Miss Hundt's native tongue. Her grandmother would have rolled her eyes had she heard her poor pronunciation after all of the lessons she'd delivered. "Will you tell her I am pleased to meet her as well and that I do enjoy most aspects of Deadwood?"

As the madam translated, Clementine caught Miss Hundt staring at the ring on her finger. A dark cloud passed over the woman's face. Clementine wasn't sure if it was recognition, but she saw traces of agitation in Miss Hundt's expression before she gathered herself and returned her gaze to Hildegard.

After the madam finished relaying Clementine's message, she glanced over her shoulder. "Ah. Your bath is ready now."

Clementine nodded to Miss Hundt and followed Hildegard to the bathing area, watching while Alexey poured steaming water into the tub. He followed it with two buckets of room temperature water from the barrel in the corner.

"Enjoy!" Alexey said and headed back to the kitchen.

"Call out if you need anything," Hildegard told her and then closed the curtain.

Clementine sprinkled a handful of dried rose petals into the water and then wasted no time undressing. She lowered herself into the hot water and sighed, closing her eyes as the water warmed her to the bone.

On the other side of the curtain, the conversation between Hildegard and Miss Hundt continued. From what Clementine could distinguish, they were speaking a mixture of Bavaria-Austrian German and Old High German. Rarely had she heard anyone use the antiquated version of the German language besides her amma, and many words were unknown to Clementine. She had been a quick study while sitting at her grandmother's table, there were so many German dialects to learn. She'd drawn the line at Old High German.

The two women exchanged small talk about the snow in the gulch and bits of news about various townsfolk and their doings for several minutes. Before long, Clementine's eyelids grew heavy, her late-night pig party catching up with her.

"The slayer has had her first encounter," she heard Hildegard say.

Clementine opened one eye. Had the madam used the German word for "slayer," or had Clementine's brain translated that wrong?

"She performed reasonably well," Miss Hundt returned, "with the exception of her misjudgment."

"Misjudgment? Are you speaking of the blow she took to her head?"

"*Ja.*"

"It was a misstep to be sure, but a small one I think," Hildegard said.

Both of Clementine's eyes were open now. A blow to the head? Were they talking about her? She sloshed her bath water around with a washcloth to disguise her eavesdropping.

"The fact remains," Miss Hundt said. "She faces a dangerous adversary and her performance indicates she is not ready."

A harrumph came from Hildegard. "She is ready."

"Fine. I will accept your judgment on this. There is also the matter of ... *Bitrog*, shall we say. She heeds the command of the deceiver."

What did they mean by *Bitrog*? Clementine was not familiar with that word. Was that similar to *Betrug*, meaning *fraud*? And who was the deceiver? She tried to push herself up the edges of the bathtub, but one of her hands slipped. She splashed down, her head submerging in the warm, soapy water. She bobbed back up, sputtering the rose-scented water.

The conversation stopped.

After a short pause Miss Hundt asked, *"Wie ist Ihr Bad?"*

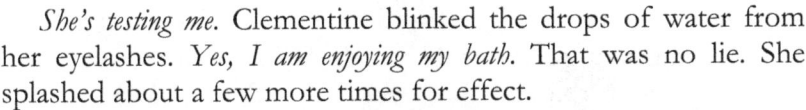

She's testing me. Clementine blinked the drops of water from her eyelashes. *Yes, I am enjoying my bath.* That was no lie. She splashed about a few more times for effect.

After another pause, Hildegard said, "As I told you earlier, her understanding of German is limited."

Miss Hundt scoffed. "*Ein Scharfrichter* that does not know the old languages?"

A *what?* That was another word Clementine had not heard before.

"She is not of German descent." A chair creaked. "Now, this second problem you mention," Hildegard continued. "I am concerned as well, but I believe she is unaware of his true nature."

"She might be vulnerable to his enchantment," Miss Hundt said. "Or in league with him. Duplicitous."

"After watching her for some time, I am relatively certain it is as I said."

"If you are correct, we must be sure that she becomes aware of his treachery before it is too late."

Several beats of silence followed, interrupted only by the crackling fire. Clementine scrubbed soap into her hair while she waited to see what came next.

"Perhaps it is time to reveal ourselves to her," Hildegard said.

"Not yet. We must continue to observe her to be certain she isn't one of his pets."

Clementine soaped her face and arms, trying to make sense of what she was hearing and figure out if it pertained to her or someone else. If she were the slayer they were talking about, why would she be someone's pet?

After another short silence, Hildegard cleared her throat. "What of the rogue? Shall we intervene?"

What rogue? Clementine rinsed her face and arms. Who were they talking about now?

"There is too much risk at present," Miss Hundt replied. "As well, the rogue has saved the life of *der Scharfrichter* once already."

There was that word again. *Der Scharfrichter.* Was it a surname?

"There is a role in this yet to be filled," Miss Hundt continued. "We do not yet fully understand their responsibilities. We must wait. There is time, of that I am certain."

"But we must watch carefully," Hildegard said. "A rogue *Scharfrichter* is a concern. To both of us. *Sehr gefährlich.*"

"Dangerous, yes," Miss Hundt agreed. "But possibly useful."

The sound of a teacup clinking on a plate broke the quiet.

"It might be even necessary for what is to come." Miss Hundt spoke again. "It is important that we allow *time* to show us whether the other is truly rogue or if another summoning occurred."

"And if there was a summoning?"

"We must know who is responsible."

"I will have Ludek see to it," Hildegard offered.

Clementine's thoughts whirled. Who was Ludek? What was *der Scharfrichter*? Who was this rogue they spoke of? Did any of their conversation have anything to do with the ring on her finger that Miss Hundt seemed to have noticed?

There was a long break in their conversation, disrupted only by the sound of Miss Hundt turning a page of the periodical occasionally. Clementine took the quiet moment to slip under the water and rinse the soap from her hair.

"I miss *Abnoba Mons,*" Miss Hundt said while Clementine was cleaning between her toes.

Hildegard shushed her. "You must refrain from using the old language so much, my friend. You risk our exposure."

"We face risks every day simply by residing in the field cultivated and sown by evil. Our task here has just begun."

Clementine remembered seeing the words *Abnoba Mons* on an old map her grandfather kept in his library. It meant "Black Forest." Was that Miss Hundt's homeland?

"I am considering changing my name again," Miss Hundt

said.

"To what this time?"

"Wolff."

Hildegard chuckled. "Hounds and wolves. I like it."

Another silence followed, longer this time.

The warmth of the water and crackling sound of the fire made her eyelids heavy again. Clementine closed her eyes and began to drift away, only to be startled awake by Alexey's voice.

"... was the biggest he ever saw. But Dmitry *preuvelichivat* ... uh, exaggerates, eh?"

"Oh, Alexey," Lulu giggled. "So do you, honey."

Water sloshed into a bathtub on the other side of the room.

"I make water just right for you, Miss Lulu."

Clementine listened to two more sloshes of water.

"And towel for you."

"Thank you, Alexey. The sushki were the best I ever ate."

"You are too kind, sweet Lulu. Enjoy bath."

Curtains swished and the door closed with a clunk.

"I'll meet with Ludek later today in your stead," Miss Hundt said more quietly now, yet still in German.

"Good. I have rooms to attend. We will speak tomorrow?"

Miss Hundt grunted in response. "*Der Scharfrichter* wears the sign of *caper-sus*. Were you aware of this?"

"The ring? It is not characteristic for her," Hildegard said. "It is likely a trophy from her last kill."

Clementine stilled, her hand squeezing the soap in a death grip. *Wears the sign* ... so they had been talking about her all of this time. What was *caper-sus*? Was that what the emblem on the ring was called?

"You are sure of this?"

"I am confident." Two sets of footfalls passed on the other side of the curtain, followed by the creak of the door leading to the kitchen.

Spear of Odin! Clementine rose from the warm water and

reached for the towel. Instead of finding out answers about the ring, she'd waded into more questions. She dried off and dressed as Lulu splashed around in the other tub, singing an old French lullaby off-key.

There was one place where Clementine thought she might find the answers she was looking for after eavesdropping.

Her stomach growled in protest. But first, roasted meat and Alexey's sushki were calling her name.

An hour later, Yellow Strike Saloon was bustling when Clementine pushed inside but the crowd was half of what it would be after the sun set. Miners worked hard, especially on cold winter days like this, and expected a payoff at the end of it, whether it was sex, cards, or drunken carousing. Most likely all three, if the day's take permitted.

"Porter." Clementine pulled up to the bar and greeted the bartender.

"Miss Johanssen," Porter replied, his tone respectful. He'd seen her handle situations most men would have backed down from and had made it clear early on that he didn't want to end up on her bad side.

"Dead shot." She thought back to what she'd overheard at The Dove and changed her mind. "Two, actually. And I need to speak with Adelinda."

"Who's that now?" He clunked two shot glasses down, pulled a bottle from under the bar, and poured the glasses full of the whiskey that she knew he reserved for special customers.

"Fannie," Clementine said, her tone full of disgust. She despised using the labels with which some of the brothel doves were saddled.

"Ah. Two Ton," Porter replied with a nod.

"I'll thank you not to use that name for her in my presence, Porter." Clementine spoke between gritted teeth.

"Sorry, Miss Johanssen." He tapped on a brass bell mounted on the bar. *Ting ting ting.* "She'll be down directly."

He shuffled further along the bar, weighing gold dust and pouring whiskey, stopping from time to time to wipe his hand on his slicked-back hair.

Further down the bar, a scrawny old man with a grizzled beard kept peeking at her and then looking away quickly when he saw she was watching him. He was muttering something under his breath that sounded like "death dealer" and "whangdoodles," but she wasn't sure she was hearing him correctly over the din of conversation.

Clementine shook her head. He must have spent too much time alone in the dark under the earth. She grabbed the glasses and headed for the nearest empty table. It wasn't long before the clip-clop of hard-soled shoes made their way along the balcony and down the stairs.

Adelinda paused partway down the stairwell, pushed up her large bosom, tilted her head to the side, and spread her arms as if to say, *Here I am!*

Clementine couldn't help but smile at Adelinda's mating dance. The girls at Yellow Strike Saloon were schooled by one of the savviest madams in the Hills, Mollie Johnson.

With a wave, Clementine caught Adelinda's attention. The woman's painted face lit up, her smile true. She waved back and scuttled down the stairs and across the room to where Clementine waited, arms wide.

"*Schön Ihnen zu sehen, Clemy!*" Adelinda slammed into Clementine, knocking her back a step.

"It's good to see you as well, Adel!" Clementine couldn't quite reach around the plump woman, but she squeezed hard just the same. She patted the chair for Adelinda to sit next to her.

"You visited yesterday, Clemy. Everyone talks about it still."

"Finnigan," she replied and grimaced. "He deserved worse. Adel, I'm sorry about Ginny."

Adelinda's eyes watered. She lowered her gaze, shaking her head. "We loved Ginny. I miss her. Miss Mollie says she's gonna bring in muscle to help protect us, but that bastard ..." she paused and glanced left and right, scooting her chair closer to Clementine before continuing in a whisper. "That bastard Angus is a tightwad. Won't spend money on us girls or the staff. *Dieses Arschloch.*"

"He is worse than an asshole." Clementine's contempt for Angus grew stronger by the day. "At least Finnigan won't be a problem anymore."

Adelinda squeezed Clementine's forearm. "I don't know what we'd do without you, Clemy."

"Adel, I'm here because I need your help. I heard a term recently that is new to me. I believe it's from your home country."

"Hmm? What is it?"

"*Der Scharfrichter.*"

Adelinda's brow wrinkled as she stared out the front window. After a few moments she snapped her fingers. "Yes, I remember this word! I haven't heard it since I was a little girl. My father would tell me and my brothers *Geschichten* ... umm, stories ... about the evil that lurked in the forest at night and terrifying beasts that were under its spell. He would talk of *ein Scharfrichter* who would battle the evil. In some stories *der Scharfrichter* would defeat the evil beasts. In some, they would die trying. I think he told us these things to keep us from wandering too far from home and getting lost."

"So *der Scharfrichter* fought the evil beasts," Clementine clarified. "Does *ein Scharfrichter* have meaning in English?"

"I think it means a killer." Adelinda snapped her fingers again. "Wait! More correctly, an executioner."

NINE

"This weather's gonna be the end of my toes!" Boone rose and stamped his feet to knock the aching cold from his legs, and then he returned to a squat.

"And my weasel," Rabbit grumbled, blowing into his cupped hands.

"The way you treat that weasel it's gonna fall off anyway. And *that* doesn't work." He pointed at Rabbit's cupped hands. "Moisture in your breath gathers the cold."

Rabbit glared at Boone and blew into his cupped hands again. "If I can't pull a trigger in that town down there, I might not succeed in keepin' you alive. Sure enough, the crippled turtle squattin' next to me ain't gonna skin iron fast enough if the situation requires."

"This ol' amphibian might surprise you. If needs be."

Boone squinted down the hill at the bleak town, which was really more a collection of shacks, cabins, and tents than a proper settlement. He wasn't at all fond of the idea that they were a pair of shave tails about to saunter into a waiting passel of nasty surprises down there.

Waiting to leave them injured.

Or dead.

Gayville promised the possibility of both.

Rabbit wrinkled his brow. "Gotta make things complicated all the time. I said 'turtle.' " He wobbled his head and with a serving of dainty added, "*Not amphibian.*"

Boone grinned in spite of his unease. "That woodcutter we met earlier is still there." He pointed down the hill. "He has a good tall pile of split wood alongside the cabin now. Might be the place to start, since he's probably had an eye on things the better part of the day."

"Yeah, but he wasn't too content on presentin' information, you may remember."

"I remember." Boone pulled his hat down lower. "But he did tell us straight. Might be straight with us again. Nobody else in that town gave us anything to whittle on."

"You're the boss, Boonedog. I'm all for headin' in. I'll freeze solid what with that sun goin' down while we're sittin' here."

Dime snorted, firing gobs of snot into the snow.

"Dime says he agr—" Rabbit stopped and bobbled his head again. "Dime indicates that he concurs." With a smirk, he added, "Told me hisself."

Boone rose from his haunches. "Still have some bad grammar in there, but I'm heartened to hear you're taking my advice on improving your vocabulary. Keep it up."

Rabbit crossed his eyes, his grin crooked. "Yuk yuk, uhh. Aws shor do thank ya for your kindly comments, Mr. McCreery."

Ignoring the clown, Boone grabbed Nickel's reins and picked a path down the hill. "How about we follow that deer trail most of the way and then cut right near that deadfall."

"Lead the way."

Rabbit followed Boone and Nickel down the slope. Dime stayed on Rabbit's heels, like a trained pup.

"Can't be as disagreeable as Lead, right?" Rabbit asked when the trail leveled out at the bottom of the gulch.

"Guess we'll see." Boone turned onto the trail toward town.

Before long, the heaviness of the place with its growing shadows and unnatural silence pressed down upon him. He took Nickel's reins in his hand, more for his comfort than the horse's. Besides, he wanted to keep his speedy horse and loaded

Winchester by his side. This little search party of theirs could have used several more gun hands, in his opinion.

They entered Gayville as the sun sank below the ridgeline. Shadows stretched from rim to rim across the gulch, leaving much of the town coated in gray. Details under the trees became obscure. There was something about the place that made Boone feel the need to keep looking over his shoulder.

Nickel's ears flicked back and forth, his upper lip curling. The horse was picking up on something—either Boone's stress or some other peculiarity that was in the air down here in the shadowed land.

"Let's find that woodcutter," he told Rabbit. "See what he knows."

Rabbit grunted in agreement.

At the north edge of town, Nickel slowed and pulled back against the reins in Boone's hand. A wave of shivers ran along the horse's sides from withers to rump. Boone knew better than to attribute that shiver to the cold. He patted Nickel, cooing to him low and steady.

A glance behind him found Dime with his head held high, alternately snorting toward town and then nickering at Rabbit.

Both horses were fully alert and ready to bolt.

"Let's settle them down," Boone said.

He clicked his tongue until Nickel, with his ears still pricked, focused on Boone's half-raised hand and then looked him in the eyes. He relaxed noticeably and moved in beside Boone, nuzzling his hand and nickering softly. Boone stroked the horse's forehead and rubbed his ears. "Okay, Big Nick. We need to go into that town. You and me. Together."

Boone looked over at Rabbit, who had commenced a calming ritual of his own with Dime.

"Ready," Rabbit said.

Dread weighed on Boone's shoulders as they started down the trail toward the woodcutter's cabin. Several of the shacks they passed seemed deserted with their boarded-up windows, but trails of smoke from hastily built chimneys proved otherwise.

"Look at all the bear traps around that one," Rabbit whispered. "You'd think the roof was made of honey."

By the time they reached the woodcutter's cabin, the sky had turned light blue. The cutter's back was turned as he stacked the last few split logs against the side of his shack, making an obvious effort to conceal and protect the canvas-clad window.

"Ho there, sir!" Boone called to the woodcutter.

A series of ragged barks rang out from a shack a few yards away. Both horses tensed and began neighing intermittently between the barks, as if conversing with the dog.

The woodcutter looked their way. His brow was drawn tight, his mouth open. "You shouldn't be—" Recognition dawned on his face. "Hey! Yer the two fellas what was headed to Lead earlier."

"There and back," Boone said. "Those boys didn't cotton to strangers. Not even a little bit. At all."

The barking and neighing continued.

"Surely no falsehoods in that statement," the woodcutter agreed with a huff.

Rabbit leaned toward Boone and spoke under his breath, "Would've been nice if someone had mentioned that fact to Uncle Mort ahead of time."

Nickel and Dime began tugging on their reins, dragging Boone and Rabbit toward the shack with the barking dog.

Boone dug his heels in, but the slippery snow offered little purchase up against Nickel's strength.

What in tarnation was going on? His damned horse was acting like a foal in new clover.

He glanced at Rabbit, nodded once, and let go of the reins. Rabbit followed suit, but not before grabbing his Sharps rifle from its scabbard.

The horses trotted over to the shack with the barking dog.

They pulled up at the door and began bobbing their heads and nickering in what appeared to be some sort of discussion. Nickel extended a leg and kicked at the door.

Boone pushed his hat back and scratched his head. "What do you make of that?"

"Those two fools are actin' like they found a bin of fermented apples," Rabbit replied, snickering. "I'm here to tell ya, there's nothin' as entertainin' as a horse drunk on hard cider."

The dog howled a few times, then returned to barking.

Rabbit grunted. "I'll get 'em." He jogged after the horses, which were now taking turns kicking at the door while the dog's yapping grew more frenzied on the other side.

"Sun's about done today," the woodcutter said, moving next to Boone. "You two should mosey on home. This ain't no place to be after nightfall."

Boone turned to the woodcutter. Something about the way the man met Boone's stare straight on without looking away made him seem trustworthy enough.

He stuck out his hand. "Boone McCreery. That's Jack Fields tending the horses. From Santa Fe."

The woodcutter took Boone's hand in his calloused palm. His handshake was brisk and sure. "Weeks. Elston Weeks. Some people call me 'Three Finger.' " He held up his left hand, minus his index finger. "Smashed it with a sledge. Listen, I mean it when I say you boys need to git by sundown. Real dangerous at night 'round here."

Boone glanced at Rabbit, who had pushed the horses back and stood with his ear against the door. He drew his Colt as he listened through the wood. What was the chucklehead doing? Boone started to step toward the dog and pony show but stopped. Nah, Rabbit had things under control ... probably.

He turned back to Weeks. "We got a little problem in a missing man. Like an uncle to both of us. Appears those hard cases up in Lead slogged him pretty good." Boone paused, swallowing a lump in his throat. "Killed and skinned his mule." The lump eased, replaced by a hot ball of anger. "Sent him back down the hill all busted up. Don't even know if he had a coat. We didn't see any sign of him between here and there."

Weeks growled in his throat. "Fuckin' bastards up there. No call to do that to a man." He buried his axe in the chopping block and looked Boone in the eye. "I should've warned you boys about that shithole."

"Maybe. But we needed to find out one way or the other, so no rough feelings toward you."

Rabbit knocked on the door of the shack.

Weeks frowned toward Rabbit. "That's Boomer's place … Jack, was it?"

Boone nodded.

Weeks called out, "Hey, Jack! Boomer's probably finishin' up down at the crick. He'll be home directly." To Boone he added, "Nobody 'round here stays out after dark."

"Boomer, you say?"

"Yep. Likes to use black powder to crack boulders. Not exactly neighborly, but it does get the job done better'n a pickaxe or sledge."

Rabbit's knocking excited the dog into a staccato of yipping.

The horses began nickering and stomping in the snow, butting Rabbit with their foreheads and pushing against him for access to the door.

What the hell? Boone scratched his jaw as he watched the comedy playing out at Boomer's door.

"You boys want some Arbuckles'? Got some fresh made inside." Weeks frowned up at the sky. "Prob'ly have time for that, anyway. Least I could do after you bein' up to that hellhole."

"Sounds good about now," Boone said, his eyes still on Rabbit, who was grunting and pushing at the horses in vain. "What's all the bootscootin' about, Rabbit?"

"Goldurn horses won't get away from the door. All excited about that critter on the other side!"

"Well, cut it out! They'll be fine. They're just curious. Mr. Weeks here kindly offered us a coffee."

Rabbit threw up his hands and headed toward Boone. "Hell with those two. I'd sell 'em both for a hot cup right about now."

"Yer horses sure have a hankerin' to be in that shack," Weeks said, heading for the door to his cabin.

Boone took one last look at the horses before he and Rabbit followed Weeks inside. To look at them, they seemed deep in discussion about the next logical step in reaching that yipping dog. He shook his head. The two nervous nellies could use a distraction for the moment while Rabbit and he downed some much-needed black water.

Inside Weeks's place, gloom had already settled in for the night. With the windows blocked by stacks of firewood and a small fire with which to cook, heat, and see by, the place felt more like a cave than a cabin. Sturdy poles leaned against the wall next to the door—barricades, if Boone had to guess. Build a palisade around the cabin and it could be called Fort Weeks.

With a warm coffee tin in hand, Boone joined Rabbit and the woodcutter at a rough-hewn table.

Weeks glanced around his cabin as if noticing the sparseness for the first time. "Not much, I know, but enough. Don't intend on spendin' my life here, just long enough to stuff the money sack and go, so to speak."

"No work animals here, horses or mules, I noticed," Rabbit said. "Not even dogs, exceptin' that noisy one."

"Can't keep 'em. Disappear. Run off scared or somethin'. Or worse, torn up and half eaten. Messy business. That's some of the reason you boys need to get yourselves and your horses out of here."

Rabbit shot Boone a frown. Back to Weeks, he said, "What? Torn up. Can't be bears."

"We noticed the bear traps outside a lot of the windows around here," Boone explained.

Weeks nodded. "Seems to do the trick. Makes 'em think a little, at least."

Makes *what* think? Boone took a sip of coffee, wincing at the bitterness.

"You mentioned somethin' about your uncle bein' sent this way by them assholes in Lead. We keep close watch around here for strangers. Haven't heard tell of your man comin' by. It's certain somebody would have noticed him."

"Any other way he coulda gone?" Rabbit asked. "Maybe found a fork in the trail that might have looked promisin' and taken it somewhere? Didn't see nothing like that ourselves."

Weeks's face scrunched up. "Well, there's the cutoff that leads up to the Bloody Bones, but nobody goes up to that mine no more. Yer uncle mighta thought that trail ended in a camp, I suppose. But you better hope he didn't go that way."

Nickel neighed loud enough for them to hear inside of Weeks's cabin. Boone heard no distress in the neigh, but took a bigger drink of his coffee. Best to hurry this chin wagging along just the same.

"The mine is all worked out, huh?" Rabbit's thoughts were riding along the same tracks as Boone's.

"Not nearly." Weeks frowned down at his tin cup. "Three brothers came out this way about six months ago and staked a claim. Called 'er Golden Echo. That's the mine's real name on paper. Wasn't 'til later they started callin' it the Bloody Bones." He took a drink from the cup. "Anyway, those boys hit a mother right quick, but that wasn't all. Story goes they broke into a patch of natural tunnels that went deep."

"How deep?" Rabbit asked.

Weeks shrugged. "So deep they tried to follow 'em and never made it back out."

Boone wondered if they hit a patch of bad air.

"After that, strange things started happenin' around here. Animals going missin' at night. People disappearin'. Dying of wounds the likes nobody ever seen before. At first folks figured it was minin' accidents, cave-ins and such, but I helped bring down one of the bodies my first week in town. Big Brody Brewster. A good man, according to all who knew him." Weeks took another swig of coffee, following it with a grimace. "He was ripped neck to groin by somethin'. Had to wrap him tight in canvas to keep his guts from spillin' on the ground."

Rabbit cursed under his breath.

"Now, when ya hear this next part ya might think I'm cracked, but I'm just retellin' stories I heard. That's all." Weeks glanced at both of them in turn. "I'm gonna tell ya anyway, 'cause I want you boys to know I ain't lying or just bein' inhospitable when I say ya need to clear out of here soon."

Boone nodded. "I don't figure you're prone to whiff, Elston, and your coffee is mighty fine."

"Finish your tale and then we'll light a shuck," Rabbit said.

"There's strange things sneaking 'round in those woods up there." Weeks looked at Rabbit. "You say it can't be bears and yer right. It's worse than bears. There are stories of folks seein' all manner of beasts out under those trees. And lots of 'em. Folks the likes you'd call bankable every day of the week. Most of 'em don't last long. They pull out of here right quick and head back to Deadwood or off somewhere else."

Weeks quieted, focusing on his tin cup again. "I s'pose you two think I'm off my nut," he mumbled and took another mouthful of coffee.

Boone raised his eyebrows at Rabbit, giving him a subtle nod.

"You ever heard one of them beasties described like a white bear?" Rabbit asked. "A white grizzly, maybe? But bigger with more teeth?"

Weeks's gaze locked onto Rabbit. "It ain't no grizzly, boy."

"So you think—"

Whump! CLANG!

Rabbit sprang to his feet and shot out the door. Boone raced after him with Weeks following.

Dime had kicked in the door to Boomer's shack and was attempting to duck through, but the saddle caught on the door frame. Nickel pushed on Dime from behind, trying to shove him through. A frenzy of barking blasted out through the opening.

"Consarn horses!" Rabbit caught Dime's reins and tugged him away from the door.

Boone grabbed hold of Nickel and towed him aside as well.

Weeks threaded in between the horses and inspected the mess they'd made of the door and frame. "A little banged up, but looks to be no harm done." He stepped inside, calling out over the barking dog, "I think the commotion we heard was the door swingin' open and hittin' Boomer's spittoon."

The barking stopped suddenly, turning into a whine.

Boone heard Weeks say, "Yer okay, doggie. That leg's lookin' better, I think."

Dime snorted at Rabbit as he tied the horse's reins to the axe-hewn end of a log jutting from the shack. "If you'd behave yourself, I wouldn't need to do this."

Dime snorted again.

"Yer a regular flannel mouth this afternoon." Rabbit scowled at Dime. "Now stay put or I'll tell Nickel you stole his apple last week." After a pat on the horse's rump, Rabbit strode to the shack's door and examined the damage himself.

The dog barked again.

Boone tied Nickel off next to Dime.

"Boone!" Rabbit shouted, his voice higher than usual. "Get in here!"

He reached Rabbit's side in a heartbeat. "What's wrong?"

"It's no wonder the horses were hell-bent to get through the door." Rabbit pointed inside the shack. "Look who's been barking her tail off."

Boone stepped inside, blinking as his eyes adjusted to the darkness. Then he saw her and his jaw fell open. "What the ... how did she ... Tink!"

Rabbit laughed. "Good ol' Tinker. She must've heard our voices when we drew up outside."

"How you doing, girl?" Boone kneeled beside their uncle's dog. As his sight adjusted even more, he noticed blood-soaked bandages where the woolen blanket didn't cover her hind end.

Tinker tried to wag her tail, but then flinched and whined.

"What's wrong, little Tinker?" Boone stroked her head and looked at Weeks for an answer.

"Boomer patched her up best he could," he explained. "Pup got shredded up pretty awful. You know this dog?"

Nodding, Boone lifted the blanket. He cringed at the blood-soaked muslin wrapped around what remained of her left leg.

"Oh, girl. What happened to you?" And where was her daddy?

She nuzzled his hand and whined, trying to wag her tail again.

"Back leg was so mangled Boomer had to take it off," Weeks said. "She's lucky Boomer's the one who found her. He's pretty handy with a knife. Much longer out there and she'd have bled to death in the cold."

Rabbit squatted next to Boone, his face drawn. "What a helluva thing, Booney." He frowned at Weeks. "Where'd Boomer find her?"

"Said he first spotted her at the bottom of the slope that leads up to the Bloody Bones. On the other side of the crick. He tried to follow the trail, but couldn't make it up the hill. Prob'ly didn't wanna find whatever it was that done that to the dog. It is a steep slope, though, and Boomer has a bit of a bum leg from a fall he took down a shallow shaft a few years back."

Rabbit cooed at Tinker and rubbed the top of her head.

Sitting back on his heels, Boone looked out the door. "Sonofabitch, Rabbit. We need to climb up and check out that mine."

"Whoa, whoa, whoa," Weeks said, stepping between them and the door with his hands raised. "Just hold on there. You can't do that right now. You're dead fer sure if you go up there. I mean, you could probably make the climb during the day since you two boys seem able to take care of yourselves, but at night? No! I told you before, you need to git before nightfall."

Boone stood. "But if our uncle is—"

"No!" Weeks crossed his arms. "You don't understand. This … this goin' up to Bloody Bones notion is no good, even in the light. At night? Worse! Worse than stayin' here. Don't do it. I mean it."

The need to find their uncle right there and then had Boone's heart pounding, but the stark fear on Weeks's face told a pretty convincing tale.

He tapped Rabbit's shoulder. "Let's talk about this for a spell outside."

Rabbit followed him out into the snow.

"We can't do it, Rabbit," Boone said after they'd reached their horses. "We got to prepare. Bedrolls. Ammunition. And better boots." He didn't doubt for a minute that Weeks was telling the truth, as he knew it.

Rabbit said nothing, but kept stroking Dime's neck.

Boone could tell by the set of Rabbit's jaw that he agreed but didn't like the fact that they were leaving their uncle to fend for himself another night in a cold and hostile world. He tried to think of something comforting to say, but drew a blank. Rabbit had suffered some awful dreams lately. Premonitions, maybe. There were no words that could salve that wound.

"We'll gather up Tinker," Rabbit said. "Head on back to Deadwood tonight and hit Bloody Bones in the mornin'."

Boone blew out a breath. Shit. First Minny and now Tink. His chest ached.

This trip to the Black Hills was turning into a nightmare.

TEN

Rabbit kept his Colt handy on the short trip from Gayville to Deadwood, but the only thing he and Boone came across after the sun had set was a raccoon that hissed at him in the moonlight and scurried off through the snow.

He reined Dime to a stop at the south end of Deadwood. The street gently sloped down and away to the north, offering a commanding view of the activity below. He tucked the wool blanket tighter around the shivering dog cradled against him.

"You want me to take Tinker?" Boone asked, pulling up next to him.

"Nah, I got 'er." A slight nudge started Dime down into the thick of gamblers and drunken miners roaming the streets. Rabbit navigated through messy stacks of lumber, crates, and barrels.

"Nails and coffee beans," he told Boone, guessing the barrels' contents. They'd played this game of speculation often over the years to kill time on the trail.

"Nope. Pickles in the smaller ones," Boone shot back.

Rabbit maneuvered around a drunk sprawled out in the road. "Deadwood's kickin' up its heels tonight," he hollered over the arguments, laughter, and shouts echoing up and down the street.

Shifting Tink carefully in his lap, he stroked her ears. She whimpered but didn't move. He frowned over his shoulder. "We gotta get this girl some help real soon, Booney."

"We're close. I remember seeing the doc's shingle down on

the left a little way. Keep her warm."

Rabbit padded Tink the best he could. "Hope the doc don't have no qualms about patchin' up critters. Let's move."

"Stay close." Boone tongue-clicked Nickel into the bustle of the street.

Rabbit steered Dime around a deep ditch obscured in shadow. "Don't have proper illumination in this town. Hope Dime can see where he's steppin' better than I can."

A short ways down the street Boone pulled up next to a one-story, clapboard building. He dropped to the ground.

"Wait here," he said and opened the door. Weak golden-orange light from an oil lamp spilled onto the boardwalk, and then the door swung closed.

Rabbit hugged Tinker's frail body against his, sharing his warmth with her. "See that sign there, Tink? It says *W.P. Wahl – Doctor & Apothecary*. Don't tell Boone I can read the word 'apothecary.' Makes him feel better when he thinks he knows more than me. *Ailments Cured,* it says. That's for you. We'll get you fixed up." He frowned at the dark bloodstains on the blanket. "Exceptin' for that leg. That must hurt terrible, but I'll make you a new one. I'll whittle a stick and strap some leather to it. You'll be almost good as new."

Tinker was still, her dark gaze locked on his face as if she wanted to believe him, but …

"Hell, enough of this waitin' bullshit." He rose from his saddle.

The door slammed open and Boone stormed out. "Goldurn doctor is checking over the girls at Yellow Strike Saloon."

"Sonofabitch!" Rabbit reined Dime around and was halfway to Yellow Strike by the time Boone had mounted up. He stopped outside of the saloon. Boone and Nickel joined him at the hitching rail. "Come here and take Tink so I can get down without hurting her."

"Why don't you wait here while I go in to get the doc?" Boone stepped down from his horse. "It's hopping in there."

"I'm tired of waitin'. Here, take her."

Rabbit handed off Tinker. As soon as his boots hit the ground, he shot toward the swinging doors. "Move it, Boone!"

"Dammit, Rabbit. Slow down so we..."

Boone's voice faded as Rabbit pushed through the doors and waded into the throng of miners gambling and drinking away the day's take. The saloon was packed to the walls and reeked of sweat and smoke.

He pushed through the crowd toward the bar. "Where's the doc?" he shouted at the barkeep, who was filling a line of shot glasses.

When the barkeep didn't bother to answer, Rabbit pushed up closer and slammed his palm on the bar. "Whiskey slinger! Where's the goldurn doc?"

A hard shove on his shoulder nearly sent him tumbling but he caught himself on the bar.

He turned and glared up at the jutting chin of the stringy-haired, rummy-eyed miner who had shoved him.

"Wait yer turn, snorter," the miner said.

Rabbit squeezed his fists tight. Since their arrival in Deadwood, Boone and he had hit nothing but rough trail. First, their lost—and possibly dead—Uncle Mort. Then Minny, brutally butchered in Lead. Now Tinker, attacked, torn up, nearly dead.

This smug mush-head had no idea whose fuse he'd just lit.

Rabbit thrust his elbow hard into the jackass's chin, sending him reeling. After bouncing off a pair of elbow-benders further down the bar, the miner crashed to the floor.

"Jack!" Boone rammed his knee into Rabbit's thigh.

"Sheeat, Boone." Rabbit hobbled sideways, rubbing his leg. "What'd ya do that for?"

"Now is not the time for fighting." His arms full with Tinker, Boone nodded toward the other end of the saloon. "The doc is on the other side of that green door back there."

Still rubbing his leg, he followed Boone toward the door.

They shouldered through the men milling between the bar and back wall.

"Stand aside!" Boone commanded to a cluster of drunks. His deep voice cleared a path.

Rabbit got the door for Boone and Tinker, closing it behind them and shutting out the loud din of drunken conversation and off-tune piano music. A hallway stretched out before them with two closed doors on each side. Men lined the walls, murmuring amongst themselves while they waited their turn for a poke.

"Doc Wahl!" Rabbit called out loud enough to be heard on the other side of the closed doors. To Boone, he asked, "How did you know he's back here?"

"I asked politely, quickdraw."

Rabbit scoffed. "Tink's dyin'. There's no time for niceties." He started down the hall. "Doc Wahl! Where's Doc Wahl?" He rapped his knuckles on the first two doors, ignoring the sounds of grunts and giggles coming from the other side. He nudged aside a pair of drunks. "DOC WAHL!"

At the far end of the hall, a door opened. A head with a mop of curly blond hair peeked from the doorway. Below her, a brunette with braids looked out at him, sizing him up. The two girls were shoved aside when a short woman with assets too large for her small frame set herself square in the middle of the hall, her hands planted on her wide hips.

Rabbit pulled up short, assessing the curvy wall in front of him. Her ruby red dress was crammed with ruffles that failed to confine a pair of very ample breasts. Arcs of pink areolas caught his attention for a couple of blinks. He dragged his gaze up to the feathery hat fastened to an unnatural amount of dark hair piled high on her head.

Rabbit had little doubt about with whom he was dealing. He cocked his head, reminding himself that he was not here to admire this lovely dove's nearly exposed bosoms. "I, uh, those ... excuse me."

He turned to Boone, who was still back at the door. Raising his eyebrows, he mouthed, *Oh my!*

Boone rolled his eyes and then bobbed his head at Tinker.

The weight of their situation returned, twisting Rabbit's guts tighter. He focused on the painted lady. "Greetings, madam. My name is Ra—uh, Jack. Fields." He bowed, not knowing what else to do. "We have ourselves a predicament." He motioned behind him at where Boone stood with Tinker. "Need the doc to patch up our dog."

She leaned to the side, peering past Rabbit. "Madam Mollie at your service, darlin'. It is apparent that you are not aware that Doc Wahl is not inclined to dispense his considerable medical knowledge on beasts," she drawled in an accent with which he had become very familiar while muleskinning freight teams through Texas. "Or Levi 'The Skunk' Simmons for that matta."

"And no Irish!" a raspy voice called through the open door beside her.

She paused to take a breath and Rabbit found his eyes drifting downward again.

"In any case," she continued when his gaze returned north of her chin. "Doc Wahl is quite engaged in tendin' to ma girls."

Rabbit eyed Madam Mollie, assessing the situation. He didn't want to upset the lady, but ... "Begging your pardon, ma'am, while I appreciate you gracing my blinkers with such a vision of beauty ..." he paused and glanced purposefully at her cleavage. "I think the doc is going to make an exception on this particular occasion. Our pup is in a bad way, and I rode for weeks through rain and snow and ice to find her."

The blond and brunette nymphs cooed, "Awwww," in harmony.

Madam Mollie smiled. "It don't matta, handsome. A beast is a beast in Doc Wahl's eyes."

Weeks of worry and frustration burned in Rabbit's chest. He took a step toward the madam, but the sound of the doc's raspy voice hollering "Madam Mollie!" through the doorway made him hesitate.

"Yes, suga?" Madam Mollie looked into the room.

"Please conclude your oral intercourse with that gentleman. There is a matter of concern here with Abigale, remember?"

The madam graced Rabbit with another smile. "My apologies for your hurt pup, Mr. Handsome, but you heard Doc Wahl. I'm afraid you need to depart." She waved toward the blonde and brunette still watching Rabbit with coy smiles from the doorway. "Unless you would care to spend some time with Pearl or Rose."

"He looks sweet as molasses, Miss Mollie," the blonde said, toying with a springy curl. "Might be I cut Mr. Handsome Jack a special rate?"

Madam Mollie shook her head. "No, but we could make a deal on two." She smiled around Rabbit toward Boone. "You both look like you could use some ... attention."

Rabbit shook off the ideas she was planting in his head. "Ma'am." He took another step toward the madam. "I'm gonna speak with the doctor and I ain't gonna let you stop—"

A low-to-high whistle he knew well interrupted him. Rabbit frowned back at Boone. "What?"

A lanky-looking fella stood next to Boone, talking with his

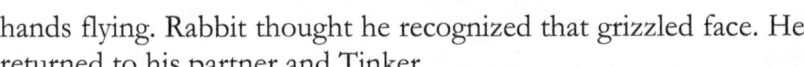

hands flying. Rabbit thought he recognized that grizzled face. He returned to his partner and Tinker.

"Ho there!" The visitor grinned up at Rabbit. "I was just havin' a drink and saw you dispatch that rummer out there. Hoo hoo! That was fun to watch. Then I saw your friend here carryin' the pooch."

"You look familiar," Rabbit said.

"Name's Hank." He started to pet Tinker, but then stopped and scrunched his face. "Aw. Poor pooch." He looked at Boone. "What happened?" He shook his head. "Never mind." He sniffed close to Tinker. "Smells like wounds have gone sour. Looks almost too far gone."

Boone scowled. "That's why we're here. Boone McCreery, that's Jack there."

"Rabbit. Just call me Rabbit."

"Thought so. Sat at the card table with you two at Belle Grande last night."

That's why Hank looked familiar.

"Why'd ya come back here with yer pup?" Hank asked them.

"We're trying to get Doc Wahl to fix this little girl up." Boone stroked between Tinker's ears, but her glassy eyes just stared at the floor.

"Doc won't touch an animal," Hank said, echoing the madam. "Kinda ornery that way. But I know somebody who can fix 'er up, right as a trivet." He opened the door to the saloon, holding it wide for them. "Let's get that pup some help."

The best thing about handling a frozen corpse was the lack of smell. Although pieces did tend to break off too easily, leaving fingers, toes, and ears to be picked up and tucked into pockets before the journey to Valhalla.

Clementine squatted in front of the wood stove in her exam room at The Pyre, using the iron claw Hank had fashioned to shove glowing cinders into a pile. She tossed a chunk of wood into the stove, then another, before closing the steel door.

Exposure, she had written in her journal upon first glance at the dead man. The daisy pusher on her table had suffered one of the many ugly ways to die in Deadwood. Unfortunately, she needed to thaw his body out in order to appease her curiosity, which meant her reprieve from the stench of rotting flesh wouldn't last long.

"That should heat you up," she told the corpse. She touched the wool blanket that was hanging on the drying rack close to the stove. It was almost warm enough.

She frowned down at the dead man. His eyelids were stuck open, giving him a surprised look to wear on his voyage to the beyond. "I know what you mean," she said to him. "I'm as surprised as you about what Hildegard and Miss Hundt said."

The slayer has had her first encounter.

First encounter. "That must be the attack at the pigsty," she told him. "They knew that I'd been surprised and struck on the head. But how?"

Ein Scharfrichter that does not know the old languages?

"If *Scharfrichter* is German for 'executioner,' why did amma always call me *ein Jägerin*?" She thought about the two names. "I think I prefer 'executioner' rather than 'slayer'. It seems more exciting."

She bent nearer, her long tweezers in hand, and clamped onto the dead man's ear, which was black from frostbite. "And *Bitrog*?" she asked, tugging lightly on the ear to have a look behind it. "What does she mean I'm heeding the command of the deceiver? Is the deceiver also the *Bitrog*, or are they two different things?"

The ear broke off and slipped from between her tweezers,

clunking onto the table next to the head.

"Oops. Too soon." She grimaced at the corpse. "Sorry about your ear."

After tucking the ear in his open mouth for safekeeping, she grabbed the warm blanket hanging by the stove and draped it over him, covering him from head to toe. "I'll get back to you later."

She washed her hands, removing the ring from her finger as she dried off. Over at her desk, she leaned close to the oil lamp, examining the ring again.

Der Scharfrichter wears the sign of caper-sus.

"*Caper-sus*," she whispered, visualizing the word in her head. Was that Latin or some derivative of it? Her knowledge of Latin was as bad as her comprehension of Old High German. If she remembered her amma's lessons correctly, *caper* meant goat and *sus* was a pig, which made sense with the image of a goat blending into a pig on the ring. But what was the meaning behind this emblem? A crest, representing a family name? Or did it have some other significance? Something darker? Miss Hundt certainly hadn't sounded happy that Clementine was wearing it.

Did it have anything to do with the *Bitrog* or deceiver?

She might be vulnerable to his enchantment.

What sort of enchantment? That word conjured images of faeries and witches in Clementine's head. Were they referring to some sort of dark magic? A spell?

One of his pets ...

"I'm nobody's pet."

At least she didn't think she was.

"Am I playing the fool?" she asked the dead man under the blanket. "Am I inadvertently in league with those bent on ruin?" The Black Hills version of *devourers*? Was she to suffer the same fate as her mother?

She focused inward, drawing on her inherited ability to sense whether someone meant her harm. A gift her grandmother had told her she must temper with caution.

Clementine replayed the conversation between Hildegard and Miss Hundt yet again, weighing their words, assessing their tones.

Hildegard was most likely to be trusted. Time and again during her interactions with Hildegard since arriving in Deadwood, Clementine had watched and listened beyond the madam's words, searching for a seed of duplicity or ill intent. Not once had Hildegard given her reason to distrust her motives, whether it was something simple such as discussing the weather or more in depth like questions about the bodies passing through The Pyre.

Did that mean Miss Hundt could be trusted as well?

The two women had spoken openly in her presence, even if in German. The truths they had known about Clementine and her actions last night at Kee Luk's pigsty gave her pause. How could they have such knowledge? Had there been another party in attendance? Were they working with the professional who'd stabbed the shooter in the alley? Or had that been the rogue they referred to repeatedly?

The rogue has saved the life of der Scharfrichter once already.

Clementine paced in front of her desk.

What if her intuition failed her this time? What if the two women were conspiring against her, playing her for a fool?

"Perhaps they are aware that I speak German," she said, looking at the dead man as if he might agree or not.

There was, after all, the possibility that their discussion was a ruse to make her question the job for which she'd contracted. To doubt her benefactor and what he represented.

She returned to her desk and dropped the ring inside the drawer. "Enough," she told it and the other two rings already in there and shut the drawer, leaning against it. She was tired of her thoughts spinning this way and that. Tired of dealing with death day after day without knowing which course she should take so

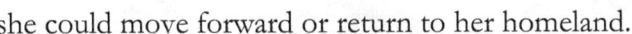

she could move forward or return to her homeland.

At least now things were growing more interesting.

"Hildegard was right. I am ready."

She'd like to go back to The Dove and talk to the madam alone, but something told her to wait to play her hand, to continue holding her cards close to her vest for a bit longer.

A rogue Scharfrichter roving about makes me nervous.

Who was the rogue Hildegard had been talking about? How many players were involved in this game? How deep was the mire Clementine had walked into here in Dead …

The front door crashed open.

She gasped, frowning down at the desk drawer.

Someone had come for the rings!

ELEVEN

Clementine rushed over and grabbed a scalpel from her instrument tray. She pressed against the wall next to the parlor entryway, lying in wait for whoever had come for the rings.

Or maybe they were here for her, since she'd killed two of their ring bearers.

Hank's voice came from the parlor room, followed by the sound of boots stomping on the entry rug.

She blew out a breath and tossed the scalpel back on the tray, returning to the frozen corpse. Her heart pounded in her ears as she waited for Hank to join her.

"… Nibbled him down 'til there weren't nothing left of him no how. Miss Clem!" He clomped into the examination room, smiling wide. "I brought ya some customers." He opened the wood stove, peered in, and slammed it shut again. "Just fed, looks like."

At the sound of the front door closing, she asked, "What sort of customers?"

"The breathin' sort. Boys, this here's Miss Clementine Johanssen." Hank held his arm out toward the parlor. "Miss Clem, these fellers are in need of a dose a yer healin' ways."

Two men stepped into the examination room, hats in hands. They were both taller than Hank with broad shoulders under thick coats. The man in front had dark wavy hair, green eyes, and a short beard. The other had blue eyes and wore a beard, too, along with sandy blond hair that stuck up in tufts here and there.

Overall, their appearance and demeanor were not that of foul or filthy trail riders, nor of rowdy miners. She noted the lines on their faces, the weariness in their gazes, and the slump in their shoulders. No, these two were sturdy men who'd been worn down either by travel or a resolve to finish whatever task they'd started. Maybe both. Clementine had seen their kind before.

Whatever was under the bloodstained blanket in the arms of the front man shifted and whined.

Hank pointed at the man with the blanket. "This here's Boone McCreery. That cowboy there is Jack Fields."

"Mr. McCreery," Clementine said. "You have a bullet hole in your hat, but none in your head. I assume my healing ways are required by the creature under the blanket then?"

"It's Tinker," Mr. McCreery said, his voice deeper than most. "She's a dog. I'd sure appreciate it if you'd take a look at her. Hank says you might be able to help."

Clementine pointed at her empty table, joining him as he lowered the wrapped dog onto the pine slab.

A whimper came from Tinker as Clementine started to unwrap her from the blanket. She glanced up at Mr. McCreery, who was rubbing his left shoulder while grimacing. "You and your friend can warm yourselves by the fire, if you'd like."

She looked over at the other man, Jack Fields, and found herself at the receiving end of a slack-jawed stare. The blond man had yet to speak, or move for that matter, since stepping into her examination room.

She turned to Hank, one eyebrow raised. "Does Mr. Fields require attention as well?"

"Ho ho!" Hank slapped his thigh. "No, Miss Clem. Seems fit as a foal. To look at him, I'd say he's smitten." Chuckling, he sent an exaggerated wink at Mr. Fields.

Jack Fields's cheeks flushed.

"Miss Johanssen," Mr. McCreery said, drawing her gaze again.

"Do you think you might be able to help our pup?" His brow was furrowed as he stroked Tinker's head. "If so, we would be in your debt and happy to pay for your services."

She stared at Boone McCreery. He smelled and acted like a gentleman. Was well spoken and easy to look at, too. And clean. Most of these traits were not common among the men of Deadwood.

"Call me Clem." She smiled. "I'll have a look now." She finished removing the blanket from Tinker. "Is she a biter, Mr. McCreery?"

"Not usually. And I'd be honored if you'd call me Boone."

The poor dog was covered in blood, her light-colored fur various shades of red and pink. Taking a pair of scissors from her instrument tray, Clementine cut away the bandages one by one. Periodically, Tinker would let out a feeble whimper in between raspy breaths.

She heard a shuffling sound and glanced over in time to see Boone smack his friend on the shoulder.

"Are you awake now, lover?" Boone said under his breath.

Clementine returned to her patient, a smile playing at the corners of her mouth. When she finished unwrapping the bandages and took a closer look at their dog, tugging gently at blood-matted fur to see the extent of the injuries, her smile faded.

"Her wounds were dressed well," she said without looking up. "But her leg is infected. There is some necrosis around the margins." She glanced at Hank. "Will you please fetch my apothecary case?"

She started toward where her apron hung on a peg, but realized her hands were covered with the dog's blood.

"Uh, could one of you help me with my apron?" She pointed at the clean leather apron hanging on the wall behind them.

Mr. Fields jumped into action. He grabbed the apron and handed his hat to Boone. "Hold this."

Boone obliged with a smirk.

Mr. Fields looped the apron over her head, his eyes level with hers. With his light coloring and tall build, he reminded her of the boys back home. Maybe he had some Norse in his bloodline.

"Could you turn around, uh, ma'am? I mean, Miss Johanssen."

Clementine did as asked, stretching her neck in an effort to pull her braid from the apron's loop. "Mr. Fields, if you could free my hair, I'd appreciate it."

His fingers were quick and nimble at her collar, but he appeared to have some problems with the apron's ties. He tugged awkwardly on one and then the other. Then both.

She glanced over her shoulder. "Under control, Mr. Fields?"

"Kinda forgot how to tie a knot. I mean, I know how to tie a knot. I tie lotsa knots bein' a muleskinner, I mean freight master and all. But it's gotta be one so's you can untie it again from behind." His chortle sounded almost cackle-like. "The leather feels like reins in my hands. Like I'm riding a horse along ..." He stopped and then cursed under his breath. "Not to say I think you're a horse, Miss Johanssen. I think you're real pretty. Prettier than any mare I've seen. What I mean to say is the leather straps feel good in ..." He stopped again and muttered, "Hobble your lip, Rabbit."

Clementine looked at Boone, whose shoulders were shaking with silent laughter. "I've not been compared to a horse before. It's good that I bathed today, or I might not have won the contest." A coating of hog shit and she surely would have come in second.

Boone laughed out loud, a low pleasant sound.

When Mr. Fields finished his bowknot, he joined his friend.

"Smooth, *hombre*. Real smooth," Boone said, grinning wide.

"*Beso mi culo*," Mr. Fields grumbled and punched Boone on the upper arm.

"Ow! That's my sore side, *gilipollas*." Boone rubbed his

shoulder again.

Gilipollas. That was one she hadn't heard before. It sounded like Spanish or maybe Portuguese.

Hank lumbered through the doorway and plunked the apothecary case on the table next to Tinker, rattling the glass containers within. "You'll be wantin' the knockout juice, I expect." Hank withdrew a bottle of clear liquid from the case and set it on the table. "I'll get you some clean muslin from the storage room."

"Thank you, Hank," she called after him. "I think he can read my mind," she told her guests, who'd settled back into quietness.

Clementine reached into the case and brought out several bottles of earthy-colored liquids and powders that when combined would help lower a fever in a human. With any luck, they'd work on a dog, too. She poured precise amounts of each into a vial and swirled it. Lifting Tinker's head, she slowly poured a fraction of the mixture into the dog's mouth.

Tinker swallowed it with some encouragement in the form of a throat rub. Another whine came from the pup's lips before Tinker wilted in Clementine's hands. She lowered the dog's head to the table, checking for a heartbeat.

It was still there, faint but regular.

"It appears she doesn't need sedation," she told the two men.

"Why not?" Mr. Fields asked, taking a step toward her. His face had paled at her words.

"Don't fret, I meant she's unconscious." Clementine brought her tray of tools to the exam table next to the apothecary case, along with the bottle of raw alcohol, and began to clean and care for Tinker's wounds.

"Not dead, though, right?" Mr. Fields pressed.

She paused to send him a small smile. "Not dead, Mr. Fields. Her body needs her to rest in order to heal."

He sighed and began to pace. "The name's Jack, by the way."

"Fine, Jack-by-the-way," she jested, trying to lighten the

mood. "I'm Clem. Or Clem-the-undertaker, if you prefer to wax eloquently."

Jack stopped pacing long enough to grin at Boone. "I knew she'd be feisty. Reminds me of you and yer fancy chin music."

Boone moved over to her desk and sat on the edge. His gaze moved from his friend, to the dog, to her.

What was taking Hank so long?

Clementine set to work trimming the dog's fur around its wounds. "I don't believe I've seen you two around Deadwood."

"We're new to the Black Hills, Miss ... uh ... Clementine," Jack said.

"We didn't plan on coming to Deadwood," Boone explained. "Our uncle Morton runs a freight business out of Santa Fe. We were scheduled to meet him in Cheyenne."

"We were comin' back with a load of freight from Laramie, so he figured on waitin' for us," Jack added.

Uncle Morton? They didn't look like brothers. Must be cousins. "You both work for your uncle, then?"

"No, ma'am," Jack said. "I mean he's not really an uncle, but we do work for Uncle Mort. Well, not work for so much as ..." His face darkened again as he sputtered.

"Tarnation," Boone said, shaking his head. "You could use a swig of tonsil oil for that tangled tongue." Boone looked back at Clementine. "What Rabbit here is trying to say is that Morton took us in when our parents died on the wagon trip west and raised us like his kin. We got to calling him 'uncle' after a while, but we can save that story for another time."

"We planned to head home to Santa Fe along with him." Jack returned to their explanation for being in Deadwood, his tongue apparently knot-free again. "But a friend of Uncle Mort's down in Cheyenne told him Deadwood was boomin', and since he had time to kill while he waited for us, he came up this way to check it out."

"He's always looking to expand his business." Boone added.

"Always expandin'," Jack repeated, crossing the room. He sidled up to the exam table across from Clementine, eyeing the blanket-covered corpse.

Clementine cut away the last of the fur around the wounds. She watched Jack tap on the corpse's chest.

"He's still a block of ice," she told him. "Died of exposure." At least that was the way it appeared. She'd know for sure when he melted and she could take a closer look.

Hank returned with an armload of rags and dumped them on Clem's desk next to Boone. "I'll tear some into strips, Miss Clem."

"Why the blanket?" Jack asked her, fingering the wool that covered the dead man. "His toes cold, are they?" He grinned with one side of his mouth.

Hank howled like a coyote, laughing at the ceiling. "That's a good'n, Jack Rabbit!" He started tearing the muslin into strips, still chuckling to himself. "Ya know, Tinker there reminds me of a pup that tagged along with the rail crew back on the Pacific Railroad headed to Utah. He'd steal yer boots and chew on 'em so's there was just scraps left by mornin'."

"Looked like Tinker, did he?" Jack lifted the blanket from the corpse's head and peeked underneath. He flinched and dropped the blanket.

Clementine fought back a smile. "First time you looked close at a dead body, Jack?"

He shook his head. "I just ain't seen one with an ear in its mouth before."

"Mr. Frost likes to talk to himself," she shot back with a straight face.

Jack did a double take. "Yer foolin' with me."

Hank howled again. "Ah, Miss Clem, that's a good one. Didn't I tell you boys that she's as bright as a penny?"

"You sure did," Jack said under his breath. His gaze meeting hers and sticking for several seconds longer than was proper.

Clementine stared back, allowing her senses to explore the air around Jack Fields. His energy flowed close to the surface, bordering on turbulent. Since he'd arrived, she'd noticed a quick confidence in his movements. She'd guess his temper matched hers—burning fast and hot. Rabbit, she'd heard his partner call him. The nickname fit well.

Boone cleared his throat twice before Jack looked away.

Clementine took the strips of cloth Hank handed her. "Will you fetch me a bowl of clean water, Hank?"

With a nod, he grabbed a bowl. "That pup was the size and color as you boys' dog there." Hank continued with his anecdote as he filled the bowl. "Plum crazy he was. I called him 'Banjo,' seein' how he was strung tight as a banjo string. Chinese named him '*Howzu*,' which is the Chinese word for monkey, on account he climbed like a monkey." He set the bowl next to Clementine on the exam table. "Didn't answer to no names no how. Climbed anything worth climbin'. Trees, water towers, ladders. Couldn't get down, though. Start to howlin' and somebody always had to go get him."

Clementine chuckled as she dabbed at Tinker's wounds. "Banjo must have thought he was a cat."

"Could be. I remember once the rascal jumped on the back of a horse. Weren't no normal roan, though. It was a bronc the rail boss was tryin' to bust. The horse was snuffy, had an extra helping of grit. 'Hades,' the boss called him, I guess 'cause he was hell to break. Well, Hades was mindin' his own business, eatin' grass, not botherin' nobody, and Banjo jumps on his back."

Clementine grabbed a clean rag and soaked it with water, and then wrung the water out on the short fur around the leg wound.

"He stayed on that broomtail, too," Hank continued. "Spread his legs so's he was belly flat to bareback, legs stickin' out each side, holdin' on to Hades's mane with his teeth. All the while Hades was twistin' and buckin', nippin' at Banjo, but that dog weren't letting go. Wasn't too long afore Hades kinda simmered down and commenced to eatin' grass again. Rail boss had worked on that bronc for two weeks." Hank let go with a belly-shaking laugh. "Li'l ol' Banjo broke him in one go." Hank slapped the table and then leaned against it as laughter rocked him clear to his knees.

Clementine stopped her doctoring and grinned at Hank. His laughter had him crying, tears and all. She started laughing along with him, a chuckle or two at first about Banjo's story, then a full-on snort followed by giggles at Hank himself as he gasped for breath.

A glance at their visitors found Jack sharing in the laughs as he watched Hank's hooting and guffawing. Boone was grinning, but his gaze was on her. Something hovering behind his eyes sobered her. Where Jack's passions appeared to ripple along the surface, Boone's emotions were still and ran deep.

"Where did Banjo come from?" Jack asked. "Was he a stray?"

Clementine returned to her task, reaching for the raw alcohol. The wound needed to be sterilized before she could put on a poultice.

"I don't know," Hank answered when he caught his breath. "Rode in one day on a supply train. Didn't come in with no one in particular. Just showed up." Hank dropped a handful of cloth strips next to Tinker. "That enough fer bandages, Miss Clem?"

"That'll do, Hank." She collected the makings for a poultice from her bag and started mixing them in the empty water bowl.

"Anyway, Banjo rode out on the supply train ever' so often, then he'd show up a week or two later, ridin' a train back in again. Visitin' on one end of the line or the other, I expect. A dog with two homes." He snorted. "Maybe he had hisself a cute li'l she-pup or two waitin' at the other end of the line, who knows?"

"Lucky dog, huh, Booney," Jack joked.

"Maybe," Boone shot back.

"Or not, dependin' on the females," Hank chimed in with

another hoot. "No offense, Miss Clem."

"None taken, Hank." Clementine began dabbing the poultice on Tinker's wounds and then had Hank help her wrap them with the strips of cloth.

Jack became restless, moving around the examination room. Clementine glanced up periodically, watching as his eyes and hands wandered.

"Mind if I sit down, Miss Clementine?" He pointed at the chair at her desk, nudging Boone to the side.

"Not at all." She tied off one of the bandages, her thoughts on Jack Fields. He might appear jumpy like a rabbit, but she had a feeling those sharp blue eyes of his didn't miss much. "So, what happened to Tinker?"

"Tracking down Uncle Morton took us to Gayville," Boone said. "A fellow there found her down the hill from the ..." He looked down at where his partner was sitting. "What was the mine called?"

"Golden Echo," Jack answered.

Hank stiffened next to her.

"That's right. Anyway," Boone continued, "that fellow in Gayville patched Tinker up best he could."

"They call that mine the Bloody Bones now," Jack said.

A grunt from Hank drew Clementine's gaze. He frowned at Boone and Jack. "That's a bad place," he said, his voice somber.

Clementine had heard the name before from some of the girls at Yellow Strike Saloon. The rumors about it sent chills through most. If she remembered right, the mine had started out bursting with prosperity and luck for some brothers, but now they were gone and nobody dared to dig any deeper. Another case of dead men told no tales, only the bodies didn't end up on an undertaker's table *if* they were found.

"Bad place how?" Boone asked Hank.

"I was hired on to help work the Golden Echo mine. Grunt work. Always had an unsettlin' feeling workin' in there. Cold and clammy like, made my guts riled." Shadows passed over Hank's face, lining his cheeks. "Wasn't there long and there was an accident deep in. They said the old boy was crushed in a cave-in, but I'm here to tell you it weren't no cave-in. Not the way the old boy looked when they hauled him outta there. Half his face ripped clean off. Strips torn deep all over his body, like big sharp claws had at him. Shredded up bad. Hard to stomach lookin' at him until we got him wrapped up. I decided that was the end of my minin' work there. Started workin' for Miss Clem not long after that. She's a good boss." He blinked away the shadows and smiled at Clementine, back to his old happy self.

Boone scowled at Jack, "I suppose that explains why the people in Gayville are holed up the way they are."

Jack was watching Clementine bandage Tinker's leg as he fidgeted with her desk drawer. "Yep. They're scared."

"For good reason, sounds like."

"Uncle Mort is probably up there," Jack said, his voice edged with tension. Anger more than fear by the sounds of it. "First thing in the morning, Booney."

Boone nodded, looking at Hank. "Is there a place in town we can leave Tinker for a day or so?"

Clementine frowned at the two men. She knew why Boone was asking. They were heading to the Bloody Bones to find their uncle, probably at first light.

"She'll stay here with me while you check out that mine," she told Boone. "I'll need to keep an eye on her for a day or two."

"You boys oughta sit and think on that," Hank warned, all signs of mirth gone from his face.

Clementine knew better than to try to change their minds. They were on a mission now. She could see it in the set of their jaw. Nothing short of hellfire or a blizzard would stop them.

She nudged Hank aside and moved to the bucket next to the stove, grabbing the soap. "Jack, can you fetch my journal from the desk drawer in front of you?"

"My pleasure." He pulled the drawer open and cocked his head. He picked up one of the pewter rings and squinted at it, turning it this way and that.

Clementine pretended to busy herself with drying her hands, but her attention was on Jack and his reaction to the ring and its *caper-sus* emblem.

With a shrug, he dropped it back into the drawer and grabbed her journal. "Here it is, Miss Clementine." He hopped out of the chair, his momentum tipping it over. "Dammit," he growled under his breath and thrust the journal into her outstretched hand. "Sorry about that. I'll go ahead and pick it up."

Jack fumbled with the chair, dropped it once, twice, and finally put it right before sliding it into place under the desk with a *thunk*. He knocked on the back of the chair with his knuckles and forced a laugh. "Must have a short leg or somethin'."

"Or something," Boone said between coughs of laughter into his fist.

Jack glared at his partner. "Shut up, Boone."

Clementine opened her journal. She'd been unable to read Jack's reaction to the *caper-sus* emblem beyond his curiosity. Was it an act on his part? Although if he'd understood the significance of the ring, he probably wouldn't have given himself away by picking it up in the first place. Maybe curiosity was all there was to it.

"Didn't know you was a bronc buster, Jack Rabbit," Hank joked, picking up the remaining rags he had carried in earlier. "All done there, looks like, Miss Clem. Won't be needin these, I'm thinkin'?"

"Nope. All finished, Hank."

Clementine scanned through her scrawls. She kept notes on all of the work she'd done at The Pyre. She knew her time here was limited, and she knew a historical record would be valuable to the next poor soul to take the job of undertaker in Deadwood. A quick scan down the last couple of weeks of known names found no notes on a man with the name Morton.

She glanced up to find Jack watching her. The slack-jawed look was back. She raised her brows. "Something on your mind, Jack?"

"Saw you at Yellow Strike Saloon yesterday," he said.

"You did?" He must have been there when … she cringed.

"Yes, ma'am. You lambasted that greasy skunk but good."

Her cheeks warmed. "Oh. That." Her grip tightened on the journal. "Upon occasion my anger gets the best of me."

"He undoubtedly deserved what he got," Boone said, his focus dipping to her hands.

"In my opinion, yes." She lifted her chin. While she was embarrassed by the spectacle she had caused during her loss of control, she was not embarrassed—or sorry—for what she did to that no-good snake.

"Never seen a woman deliver a slogging that good." Jack grinned. "I'd wager that foul-mouthed fool was luckier than he realized." He pointed at Tinker, who was starting to stir. "She's gonna make it, then?"

Clementine wasn't sure. "That's up to her now. I did all I could."

Jack walked over, worry lining his forehead as he stared down at the dog. "You did a first-rate job on her, I'd say. Thank you."

Boone joined Jack at the table. "Little Tink," he said, his touch tender when he stroked her head. "We'll come visit you later tomorrow. First, we have to find your pa."

"I still think you boys oughta give it some more noggin time before ya—"

"We're as good as there, Hank," Boone cut him off, his hard tone leaving no room for debate.

Jack patted Hank's shoulder. "Don't worry none about us, we're heeled."

"I get ya. I'd go and help out, but I gotta be in Galena tomorrow. If'n you could wait a day, I'd—"

"Hank," Clementine said. When he looked at her, she shook her head. "This is their business. Leave them to it."

Hank nodded once, looking out the window with a scowl. Clementine didn't like the two men going up to the Bloody Bones any more than Hank did, but she knew better than to try to stop them. Their uncle was somewhere out there. She just hoped he was in better shape than their dog had been when they found him.

If they found him.

"Miss Clementine," Jack said, scratching under Tinker's muzzle. "If we don't make it back tomorrow for some reason …"

"Don't worry about your dog. She'll be here when you return."

Boone stared at her for several beats, his expression intense, yet guarded. Then he turned to Jack. "We should be on our way. The horses need a meal, and so do we." He stepped away from the exam table and slapped his hat on his head. "If there's anything you need, we're at the Custer Hotel."

She nodded. "Good luck."

"Got my hat," he said, pointing at the bullet hole. "We have all the luck we need."

Clementine watched them go. "I hope he's right," she said after the door shut in their wake.

"Me, too, Miss Clem," Hank said, frowning after them. "But the Bloody Bones swallows men whole."

TWELVE

"I'm shootin' somebody today," Rabbit grumbled from his horse behind Boone. "A lot!"

"Okay." Boone continued leading the way toward Gayville, his head lowered against the cold wind.

Rabbit had started the day downright surly. He'd continued the testament to his beleaguered presence in the Hills as they'd traveled through the windblown sleet that stung cheeks and froze fingers, not to mention that it made seeing the trail a pain in the ass.

"And keep Nickel walkin' the chalk," the snarly wolf riding behind Boone added. "Can't hardly follow through this snow with you weavin' all over."

"Right."

Ordinarily, Boone might have snapped back at his partner in return for a comment like that, but he was giving Rabbit more rein than usual this morning. The crabby cuss had woken at the break of dawn with a shout, thrashing about from another one of his nightmares. After Rabbit had steadied his breath and gathered his senses, he'd described another grisly vision of Uncle Morton's lifeless body and milky, unseeing eyes with a steady voice. But his hands hadn't stopped trembling until midway through breakfast.

While Boone tried not to let on as they ate and prepared for their man-hunting trip to Gayville, Rabbit's visions had darkened the outlook for the day even more, leaving him chilled to the bone about what they might find at the Bloody Bones mine.

In the past, visions had come to Rabbit on occasion, so his prophetic dreams were not new to Boone. Unfortunately, those visions were often more accurate than not, at least as a whole if not in detail. The grim images Rabbit had described upon waking were now stuck in Boone's mind, probably the same as they were in Rabbit's.

If Uncle Morton were indeed dead, then Boone would hunt down and kill the bastard responsible for his demise. Whoever, or whatever, would suffer the same fate as his uncle.

Revenge aside, there were other dark clouds filling the horizon that had Boone's nerves strung tight as he cut a trail through the snow to Gayville. This particular growing storm had nothing to do with the damned sleet and snow currently swirling around them, but rather Rabbit, who was chomping at the bit behind him. Boone could feel the unbridled rage rolling off his sidekick, and history had shown that when riled, Rabbit's common sense was left stabled in the barn in favor of impulsive, ill-considered deeds. Sooner or later, Rabbit's recklessness would most likely see him hurt.

Or killed.

And Boone couldn't allow that. He wouldn't.

Uncle Morton had seen it in Rabbit, too, of course. The old freighter hadn't missed much when it came to the two of them. He didn't dare take his eyes off of Boone or Rabbit for too long, or one of them would land up to their necks in trouble. He'd once told Boone that at times raising two curious boys was like holding a skunk by the tail. Boone could believe it. Hell, Rabbit alone had enough starch in his britches to drive a preacher to cuss most days, especially once he'd started filling out his boots.

Boone thought back on a day years ago when the three of them were out sinking fence posts. Uncle Morton and he had watched Rabbit chip away at a hunk of granite buried in the rocky ranch soil with a pickaxe ...

"That's futility, pure and simple, Jack Rabbit," Uncle Morton said.

Boone snorted in agreement, holding up a shovel. "Move to the side, lunkhead."

"Nope! Fence post is goin' right here!" Rabbit said, pointing at the granite.

Uncle Morton chuckled. "He'll try 'n plow through a stump lessen you help him steer around it, Boone."

"I know, stubborn as hell. He'd have made a good ox. Yet he'll spend a day finding homes for a litter of kittens."

Uncle Morton's grin widened. "Rabbit is one of a kind. Unfortunately, the boy is short a dose of your temperament."

"Avast, ya fuckin' scurvy granite!" Rabbit shouted, threatening the rock with his pickaxe. "I'll piss on yer poop deck and feed ya to the fishes!"

Laughing, Boone buried his shovel in the dirt. "He's been knocked upside the head with a frying pan too many times."

That had made his uncle hoot and …

"I don't remember it bein' this fuckin' far." Rabbit's grousing pulled Boone from his rumination. "We got sleet but at least the damned wind ain't blowin' … oh, my mistake. It is." The growl in his voice was a sure sign Rabbit was spiraling into a pit.

A diversion was in order, and Boone knew just the trick. He slowed Nickel until he was neck-and-neck with Dime and Rabbit. "That Clementine … what was her last name?" He pretended not to remember.

"Johanssen."

"Yeah, Clementine Johanssen. She did some nice work on Tink."

"Yep."

"She looked good this morning."

"She surely did."

Boone grinned. "Tink, I mean."

"Both of them, actually." A smile crept onto Rabbit's face.

"Tink awake and waggin' her tail. That was heartliftin' to see." Rabbit patted Dime's neck and then settled back into his saddle. "Looked like Tink wasn't even boogered up that much, exceptin' her leg."

"That must be some kind of miracle snake oil Miss Johanssen has in her bag."

"She's got some miracles in her bag, all right." Rabbit waggled his frosty eyebrows.

Boone chuckled, warmed to see easygoing Rabbit back at the reins. "You're not wrong about that," he said after bracing through another blast of breath-stealing sleet and wind. "She has charms hard for a man to resist."

"Now don't get your hopes up, ol' boy. We was sparkin', in case you couldn't tell. Her eyes told a story of me and her."

"Could be. Handsome man such as yourself." Boone smirked. "You were certainly as smooth as blackstrap molasses last night at The Pyre."

"Shut up."

Boone's laughter was muffled by the wind.

"She can fight," Rabbit said after a spell. "Stomped that bastard in the bar without workin' up a huff."

"She did that."

"She can heal a dog that's next to dead, probably do the same thing for a person, too."

"I bet so."

"And got the looks."

"Surely."

"I been thinkin', Booney."

"Uh-oh."

Rabbit held up his fist, threatening Boone, which made Boone laugh again.

"I been thinkin' about the business," Rabbit continued. "If we open up a depot in Deadwood, I could run it."

"Hmm …"

"I could settle down with Miss Clementine. I mean, I don't like the undertakin' business so much, but maybe she could help run the freight depot we open up."

"Are you saying you'd move to Deadwood for a sage hen, Rabbit?"

"Well, facing reality, if Uncle Mort is gone ..." Rabbit paused, shaking his head, and then pushed through. "If Uncle Mort is gone, we'll need to change things up some. You've been chewin' on the idea of startin' a ranch, but I'd rather run the depot. Why not around here?"

"I have a few concerns about that."

Rabbit guffawed. "Ain't like you to go and overthink a thing, Mr. Tortoise. Go ahead, tell me your all-fired problems with my idea."

"I seem to remember somebody being mad as a hornet whenever Uncle Morton sends him north of the New Mexico territory line in the winter. 'I freeze my prairie oysters off up there!' he says every time."

"Aren't you the funny one? Every time? I said it *once*. And that was a long time ago. Things are different now."

"Different how? Tall? Ass-kicking? Auburn hair? Pretty?"

"Suck eggs." Rabbit shot Boone a stupid grin. "Maybe. She is a vision, ain't she, Booney? And she's got a good helpin' of smarts, too. Clementine." He rubbed his beard. "Even her name is pretty. Everything I'm lookin' for, plus a little."

"I'd say you're overshooting on this one, considering your list of qualifications for a suitable woman usually consists of one thing—willing."

"Considering my list usually consists of one thing," Rabbit repeated with a squint. "Listen, buzzard. I told you, we sparked. Besides, you're wrong. It's two things—breathing and willing."

"Oh, you sparked, all right." Boone grinned. "The first time you knocked that chair over last night, I could tell she was ready for some courtin'. By the second time, she was itchin' for a hitchin'."

Rabbit took off his hat and smacked Boone on the shoulder with it. "You're a jackass," he said as he jammed it back on his head.

"Okay, okay." Boone laughed at his partner's glare. "I'm done tying knots in your lasso. You're right. She has the curves to make a sculptor cry, no doubt there." Boone sucked air through his teeth at the thought of her shape. "Truth be told, she's a wonderment."

"All around impressive, I reckon you mean. You said a 'few' concerns. What else are you worried about?"

Boone shifted in his saddle. "Every time you run a load of freight out of Santa Fe, what do you see?"

"Javelina."

"No."

"Rosalita."

"Now who's the funny one?"

Rabbit held his hat on tight as a gust of wind blasted them. "Then what, oh, wise prairie dog?"

"Trains," Boone said. "New lines are appearing all the time."

"Jehosephat! You ain't startin' in on that again."

"Rabbit—"

"Trains might do away with long-distance runs, maybe. Still need to get the goods to towns a ways from the rail line."

Boone shrugged. "We'll talk about it later. Gayville is around the bend up there." He nudged Nickel back to the front of the line, leading the way around the craggy outcropping of rock and pine trees. A strong wind slammed into him as the small town came into view.

"What if Weeks ain't home?" Rabbit yelled from behind him.

"We'll go looking for him."

"In this mess of weather?"

Rabbit had a good point. The sky had grown darker as they neared Gayville. The whipping sleet and snow seemed determined to turn them away. "Maybe somebody else in town will know how to get to the mine."

Boone held his hat as another gust rocked them in their saddles.

"This fuckin' wind!" Rabbit shouted. "Gettin' even worse. I swear, this town is cursed."

"We rounded the bend into the wind is all," Boone hollered back over the howling wind.

Rabbit might be right about the place being cursed, though. Riding into Gayville certainly made Boone cringe and shiver even without the blinding snow and sleet.

They pushed into the small grouping of cabins and shacks, heads bent against the wind. Up ahead, Weeks's place was a blur through the churning snow that blunted Boone's instincts along with his senses. He just needed to escape the freezing gales and warm his hands for a moment.

He led Nickel to the side of Weeks's cabin where he'd be partially shielded from the worst of the gusts. Boone dropped into the snow, holding onto the saddle horn so he didn't land on his ass. Rabbit pulled up beside him.

"Here." Boone handed Nickel's reins to Rabbit. "See to the horses. I'll get Elston."

"Do I look like a stable boy?" Rabbit called to his back.

He peered around the side of the cabin, gearing up to face the wind. "Door is open a crack," he told Rabbit, who'd managed to tug his boots free of the icy stirrups and land in the snow upright between Nickel and Dime.

Boone cupped the side of his mouth with his hand. "Elston Weeks! You in there?"

Besides the whistling wind, he heard no reply. He stepped around the corner, leaning into the frigid gust.

"Hold up, Boone!" Rabbit called.

As Boone neared the door, something crashed inside the cabin. He hesitated. "Everything all right in there, Elston?"

Again, no reply.

Something didn't sit quite right with this situation. Boone took a step back and pulled his pistol. He pointed it at the door, aiming about heart-level.

Off to his side, he saw Rabbit edge out from the side of the cabin. "Consarn it, Boone! Would you just wait a second? I need to secure the reins."

Elston might not have a second. Boone kicked the door open. It flew wide, hit the wall with a bang, and slammed shut in his face.

"Beautiful," Rabbit said, wrapping the reins around the log jutting from the corner of the cabin. "Let me show you how that's done."

Boone ignored him and kicked again, rushing into the dark cabin. He hesitated inside the doorway, temporarily blinded while his eyes adjusted from the bright white world outside. His gun ready, he took another step into the room. "Elston?"

He saw a shift in the shadows to his left a split second before the side of his head exploded in pain.

He staggered. "I can't ..."

His legs gave way and he crashed onto the sawdust floor to the side of the door. When he struggled to sit up, his head reeled in pain. He fell back again and rolled onto his side.

A blur of movement in front of the door spurred him to push up onto one arm.

"Rabbit?" He blinked to clear his vision.

A figure leaned over him, blocking out the light. Though the edges of his vision were blurry, he could make out a pale face.

No, not Rabbit.

At first it appeared to be a man, but the skin was so white.

Long, stringy hair draped around jutting cheekbones.

A closer look made Boone's heart pound. There was something wrong with the shape of his face, his nose and mouth forming a beak-like snout.

Boone's gaze lifted. Red eyes stared back at him with dark vertical slits for pupils. Snake eyes! He recoiled.

Long skeletal fingers reached toward Boone. A cold hand clamped over his mouth and forced his head to turn to one side and then the other. Leaning closer, the pale devil sniffed along Boone's neck.

"Common livestock." The voice that spoke in his ear was low and gravelly, the accent heavy. "I can hear your heart quiver."

Boone cringed at the rancid smell of death on its breath.

A war cry sounded from the doorway.

Rabbit barreled toward them and rammed into the pale devil's back. The two of them tumbled over Boone, rolling across the floor.

The devil came out on top, rising while Rabbit clung to his back with one arm wrapped around his neck. He landed several kidney punches while the devil tried to shake him loose.

Boone tried to stagger to his feet, reaching toward them. A stab of pain in his head tipped him sideways. He held onto the table leg, watching, helpless.

The pale devil grabbed the sleeve of Rabbit's coat.

For a moment, Rabbit froze. His eyes widened. His snarl of rage shifted to a bewildered gape as he stared at the white, skeletal hand clamped onto his sleeve.

A roar filled the cabin.

In a blur, Rabbit flew across the room over Boone's head. He slammed into the log wall of the cabin. No sooner had he hit the floor, he bounced to his feet, pistol pulled. The barrel flashed, and a clap of thunder made Boone's ears ring.

Boone went for the iron at his hip, but his holster was empty.

Rabbit's hammer clicked back again. Before he could get off another shot, the pale devil flew out of the cabin and disappeared into the snowy world outside.

"Shit," Boone said, blinking. Nobody could move that fast. At least not on two legs.

"Tagged him in the shoulder, damn it!" Rabbit limped after the devil. "Don't move, Booney."

"Rabbit, no!" Boone tried to stop him, but the trigger-happy cuss disappeared out the door, too.

Boone struggled to stand again and go after his partner. The room spun out from under him and he landed on his back.

Everything went dark ...

Boone's head throbbed.

A blast of freezing air swirled around him, sprinkling him with snow. The side of his neck was so cold. It felt wet.

He groaned, opening his eyes, staring up at a wood plank roof.

What am I doing on the floor?

The wind whistled and growled outside.

Where am ...

In a blink, it all came back. The snowy ride to Gayville. The open cabin door. The pale devil with snake eyes. Rabbit racing out the ...

"Rabbit!" He winced at the loudness of his own voice in his aching skull. Squeezing his eyes shut, he tried to shake off the fog dulling his senses.

What in the hell was that thing?

"Shit!" He needed to go after Rabbit. Struggling to his knees, he held onto the table until his head stopped spinning.

Before he'd made it to his feet, Rabbit limped into the cabin, closing the door behind him. He leaned on the table next to Boone, his breath coming in huffs. "You still resting, ol' man?"

"My head hurts. Went out for a spell, I think." Boone started to lift his hand to touch the side of his head.

Rabbit caught his wrist. "Let me take a look at that hard head of yours." He leaned down, gently turning Boone's jaw to the side. "You have an ugly gash next to your ear leakin' blood down your neck."

Well, at least he had something to show for the throbbing pain on that side of his head. "Lost the pale devil, did ya?" Boone winced as Rabbit cleared his hair from his wound.

"I commenced the pursuit, leastways."

"What happened out there?"

"I saw him cut around the cabin and head toward the crick out back, but I lost sight of him through the bushes. Got to the crick and caught a glimpse of somethin' taking big jumps through the drifts up the hillside." He paused, looking toward the door. "Must have been him. Looked like his coat from the backside anyway, but the fallin' snow makes it hard to see out there." He looked at Boone. "Then he was gone real quick. No way I could've caught him. Not with him movin' so fast."

The way the devil had raced out of the cabin replayed in Boone's mind. Moved like the wind, just a blur.

"I've never seen a man leap like that uphill," Rabbit said. "Let alone through the snow."

Boone wasn't certain they had been dealing with a man. Not with those eyes and that face. " 'You have adventurous, troublesome ways,' " Boone repeated a line from one of his favorite authors. "You shouldn't have taken off after him like that."

"I thank you for your concern, Mr. Clemens." Rabbit smirked, playing along. He'd been on the receiving end of quotes from Samuel Clemens's writings many times during their trips to and fro.

"You might have needed my help."

"True, but you weren't exactly hopping around after he left."

Rabbit turned his attention back to Boone's injury. "Cut isn't too big. Some thread and a needle will fix that right up. It's in the hairline so you'll still be pretty."

He helped Boone to his feet and guided him to one of the chairs, falling into the one next to him.

"You've picked up a limp." Boone tipped sideways as far as his pounding head would allow and took a closer look at Rabbit's leg. "No blood."

"Gathered some lumps when I got tossed into the wall by that big ..." Rabbit put his elbows on his knees and leaned toward Boone. "What in tarnation was that thing? It looked like a man, but it didn't move like one."

Boone was still trying to decipher what was real and what might have come from being hit too hard on the head. "Did you look into his eyes?"

"Nope. I never felt nothin' that strong, neither. He threw me, Booney. Sent me flying through the air like a tiny birdy." Rabbit snorted. "Until I hit the wall."

Boone glanced around the cabin, noting a pot of bubbling soup over the fire. A spoon and clean bowl sat at the other end of the table. He pointed at the soup. "Looks like Elston skedaddled before his visitor arrived."

"Or that troublemaker got hold of him, dragged him out of here, and came back for something he'd left behind."

Boone scanned the rest of the room. A pile of bedding was pushed up into the far corner. A frying pan hung from a nail in the wall nearest them, along with a washboard and a piece of deer hide. A pair of boots sat next to the fire, rusty sluicing pans lay scattered around them.

"Looks like the pale devil was looking for something," he said, spying his lucky hat in the corner. It must have taken flight during the scuffle. "I expect Elston had been ready for something like this. But didn't he describe a *beast* to us? It seems to me this thing was more man than beast, but maybe a smidgeon of both."

"What the fuck have we got ourselves into, Booney?"

Boone held his head in his hands, careful not to touch his wound. "I don't know, but I don't think either one of us is up to climbing the hill to find that devil-man or the damned Bloody Bones mine. Besides, we're greenhorns here without Elston's help."

"Son of a dough-belly." Rabbit slammed his fist on the table. "Back to fuckin' Deadwood we go."

"Yep. If Uncle Morton is still alive, he'll need to stick it out one more night in the snow."

"And if he's dead, no sense in adding us to the tally."

"Exactly. Makes the most sense. You can rest that leg and I can get my head sewn up. Maybe Clementine has the knowhow for that, too."

Rabbit frowned.

"We can see if Hank is willing to guide us up to the mine tomorrow." Headache or not, Boone needed to check out that mine. "Hank seemed willing to join us last night. A more agreeable fellow than most around here."

Leaning back, Rabbit glanced in Boone's direction. "We got us another problem."

"What's that?"

"While Miss Clementine was workin' on Tink last night, I noticed some pewter rings in her desk drawer. They had some kind of animal symbol on them. Like a mix of a pig and a goat."

"Why's that a problem?"

"I saw the same sort of ring on the finger of whatever that thing was that knocked you silly and tossed me across the room."

What the hell did that mean? Was there a tie between the undertaker and the pale devil? Or was it a peculiar coincidence?

Boone was beginning to feel like he and Rabbit were stumbling into trouble.

"You up to riding?" Rabbit asked.

"No, but I sure don't feel like sticking around here to wait and see if Elston returns." He pushed to his feet, feeling more himself than not in spite of the pain. "Elston's on his own for now. Let me grab my lucky hat."

The trip back to Deadwood took twice as long as the ride out thanks to the blinding snow and Boone's throbbing head.

It was midday by the time they reined up at The Pyre.

"Back in fuckin' Deadwood," Rabbit grumbled. In spite of the biting cold wind, he was apparently steam-engine hot. As they'd plodded along through the snow, his surly disposition had grown horns, becoming downright ugly.

Boone glanced his partner's way. Based on the brief exchanges they'd shared on the return trip, he had a feeling whatever was chafing Rabbit had something to do with the pale devil back at Elston's, that ring, and a certain undertaker.

"Remember what we discussed," Boone said. "No mention of the ring or what we encountered back in Gayville until we suss out who the undertaker really is. As far as she's concerned, we fell off our horses. I hit my head on a rock and you landed on your side."

There'd be no mention of the snake eyes or the pale devil's odd facial features, either. Those were pieces of information he'd kept from Rabbit, uncertain of what exactly he'd seen. That blow to his head might have made him see funny things.

"I remember *you* discussin' that particular topic. Don't remember volunteerin' a yea or nay." Rabbit yanked off his hat, beat it against his leg to knock off the snow, and then jammed it back down tight. "The rings could be off of her customers. You know, the dead ones."

Boone sighed. He could use a moment away from Rabbit's sour personality this afternoon. "I'm gonna head inside and see if she'll stitch me up. Might be better if you go on back to the hotel. Get a meal in your belly." Uncle Morton had often said that a hearty meal tended to bring out the sun when Rabbit got too stormy.

"I don't have the patience for that." Rabbit flung his leg over Dime's rump and dropped to the slushy snow-covered street. His boot heel hit the ground hard and skidded underneath Dime's belly. His other leg twisted, wedging his foot in the stirrup.

"Aoow!" Rabbit howled as his legs stretched further and further apart until his elbow landed in the thick slush and stopped his fall. He tugged at his boot trapped in the stirrup but it wouldn't budge.

"Pffft!" Boone tried to hold back his laughter while he climbed down off Nickel. In a flash he was at Rabbit's side, lifting him under the arms.

Rabbit yanked against the stirrup again, which made Dime whinny and sidestep. His foot pulled free of the boot, landing in the mud and snow with a *sploosh*. His sock soaked, Rabbit scrambled to his feet, grabbed the boot from the dirty slush, and threw it onto the boardwalk in front of The Pyre.

He whirled and pointed his finger at Boone's face. "Not a damned word, McCreery."

Boone turned away, focusing on a building farther down the street, his shoulders shaking with silent laughter.

Rabbit laced together a symphony of curses as he climbed the steps, grabbed his boot and threw it down again, then picked it up and shoved it on his soggy socked foot. Still grumbling, he followed Boone through the front door of The Pyre.

Clementine joined them in the front parlor before they had a chance to take off their hats. She was dressed in the same red shirt and brown pants as she'd worn this morning when they'd stopped to see Tinker. The same warm smile creased the corners of her eyes, too. A man could get used to such a greeting. It was no wonder Rabbit was daydreaming about setting up shop in town.

"You've returned," she said, her gaze traveling over Boone,

and then shifting to Rabbit as he closed the door behind him. "In one piece, at that." Her focus hovered north of Boone's eyes. "Although your lucky hat is crooked and Jack has a limp."

Hell, she certainly didn't miss much at a glance.

"That's sort of why we're here," Boone said, carefully taking off his hat. Boone looked at Rabbit, who was fidgeting with his troublesome boot. That wet sock must be giving him some grief. "Maybe take that boot off and dry your sock by the fire."

Rabbit eyed Boone like he was contemplating throwing his boot at his head. He opened his mouth, but then seemed to remember where he was, or rather in whose company he stood, and closed it again. A big, fake smile filled his face, and he turned to Clementine. "That'll be okay with you, Miss Clementine?"

"Help yourself, Jack." Clementine indicated the two cushioned leather chairs near the parlor room stove. She stared after Rabbit as he limped to the chair and then looked back at Boone with one dark eyebrow raised. "Was I correct that you've suffered a head injury?"

He nodded and winced. She stepped closer, but hesitated. "Do you mind if I take a look at it? I might be able to help."

"I was hoping you would." He tilted his head and pointed at the wound. "Rabbit says it's in the hairline."

Her touch was soft yet deft. She smelled of raw alcohol with a hint of something sweeter underneath, flowery almost. He leaned closer and breathed deep. She smelled of biscuits, too. Or maybe he was just hungry.

"A flesh wound," she said, stepping back. "Deep, but it should heal quick enough. I'll need to clean and suture it, though, and then apply a poultice and bandage to keep infection away." She pointed toward the wooden chair by a desk in the corner. "If you'll take a seat, I'll go get my suture kit." She left him, heading down a dark hallway at the back of the parlor.

Boone moved to the desk. Tinker lay curled up on a blanket next to it, her bad leg wrapped in clean muslin, her tail thumping on the floor when Boone bent down and petted her head. "Feed that fire, huh?"

"Doesn't need it," Rabbit said, rubbing his sore thigh. His wet sock was draped over the drying rack behind the stove.

"That makes three now," Rabbit said. "Two for you and one for me." He propped his good leg on the arm of the chair, dangling his naked foot near the stove. "One sore leg, one damaged shoulder, and a bump on the head."

"And we've barely even gotten started." Boone lowered himself into the wooden chair at Clementine's desk. He glanced down at the drawer, thinking about the pewter rings Rabbit had found in the desk in her workroom.

Clementine returned shortly, carrying a small box, a piece of muslin, and a bottle of alcohol in one hand. In her other was a cloth bag, which she held out to Rabbit. "Hungry? I have some leftover biscuits that Hank brought by before he left for Galena."

"Yes, ma'am. Thank you." Rabbit dug into the bag.

"How's your tolerance for pain?" she asked Boone, tearing off a strip of cloth. She tipped the bottle to wet the strip.

"I'm no two-day-old pup."

Rabbit snorted and shoved a small biscuit in his mouth.

"Good. Because this is going to hurt." She dabbed at the gash beside Boone's ear.

"Owww!" Boone's eyes watered, the cut stinging and throbbing at the same time.

The corners of Clementine's mouth curled. "You'll live to see another sunrise, I promise. So what happened in Gayville? I didn't think you'd return until this evening."

After sending a warning squint in Rabbit's direction, Boone answered. "Well, we ran into a peck of trouble there."

While Clementine tended to his head, Boone recounted the morning's trials in between his grunts of pain.

Rabbit sat with his foot in the air, eating biscuits, watching Clementine work.

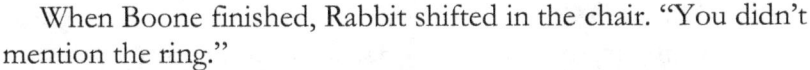

When Boone finished, Rabbit shifted in the chair. "You didn't mention the ring."

"What ring?" Clementine asked, lowering the cloth.

Boone glared at his partner.

"Those pewter rings in your drawer." Rabbit thumbed toward the doorway to her work room. "They yours?"

Clementine stared at Rabbit, brow creased. "Why do you ask?"

Rabbit shrugged. "Saw one on a big, pale-skinned desperado who ambushed us in Gayville. Boone forgot to mention that part, I guess."

Their hostess looked down at him, her gaze narrowed, measuring. "Boone?"

Boone sat back in the chair, aiming a scowl at Rabbit. "I guess it's probably best to lay the cards out."

"There's the plan I agreed on." Rabbit grinned back with a bit of his usual sunshine, wiggling his toes close to the stove. Apparently those had been *magical* biscuits Clementine had shared.

Stepping between Boone and Rabbit, Clementine blocked his view. She crossed her arms. "So you chose to omit that particular detail in your storytelling? I wonder why that might be, Boone?"

Boone held her stare. "Well, to speak plainly, no offense intended, but I ... we don't know who you are, really. You seem honorable and all, but I thought it wiser to figure those details before we start confiding in you with our troubles. I reckoned Mr. Wetfoot over there was riding alongside me with that idea, but it turns out he prefers to run his big yodeler instead."

Clementine contemplated Boone for a few seconds, her expression unreadable. He'd sat across the table from high-stakes gamblers with more tells than the undertaker.

"Jack," she said without turning. "I appreciate you confiding in me."

Rabbit leaned back in the chair to peek around Clementine's

back, grinning at Boone. "You're welcome, Miss Clementine. You seem the trustworthy sort what with the way you took care of Tink without a fuss."

Boone rolled his eyes.

Clementine walked into the other room, returning a few seconds later. "As for these rings," she said, setting one on the desktop next to Boone. "I took them off men who attempted to kill me and failed."

Rabbit's jaw dropped. "Holy sheeat!" He sat forward, his bare foot hitting the floor.

"Kill you?" Boone repeated, frowning up at her.

Her deadpan expression told nothing. "That's what I said." She moved to Rabbit, holding out another ring toward him.

"Ah, sorry, Miss Clementine." He took the ring, inspecting it in the light from the window. "So, maybe the bastards who tried to kill you have something to do with the pale cutthroat that tried to kill us in Gayville?"

"It's possible. The symbol on those rings is something I've not seen before. Now there are several exposed in a matter of days. Surely there's a connection to be found."

"A troubling one at that," Boone agreed, taking a closer look at the ring she'd placed on the desktop.

"Three assassins were present the night I collected these rings. Two are accounted for, one escaped."

"Could be that third one was our man in Gayville then," Rabbit said.

"Possibly." She opened the small box she'd brought out with the bottle of alcohol, lifting out a needle and string. "Let's stitch up that wound, Boone." She closed one eye and threaded the needle. "What's the extent of your injury, Jack?"

"Just a few bruises and a soggy sock, Miss Clementine."

She glanced down at Boone, a smile playing at her lips. "He was the lucky one, it appears. Were you not wearing your hat?"

"It softened the blow," he said, grinning back.

"Hold steady now, this won't feel too pleasant." She bent closer and began suturing the gash in Boone's head closed.

He winced and grimaced at the sharp pain and small tugs, but held still. This wasn't his first set of sutures. With the hornets' nest they'd stumbled into here in Deadwood, it probably wouldn't be his last, either.

"Hank will need to guide us," Clementine said as she stitched. "He'll be back from Galena late today, so we can't leave until tomorrow morning."

" 'We,' Miss Clementine?" Rabbit asked.

Boone grunted. It was all he could manage through clenched teeth.

"If Hank is going with you," she explained, "and he needs to since he knows the way to Bloody Bones mine, then so am I. I can't have anything happen to him. He knows where to find the best biscuits in town." She gave Boone a wink when he glanced her way.

"This isn't a Saturday shoot or a Sunday picnic, Miss Clementine," Rabbit said, his chair creaking.

Boone grunted again, managing to add, "Considering what we've heard and been through, it's likely we'll run into more adversity."

Something snipped next to his ear.

Clementine stood upright, angling her head to the side as she inspected her work. "Don't worry, Jack. I'll keep you and Mr. *Leery* McCreery here safe."

Rabbit chuckled at her new nickname for Boone. "I like that. Seems fittin' for the tortoise." He tossed the cloth bag of biscuits to Boone.

"Flap those gums some more, Rabbit," Boone shot back, pulling out a cold biscuit. "And I'll stuff that wet sock between them."

"Besides, do you two really think you can stop me from coming along?" Clementine set the needle down on her desk and walked into her exam room. She came back with a bowl. "This ring you saw, it's a solid lead." She dumped alcohol in the bowl and then dropped the suture needle in it. Her eyes were hard when she looked at Boone. "And I aim to find out what son of a bitch is trying to put me in the ground."

Boone took a bite of the biscuit, tasting pork amid the flour and butter. He swallowed. "You might regret it." He held her stare. "But it'll be good to have you along, just the same."

THIRTEEN

Clementine finished her job of undertaking for the day and sank into the cushioned chair Jack had occupied earlier. It was one of the few luxuries she'd splurged on since coming to Deadwood, and she loved the feel of the soft, smooth leather.

She scooted the chair closer to the wood stove. Earlier, after the snow had finally stopped falling, she'd moved Tinker and her blanket nearer to the heat, tucking the thick wool around the sleepy dog. Now, Tinker was awake and eating the scraps of bread and fatty meat Clementine had bought from the café three doors down. The dog's appetite was back in full force, a good sign along with her occasional tail wags.

Tinker glanced up in between bites, licking her chops.

Clementine scratched between her ears. "I'll bet you could tell me a story or two about your friends from Santa Fe."

Too busy eating to chat, Tinker returned to the bowl of food.

Clementine sipped hot honey water from a cup she'd warmed on the stovetop, staring at the ring she'd slipped on her finger again after Boone and Jack had left to tend to their horses and return to the hotel. "My intuition tells me I can trust them."

Her intuition had also told her to thaw out that frozen man yesterday, and by this morning she'd been able to peel his clothes away and search for other possible means of death, such as a strategically placed knife wound. In the end, she'd found no evidence of anything other than a cold, miserable death from exposure.

Was she losing her touch when it came to listening to her instincts? Was common sense cautioning her to be more careful from now on and begin double-checking the dead rather than rushing them through The Pyre? Was it intuition warning her to be more diligent and watch for a sign of what was coming?

She pulled a piece of jerky from her shirt pocket, her thoughts returning to Jack and Boone. "Maybe I can trust them, but with how much?"

Boone had withheld information from her. She'd seen the shadows behind his eyes when he'd told her the events that had happened in Gayville, and she'd wondered what he was keeping from her.

Another ring with the *caper-sus* emblem—that had been a surprise. She'd expected Boone to be shielding her from a report of a gruesome murder. Something a gentleman wouldn't want to share with a lady. But she was no "lady," at least not when it came to blood and death. Not before she came to Deadwood, and certainly not after months of playing undertaker in this often-barbaric town.

Clementine chewed on the jerky, thinking about Boone's resistance to open up, unlike Jack. She could respect his hesitation. Why should he trust her? Because she'd helped save his dog? That didn't make her any sort of saint. His propensity to lean toward caution might save his life someday, and Jack's, too.

"He was still hiding something when he left," she said to Tinker. She could see it in the way he'd frowned when he thought nobody was watching him. "Something about the fight at that cabin appears to be lingering in his thoughts. That's my guess, anyway. What do you think?"

Tinker rolled onto her side, injured leg in the air, and wagged her tail.

Chuckling, Clementine reached down and scratched her round belly. "I'd share a bite of my jerky with you, but it looks like you've had enough for now."

Tinker rolled back onto her stomach, trying to sit up. She whined when she tried to put weight on her back end.

"Stay down, girl." Clementine leaned over and coaxed Tinker back into a lying position. "You need to let that heal more. Amma's poultice works fast, but it's not magic. Rest now that your belly is full and I'll check on your leg in the morning."

Once Tinker had calmed down again, resting her muzzle on the bunched blanket, Clementine returned to her honey water, jerky, and contemplations. The fire crackled in the stove, the wind whistled outside the front door. The light outside had faded to dark, night settled into the gulch.

"There are two things that puzzle me," she told her furry companion. "First, why are these rings suddenly showing up around Deadwood?"

What was their meaning? Not just the goat-pig emblem, but why so many rings all at once? She took another bite of jerky, chewing on her thoughts.

Tinker scooted closer, sniffing Clementine's pant leg.

Resting her elbows on her knees, she stared at Tinker's bandage. "And what did Hildegard mean? How am I being deceived? Does she think that I'm being duplicitous as well?"

How much did Hildegard know about Clementine's reason for coming to Deadwood? Who was her source?

"Apparently I have more than two unanswered questions," she told Tinker and popped the last of the jerky in her mouth.

She stroked Tinker's head. "I can't go riding into Gayville without having an inkling about what your masters stumbled into back there." Hell, she wasn't even supposed to go to Gayville. It was one of the locations she'd agreed to avoid when she'd taken on the task. A quick trip there and back shouldn't cause any ripples, though. As far as she was concerned, figuring out the story behind the rings was part of her job.

"Boone and Jack are capable men, wouldn't you agree, Tinker?" The dog whined, looking up at her. "And there is far more to Hank than most know. I'd lay odds that all three are good in a fight, too. But if the opponent they met is one of the *others*, as I suspect with the way Rabbit was tossed about like a feather, then these men are up against more than they appreciate. Far, far more."

She pulled the ring off her finger and tucked it down into the pocket she'd sewn in her chemise. She could think of one person who might have answers for her. The biggest question was, could Clementine trust her?

There was only one way to find out.

She wrapped the blanket tighter around Tinker, fed the stove, turned down the oil lamp, and grabbed her wool coat and hat. With one last check on the now-sleeping dog, she stepped out into the darkness. Head down, she rushed through the wind and slush.

The Dove's red velvet embrace welcomed her with warmth and the smell of baked bread. Jurgen helped her out of her coat before heading off to find Hildegard, leaving Clementine to wait in the kitchen where Alexey had left several loaves of fresh baked bread on the work counter and a pot of boiling water on the stove. Another bath would feel wonderful, but there was no time for that tonight.

Clementine was licking her chops over a loaf of bread when Hildegard stepped out from the private bath area. She wore a dark blue satin gown with a high waist that made her look taller than usual. Her white-blond hair was tied back with a gold ribbon. Her cheeks blushed pale pink. A finer madam of a brothel Clementine had not met.

"I'm pleased to see you again so soon, Clementine. Come with me."

She waved for Clementine to follow her back through the safe room door and turned right, her dress swishing as she led the way down a long hall to an open doorway at the end.

"Jurgen mentioned your need to discuss an important matter

with me." Hildegard smiled, holding the door open.

Clementine paused at the tinkling sound of laughter from a room two doors away.

"Come. These are my private quarters and quite safe from stray ears, I assure you." Hildegard motioned her into the room.

Unlike the colorful main parlor and the few ornately decorated public rooms Clementine had viewed at The Dove, Hildegard's room was understated. It was spacious, yet conveyed comfort, warm with the subtle scent of sandalwood and something floral. There were parts of Hildegard's chambers that reminded Clementine of her home in Scandinavia and neighboring Germany, but the décor was an eclectic mix of cultures.

A stove sat at the side of the room flanked by a pair of well-cushioned reading chairs covered in green velvet. Thick animal furs surrounded a bed of elaborately carved hardwood, stained dark. Large tapestries depicting scenes of armored huntsmen slaying all manner of beasts decorated two full walls. On another wall, an ornate wooden cuckoo clock hung above a china hutch, which was filled with porcelain figurines and neatly stacked books. Smoke spiraled from a burning stick of incense, like those sold in several stores down by Kee Luk Laundry. That explained the fragrance in the air. She should have Hank pick some up for her parlor at The Pyre. Maybe they would help mask the odor of death.

Hildegard fetched two teacups from the hutch and set them on the marble-topped table between the chairs near the stove.

"Please, join me." She poured steaming, amber-colored liquid from a teapot on the stove into each cup and then sat in one of the chairs.

Clementine lowered herself into the soft chair and took a cup from the table. Cloves, cinnamon, and other scents she couldn't identify rose from the liquid. This was not tea as she would have expected coming from a teapot. A memory with her grandmother flitted through her thoughts. "Is this mulled wine?"

"Yes. One of the comforts from home I'm not inclined to relinquish."

Clementine sipped the spicy-sweet wine and relaxed into the chair. "*Relinquish*. An interesting choice of words."

Hildegard ignored the implied question. "I miss the juniper berries from the Black Forest. But still, this is pleasant, don't you think?" She waved her hand around, indicating not only the wine, but the room as well.

Nodding, Clementine let the wine sit on her tongue as she tried to figure out a way to ask the questions that had led to her paying Hildegard a visit tonight.

Oh, just come out with it. "Are you saying your homeland is the Black Forest in Germany?" she asked.

"Indeed. But we can discuss that later. What is really troubling you, Clementine?"

"I'm not entirely sure how or where I should start." She stared at her cup of wine. "It's ..." She looked up at Hildegard. "*Ich spreche Deutsch*." She searched the madam's face, watching for any reaction to her announcement, adding in a low voice, "And many other languages as well."

A smile spread across Hildegard's face as she leaned closer. "If your intent this evening was to surprise me about your multilingual abilities," she said in a conspiratorial tone, "especially concerning your knowledge of German, then you will be disappointed. I've suspected as much since your first visit to The Dove when I overheard you helping Jurgen with his English. You understood his native tongue much too well."

"Ah, shit."

Hildegard laughed. She patted Clementine's knee. "I'm glad you came. It is time we remove some of the mysteries between us. Who knows? Perhaps we can help each other."

Clementine wanted to have someone with whom she could confide, but she'd been taught early on that her profession was one of solitude. Her kind was strongest when focused only on the task at hand. Companions of any sort offered only distractions. Those of her ilk who lived the longest worked and existed alone.

She sipped her wine. "I listened to your discussion with Miss Hundt while I bathed, of course."

"As I expected."

"I apologize for the deception, but in my line of work, I cannot be sure whom to trust."

"It is wise to be wary."

"To be frank, I'm still not sure if coming to you is sensible, but I need answers, and intuition tells me you are the one who can give them to me."

Hildegard's forehead tightened. "I have no desire to cause you harm, Clementine. I know what you are. I understand that you could slay me in a heartbeat and with little effort. Few *others* could. Yet even aware that I continue to breathe at your will, I invited you into my private chambers. If that does not speak of my trust in you, then I do not know what would."

"I kill only when necessary, Hildegard." Her grandparents had instilled her with morals in spite of her profession.

Sitting back, Clementine relaxed into the cushions and tried to organize her thoughts and questions. She had not spoken so openly in someone's presence for much too long. At least not someone living. If the dead could talk, she would've had to leave town months ago.

"Such as when attacked while spying on a hog sty?" Hildegard asked, a small smile playing on her pale lips.

Clementine sighed. "That was not one of my finer moments."

"You were ambushed in more ways than one."

"It's obvious you know much already concerning my presence in Deadwood."

Hildegard nodded. "As I said, I understand your profession. And to a lesser extent, your presence in the Black Hills."

"What exactly is your purpose here? Other than running The Dove?"

Hildegard took a drink of her wine before answering. "In short, you can compare what I do to that of a lookout."

"You spy for someone?"

"No. I observe circumstances in an effort to keep the balance."

"What balance?"

"The balance that keeps time progressing as it should."

"Do you report to a benefactor or master?"

"Like you, I am usually self-driven. However, I do tend to lean in one direction or another, depending on the situation."

Clementine chuckled. "Hildegard, you must excel at games of wit and strategy."

The madam shrugged. "If I didn't, I would be dead by now."

"Is Miss Hundt in the same observation business as you?"

"Yes, but no. It is not my place to explain her occupation. That is left to her when she wills it."

"She does not trust me as you seem to." It was a statement, not a question.

"Miss Hundt is more deliberate regarding trust. Her preference is to wait until your character becomes more evident. In Deadwood parlance, she waits for you to show your hand."

"Yet you feel different even though you two appear to be old friends."

Hildegard didn't deny either part of Clementine's statement. Her gaze drifted to one of the tapestries. "A cautious approach on her part is justifiable when dealing with an Executioner, I assure you. More so than mine." She turned back to Clementine. "Like you, I place great value on my intuition. I've observed you longer than she, and I feel strongly that you and I are in alliance. As such, you need to be made aware of certain things." She held up the teapot. "More wine?"

Clementine nodded and held up her cup.

"This is delicious, thank you," Clementine said. "My diet here in Deadwood hasn't improved much beyond simple nourishment. Although the biscuits my assistant brings me from Grand Central Hotel are quite good."

"You've made a prudent choice in hiring Mr. Varney. His depth of character is exceeded only by his innate kindness."

Clementine raised her cup in toast to Hank. "He also tells one hell of a tale."

"He has lived many lives in his time." Hildegard's eyebrows inched up. "So, what other concerns have brought you here today?"

Clementine pulled the pewter ring from her chemise and set it on the table between them with the emblem facing her host. "What is this?"

Hildegard picked up the ring, studying the markings next to her oil lamp. "*Caper-sus.*"

"That was the word you used before while I was bathing."

She set it back on the table. "It's an emblem employed by a cult of *others* and their livestock as a means of identification. I've seen it on rings and other jewelry, as well as burned into flesh—especially on livestock. A branding, if you will."

"What do you mean by 'livestock'?"

Hildegard frowned at the ring. "These particular *others* think of humans as livestock. To be used as pets for their pleasure, as slaves to perform menial tasks, as sacrificial animals when needed, even as food at times. This specific cult also uses them to help fight—"

A soft rap on the door interrupted Hildegard.

"Yes?"

"It is Dmitry, madam," a muffled voice with a heavy Russian accent called through the door.

"Come in," she said, rising from her chair.

Dmitry opened the door and paused on the threshold. "Clementine! Greetings!" He waved as if to someone far away.

"Good evening, Dmitry. I almost took a bite out of the bread in your kitchen earlier."

"I will cut slice for you when you finish here. Alexey made fresh apple butter earlier today." He turned to Hildegard. "Ludek is here. He eats in kitchen but wishes to speak to you."

"Thank you, Dmitry. Please tell him I'll be there as soon as I can."

Dmitry backed out the door, sending Clementine a wink before closing it.

Hildegard walked over to the china hutch and picked up a dish mounded with shiny pieces of candy. "Would you like a piece? It's an old recipe I brought over from my homeland."

"Yes, thank you." It had been months since she'd had the opportunity to indulge in sweets.

Hildegard placed the dish of candy on the table, taking one and putting it in her mouth. "I must warn you, though," she said around the piece. "There might be a side effect to the candy. Whether pleasant or disconcerting, that is determined by your state of mind. The desired result is resistance to various maladies present here in Deadwood, and I find that it often makes me feel somewhat spooney for an hour or two after I eat several."

"So a handful could make me drunk?"

"Possibly. You're different from me, though. They tend to send my girls into a deep sleep."

Clementine popped one into her mouth, savoring the tart, sweet taste.

Ludek was waiting in the kitchen, Dmitry had said. Hildegard had used that name in conversation with Miss Hundt, using words that made this Ludek sound like an assistant or attendant. Someone in a role similar to Hank's.

Could Ludek be the rogue? No, they had spoken of the rogue as of someone unfamiliar. Possibly summoned they had said, the same as Clementine.

She waited for Hildegard to sit back in her chair. "Ludek was at Kee Luk that night."

"Correct."

"Did he kill the man in the alley?"

"No. His sole purpose regarding you is observation. I believe the rogue was present at Kee Luk and is responsible for the execution in the alley, but Ludek did not witness that, so I cannot be sure. I am also uncertain whether the rogue's agenda was to kill you or save your life, but I'm leaning toward the latter."

Clementine scowled. "I did not need a savior. The situation was well in hand."

Hildegard raised her brow.

"Okay, mostly in hand."

A frown played at Hildegard's lips. "Please do not be offended. I meant you none, Clementine."

She waved off Hildegard's concern. "None taken." She pointed at the candies in the dish. "May I have another?"

"Of course, but remember—"

"I might get drunk or sleepy." She would stop at two. Tomorrow's business in Gayville would require steady thoughts and hands. She leaned forward, seeking a few more answers before leaving Hildegard to her dealings with Ludek. "What do you know about the Golden Echo mine?"

"You mean Bloody Bones?"

"So you've heard the stories. I'll be going to the mine tomorrow with Hank and two gun hands."

Hildegard rose from her chair and began pacing. "I must warn you, Clementine. Men dug deep into the hillside there. Too deep. Rich veins of gold beckoned to the miners to penetrate the earth until they reached passageways and caverns that should not have been opened. You've no doubt heard of the goings-on in Gayville."

Clementine nodded. She had heard stories. Most were from Hank, some were from drunken miners at Yellow Strike Saloon, and a few from a handful of sober miners there, too.

"These are not random occurrences. Gayville is plagued by the *others* and their pets." She stopped pacing and frowned down at Clementine. "Golden Echo is the source."

The source of what, exactly? "The one who summoned me to Deadwood," she started.

"He is not to be trusted," Hildegard interrupted.

The deceiver. Miss Hundt and Hildegard's previous conversation echoed in her thoughts. She set her empty cup down. "So you've said. He forbade me to enter Gayville."

"Forbade an Executioner?" Hildegard scoffed.

Clementine shrugged. "Apparently he is under a delusion regarding his influence over me. I allow it to continue for the time being."

"Understandable."

"Anyway, there must be a connection to his restriction and the Bloody Bones mine, don't you think?"

Hildegard knelt at her feet, clutching Clementine's knees. Her eyes were wide, her expression earnest. "You must be cautious, Clementine. Your summoner cannot be trusted. Do you understand?"

"As I told you before, in my line of work, I don't trust easily."

"Good."

"Why can't I trust Masterson?" When Hildegard continued to frown at her, she added, "What is it you know about him that has you and Miss Hundt so concerned about me?"

Hildegard sat back on her heels. "From what I've learned since coming to town, there is a war brewing between him and another of his creed."

"What does that have to do with me?"

"Going to battle with an Executioner in his ranks makes him nearly undefeatable."

FOURTEEN

"Now I see why you wanted to have breakfast here." Rabbit held up the last bite of what used to be a fist-sized biscuit, happy to start the day with a full stomach.

Boone nodded, setting his spoon on his empty plate. "Hank told me where he gets his biscuits."

The food matched the pleasant air in Grand Central Hotel. The décor was modern enough with lacy curtains and white table linens.

Rabbit scraped up the gooey egg yolk from his plate with the last morsel of flour and lard. "These biscuits are as good as Lupe's back home. But these eggs got a smell to 'em." He wrinkled his nose, stuffing his mouth full of biscuit anyway, barely able to close his lips around it all.

"Don't tell Lupe that," Boone said. "She'd string you up by your *cojones*. I miss her *chile verde con carne*. Hank knows a good biscuit, though." His chair creaked as he leaned back and took a swig of coffee.

"Mmm-hmmm," Rabbit agreed with his mouth closed. He remembered the last time he'd enjoyed Lupe's food. It seemed a lifetime ago. So much had happened between Santa Fe and now, including a heap of snow. "Aw mith the rwanchth," he said through a mouthful of biscuit. Crumbs flew at that last word.

"Tarnation, Rabbit." Scowling, Boone flicked biscuit specks from his brown shirtsleeve. "I think I'll head to the stable. Finish breakfast there."

"Hmmm?" More crumbs escaped Rabbit's lips, falling on the table.

"Nickel has better manners than you. At least I don't end up wearing *his* breakfast."

Rabbit shook his head at Boone's testy tone. He'd woken up prickly this morning, easy to rile. Things hadn't improved since they'd washed up and gotten dressed.

"And he's sensitive to my needs," Boone added.

Rabbit snorted and then coughed, spraying more crumbs across the table. He took a swig of coffee between sputters. "You made me ..." He coughed again. "... Swallow wrong." He blew his nose in one of the linen napkins. "Got up my nose. Damn, that burns."

"I bid you good morning, gentlemen." A pudgy man sidled up to the table. He plunked a wooden crate down in front of Boone hard enough to rattle the flatware on their empty plates.

Rabbit sized up their visitor while taking a sip of coffee. His black frock wasn't very long, but even so still grazed the floor. A matching small bowler hat teetered atop his head. Dried sweat stained the brim, leaving a white outline.

"Mr. McCuddle at your service." The stranger bowed, gracing Rabbit with a sharp scent of something medicinal.

After a moment's hesitation, Boone took the visitor's outstretched hand. He squinted up at Mr. McCuddle, his upper lip wrinkling.

Rabbit grinned. Years of travel from small town to big city had exposed him to every manner of scoundrel, card sharp, charlatan, and fraud. He knew this man—or rather, this type of man. Wiping his fingers on his napkin, he shot out his hand. "Salutations, Mr. McCuddle! I'm Mr. McDoodle."

Mr. McCuddle's slick smile dipped at the corners. "McDoodle, you say?"

"Yep." He gave the visitor's clammy palm a hard squeeze and shake. "I'd wager you have an immeasurably wonderful opportunity for my companion and me." He pulled free and pointed at Boone. "That handsome devil is the Santa Fe Sidewinder."

McCuddle paled at the gills, but he held his chipper expression with only a slight wobble.

Rabbit leaned toward McCuddle, putting his hand to the side of his mouth. "Whatever you do," he said in a loud whisper, "don't look the Sidewinder in the eyes."

"I, uh ..." McCuddle blinked rapidly. He tugged at his collar and licked his lips. "From the farthest reaches of Europe and the remote jungles of Africa, this is *the* elixir to address the darkest ailments known to mankind." He opened his crate and extracted a bottle filled with dark liquid. "This, gentlemen, is McCuddle's Original Magical Tonic. Patented."

Rabbit covered his mouth, turning to Boone with wide eyes. "Did you hear that, Sidewinder? A cure for your big red—"

Boone lifted his hand to halt Rabbit, then raised his coffee tin to his mouth, hiding the grin that was spreading across his face.

McCuddle struggled to avoid setting eyes on the Sidewinder. His gaze drifted in Boone's direction, but then he'd catch himself and look back at Rabbit. The small bowler on his head threatened to fall off each time his head moved, requiring continual adjustments.

"You, sir," he said, focusing on Rabbit. "May I inquire as to your profession?"

"I'm a pirate," Rabbit answered, straight-faced.

McCuddle sputtered. "Uh, pirate, you say?"

"Yep."

"In Deadwood, sir?"

"Okay, then." Boone lowered his coffee to the table. He pulled a coin from his vest pocket. "Should be enough for a bottle," he said and flipped it onto the table in front of McCuddle.

The salesman scooped up the coin before it came to a

standstill. "Thank you, good sir ... er uh, Mr. Sidewinder, I mean." He looked everywhere but at Boone while he closed up his crate of magical elixirs. "I'll presume to find you in good health at our next encounter."

Rabbit sat back, crossing his arms.

"Good day, gentlemen." Mr. McCuddle picked up his crate and shuffled to a trio of finely dressed men on the other side of the dining room.

Rabbit glared across the table. "I wanted to hear him speak. Could be a daisy."

"I'll never understand why you feel the need to listen to swindlers."

"Next elixir might be magical. No harm in keeping an open mind about such possibilities."

"It's alcohol with flavors added."

"I know."

"Then why d—"

"Alcohol has a positive effect on me."

Boone smirked. "Opinions vary on that."

"Plus, sometimes those flavors are pretty good. And it may be the next guy's tonic *is* magical. You don't know."

"I do know."

"That Bernhardt's Herbs and Famous Tincture had me feelin' better than fair to middlin' when I had that toothache in Albuquerque."

"That's because you passed out."

"Yeah, but after I woke up ... Wait, that's not such a good example. But there's been others."

Boone laughed. "Right, Captain Blowhard." He nudged his coffee tin aside, his expression sobering. "We have important things to discuss. Namely, what to do about Miss Clementine Johanssen."

"I have an idea or two about that." Rabbit rubbed his hands together, trying to lighten the gloom that had returned to

Boone's countenance.

"I'm not so concerned about Hank," Boone continued. "He should be good in a brush-up, and he assured me he'll come well heeled. But Clementine ..."

"It's raised some concern in me, likewise," Rabbit admitted. "Might be a liability. Might get herself killed. Or get us killed tryin' to keep her from gettin' killed." He swirled what was left of his coffee. "Been thinkin' on what happened in Gayville. If we come up against the likes of that pale-faced devil, we could end up in a hell of a pickle, and you're already hobbled by a sore head and bad shoulder, old man."

"My head and shoulder are fine, wiseacre. But if we're hobbled by a woman, my mind is conjuring all manner of trouble. Could be keeping her safe takes that sliver of time you or I need to stay alive."

Rubbing the back of his neck, Rabbit pondered the situation. "I don't know, though. Don't forget what happened when we got to Deadwood. That sorry sack she slogged in the bar. Finnigan, wasn't it? He didn't get one lick in."

"She's strong, that's for sure. Finnigan had no chance." Boone flashed a crooked smile his way. "Wouldn't mind seeing that again."

"Any case, I think we're stuck bein' in the company of a sage hen this trip." Rabbit popped the cork off the bottle of McCuddle's Magical Tonic. "I for one ain't *too* unhappy about our situation. If I die, I wouldn't mind her smile bein' the last thing I saw rather than that forty miles of rough trail you call a face." He raised the bottle of tonic in a toast.

Boone grabbed Rabbit's wrist before he could try a sip. "Don't drink that, lunkhead."

"Suppose you're right." He lowered the bottle, corked it, and slid it into his saddlebag. "I'll wait 'til later. But it might make me even faster with my lead pusher." He drew his Colt in a flash and placed it on the table pointed at Boone.

"You get the cartridges?" Boone asked, nudging the barrel so it was aimed at the wall instead of him.

"Yep, the .44-40s, anyway."

"Not for that buffalo cannon of yours?"

"Ain't no .50-90s in town that I could find for the Sharps. Probably won't need it anyway. That's not the problem."

"What's the problem?"

"I couldn't find one goldurn cartridge in this fuckin' town for the smoothbore. Merchants have something against sawed-offs around here, I guess."

A skeleton of a girl approached them. Her eyes focused on the floor as she placed a cloth sack on their table. "Here's yer biscuits, sir," she said barely above a whisper.

Her neck had dark bruises in the shape of fingers, still fresh, unlike the bruise on her cheek that had turned a greenish yellow. Her hands trembled at her sides. How old was she? Not more than fourteen or fifteen, surely.

"Thank you kindly, miss." Rabbit handed her a couple of coins worth twice the cost of the biscuits.

"Thanks, m-mister." She dipped her head, her smile missing a tooth, and limped over to a nearby table.

"You're gonna run out of money, big auger," Boone said.

Rabbit watched the poor skirt collect the plates at the empty table. She caught a slap on the ass from a greasy boot-licker at a crowded table of miners on her way to the kitchen.

"Poor thing's killin' herself," he said more to himself than to Boone. "Lotta scalawags need beddin' down in this town." He closed one eye and sighted down his index finger, taking aim at the slap-happy miner.

Boone leaned forward. "Don't shoot him with your finger, tough guy. They'll put you in the calaboose."

"Ain't no law in this town, Booney." Rabbit cocked his thumb. "Bang."

"Aw, ya missed."

Life at the Coffin Joint

"No, I didn't."

"Listen, Rabbit, don't get sidetracked by that poor kitten. She has a better job than most of the women her age in this town. Remember why we're here." Boone held up the sack of biscuits.

"For the road, I'm guessing?"

"Maybe."

"Why, Jack Fields," Boone said with a grin. "Are you courting Miss Clementine?"

"Shut up, mutton mouth." He picked up his Colt and holstered it. "If you're done with your chin waggin', ya scurvy dog, let's boom along."

"Boom what?" Boone collected his lucky hat from the chair between them.

"Boom along. Pirates say it. It means get movin', quick like."

"Right." Slinging his coat over his shoulders, Boone headed for the door.

"You should read more, Booney. I got some stories about pirates you might like." Rabbit followed, pausing on the threshold to cast one last glare toward the miners. "Bang, bang, bang," he said under his breath, finishing off the rest of them.

Clementine stood in the cold morning sunshine while she brushed Fenrir's long neck and muscled shoulders. Rays glinted off the polished saddle buckles, d-rings, and stirrups, adding some sparkles to the dark horse.

She'd come to the livery early, wanting to spend some time petting and bolstering her horse before Boone and Jack arrived. Hank was already at the livery when she showed up. Never one to sit for a length of time, Hank had not only brushed and saddled Fenrir for her, but also fetched, brushed, and saddled

Nickel and Dime.

By the time Boone and Jack joined them, Hank had their horses hitched next to Fred the mule at the rail.

"Hallo, boys!" Hank waved a salute. "I got yer mounts all dressed for the shindig. That's got to be one of the purtiest rifle scabbards I ever seen, Jack."

The two men paused, taking in Hank's preparations.

Rabbit smiled wide. "I like workin' leather when I get the chance. It's relaxin'. Tooled these, too." He hefted his saddlebags onto Dime's back.

Hank studied the patterns in the leather and then shot Jack a quizzical look. "Ute?"

Jack shook his head. "Good guess, but it's Navajo."

"I notice your gun rig and Boone's is all tooled up, too. Real fine work, Jack."

"Thank you kindly, Hank." He pointed at old Fred. "Is that a bow and a quiver of arrows strung on your mule?"

"Hee hee. Yessir. That there's a Sioux bow. Same feathers as them on my bone breastplate. Traded for both. Had to give up my favorite bugle, but they're worth it." He patted Fred's rump. "Stretches your brain most like, but archery comes kinda natural to me. Took a lick of practice to get real good at it, though. I ain't got much use for a rifle no more."

Neither did Clementine, not that firearms had ever been part of her repertoire anyway.

"I'd like to see you use that, Hank." Jack looked her way, tipping his hat. "Mornin', Miss Clementine. How's Tink doin' today?"

"Hungry. She's eating like a horse." She tossed the brush in the bin where Keller kept his supplies. "Ling and Gart are going to swing by around noon and check on her."

He regarded Fenrir, front to back. "That's a majestic animal. What is she, a Morgan?"

Clementine nodded. "Hank found her for me."

"Fifteen hands?" Jack said with a wink.

Fenrir turned her head to Jack, as if she understood the slight. Clementine laughed.

Hank pointed his thumb toward the sky. "More'n that."

"She's got ya by a little, Dime." Jack scratched his buckskin between the eyes.

"Morning." Boone shook Hank's hand and then leaned against Nickel. He tipped his hat. "Clementine." He pointed his chin toward the well-muscled Morgan. "What's her name?"

"This is Fenrir. Hank has done a wonderful job of rehabilitating her."

Boone studied her horse. "Wasn't Fenrir the son of Loki?"

Impressive. Not many in these parts knew Norse mythology, unless they emigrated from regions near or in Scandinavia.

"I thought you said it was a big wolf," Hank said to her.

"Fenrir was both of those in Norse mythology. I took liberties." She stroked the Morgan's neck. "Now she's like me."

"One of those Amazon women?" Rabbit asked.

Boone groaned, "Oh, Lord. Get that from your pirate books?"

"That's Greek mythology, Mr. Reads-a-lot."

Clementine laughed. "Well, I was going to say a shieldmaiden, which is also from Norse mythology, but we'll take the Greek version as a compliment, won't we?" she said, scratching Fenrir along her thick mane.

The horse lowered her head and nuzzled Clementine's hip.

Boone grimaced. "Looks like some bastard took a bullwhip to her."

There was no hiding the scars running up and down the horse. "Yes, *he* did, and Fenrir still holds a grudge about that, so I'd step carefully around her if I were you. She has no use for men, except for her rescuer and hero." Clementine smiled at Hank, who shrugged and grinned sheepishly.

She grabbed a carrot from a bag hanging from Fenrir's saddle and tossed it to Hank. He hid it in his coat pocket.

"Hey, Fred. Fred!" he called to the mule. "Where's the carrot, boy?"

Fred pricked up his ears and looked up and down the street.

"Naw, it ain't out there." Hank moved closer. "Come on, ya silly mule. Where is it?"

Boone's horse, Nickel, shuffled over to Hank and began snuffling around his coat pocket.

"Hey now!" Hank laughed. "I coulda swore I hitched you."

"Catch, Hank." Clementine tossed another carrot to Hank, who held it in his palm under Nickel's muzzle.

"Untied yerself, did ya?" Hank asked as Nickel lipped the carrot into his mouth.

"He's never taken to being tied up," Boone said, scratching back and forth across Nickel's rump. "Can't keep him in a stall either, if he doesn't want to be there."

Hank's grin widened. "Trickster. An' a smart one at that."

"Dime neither," Jack said, pointing at his buckskin, who was working on his tied reins with his lips and teeth. "But he ain't so good at escapin' yet. Takes him longer than Nickel." Jack nudged Dime's mouth away. "You're tuggin' on the wrong part. Here, like this." Jack pulled on the rope tail and the knot fell free.

Dime whinnied and headed for Hank, sniffing at his pocket.

"I don't know," Clementine said with a chuckle, tossing Hank another carrot. "Looks to me like Dime has an escape plan of his own that includes you and your fingers to save him time."

Boone checked his rig, the tightness of straps and buckles, and the Winchester rifle in its scabbard. "I think Nickel is teaching Dime while we're not watching."

As if to prove Boone's theory, his horse took the carrot from Hank and then turned, holding it out to Dime. Jack's horse took half, bumping Hank for more before he'd finished chewing.

Life at the Coffin Joint

"Get back here, ya broom tail," Jack grumbled.

"Hank," Clementine said, cinching the bag of carrots closed. "Fenrir is ready to plough snow. When you're done horsing around, we should hit the trail."

Her play on words had Hank grinning wider yet. He moved over to his mule and opened one of his saddlebags. "Jack, figured you'd need some shells for your smoothbore." He tossed a box of shells to Jack. "Tough to come by in Deadwood these days, but I know a place that's got 'em."

"Well, that's just fine! Thanks, Hank. That'll do it." He began filling the bandoleer slung over his shoulder with shells.

Fenrir stomped at the ground. Clementine felt the same way. It was time to go. Daylight was wasting. "Are we prepared now, gentlemen?"

"Here," Boone stepped next to her. "Let me help you up."

Hank snorted. He leaned toward Jack, who had finished filling his bandoleer. "Watch this."

Clementine looked at Boone's outstretched hand and

chuckled along with Hank. "Like I said, step carefully." She grabbed the saddle horn. "Ready, girl?" she said to the horse, waiting for Fenrir to brace herself. With a leap, Clementine sprung upward and onto the horse, who adjusted to her weight with a nicker.

"Holy ... all right then." Boone shook his head and climbed into his saddle the old-fashioned way.

Once he was settled in, he brought Nickel alongside Fenrir. "I'll lead the way until we get to Gayville, Clementine." Over his shoulder, he told Hank, "You take—"

Fenrir whinnied and reared, fighting Clementine's pull on her reins. The horse apparently had a strong urge to feel her legs. Holding her in check would be futile. Clementine had learned her first few times on Fenrir's back that when the horse had a whim, the wisest course was to let her have the reins.

Clementine leaned forward and whispered in the horse's ear, "Let's see if all these boys can keep up with a girl." She held on tight. "Fly!"

FIFTEEN

Fenrir shot out of the livery with Clementine leaning into the wind. Snow sprayed from the mare's hooves as they flew down the nearly empty street.

A glance over her shoulder found Boone galloping behind her, a twinkle in his eye.

Jack followed, his hat crooked, his grin wide. Further back, Hank and Fred the mule were trotting along in no apparent rush. He leaned forward and rubbed Fred's cheeks, which always seemed to make the mule move a little faster for some reason.

At the edge of Deadwood, Fenrir slowed. Her breath steamed in the air, her muscles relaxing. Boone pulled up next to Clementine while Jack followed several lengths behind, waiting for Hank to catch up.

"Cloudless sky today," Boone said. "Makes for calm weather for a change."

Clementine wasn't interested in discussing the weather. "I know you and Jack are trying to find your uncle, and I'll help in any way I can, but I have a different purpose here today."

"The ring," he said.

"Exactly." She looked at Boone, who stared straight ahead, his face unreadable. "Hank has nothing to do with any of this. He's showing us where the mine is and that's it, right?" Hank didn't need to be dragged into either of their problems any more than necessary.

"Agreed." He glanced her way. "Then again, he's a grown

man. He seems to make decisions on his own without your help. Won't be me that tells him one way or the other."

Clementine sighed. "He makes decisions based on his oversized heart. They aren't always the best, but he appears to have nine lives." She turned in her saddle as Hank caught up to their group.

"Hey, Jack!" he said. "Fred the mule decided he wanted to join ya finally."

"Friends call me Rabbit, Hank. That means you."

"All right! Jack Rabbit it is, then." He shot a grin at Clementine. "My friends call me … uh …"

"Hank," she supplied.

"Yeah, I guess they call me Hank. You got quite a two-gun rig there …"

The two trailed along behind her while Hank told Jack about a fancy rig he'd seen down in Colorado. Clementine had a feeling it would probably be a long story. They usually were.

She turned her attention back to Boone. "At The Pyre, you mentioned that Morton took you in when your parents died."

"Yes, ma'am."

"May I ask how they died?"

After hitting her with a hard stare for several seconds, Boone lowered his gaze. "We started out in Ohio. My family, anyway. Rabbit's … I mean Jack's family came from Virginia. The caravan formed in St. Louis and struck out for California by way of Santa Fe. Morton was the wagon master."

They rode along for a moment in silence. She kept quiet, giving Boone room to open up further or leave it at that.

"We must've had, oh, a hundred or so wagons," he continued. "Most were families, well behaved, but some were scoundrels and rascals. Jack and I got to know each other pretty good. Our pappies even took to keeping our wagons close so we'd keep each other busy and out from underfoot. Morton did a fine job keeping the caravan together and safe in spite of two

Indian attacks, typhus, broke-down wagons, dead draft animals. He kept us going, always wearing a smile. Helping any way he could to lift people's spirits."

Clementine smiled at the picture he painted with his words. What would it have been like to ride in a wagon train? Even more of a wonder, to have a childhood friend? She'd been alone since her mother died, her grandparents always caring, but mentors and protectors first and foremost.

"I don't know if you've heard about the Santa Fe Trail." Boone's voice interrupted her memories. "But most of the caravanners wanted to take the Cimarron Cut. That cut shaves sixty or so miles but you run into a lot more adversity. Indians and plenty of rough country. But the worst thing about it? No water. Not enough anyway. A lot of people don't make it. Some do, but they end up leaving everything they own behind on the trail."

He paused, looking back at Jack and Hank, his brow lined under the brim of his hat. "Just like Morton warned," he said, focusing forward again, "everybody's water barrels were empty halfway through the Cut. Nobody had listened, not even my folks and Jack's. We came on a water hole. Morton knew it was bad. He always just knew things like that somehow. Experience, I guess. He tried to stop them, but people drank it anyway. We were so parched."

He looked at her, his mouth a thin line. "It was quick. Whatever was in that water made man and beast spill their innards from both ends. Two days later, most in the caravan were dead already, including kids and babies, my folks, Jack's folks. Almost everybody. Even most of the animals. There were hundreds left laying beside the trail." Boone blew out a breath, shaking his head. "Jack and I got real sick, but Morton, well he was trying to save anybody he could. He nursed Jack and me as much as he was able. Good enough, I guess, since we're still putting our boots on every morning. Morton blamed himself, though. He never took another caravan after that. Started up his freight business in Santa Fe, always saying, 'Can't kill freight.' Said that for years. He had a heaviness in his heart that wouldn't go away, I figure." Boone gazed along the ridgeline above them for several seconds. "He tried to stop them from drinking. Just another twenty miles, he said, but they wouldn't listen. The terrible part was, he was right. There was a clean water hole not twenty miles up the trail."

Clementine's heart ached for Morton. What a weight to carry for the rest of his life. For the boys' lives, too. "I'm sorry, Boone."

He cleared his throat. "Long time ago."

She let the emotions he'd stirred up settle, enjoying the sunshine and crisp air free of the smells ripe with humanity that often filled Deadwood's gulch.

After several minutes of comfortable silence had passed, she leaned toward him. "How did Jack get the nickname 'Rabbit'?"

The ghosts of Boone's past were missing from his eyes when he grinned at her. "You can't tell?"

"I wasn't sure if it was really that easy. Do you have a nickname?"

"Yes, ma'am."

"I haven't heard Jack use it."

"He doesn't, usually." He added, "We'll save it for another time."

She nodded once. A hawk screeched overhead, landing in the trees along the creek in front of them.

"We may be in for a fight," Boone said in a low voice for her ears only. "Just to warn you."

Clementine focused on him, deadly serious. "I'm counting on it."

He sat back in his saddle, one eyebrow raised. "The devil you say. You sound excited about the idea."

"I've waited long enough." Her patience had worn thin while

one corpse after another passed through her hands.

"Jack's always on the shoot, and now you. I think I'm in a heap of trouble."

That made her chuckle. "Let's hope so."

"Yet you're concerned about Hank."

"Well, he can handle himself, but this isn't his fight. It's yours and mine."

"True. Maybe he can act as our lookout."

Whatever it took to keep Hank out of harm's way sounded good to her. She shifted in her saddle, needing to broach a more delicate topic but unsure how to come around to it. She glanced his way several times, trying to read his body language without success.

"I'm not sure what you're prepared for today, Boone," she said in a quiet voice. "But I need to warn you and Jack about some of the evils we might encounter."

Boone met Clementine's gaze head-on. "What sort of evils?"

"Creatures that we might find ourselves up against in or around the Golden Echo mine."

His eyes narrowed. "Listening."

She licked her lips, considering her words before speaking. "These creatures may not be affected by the weapons you carry."

"Affected?"

"Mortal weapons," she said slowly, letting her meaning sink in. "Carried by mortals."

"Gotcha." He took off his hat, looked at the bullet hole, and then jammed it back on his head. "What does that mean exactly?"

She decided to come at the truth from the side. "Tell me more about the man who attacked you in Gayville."

"I'm not sure that was a ..." He frowned at her. "Hey! Are you trying to tell me ..." He trailed off again, his mouth opening and closing several times.

"Was he unnaturally strong?"

"Threw Jack across the room like he was a rag doll."

"Did he have distinctive features?"

"Uhhh, I'm not inclined to say. "

"Boone," she pressed.

"Well, he, I mean it, was really pale, almost white."

She nodded. "What else?"

After a moment of thought, he continued. "The really strange thing was …" She could see in his face his struggles with speaking the truth.

"I've seen strange things myself," she told him. "Tell me."

"All right, but remember, I got knocked on the head first thing." He rubbed the side of his head near the cut she had tended. "So my recollection may be slanted."

"I understand."

He glanced back at Jack and Hank, and then urged Nickel closer to her. "He had kind of a beak-like snout," he whispered. "Reminded me of a dog, a bird, too. And it had red eyes. But the dark parts in the middle were black slits. Not round. Not human. Up and down, like you'd see on a cat."

Clementine knew exactly what he meant. She'd seen his attacker's kind before. "Did it speak?"

In her experience, they usually did.

"Yeah, but it was hard to understand. Voice was deep and rough, with a strong accent. Some kind of northern European, I'd guess, but I don't claim familiarity with much other than German."

She'd have to ask Hildegard what she knew about such *others* roaming these parts.

"I can tell you this." She pointed at his pistol. "If we run into anything like him again and you skin that iron, shoot for the head. Knives sometimes work, if you can cut them in the right places, or take the head clean off."

Boone's jaw dropped so low that Clementine thought he might want to dismount to pick it up off the ground. "Take the head off?"

"Yes. You should tell that to Jack, too."

He reined Nickel to a stop. "There's a lot I don't know about you, Miss Johanssen."

She looked back at him with a smile. "Well, we've only recently met, Mr. McCreery."

He clucked Nickel to a walk again, catching up to Fenrir. "Rabbit will like hearing that, at least. He'll take it as a challenge."

They walked in silence for a few hoofbeats.

"Told me he winged the pale devil," Boone said. "It didn't drop, though. Now it makes sense. Rabbit usually doesn't miss."

"This isn't a game, I hope Jack knows that. They will kill him with no hesitation."

"I'll make sure he understands."

She sniffed in the cold, smelling a hint of wood smoke. Gayville must be near.

"I should tell you," Boone said. "On the trail not far out of Deadwood we ran into another kind of beastie. We did a little more damage to that one, but it still got away."

"How was it different than what you witnessed in Gayville?"

"We thought it was a cat for a while, but it looked like a bear. It tracked us, stayed out of sight for the most part."

Clementine did a double-take. "It *hunted* you?"

"I think so. It waited until we were incapacitated and jumped us. I stuck it in the leg with this." He patted his Bowie knife. "Rabbit stuck it through the ribs and lost his knife when it went over the cliff. Must've fallen a hundred feet, through branches and such, then moseyed away, easy as you please."

So there were predators amidst the *others*. Clementine pondered this news. Were they connected somehow? Pets? Guard dogs, maybe? Either way, this meant trouble was more widespread than she'd realized.

"It was all white, too," Boone continued. "Hard to believe Rabbit didn't kill it. He sank eight inches of blade between its ribs."

There were some creatures that were nearly impossible for humans to kill. It sounded like Boone and Jack had found such a beast.

"You might get the same results with bullets." She could feel his gaze on her. She wasn't sure how much she could risk telling him beyond what he needed to know for their visit to the mine.

"How do you know about all of these oddities?"

What would he think if he knew the truth about what she was? She'd been called all sorts of names in her time, some true, others harsh but also accurate, some exaggerated. Did she care about his opinion?

Before she had a chance to answer, Jack rode up. "Hey, Booney! Hank here says he met James Butler Hickok!"

"Sure 'nough!" Hank and Fred the mule closed the distance, edging up next to Clementine when the trail widened. Fenrir neighed at Fred, who nodded back at her several times.

As they approached Gayville, Jack reined up next to Boone, their horses bumping close.

"Well, I'll be," Boone said, after a moment's pause. "Hickok's always been a curiosity to me. He ran freight around New Mexico and thereabouts, but I never met up with him."

"Yep." Hank sniffed, sitting up tall in his saddle. "Stood and watched while the mush-headed jury let that no-good McCall walk away. Weren't too many citizens happy about that. Circus is what it was. Weren't no darn trial."

"Was he as fast as they say?" Jack pressed.

"Never saw him draw his iron. Always drinkin' and cards with Wild Bill. Had a kinda way about him. How he strutted ever'where, like he owned ever'thin'." Hank pursed his lips. "Guess a man could describe me that way, too." He let out a belly laugh.

Clementine leaned over and squeezed Hank's shoulder. "I don't know about that, Hank. My description of you would be a smidgeon different. I'd include several of your finer qualities." She knew well enough what Hank's strengths were, and there were many.

"Like what?"

"For starters, I'd make sure to add how good of a storyteller you are. That always makes for good company." Hank snorted and glanced away, his cheeks a shade darker. "And nobody can sniff out good biscuits and vittles like you."

He snickered. "I've had my share of some awful grub, that's for sure."

"I think Miss Clementine has you pegged, Hank," Jack said.

"Gayville is around the bend up there," Boone cut in, his words sobering even for Hank. "Soon as we get there, I'll pay a visit to Elston Weeks. See if he's healthy." Boone exchanged frowns with Jack before he continued. "Then you can lead the way to the mine, Hank."

Hank grunted in agreement.

Boone was a natural at taking control, and Clementine was inclined to let him.

For now.

A few minutes later, they stopped at the edge of a collection of cabins, shacks, and tents.

Clementine shielded her eyes from the sun, surveying each structure. Gayville appeared to be like any other growing mining camp on the surface, but there was a silence about it that lifted the hairs on the back of her neck. No one. Not a soul. Not visible anyway. The smell of wood smoke lingered in the air.

"Meat seats ain't complaining much about the weather." Jack cast a sideways glance at Clementine, and then grinned.

"What in Valhalla is a 'meat seat'?"

"Horse," Boone clarified. "He thinks it's funny."

Hank chortled. "Meat seat. Good one, Jack Rabbit."

Jack was right, the horses seemed to be doing fine with the snow, but the effects from the mining town were another matter.

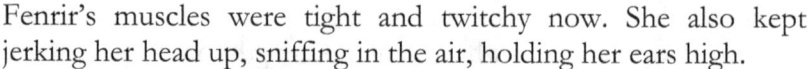

Fenrir's muscles were tight and twitchy now. She also kept jerking her head up, sniffing in the air, holding her ears high.

"At least the wind ain't blowin'," Jack said, nudging Boone. "Prob'ly pick up in a minute or two, knowing this place."

"Wind cottons to the gulch up this way, usually," Hank said, his voice solemn. "Gets down into yer bones, pert near. Not so bad come summer, though. I remember one time—"

"Hank." Clementine stopped him before he got on a roll. She scanned the ridgelines and outcroppings. "Where is the mine from here? Is it visible if we know where to look?"

"Uh ... well, let me ponder that. If I 'member right, Ol' Fred here lost his balance the last time we was headin' up there." He hooted hard enough at the memory to bounce in his saddle. "I think he was sauced. Found him earlier that mornin' out back of Boomer's shack guzzlin' from a half-empty whiskey bottle. He did the darnedest thing. We was on the other side of Gayville there, up thatta way." He pointed to a patch of stumps on a hillside up the trail heading out of town. "Cuttin' trees fer—"

"Hank." Clementine stopped him again, smiling to take any sting out of her interruption. "The mine, please. These men are in a hurry."

"Oh, yeah. That's a story for later. It's up thatta way on the other side of town there." He pointed toward the top of the steep slope behind Gayville. "Can't climb that, though. We gotta go 'round, up past town, and cut back."

"Weeks mentioned there was a trail up to it." Boone clicked his tongue, urging Nickel into a slow trot toward the center of town. "His cabin is up ahead."

Clementine followed. She reined up beside him when he stopped next to a cabin practically surrounded by split and stacked firewood.

"This is Elston Weeks's place," he said in a low voice. "Where Rabbit and I got bushwhacked."

She scanned the shacks and cabins surrounding Weeks's

dwelling. Many had firewood stacked clear to the roof, covering windows. Large metal traps were scattered about in the snow around the doors, boarded-up windows, and woodpiles.

"These people are determined to keep something out," she said, grimacing at the lengths to which they'd gone for defense. This wasn't right on many levels in her book.

"According to Elston, they've had run-ins with the same kind of beast Rabbit and I did on the trail into Deadwood. Other creatures too."

She searched the ridgeline behind the cabin for signs of movement. "How far do you figure it is to Hillyo?"

"My guess, fifty miles." Boone cleared his throat, gaining her attention. He tilted his head toward Elston's cabin. "Door is open a crack." He slid from Nickel's back and then pulled his pistol. "Just in case." Pointing the business end at the sky, he eased toward the open door.

Clementine hopped down from Fenrir. She unbuttoned her coat and waited, her hand sliding inside the Eagle Claw secured to her belt.

"Elston!" Jack bounced from Dime's back, pulled his sawed-off shotgun, and positioned himself with an unobstructed view of the door.

Boone aimed a glare at Jack. "Thanks, Rabbit. Now we surely got the drop on whatever's in there."

"We don't need no repeat of our last visit." He cocked his shotgun.

Boone nudged the door. It swung wide with a long squeak.

Clementine glanced at Hank and Fred the mule to make sure they were out of the line of fire. They'd stopped near the shack next door. While Fred nosed through the snow for something to eat, Hank pulled his bow, tucked himself around the corner of the building, and aimed an arrow at Elston's door.

She really needed to stop underestimating Hank.

Jack started toward the door, too. "Well, go on, Booney.

Unless you went tenderfoot and need me to take the reins."

Boone yelled, "Arrrrgh!" and raced into the shadows.

A loud crash rang out through the doorway a heartbeat later.

Clementine rushed the cabin, her Eagle Claw on and ready. Jack dashed toward the doorway, too, but Clementine beat him inside. A scan from corner to corner found the cabin empty except for Boone, who was bending over next to the wall.

"Are you hurt?" She tucked her claw back into her belt.

Boone held up a frying pan. "Came in too fast and knocked this off the wall. It's hard to see the darn nail in the dark."

"Now who's the pirate, Booney?" Jack stood in the doorway, grinning from ear to ear. "Arrrgh!" he repeated what Boone had yelled, chuckling. "You give your pistol up for a pan? Feelin' like you want to cook me a steak?"

"How about I knock you upside the head with this here pan instead?" Boone joked. He hung the pan on the wall and turned, sizing up the cabin. "No Elston, but his boots are gone. Bedding's gone, too."

"No soup," Jack added. "Fire's dead."

"Yep. The place is cleaned out."

"Soup?" Clementine asked.

"Soup was in a kettle last time we were here," Jack explained.

Boone cursed under his breath. "Either Elston cut and run, or the pale-faced devil got him and the neighbors pilfered his belongings."

"My bet's on cuttin' and runnin'," Jack said.

"We should get gaited then and find that mine." Boone was apparently satisfied and done with this mystery. He headed out the door with Jack trailing.

Clementine took another look around the cabin. What could the pale-faced *other* have wanted in here? Had this Elston found something in the area while out panning gold and brought it home? Worse, had Elston witnessed something he shouldn't have? An altercation involving the *caper-sus* cult? Whatever the reason, Boone and Jack had bad timing. Now that they'd seen what they called the "pale-faced devil," were they at risk of being hunted down and killed?

She joined the men outside. They were on their mounts, waiting for her.

"What are you guys lollygagging around for?" she jested, tightening the cinch on Fenrir. "Let's get to the mine."

She popped up on her horse and waved at Hank to lead the way.

"Get a wiggle on, Fred." Hank bumped Fred's shoulders with his knees and they were off.

"Let's go get Uncle Mort." Jack followed, nudging Dime into a trot.

Boone and Clementine brought up the rear.

They weren't far outside of Gayville when Hank slowed and began to search the right side of the trail, scrutinizing the trees and hillside. From time to time he would give a "whoa" to Fred, adding a "Right in here," or a "Looks to be," followed by, "No … not here." Then he'd continue on up the trail.

After the third such occurrence, he growled, "Dadburned snow is obfuscatin' the terrain."

"What was that, Hank?" Jack asked.

"You know, obfuscatin'. As in disguisin' or concealin'. Hidin' the ground."

Jack's furrowed brow made Clementine grin. Time and again, Hank would make a person scratch their head. He truly was an enigma in plain clothes.

"Have you ever done any tracking, Hank?" Boone asked.

"I did some scoutin' for the army when I was a youngster. I remember this time when a pipsqueak of a lieutenant had a real sleek mustang gelding. Fury, I think he was called. Well, this lieutenant was givin' him a real jessy—Whoa, Fred!" He shaded his eyes and leaned forward, squinting.

"You see somethin'?" Jack asked, pulling his pistol.

Hank muttered something Clementine couldn't decipher. He used his hand to site a straight line up the slope through the trees.

"That's it!" He turned to her, his eyes bright. "We need to push some snow. Ain't too deep, though." He leaned against his mule's mane and rubbed him between the ears. "Just up to your knees, huh, Fred? You gone through deeper yesterday."

Fred answered with a laughing whinny-haw.

"Thatta boy!" Hank reined the mule into the snow.

Clementine fell in line behind them, using Fenrir to widen the trail up the slope for Nickel and Dime.

"Keep yer top lights on for any sign." Hank looked left and right, checking the ground to each side of Fred as they plowed through the powdery snow.

The sunlight pierced the tall evergreens here and there, illuminating the snow with dappled patches of sparkly brilliance amongst the gray shadows. Clementine squinted through the alternating light and dark as Fenrir labored and steamed up the slope. The horse nickered occasionally, rearing her head this way and that, making it clear that she'd prefer to be any number of places rather than where they were. Judging by the snorts and whinnies coming from behind her, Nickel and Dime were no more thrilled at the climb than Fenrir. Fred the mule, however, plodded onward and upward at a steady pace while Hank cooed him along. What that mule lacked in smarts, he made up for in gumption.

They worked their way up the slope along the trail past giant stumps, fallen trees, and large outcroppings of rocks. From time to time, they'd dismount to navigate particularly steep or treacherous stretches.

"Are we up behind Gayville yet, Hank?" Clementine asked after one particularly difficult patch of deep snow.

"Yes, ma'am. Gayville is just over that rise to the right, through a small gulley, and over another rise, then down a steep slope. The Bloody Bo ..." He hesitated, glancing back at Boone and Jack. "I mean the Golden Echo is up a little ways farther, and back yonder." He pointed in an arc, indicating it was well over the ridge top they were nearing. "There's a cabin 'tween us and the mine. Could be yer Morton made it that far."

"From up here, the mountains seem to go on forever." Clementine gazed out across the miles of evergreen forest. She'd not seen the Black Hills from such a high vantage before now. Her time had been spent at The Pyre in Deadwood since her arrival. Thanks to the smallpox run, she'd had no spare time left for exploring before the weather turned foul. Who'd have figured the work of an undertaker in a frontier town was so demanding?

And time consuming.

And exhausting.

"We got ridges around here, more than mountains," Hank said, following her gaze. "Like wrinkles on the *oli-phant* I saw at the circus."

"Are we almost to the cabin?" Boone looked up the trail.

With a nod, Hank led onward through the trees.

Fifteen minutes and a scramble up and over the crest of a ridge later, they stood up to their knees in snow in front of a tumbledown log shack. The door had been torn away and one corner of the roof had collapsed, allowing weather to completely inundate the interior.

Boone headed inside, hollering from the doorway, "Rabbit, check for tracks, huh?"

Hank patted Fred's neck and then followed Boone inside.

Clementine nuzzled Fenrir's nose, giving the horse a few accolades on her hard work. She loosened the tie-string on the bag of carrots, listening to the deep drone of Hank's and Boone's voices coming from inside the cabin.

"Hey, Jack," she said, grabbing a handful of carrots. "You want to give some of these to ..."

Where did he go?

Clementine handed a carrot to Fenrir and then stepped back, looking around the horse, searching the tree line. She spotted Jack in the shadows to her left. He was staring deeper into the trees.

"Jack?" she called as Nickel nudged her hand, looking for his carrot. She held carrots out to both Nickel and Dime, watching Jack as the horses lipped them from her palms.

Jack took a step forward into the shadows, reaching out toward the trees beyond.

Something wasn't right.

Clementine held still, listening. The pines whispered in the breeze, Hank's voice rumbled from the old cabin, Dime and Nickel crunched on the carrots.

"Jack?" she called again, starting toward the tree line.

"Wait," Jack said.

She stopped. What? Was it a mountain lion? Or something worse? She reached inside her coat for her claw.

Jack sprinted into the trees.

SIXTEEN

Rabbit slid to a stop, leaning against the rough bark of a spruce. The frigid air burned his lungs. Pain stabbed his side as he searched the ridgeline above him.

"Where'd," he gasped, "you go?"

The trees thinned near the top, sparse in the shallow gap leading up the side of a further rim.

"Musta gone over and down the other side."

He pushed onward, walking now rather than running. The knee-deep snow pulled at his legs, much as water would, and made his thighs ache. "Damn this snow. Ain't …" He paused to take a few lung searing breaths. "… One single, solitary good fuckin' thing about it."

He huffed through the trees, grumbling as he trudged up the slope. "Cold and wet!"

Rocks and branches concealed in the snow snagged the toes of his boots, bringing him to his knees more than once. He stopped at the rim, catching his breath as he searched the shallow gully below.

He shivered. "Cold. Fuck!" He'd said that already, but it deserved mentioning twice.

Further up the side of the next slope, Rabbit caught sight of a massive pile of gravel and rocks.

Tailings. A mine!

"Gotta be Golden Echo."

Something moved at the edge of the entrance to the mine. He

squinted in the sunlight, shielding his eyes.

It was a man. The one he'd seen through the trees back at the cabin that sort of looked like …

"Uncle Mort!"

The man stared across at Rabbit. He sure looked like Uncle Mort.

Rabbit started down into the gully, keeping his eyes on the figure as much as he dared. He ran, lurched, and teetered, stumbling through a cobble-strewn streambed blanketed by the snow.

His heart pounded. His lungs were aching.

"Uncle Mort," he called again. "Hold up, I'm coming!"

At the base of the slope, he tripped over a hidden rock, tumbling head over heels, his hat flying. He submerged nose-first into a drift, snow packing into the collar of his coat.

"Blasted, cold wet shit!" He sprang to his feet, shaking and brushing off the snow.

"Jack!" he heard Clementine's voice echo through the gully.

He looked back the way he'd come. She stood at the top of the ridgeline, waving at him. Rabbit's focus returned to the mine. The figure was still there, resembling his uncle more than ever, red suspenders and all. But where was his coat? What was he doing up there?

Uncle Mort turned away, toward the mine's entrance.

"Wait! Uncle Mort!" Rabbit grabbed his hat and started scrambling up the slope.

His uncle walked into the mine.

"Sonofabitch! Would you just hold your damned horses?!" Rabbit bounded up the slope, skirting the edge of the tailings. He reached the entrance and peered into the mine's throat. Lack of oxygen and light had stars dancing in his vision.

He took a step inside but then hesitated.

The rocky ceiling arched, allowing space for a tall man to stand upright. Timbered walls were wide enough to walk two abreast. The floor descended out of sight into the shadows.

"Uncle Mort," he called out. His voice echoed, making him wince. He stepped deeper into the throat. "Uncle Mort?" he repeated, a loud whisper this time.

Rabbit squinted into the deeper dark, listening for signs of life coming from further inside.

All manner of beasts, Weeks had said in his tales of this place.

He took another step, his boot crunching on loose pebbles.

The old boy was crushed in a cave-in, he could hear Hank say. *But I'm here to tell you it weren't no cave-in ... Half his face ripped clean off. Strips torn deep all over his body, like big sharp claws had at him.*

As his eyes began to adjust, he could see outlines of the tunnel's features. Several feet farther on, the miners had dug out an enlarged cavity. It was a bulge in the tunnel. He felt sort of like a rodent in the belly of a snake. He found the seam of white quartz they were following, a clue that usually led to gold. Side drifts branched off to the right and left.

Watch for shafts in a mine, boy, his uncle had warned long ago when he'd found out Boone and Rabbit had been playing hide and seek in a silver mine just north of his ranch. *Drop you to China.*

"Hellfire." Rabbit tiptoed along, watching the floor for holes waiting to swallow him up. The shadows thickened with each step. "When you think it's bad, it gets even wor ..."

Movement up ahead stopped him.

The figure disappeared into a side drift on the left.

"Uncle Mort?" he said in a loud whisper, starting after him.

As he neared the side tunnel, a draft of cold air moved past his face, making his skin tingle. He rounded the corner and stepped into the deep dark.

The mine was warmer here, more cocoon-like. He could hear water trickling and touched the wall, his fingers coming away wet. He looked up at the ceiling, but he'd need a light to see any fissures or cracks.

He inched deeper, feeling his way along the wall. He fished his matchstick tin from his vest pocket, but held off on lighting any matches. The longer he could go without a flame, the better. He didn't have many matches left.

Rabbit caught a whiff of rotting meat. Two steps farther, he sniffed again. Sure enough. The rank odor of decay mixed with the musty air.

His pulse pounded in his fingertips as he opened the matchstick tin and struck a match. He held the flame out in front of him. Rock walls, ceiling, floor, nothing more. The wall glistened with dripping water. He mapped the drift's features in his mind. Twenty feet and then he'd need to turn right.

The fire burned down to his fingers. He dropped the match and stepped further in the drift, feeling his way along the wall.

Light another one, he thought.

I don't have that many, lunkhead.

Up to the corner and light another one then.

Shut up.

After Rabbit rounded the corner, he struck another match and held it up. The tunnel ended not fifteen feet away. At the end stood his uncle in red suspenders, his back to Rabbit.

The match shook in his trembling fingers.

His heart slammed against his ribs.

"Uncle Mort?" he whispered.

Without looking his way, the figure pointed at a pile of rumpled clothing on the ground.

The flame reached Rabbit's fingers. He cursed and dropped the matchstick. He reached for another with shaky fingers, fumbling with the match tin. It slipped from his grip and clanged when it hit the rock floor.

"Damn it to hell." Rabbit fell to his knees, scrambling for the match tin. The stench of death was stronger at floor level, making him gag.

His ears rang in the silence.

His fingers touched the cold metal.

Please, don't let it be him.

He palmed the tin. It was empty. "Shit."

A scuffling sound came from the main tunnel. He pressed back against the wall, reaching for his pistol.

"Jack!"

Clementine's voice was music to his ears.

"Jack, are you in here?"

"Down here!" He slid his pistol back into its holster. "First left about thirty feet inside the entrance!"

He waited for her, his eyes closed, trying not to think about what or who might be waiting there with him.

"Jack?" she said in a quieter voice, closer.

"There's someone else in here," he said, wiping the sweat from his upper lip.

"Who?"

He hesitated to tell her. She'd probably think he'd gone *loco*. He snorted. Hell, maybe he had. "It might be Uncle Mort, but he won't answer."

"Hold steady. I'm coming, and Boone's not far behind me." Her voice was louder now.

Rabbit saw a steady glow before she rounded the corner. She must have a candle or a tinderbox. He heard her sniff several times. Then she was there, kneeling next to him.

"Are you hurt?" She held the tinderbox at chest level, searching his face and neck.

The glow from the flame eased the panic that had gripped his chest. "No. Dropped my damn matches. Can I see your light?"

Tinderbox in hand, he turned toward the end of the tunnel.

The figure was gone.

"There's something on the ground." Clementine went to take a closer look, covering her nose with her sleeve as she squatted next to it.

Rabbit followed slowly, his stomach heavy.

She stood, blocking the path. "Jack, give me the light."

Something in her tone made him hand it back without hesitation.

"What is it?" he asked.

But he already knew.

"Maybe we should wait for Boo—"

"No." He pushed her aside. In the tinderbox light the pile of clothes became more distinct, the greens and browns more visible.

Red suspenders.

Gray hair.

Mottled flesh, blackening with decay.

"No," he whispered, covering his nose as Clementine had. His stomach churned and heaved.

"Jack," Clementine said, trying to pull him away.

Rabbit tugged free of her hold and stared down at the crumpled body of the man who'd been more of a father to him than his own. His vision blurred. "No, no, no, no, no …"

"Your uncle," Clementine stated quietly.

Rabbit turned away and lurched down the tunnel a few steps. He bent over, dry heaving.

"Rabbit! Clementine!" Boone's voice echoed from the main tunnel, followed by the sound of his boots on the stone floor.

"We're in the first drift on the left," Clementine called. She touched Rabbit's shoulder. "I'm so sorry, Jack."

Boone appeared from around the corner, an oil lamp in hand that lit the drift with a bright glow. He was breathing heavy, his face dripping with sweat.

"Damn it, Rabbit! What in the hell is the idea, bolting like—" He leaned closer, his brow wrinkling. "What is it?"

Rabbit wiped his face with his sleeve and stood upright. "It's like what I saw, Booney. Just like my dreams."

"What?"

"Mort's gone," he whispered, pointing toward the pile of rags and flesh.

The pain in Boone's eyes mirrored the ache in Rabbit's chest. He took a step toward the body.

Rabbit caught his sleeve and shook his head. "Don't."

Boone shook him off. He walked to the end of the drift, holding the oil lamp over what was left of Uncle Mort.

Rabbit sucked in a ragged breath. "I saw this, Miss Clementine." He pointed at the body. "I saw it in my dreams."

Clementine studied him, her forehead lined. "You did?"

"Yeah. Dammit."

Boone stood next to the body for a few moments, his back to them. Then he shook his head and returned to Rabbit, his face drawn and pale.

"The clothes look like his," he said, "but I can't tell it's him. Are you sure, Rabbit?"

Rabbit nodded, swiping at the tears wetting his cheeks. He grabbed Boone and hugged him tight. "Aw, Booney. Who did that to him?"

Boone patted his back, comforting him the same way he had when they were kids standing over their parents' graves. "I don't know, Rabbit, but we'll find who did this. We'll set this right."

Clementine offered to carry Morton's body out of the mine. Moving corpses was what she'd done for the last few months.

Boone thanked her, but insisted on doing it himself, wrapping what was left of his uncle in his tattered, bloodstained clothes as best he could.

"Miss Clementine," Jack said, watching Boone with a solemn gaze. "Will you hand me the lantern, please?"

She did as asked, watching as he walked over to the body. He squatted next to Boone and pulled something from around his uncle's neck.

"The necklace?" she heard Boone ask.

Jack nodded and stuffed it in his coat pocket. He returned to Clementine, lantern in hand.

"May I see it?" she asked, curious.

He pulled it from his pocket, holding it in the lantern light.

Clementine admired the silver pendant shaped like a bear hanging from the strip of leather. "Is that turquoise?" she asked, pointing at the stone in the middle.

"Yep. An old Navajo gave him this when he was still working as a wagon master. Told Uncle Mort it would bring him strength and protect him from the evils of the world."

"It's excellent craftsmanship."

Jack scowled. "Didn't seem to work for Uncle Mort on the strength and protection business, but I reckon it'll be good to have in the years to come when I'm missing him."

She reached out and hugged him.

Jack stood stiff for a moment in her arms, and then relaxed and hugged her back. "Uh, Miss Clementine, you got backbone of steel?"

She chuckled and stepped back. "It's a hardwood baton, but Hank likes to call it my thumper. I brought it along just in case."

"In case of what?"

"In case of trouble."

"You two ready?" Boone asked. He scooped up his uncle's remains.

Clementine took the oil lamp from Jack and led the way out of the mine into the bright sunlight. Boone set the body down under a tree, then walked to the edge of the slope. He stared out over the gully for several breaths, rubbing his shoulder.

"Hank should be here shortly with the horses," she said to both of them. "You two have seen enough today. Take your uncle's body back to The Pyre and we'll give him a proper burial tomorrow." That was if she made it back in one piece. She drew out her Eagle Claw, slipping it on her left hand. "Have Hank use Fenrir to carry Morton. He can come back with my horse later. Tell him to wait for me in Gayville, but if it gets dark, he needs to leave."

Boone turned toward her, his gaze held on the claw. "What are your intentions?"

She pointed at the mine. "I'm going in there to find the bastard that did this to your uncle and rip its damned throat out." She clicked her finger blades together and smiled. "If I learn more about what is going on in Gayville and the meaning behind the multiple appearances of this *caper-sus* symbol in the process, so much the better."

Boone shook his head. "You're not going in there alone."

"Trust me, you two should walk away from this."

"We ain't doing nothin' of the sort," Jack said, adjusting his bandoleer.

Clementine sized them up. She didn't doubt their shooting abilities. The fire in their eyes told tales of fury fueled by grief, powerful emotions indeed. However, she had an idea what she would be facing in there. They didn't.

"You're out of your depth here," she told them. "If you go in there with me, your uncle might not be the only one carried out today. I recommend you both take care of Morton and leave this to me."

"Ha!" Jack scoffed. "You're a real peach, Clementine Johanssen." He grabbed the lantern and marched into the mine under a healthy head of steam.

Boone started after him. He paused at the entrance and looked back at her. "You coming?" He didn't wait for her to answer, trailing Jack into the darkness.

"*Verdammt!*" she cursed at the blue sky and then jogged after the two firebrands.

When she caught up, she blocked them with her arms held

out wide. "Since you two won't listen to reason, understand this. I'm in charge now. Do what I say when I say it."

"Yes, ma'am," Jack said.

"Like I told Boone earlier, heads are the weak spot. A stab or bullet anywhere else might slow them down, but nothing more. You already experienced a taste of what's to come—twice. Be efficient in your movements and don't stay in one spot too long. Oh, and keep an eye on each other."

"Anything else?" Boone asked, peering over her shoulder into the darkness.

"Yes. Don't worry about me. I can take care of myself."

Jack twirled his pistol. "What if we run into that pale-faced asshole?"

"Leave your white devil to me." Clementine looked down at his firearm. "If you're going to use that, watch out for ricochets. More important, don't shoot me."

"What will happen if *you* take a bullet?" Jack asked.

"I'll be snortin' mad."

She started down the adit. "Jack, walk beside me and shine the lantern up ahead. Boone, watch that no one sneaks up on us from behind."

As they made their way deeper into the hillside, Clementine thought about Gayville, the way the cabins and shacks had been surrounded by barricades and traps. That was no way to live. Ah, but gold was seductive, and according to what she'd heard, Gayville sat on top of a rich vein. Men would try to move mountains to plunder the Black Hills for the precious metal, she had no doubt. But at what cost? In a land plagued by *others* and their pets, the price would be steep.

She cast a frown at Jack. His rage and stubbornness fueled his courage, but would it be enough? If she was right about the tracks she'd noticed outside, this could be the end of him and Boone.

She prayed that Odin didn't see fit to put an end to her today, too. If what Hildegard said was true about the Golden Echo mine being the source of the infestation, Clementine's work here had only just begun. Before this was all over, she'd need to seal this gate and cleanse the surrounding hills of all those who had slipped through.

The adit arced to the right. The stillness was interrupted only by their footfalls scuffling on dirt and rock.

"Almost feels warm in here," Jack whispered, breaking the silence.

Boone shushed him. "We need to listen to the mine."

"Actually," Clementine said, "I'm more interested in listening for whatever made all of these tracks in the dirt. There are so many they blend together." They sort of looked like wolf prints, but the paws were larger, the claws longer. They mirrored what she'd seen outside in the snow.

Jack crouched with the oil lamp, reading the prints. "Maybe a small bear. Pretty fresh, looks like."

"Whatever it is," Boone said. "There must be a lot of them."

"Those aren't bear tracks," Clementine said, continuing along the tunnel.

Jack caught up with her. "How far in are we? Couple hundred feet?"

Boone had drawn his knife and was practically stepping on Jack's heels. "Some breed of big badgers, maybe?" he said under his breath. "No, can't be right. They tend to be loners."

"Wait," Clementine whispered. She stopped, grabbing Jack's coat and tugging him back several steps.

"What is it?" he asked.

"Listen."

A staccato of clacking echoed from the darkness ahead.

The sound of quick huffs came next.

"Here it comes." She flexed her claw. "Get ready."

She drew the hardwood baton from her back holster, gripping it in her right hand.

"I don't hear anything," Jack whispered.

"Take my word for it." She pointed her baton at his sheath. "Draw your knife. No guns yet."

Jack pulled his Bowie knife free and held it at the ready. "Booney, take the lamp."

"I hear it, too. It's coming fast." Boone grabbed the lamp and held it over Jack's shoulder.

Clementine swung the baton in a series of swoops, warming up her muscles. She rolled her shoulders and stretched her neck from side to side.

The huffing and clacking grew louder, mixed with grunts.

"Consarn!" Jack whispered. "I hear it. Giddyup, fucker. Let's have us a hoedown."

Clementine's blood raced, her body gearing up for a fight.

Boone moved up next to Jack. He held the lamp high in one hand, his knife gripped in the other. "It sounds like a charging bull."

Suddenly, the clacking stopped.

Two eyes glistened at them from the shadows.

"Jack and Boone," Clementine said in a level tone. "Step behind me."

The dark furred creature stalked closer, taking shape in the dim light. It skulked toward them on four stout legs. Its paws were huge. Its shoulders were nearly as massive as Fred the mule's. Its thick neck rippled with muscles. A long snout opened wide. Its lips curled back, revealing dagger-like fangs.

Jack cursed. "Is that some kind of wolf?"

"It looks more like a deformed calf, only bigger," Boone answered. "And longer. Look at that tail."

Clementine studied the beast, her mind flitting through memories of her grandfather's drawings. "Great Odin's spear," she said under her breath. "That's a *Bahkauv*."

"A what?" Jack asked.

"She said 'bah-cough,'" Boone whispered.

"I heard what she said, Booney. I don't know what it is."

Clementine flexed her Eagle Claw. "It's a menace, that's what."

The *Bahkauv* leaped in their direction and landed not ten feet in front of them. Its thick tail swished from side to side, thumping against the mine walls.

"Watch out!" Jack switched his blade to his left hand and jerked his pistol, aiming at the creature.

"No!" Clementine knocked his gun away with her baton. "Get back, now!" She squared her shoulders to the beast.

It snarled and sprang at her. The fur on its back brushed against the top of the tunnel.

She lunged toward it, ducking low.

Its front claws extended mid-air, jaws open wide.

Clementine slammed her baton down and knocked its front legs aside. She swung upward, driving her razor-sharp finger blades into its throat, and smashed its head into the rock ceiling. Dark blood ran down the blades of the Eagle Claw.

She pulled her blades free, letting the beast fall to the ground. It stared at her, its legs twitching.

"Which one of you wants to finish it off?" she asked them. If they were going to join her in battle, she needed to know that they could stomach the task.

Jack stood motionless, pistol and knife hanging at his side, gaping at her.

"You already did," Boone said, grimacing down at the beast.

"It will recover if we don't finish it." She looked from Boone to Jack. "This is likely the creature that killed your uncle. Or one just like it did."

Boone frowned at her while Jack squinted at the injured *Bahkauv*, neither volunteering to finish what she'd started.

"If you aren't up to it, I can send it back to the earth instead, and you two can wait for me outside where it's safer. I cannot waste energy protecting you in the thick of battle if there are more of these creatures."

According to what her afi had taught her about the *Bahkauv*, they roved in groups. She wished he were here to help her fight them.

Jack holstered his pistol. "I'll kill the sonuvabitch." Knife in hand, he bent down next to the creature.

"You need to stab it in the brain or take its head."

"Just like skinnin' and preppin' a critter for eatin'." His cuts were deep and efficient. He tossed the head aside and wiped his blade off on the fur. Standing, he sniffed. "Good enough?"

"That will do." She blew out a breath, frowning toward the shadows. "To be honest, I was sort of hoping for a different ending."

"Different how?" Boone asked, looking at her as if she might morph into a *Bahkauv* herself.

"One with less death." She nudged the carcass with her toe. "This creature is not normally of this plane. Hildegard was right."

Trouble was brewing in the Black Hills—the sort that made for dark legends of death and destruction.

Jack's brow wrinkled. "Who's Hildegard?"

"It's not important right now." She wiped her blades on her pants. "That's one down."

"That fella in the bar ... Finnigan," Boone said. "He was lucky, wasn't he?"

"I don't kill out of anger." At least she tried not to, but she didn't always succeed. *The rage of a Slayer makes you strong,* her afi had told her many times. *But you must not let the bloodlust control you.*

That was easier said than done.

A lopsided smile crept onto Jack's face. "I was right. You're an Amazon."

"Not quite, Jack."

Amazons were warriors. She was just a killer for hire with a short fuse for no-good assholes who murdered innocent Uncle

Mortons and others like him.

Her amma's words of advice on her temper issues were more of a mantra to repeat while meditating:

Strength of the mind grants strength to body.
Strength of body follows strength of mind.

Hot temper aside, she had a feeling that today would require great focus and strength—both body and mind.

"I'm sorry I struck your gun hand, Jack, but we might still be able to surprise the rest."

"Rest of what?"

"The rest of those." She pointed her baton at the *Bahkauv*. "You two ready?"

SEVENTEEN

Boone followed Clementine and Rabbit deeper into the mine, glancing behind him every few seconds. It was quiet again, save the occasional plink of water and scuff of a boot on rock.

Clementine still wore the claw-like weapon. He lowered his lamp down next to her hand to get a good look at how the finger blades were attached to the leather. What was that weapon called? He hadn't seen anything like it before. He eyed her long legs, strong shoulders, and braided hair. Come to think of it, he hadn't seen anything like *her* before, either.

"What'd you call that beastie?" Rabbit asked in a quiet voice. "Wasn't like that white grizzly on the trail, but it was just as disagreeable."

"*Bahkauv*," she answered. "Most people believe they're only fairytale creatures."

Boone shook his head. More like nightmare fodder.

"Ain't like no fairytales I know."

"Shhhh." Clementine stopped and held up her hand. "Do you hear that?"

Boone waited, breath held, listening. Blood pulsed in his ears, blocking whatever it was she was hearing.

Up ahead, the tunnel arced to the right and then continued out of sight. The shadows played with his imagination.

"Guns now," Rabbit whispered. He sheathed his knife and drew his pistol.

Clementine frowned at Rabbit's pistol but didn't argue. She

inched forward, staying close to the inside wall of the curve.

Boone and Rabbit followed without making a sound. Around the bend, the walls of the passage went on for about thirty feet or so and then gave way to blackness.

"There's a cavern ahead," Clementine said. "Wait here for my signal." She ran ahead hunched over, stopping where the tunnel widened into the cavern. She pressed back against the wall. One of the blades of her claw clinked on the rock.

Rabbit leaned close and said, "We're just gonna wait here?"

Boone shrugged. This was his first time hunting fairytale creatures in a mine with a sharp-clawed woman. "Like she said, wait for her signal."

They watched Clementine slip around the wall and vanish into the dark cavern.

"I don't like this." Rabbit wiped his brow with his wrist.

Boone smirked. "I've been rethinking the whole idea of visiting the Bloody Bones mine since I saw that *Bahkauv*."

Seconds later, Clementine returned from the shadows and waved for them to join her. They hurried to her side.

"Light it up," she said to Boone, pointing toward the darkness.

He stepped around her and swung the oil lamp in an arc at arm's length. The cavern glittered from top to bottom.

Rabbit peeked over his shoulder. "I reckon we found us the mother lode."

He was right. The light revealed outcroppings and veins of gold and white quartz in the ceiling and walls.

"Sixty feet long, maybe thirty feet tall," Boone whispered, sizing up the cavern.

"Bigger even, maybe."

He lifted the lamp higher. "Look at the ceiling in the back."

Long, slender stalactites dripped water. The minerals seemed to glow in the lantern light. Boone followed the droplets down to stalagmites sticking up amongst cobble- to wagon-sized boulders.

"I'll be." Rabbit wandered a few steps into the cavern, and spun in a slow circle. "This cave is a wonderment."

"Rabbit!" Boone whispered. He tiptoed behind the lunkhead, who was drifting further into the cavern. Rabbit stopped to run his fingers over the smooth wet surface of a stalagmite.

Boone looked back at Clementine.

She pointed to her chest, then to the right along the wall, and dashed into the shadows.

"Look at all the gold in here, Booney."

Before Boone could shush him, a bloodcurdling screech shattered the stillness. The cry came from the same direction Clementine had gone.

Boone raced toward the sound. Rabbit rushed past him with his knife and pistol both out and ready for action.

"Clementine?" Boone said in a hushed voice.

"That wasn't her screamin' we heard."

They rounded one of the larger boulders, skidding to a stop at the sight of Clementine wiping off her claw blades. She stood next to a small mound of dirt and rocks.

She kicked the pile with her boot, scattering the stuff across the floor. "That's two."

"Two what?" Boone asked. *Bahkauv?* If so, where was the second one?

A shrieking howl blasted through the cavern.

Scratches on the boulder behind him made Boone's blood rush. He turned, lantern raised, and found himself face-to-face with another of the long-fanged beasts. It crouched on the boulder, not five feet away.

The *Bahkauv* lowered its head, set Boone in its sights, and shrieked again.

"Fuuuck!" He raised his arm, cringing.

WHAP!

In a blur of movement, an arrow pierced the beast through the side of the head. It screamed and fell off the boulder next to him, its legs flailing.

Boone lowered the lamp, squinting into the shadows.

Hank rushed over, drew his knife, and sank it into the neck of the beast, slicing clear through. "Cut yer spine, didn't I, you devil." He wiped his blade clean on the *Bahkauv's* shoulder.

"Hank!" Boone and Rabbit cried.

"Perfect timing, Hank," Clementine patted him on the

shoulder. "Boone owes you a shot of gut warmer for that one."

"Gladdened to see the three of you still breathin'." He scowled at Clementine. "You ought not come in places such as this, Miss Clem, without me nohow. Oo." He snapped his fingers. "I brought more lanterns fer us. Set one on the boulder back there to take my shot." He mimed shooting his bow and then hurried off, returning with another lantern, which he handed to Rabbit.

"Noticed your handiwork in the adit back there, Miss Clem." He tilted his head to study her claw, and then smiled at Boone and Rabbit. "Somethin', ain't she?"

Boone was still searching for his tongue after having the hell scared out of him.

"Actually, that was Jack's handiwork," Clementine said. "I just helped a little."

Rabbit scoffed. "A little?"

The clatter of pebbles hitting stone echoed from the far side of the cavern.

"We're not done yet," Clementine said. "Set the lanterns so each shines in a different direction to light up the place as much as possible." She shot Rabbit a tight smile. "Remember, don't shoot me." She ran off, rounding the boulder, and faded into the darkness.

More pebbles clattered near the entrance tunnel, then off to their right in the shadows.

"They're trying to surround us," Rabbit said, setting up the lanterns per Clementine's instructions. "Cut us off."

Hank whistled low. "Look at 'em move. Gonna be tough to hit when they're on the go."

The shadows rippled as the *Bahkauv* raced into the cavern. Boone placed his lantern on the boulder beside him and then drew his knife with his left hand. "If I can't hit 'em, I'll stick 'em."

Huffs and growls echoed all around them.

"Jehosephat," Hank said. "How many of them nasty buggers are in here?" He set his quiver and bow next to his lamp, and then pulled his pistol. "Let's get to cleanin' up before this winds up bein' our tomb."

Rabbit jerked his sawed-off shotgun and cradled it in his left arm and cocked his Colt in his right.

"Careful with that artillery." Boone shot a glance at the scattergun. "That thing hurts."

Rabbit squinted toward the far reaches of the cavern. "Never let me forget, will ya?"

A screeching roar echoed from somewhere deeper in the mine. On the other side of the chamber, a *Bahkauv* crept around a boulder and stalked toward them. Another leapt onto a boulder. Another emerged from the shadows. And then another. And another.

"Shit! They're everywhere!" Boone peeked around the boulder, his revolver ready to fire, but he hesitated. They were moving so fast now, like dark blurs across his vision. If he missed, the ricochet could be deadly.

"Sounds like a pack of demons," Hank hollered above the snarls and hisses and howls. He stood with his back to the boulder. Boone saw him spin the cylinder on his revolver in the flickering light.

Rabbit's pistol exploded to the left of Boone in an ear-splitting *BOOM!* that echoed throughout the chamber.

One of the creatures that had been slinking toward Hank stumbled. Then it keeled over, dark liquid pooling under its head.

"Take that, ya cur!" Rabbit yelled. "Shoot somethin', Booney."

Boone let his pistol sing as one charged him, its teeth bared. *BOOM!* He hit the beast in the shoulder. It shrieked and scuttled away.

Across the cavern, a commotion of screeches, snarls, and shrieks told a tale of death dealt by Clementine and her claw. At least he hoped that's what was happening.

BOOM! Hank was letting loose.

"Give 'em hell, Hank!" Rabbit shouted. *BOOM!* "Like shootin' prairie dogs!"

"Big damn prairie dogs!" Boone hollered. One of the creatures lunged out of the shadows straight for him. *BOOM!* His shot was low, hitting its chest. The creature screeched and slipped away into the darkness.

"Damn it!" he yelled.

"Aim for the head!" Rabbit shouted.

BOOM!

A beast landed at Boone's feet, its skull half blown away.

"Took care of that—*BOOM!*—for ya!" Rabbit hollered over Hank's gunshot.

"Jackass," Boone muttered.

"Gotta reload, Booney. Cover me!"

Boone fired at a beast that leapt onto a boulder directly in front of Rabbit, but it dodged. The bullet ricocheted into the ceiling, sending pebbles raining down on Hank, whose spent pistol lay at his feet while he shoved his blade through the neck of a creature. He kicked at another, landing a solid blow to the side of its head, knocking the *Bahkauv* sideways toward Rabbit.

He heard the click-whizzzz of a cylinder locking into place, and then *BOOM!*

Rabbit was back in it.

"Checking on Clementine!" Boone ran to the other side of the boulder and nearly dropped his pistol at what he saw.

With one of the bastards skewered on her blades, she spun and smashed another across its jowls with her baton, sending it flying into the wall headfirst. It crumpled to the ground and lay twitching. She twisted her claw and tore the head off the one she'd skewered. Then she ran and jumped, springing off a boulder. She landed behind another *Bahkauv* and drove her blades through the base of its skull. It collapsed at her feet. She turned and pierced the chest of yet another mid-lunge. It slumped next to the others.

"Holy hell," he said, trying to keep up with her movements as she shredded one *Bahkauv* after another.

She dashed around a boulder, chasing down another.

"Look out!" Rabbit crashed into Boone's side. They both fell to the ground.

Rabbit's pistol flew from his holster. It clanked against a rock a few feet away. He rolled and popped up, the scattergun in his hands. "Get up, Booney!"

Boone shook the stars from his head and scrambled upright in time to face off with Rabbit's shotgun.

"Down!"

Boone dropped flat on his stomach.

Rabbit pulled the trigger. BOOOOM!

The concussion from the double-barreled blast shook Boone's world, blurring his vision. He pushed up to his hands and knees. The front half of a creature landed directly in front of him with a squishy thump.

He recoiled. Damn that fuckin' scattergun.

The screeching roar sounded in the distance—the same one that had started it all. The beasts retreated, their claws clattering down the tunnel at the back of the cavern.

Rabbit took off after them.

Boone pushed to his feet.

"Jack, stop!" Clementine yelled.

He did as ordered, but took aim down the tunnel and fired. *Click.* "Fuck! I didn't reload."

"Don't waste cartridges, Bunny Rabbit," Boone shouted, picking up Rabbit's gun. "And take your revolver."

Rabbit jogged back and grabbed his revolver, holstered it, and began reloading his shotgun. He moved close to Boone and said under his breath, "I know you got some feelin's about killin', but you gotta, Booney. You gotta aim for the head." He started to

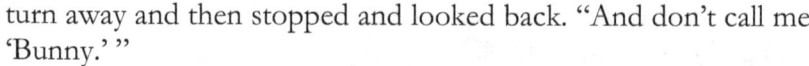

turn away and then stopped and looked back. "And don't call me 'Bunny.'"

Hank joined them, taking a moment to reload his pistol.

Boone surveyed the destruction around them. Bodies littered the ground in front of him, thanks to Rabbit's and Hank's handiwork.

"It looks like a massacre," he said over the ringing in his ears.

He walked over to a *Bahkauv* Clementine had slain. It looked different, crusted over somehow, like a statue frozen in a death pose. He bent closer. The dark fur had faded to a light gray. A touch confirmed the crust notion. It felt solid. What the hell?

Clementine joined him, standing over the dead beast. "Back to the earth with you," she said and hit it with her baton.

The statue shattered into a pile of pebbles and coarse grains of dirt. She kicked the remains with her boot, scattering the stuff across the floor, and moved on to the next.

Boone stared after her, watching her repeat the performance several more times. More dirt and dust flew. Hank joined her, hitting and kicking. "Why do they turn to dust when you kill them?" Boone asked her.

Clementine returned to his side. "That's not important right now. We have a problem. You should reload."

Boone frowned, but started loading his pistol.

"Didn't we just get rid of our problem?" Rabbit asked.

Clementine looked toward the tunnel at the back of the cavern. "They were called back."

Hank sneezed. "Durn dust got up my nose." He sneezed again, and then leaned to the side and buck-snorted. "Ain't right, that critter dust up in my nose holes. Might be it turns me into one of 'em."

"Breathing their remains won't turn you into one, Hank."

How in the hell was that dirt and dust their remains?

"Did anybody get hit?" Boone did a quick survey for injuries.

"Took a whack to my side." Hank rubbed his ribs under his

left arm. "Didn't get stabbed or stuck, though, so I'm fit to fight."

"No injuries here, only a scratch or two," Clementine said.

"Hank had my back."

"That's my job, but I reckon you really had mine." Hank pointed at Rabbit. "I got a bone to pick with you, Jack Rabbit. That scattergun pert near turned me into a siftin' pan."

"Sorry, Hank. I had to save Booney's life. Again."

Boone rolled his eyes. "If I had a nickel for every time you—"

"*Scharfrichter.*" A gravelly voice echoed out from deep within the mine.

Boone turned, staring at the tunnel that led deeper. "That's downright disturbing." He finished reloading his revolver and spun the cylinder.

"I smell you, *Scharfrichter.*" The voice was closer now.

"Is that another one?" Rabbit holstered his shotgun. He drew his pistol, squinting into the darkness. "Anybody hear one of them beasties talk? Or is this somethin' new?"

A screeching roar filled the cavern.

The shadows came to life again.

"They're back!" Boone turned to cover Hank, who was still loading his revolver. Over Hank's head, he saw a blur of movement across the upper wall of the cavern, scurrying along like a lizard. Before he could get a word out, the form dropped to the floor in the shadows behind Clementine.

He started to call out to her.

BOOM!

"Gotcha!" Rabbit was at work again on the *Bahkauv.*

The creature stepped out from the shadows.

Boone gasped. The pale-faced devil! Snake eyes locked onto Clementine. His hand shot out, but she dodged and spun, leading with her baton. It slammed into his jaw.

He roared with rage.

Hank leapt from one of the boulders, his knife in hand, and

landed on the back of the pale devil.

"Booney!"

He turned to see Rabbit surrounded by three of the beasts. He pointed his pistol at one.

BOOM!

The bullet hit the *Bahkauv* in the ribs. It stumbled, but continued to stalk Rabbit, who was slashing at the other two snarling creatures with his knife as he was backed toward the wall. Where was his gun?

Boone aimed for the head and fired. One of the two that Rabbit was trying to knife crumpled to the ground. Rabbit pitched sideways as the second beast leapt at him. It crashed into the boulder behind him. Boone locked onto the stalker's head and fired again, blowing off the backside of its skull.

Rabbit rushed the other one as it tried to stand. He delivered a series of slashes to its neck and ribs. Then he raised his knife and buried it in its cheek. The creature collapsed at his feet.

Boone turned back to Hank, who was on the ground next to the wall. How'd he get over there? Hank rolled onto his stomach and pushed off the ground, rubbing his hip.

Movement near the stalagmites caught his eye. Clementine was there, crouched low, her fingertips touching the ground. The pale devil rushed her. She shifted back. Her leg shot out, connecting hard enough to send the devil stumbling. He caught his balance and flew back at her with another roar. She tried to duck again, but he delivered a blow to Clementine's shoulder that sent her through the air. Her back slammed into a stalagmite, breaking off the top.

"Miss Clem!" Hank took aim at her attacker. *BOOM, BOOM, BOOM!* When the bullets didn't slow the devil, Hank charged, knife first.

The devil faced Hank, a small black sword in hand. Its blade curved backward, twice as long as Hank's Bowie knife. He raised it high as Hank lunged.

"No!" Clementine struggled to her feet.

Boone raised his pistol. His finger tightened on the trigger as he took aim at the devil. Before he could shoot, a *Bahkauv* slammed into him. He reeled and fell, pushing at the beast while its jaws snapped in his ear.

BOOM!

The beast's head kicked back, and then it collapsed onto Boone's chest.

"He's a goner, Booney!" Rabbit yelled.

Did he mean Hank or the *Bahkauv*?

Boone shoved the carcass aside in time to see the pale devil's sword slice down Hank's chest.

Hank stumbled backward into the wall.

BOOM!

Rabbit's gun blasted again, acrid smoke burning Boone's nose as another beast collapsed nearby.

Clementine rushed the pale-faced devil, knocking away his blade with her baton as he swung. She spun and swept her claw down, slicing through his arm, severing it clean off. The limb fell to the ground. The sword clanged against a rock next to it. The pale devil howled in pain, his face elongated with the snout Boone had seen at Weeks's cabin. The devil swung his free arm at Clementine, his lips pulled back with rage. She deflected his hand with her baton and thrust her claw into his stomach, plowing him into the wall.

He grabbed her by the throat with his remaining hand, pulling her close as he muttered something to her in another language, his spit and blood peppering her face.

She twisted her claw deeper into his torso.

His shriek of pain chilled Boone.

"They're gettin' away!" Rabbit ran after one of the *Bahkauv*, following it into the shadows.

Boone pushed off the carcass pinning him to the ground and scrambled to his feet. He stared into the shadows. "Rabbit!"

Every damned time.

Hank groaned from where he lay over by the wall.

Hank!

"Shit! Rabbit, get back here!" Boone rushed to Hank and knelt beside him. "Hank?" He searched his chest for wounds.

BOOOOOM! Rabbit's sawed-off shotgun exploded in the distance.

A deep rumble filled the cavern and the ground trembled. Boone looked at the ceiling, expecting to see the rock fracturing before his eyes. Pebbles spattered his face as the rumble echoed around him. Crashing rocks thundered from deep within the mine.

He was going to kick Rabbit in the ass if they made it out of this alive. He turned his attention back to Hank, yanking open his partially shredded wool coat expecting to see a death gash down his chest. Underneath was the Sioux bone breastplate he'd mentioned earlier. Several of the breastplate bones over his sternum were broken, but there was no blood.

"Hank?" Clementine joined them, kneeling next to Boone. She touched Hank's chest. "Where's he injured?"

"I can't see anything." Boone ran his hand over Hank's head, coming away with only a small smear of blood. "Back of his head must have hit a rock."

A roiling wave of dust swelled around them. They coughed and sputtered.

"Cave-in," Boone said between coughs, rising to his feet. "I have to find Rabbit."

Clementine nodded, but her focus remained on Hank.

Hank's body shuddered once. Twice. Then his eyes opened. He let out a shout, raising his arms in front of him.

"Hank!" Clementine pulled his arms down and turned him to face her. "You're okay."

Hank looked side to side, eyes wide. "Where's the bastard with the big knife?"

Clementine pointed at the pale-faced devil. She'd left him pinned to the wall across the room, her Eagle Claw stuck clear through him, blades lodged in a crevice in the rock.

Rabbit came running from the mine tunnel. He was covered with dust. "Saw at least two go down a tunnel further back in there before the roof fell." He pointed behind him. He holstered his sawed-off and scrubbed his hands through his hair, sending more dust into the air.

"That damned shotgun is going to get us all killed."

He waved Boone off. "What happened over here?" He looked at each of them in turn, then he noticed Clementine's wall decoration. "That's a different sort of hangin' method."

Clementine strode over to the pale devil, scooping up the curved blade on her way. She grabbed a handful of white hair and lifted his head.

He opened his snake eyes and hissed at her.

"You ... have defied ..." He sucked in a ragged breath. "The Master, *Scharfrichter*. You will be—" His eyes fluttered closed.

Clementine slammed his head back against the wall.

A creaky groan leaked from his lips.

"Wer befiehlt dir?" she asked.

"What'd you say?" Hank limped over to her.

"I asked him about his master."

"What is he, Miss Clem?"

"A pest."

The pale devil croaked out a laugh. "You have exposed yourself. Your flesh will be torn from your bones." He began chanting, weakly at first but louder with each iteration. *"Ich beschwöre den Verschlinger. Ich beschwöre den Verschlinger. Ich beschwöre den Verschlinger ..."*

"Enough!" Clementine said and thrust his own sword up through his chin.

Boone watched in amazement as the pale devil's features began to decay and turn gray and then black, almost as if he were being consumed by an invisible fire.

Clementine turned away right before he exploded into a swirling cloud of ash that expanded and joined with the dust and gun smoke in the air. The devil's blade and her claw clanged to the shadowed ground at her feet.

She bent to collect both, pausing for a moment with her head cocked to the side. Then she slid on her claw and walked over to the three of them. Rabbit's eyes were wide, Hank's forehead furrowed. Boone needed a drink. Maybe three. Plus, his ears were still ringing from that damned sawed-off shotgun blast.

"This is a gateway." Clementine pointed the devil's blade toward the tunnel at the back of the cavern. "We'll need to seal it, if Jack didn't already."

Boone looked at Rabbit, feeling every bit of the shock he saw on his face. He rubbed his aching shoulder and walked over to grab his lucky hat that lay next to the dead *Bahkauv* Rabbit had shot in the head.

"What just happened?" Rabbit asked. "Did I see that?"

"Tarnation, Miss Clem," Hank chuckled. He strapped on his quiver and slung his bow over his shoulder. He picked up an oil lamp and handed it to Rabbit. "I swear, you are above the bend."

Boone scratched his jaw. Who was Clementine Johanssen? Better yet, *what* was she?

"Hank, how much dynamite would it take to seal this mine at the entrance?" Clementine stuffed her claw in her coat and tucked away her baton. She carried the pale devil's sword at her side.

Hank winced as he reached for the lanterns. He handed one off to Boone. "Well, I reckon it shouldn't take more'n a keg. Seal this adit and prob'ly bring down the roof of this cavern and all the stopes too, since ain't none of them been timbered like they did at the front of the mine."

The mine rumbled again as a distant cave-in shook the hill's guts. Dust and pebbles peppered them.

"Time to mosey," Clementine said, leading the way.

Hank followed, with Boone falling in beside Rabbit.

"Where are you going to get a keg of blasting powder?" Boone heard Clementine ask Hank.

He snorted. "Might be we could borrow some from Boomer down in Gayville. If not, I believe I might could rustle us up enough to get the job done." Hank looked over his shoulder. "That was a real hog killin', weren't it, Jack Rabbit?"

"Yeah. I guess."

Boone frowned. Rabbit's tongue being idle was a rare occasion.

As they made their way back out of the mine, Rabbit exchanged uneasy glances with Boone.

I know, Boone mouthed, his thoughts still reeling. He looked at Clementine and then back at Rabbit. What had Uncle Morton gotten them into? Damn, he'd picked a hell of time to give up tobacco.

"Never seen such a sight," Hank said to Clementine. "Shame to seal up all that glitter in there." He snickered. "There was this time I was a workin' on the railroad …"

EIGHTEEN

Clementine stoked the fire in the stove and then sat on the floor next to Tinker. The dog was obviously confused by this afternoon's events. "You poor little girl."

At first Tinker had yipped and shook her backend as Boone and Jack had carried Morton's bundled body to The Pyre's exam room. But her wagging tail had stilled when they'd returned to the parlor without her master, her head tilting sideways as she looked from one to the other and then watched them head out the door. Now, she rested her chin on her paws, glancing back and forth between Clementine and the doorway to the exam room.

"I know you don't understand why your master isn't coming."

Tinker whined softly, aiming another look toward the exam room. Periodically since the men had left, Tinker would freeze with her ears perked. Clementine had a feeling the dog was listening for Morton's footfalls, as she must have done countless times in the past.

"Ah, sweetie. This must be so confusing for you. I wish I could make you understand that he's not coming back." She stroked Tinker's head. "But the boys will be back in the morning to see you again."

Tinker whimpered, covering her nose with her paws.

Clementine tucked the blankets tightly around her. "There's a chill in the air but that stove will warm us up directly." She rose and smiled down at Tinker. "I promise I'll take good care of your master and give him a sendoff worthy of a great Viking *jarl*."

She nudged the knobby bone Hank had dropped off earlier under Tinker's nose and left her to rest. In the exam room, Clementine peeled back the waxed canvas and gently laid out Morton on the table.

Her thoughts returned to the Golden Echo mine ...

After they'd emerged from the mine, Boone and Rabbit had bundled Morton's body in a waxed canvas Hank carried on long trips "just in case." Then they'd loaded him onto Fred the mule behind Hank for the ride down to Gayville and back to Deadwood.

The sun dipped toward the western horizon during the trip, the growing shadows accompanied by cooler temperatures. Conversation had been a commodity in short supply other than Hank verbally evaluating the strengths and shortcomings of oxen versus mules as draft animals. By the time they reached the outskirts of town, Clementine was reasonably sure that not only were mules the proper choice on short smooth roads, but also a sure-footed mule was preferable to a horse.

After helping deliver Morton's body, Hank gathered Fenrir and Fred the mule. "I'll take care of these two, Miss Clem. After, I believe I'm feelin' the need for a nip of Kansas sheep dip." He must have read the question in her eyes. "That's whiskey."

"Thank you, Hank. I'll see you in the morning." After the day they'd had, she could use a tall glass of whiskey herself—and not that watered-down tongue oil they served drunkards down at Yellow Strike Saloon.

Hank started to lead the horse and mule away, but then stopped and looked back. "You done real good today, Miss Clem. I'm heartened you're okay after that ruckus." With a wink, he was on his way down the street toward the stable.

After a short discussion, Boone and Jack agreed Clementine should be the one to prepare their uncle's body. They would hold his service the next morning up at the graveyard. Boone and

Rabbit said their farewells after paying a visit to Tinker. Clementine watched them cross the slushy street, her heart heavy. Distancing themselves from their uncle's body for the night, given its condition, was probably for the best. They were fortunate to have each other to lean on during their grief.

... Clementine frowned down at what remained of their uncle. "I'm so sorry, Morton. This wasn't your fight."

She extracted the tattered undergarments from his torso, cringing slightly at the stench of decay on the cloth. They would need to be burned.

"They set you adrift in the cold."

She had a feeling it was the dirty animals passing for men in Lead that Boone had told her about on the trip back to town who were responsible for beating Morton and robbing him of his belongings. She wanted to gut them for what they did to his poor hinny. Was what they'd done to Morton simply the heartless act of greedy men? Or was it the result of something more sinister? A thoughtless killing? It could have been a sacrifice. The assholes in Lead must have known what would happen to this poor man. Either death from exposure or worse. It was nothing short of torture.

No, murder.

Her fists clenched, anger welling.

Besides his battered face and broken nose, she found multiple parallel lacerations on his torso. Deep cuts, undoubtedly caused by the claws of a *Bahkauv*.

The horror he'd felt in his final moments were visible by his gaping mouth and wide eyes. She closed his eyelids and placed coins over each, her hands trembling from rage.

She looked away, taking a calming breath, and thought of her amma's words: *Strength in serenity*.

Why was this man's death affecting her more than usual?

Could it be she knew too much about him from his nephews? Or was it simply guilt?

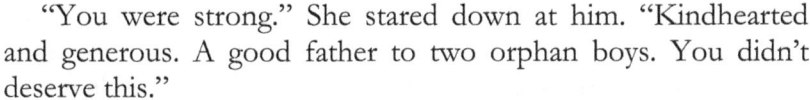

"You were strong." She stared down at him. "Kindhearted and generous. A good father to two orphan boys. You didn't deserve this."

Clementine closed her eyes, trying not to think about the injustice suffered by this innocent. *"Strength in serenity,"* she repeated several times. Her body relaxed, the tension in her muscles easing.

She began cleaning and closing up Morton's wounds as best she could, preparing him for the morning committal. She had the perfect item to place in his casket to help him have a safe journey to the afterlife—a small knife she'd picked up in her travels. The handle was made of bone with a ship carved into it.

"Why did you leave the trail and head toward the mine?" she asked as she worked. "Did you see something up there? Or did one of the *Bahkauv* chase you into the mine? Or drag you there?"

Her job would be so much easier if the dead could talk.

A short time later, Tinker whimpered in the parlor and then barked softly.

Clementine stilled. A rush of air moved past her. Someone was in The Pyre with her.

She grabbed her Eagle Claw from where it lay on the other exam table and slipped it over her hand. She hadn't yet taken the time to clean off the sticky blood.

She flattened herself against the wall near the entrance to the hallway, clawed hand raised and ready to strike.

The soft clunk of sturdy heels on wood approached from the back door. The footfalls stopped on the other side of the entryway.

The scent of sandalwood tickled her nose.

"Clementine?" Hildegard said, her voice calm and steady.

Blowing out a breath of relief, Clementine lowered her claw. She stepped into the hallway. "Good evening, Hildegard."

Hildegard's eyes widened when she saw the Eagle Claw. "I'll endeavor to be more careful henceforth." She smiled, but her gaze remained on the claw.

"Come," Clementine said and led her visitor into the parlor. Once there, she motioned her to sit in the chair next to Tinker's bed and the warm stove.

"I presume the injury you suffered at Kee Luk has healed?" Hildegard settled into the chair.

"It was merely a flesh wound, and I am *ein Scharfrichter*, after all." Clementine used the name Miss Hundt had called her, liking the guttural sound of it. "I assume you are familiar with an Executioner's robust constitution?"

"It is a strength revered and yet reviled by many *others*." Hildegard laced her fingers together. "I apologize for the intrusion this evening."

"It's quite all right." She slipped off the claw and set it on the parlor desk.

"I'm sorry about greeting you like that," Clementine said. "After today's activities, I'm still swinging at shadows." She sat on the corner of the desk.

"I'm anxious to learn of your adventure." Hildegard stared at Clementine's bloodstained pants. "Or, judging by your appearance, is *ordeal* a more accurate description?"

"*Test* is more correct." Clementine frowned down at the Eagle Claw and, without wasting any more time on niceties, recounted the day's events to Hildegard. She left nothing out, pausing only to offer hot tea from the stovetop to her guest.

Hildegard made no attempt to interrupt Clementine, offering nothing in reply except a furrowed brow and a nod occasionally.

When Clementine had finished, Hildegard sipped from her teacup and gazed at Tinker, who was dozing with her nose under the blanket. The dog had apparently grown bored with Clementine's tale.

"This is Mr. Morton's canine?" she asked.

Clementine nodded.

"And you have prepared the man for burial?"

She nodded again. "I was almost finished when you arrived."

"Since leaving the mine, have you experienced anything peculiar? Any occurrences that you would find difficult to describe or explain?"

She thought of the return trip to Deadwood. "No. Nothing."

Hildegard continued to regard Tinker. "The presence of *Bahkauv* does not surprise me. You are perhaps aware that they are often used in packs as a show of force."

"I am now." Clementine hadn't battled a *Bahkauv* before today, only heard and read about them.

"They are quite capable combatants." Hildegard shot her a quick smile. "Unless challenged by an Executioner, that is."

"They made good practice."

"And your companions returned unscathed as well." It was a statement rather than a question.

"Mostly." Hank and Boone had both been bruised, sure to feel the pains of their battles in the morning. "Worthy men, all three."

"But the pale devil you mentioned, I believe you are referring to what we have long called *ein weißer Hund*."

Clementine crossed her arms. " 'White dog,' huh? Where do they come from?"

She shrugged. "Their kind came to the Black Forest long before my time. Their history is generally unknown. Most are now used as guard dogs, obeying their master's wishes."

Clementine repeated the name in German. "White dog" seemed far too tame for an *other* of his strength. Boone's "pale devil" seemed more fitting.

Hildegard set her teacup down. "Due to their unbending loyalty and ferocity, they are often given greater responsibility."

"The *Bahkauv* were certainly at his command."

"Your patron, Masterson," Hildegard said, staring out the window, her brow furrowed in thought. "He forbade you to go to Gayville. Why would he do that? If you did …" She paused, tapping her fingertips together. Her gaze returned to Clementine. "Naturally, you would perform your duties and destroy any *others*, at least those forbidden to use the gate, as well as their pets. This would then leave the gate unguarded. He'd know that by simply performing the duties you were born to, you would jeopardize his machinations."

Clementine had thought this idea through as well upon leaving the mine. "I believe the white dog's presence at the mine was Masterson's attempt to control and guard the gate in the Golden Echo mine."

"You are certain Masterson directed *der weißer Hund*?"

You have defied the master, the white dog had said, indicating that they shared a benefactor. Then he'd kept repeating, *I implore the devourer*, which had reminded Clementine of her mother and spurred her rage, so she'd executed him. But back to Hildegard's question ...

She nodded at Hildegard. "It would seem so, but what of this?" She pulled the *caper-sus* ring from her waist pocket and handed it to Hildegard. "I took this from the ashes of the white dog. The gun hands ..." Clementine hesitated at the sound of the expression, and then corrected herself. "The *men* accompanying me into the mine had also seen this on the white dog's hand prior to today's event."

Hildegard took the ring and studied it. "I spoke again with Miss Hundt since you and I last talked. One of her many roles is a keeper of historical records." She handed the ring back to Clementine with a scowl. "*Caper-sus* is the coupling of *Bovidae* and *sus Scrofa*, in more general terms, goat and swine. Long ago in the old country, this signified the wearer's loyalty to a master. But it was more than loyalty—it was fidelity. Devotion. Total obedience. The wearer of this symbol would gratefully sacrifice their life for their master. It was considered an honor to do so. In time, imaginative individuals became involved whose unique roles were to devise sadistic, tortuous deaths for the entertainment of the masters."

Hildegard dropped her gaze to the ring in Clementine's hand, her forehead drawn. "It is also representative of the cloven-hoofed. It was believed by some that *Bovidae*, specifically a unique type that could be described as goat-like, were used to pull the chariots of the *others* from one world to the next, allowing certain individuals to travel freely between worlds."

Clementine held the ring under the light from the oil lamp, scrutinizing it yet again. "This symbol is ancient?"

"Perhaps. Perhaps not. There were many variations. It was once thought the symbol bestowed the qualities of a warrior on the wearer. Some also believed it was ceremonial. That it could be used to aid in summoning."

"The summoning of what?"

"Creatures that should remain gone from this plane of

existence." Hildegard shrugged. "In any case, it fell into disuse over the years. According to the scrolls of time, its believers destroyed each other or simply died out."

While Clementine pondered this news, Hildegard stood and walked to the window. "Miss Hundt and I discussed the recent appearance of the *caper-sus* symbol at length. Neither of us has seen it for many years. We believe it is possible that the *caper-sus* has been resurrected to signify a shifting of sovereignty and dominion. That it is meant to intimidate and repress any who oppose."

Clementine lowered the ring. "Masterson is preparing to … what?"

"We are not certain. But someone is attempting to stop him." She glanced at Clementine. "Or it could simply be a struggle for dominance."

"The men who tried to kill me at the Kee Luk pigsty were each wearing one of these rings."

"It is possible you were simply in the way. If you recall that night, the initial blow you took to the head didn't kill you. It is conceivable that you were intentionally left alive."

"There was a severed hand with the ring *inside* the pen."

Hildegard gazed down the street. "Deception is not unheard of among *others*, same as humans. Perhaps someone was cleaning house, as it were."

"If I—"

"*Ruhe!*" Hildegard shushed her. She stiffened for a moment, and then rushed over to Clementine's side. "It has begun, *Scharfrichter*. You must be extremely careful now. Remember, trust is dangerous." She glanced at the front window and then back at Clementine. "It would be beneficial for both of us if our conversations remain unrevealed to others."

Without further explanation, Hildegard dashed out of the parlor down the hall leading to the back door.

Bam!

Something slammed into the front door.
Clementine stood. Tinker raised her head.
Bam! The door rattled in its frame.
She grabbed her Eagle Claw. Tinker growled and tried to rise.
Bam! The front door of The Pyre flew open and banged against the wall. Cold gusts from the street swirled into the room. A dark figure filled the doorway.

Chills spread through Clementine's limbs for more reasons than the weather. She slipped her fingers into her claw.

"Miss Johanssen." Masterson stepped into the room, closing the door behind him. The dim light from her lantern didn't penetrate the shadows under the brim of his black top hat. "Greetings."

Her stomach clenched as he walked closer. "Good evening, Mr. Masterson. I wasn't expecting you to stop by and attempt to break down my door. Did you find the handle unsatisfactory to the touch?"

He waved off her sarcasm. "I trust you have finished your work for the evening. Surely you've accomplished enough for one day." He moved over to the wood stove.

Tinker snarled up at him as he neared. When Masterson stopped and looked down at the dog, she whimpered and lay down, burying her nose in the blankets.

"What's this?" he asked. He bent over and pulled the blankets away from the dog's body. "You've been in a tussle." Tinker whined as he stroked her head, glancing toward Clementine. "Deadwood is dangerous," he continued. "But you already know that."

Clementine watched as he grabbed the iron fire poker Hank had fashioned, opened the stove's door, and shuffled the glowing coals. Tinker jumped when he slammed the small door shut.

Masterson stood, still holding the iron poker. He looked at the piece of metal, appearing to study it. "Interesting. Well crafted." He tested its heft. "You've been busy, Miss Johanssen."

When his gaze lifted to her, his face showed no emotion, his dark eyes watchful from under the brim of his hat.

"Of course," she said. "Tending the dead is a booming business in the Black Hills."

"True. So little time for the refinements or diversions that might otherwise supplement one's life."

He knew what had happened today at the Golden Echo mine, of that she had little doubt. The question was, what did he plan to do about it? His *white dog* had not finished his prediction of what the "master" would do about her insubordination before she delivered her swift execution.

"I find that spare time is a rarity these days," she said.

"No fine meals." He continued as if she hadn't spoken, and walked toward the front window where Hildegard had stood moments before. "No cordial libations with acquaintances." He sniffed several times, while he stared into the darkness beyond. "No carnal embraces." He strolled across the room, brushing the snow from his fancy black frock coat. He took another deep breath at the end of the hallway that led toward the back door, searching the shadows.

While he was busy playing hound dog to Hildegard's fox, Clementine extracted a clean rag from her desk.

He turned to face her. "No travel, then?" he asked, slowly shaking his head as if her situation saddened him.

She inspected her Eagle Claw, pretending boredom at their conversation topic. "What is it I can help you with this evening, Mr. Masterson?" She raised the claw to examine the blades in the light of the lantern, scrubbing the muslin across the dried blood.

A glance his way found his attention fixed on her claw. "My reasons for this visit aren't entirely social in nature, Miss Johanssen. I mean to—"

"Excuse me for a moment," she said, interrupting what he surely meant to be an impressive and menacing speech. She slipped past him, ignoring the foul scent of his kind, and stepped into the exam room. She returned to her desk in the parlor a moment later with a bottle of alcohol. She soaked the muslin with alcohol, taking a long swig herself before clunking the bottle on the table. "Please. Do continue with your lecture."

She began scrubbing the metal to a shine, meeting his gaze over the blades periodically as she worked.

"You have little time to spare for niceties, yet you find time to travel to Gayville," he finally continued.

"I wouldn't consider travel to Gayville a nicety."

"And still, you went."

"I did."

"Against the conditions of the contract. I was specific. Gayville was to be left untouched."

"I simply traveled through Gayville. I conducted no business in that town."

His nostrils flared. " 'Gayville and its general locale,' if I remember the wording correctly."

Clementine shrugged. "In my estimation, my business was not in Gayville or its *general locale*. Therefore, I have abided by the contract." She cocked an eyebrow, holding one shiny blade up in the lamplight. "Out of curiosity, why is it you are so adamant about my need to avoid that place?"

"Simply a concern for your health."

"My health. Of course."

He pulled a gold pocket watch from his vest, checked it, and snapped it closed. "Keep to the business of the contract, Miss Johanssen. Abide by the agreement." A vein pulsed at his temple. "Executioners are rare. The necessity to find another would irritate and distress me greatly."

Clementine worked the fingers of the claw. A little oil, perhaps. "I will abide by the agreement." By her interpretation of the agreement.

"Excellent."

"Oh, that reminds me." She pulled the ring with the *caper-sus* emblem from her pocket and tossed it to him. Hildegard and she could spend days speculating, but Clementine's patience was running thin. "This belongs to you?"

He stepped closer to the lantern and examined the ring, his upper lip curling. "*Ego rip a corpore eius faucium.*" He growled under his breath.

"What was that?" Clementine played dumb.

She hadn't expected the threat of such violence at the mere sight of the ring. *Why would he threaten to rip my throat from my body?* Like what happened to Morton in that damned mine? Her body tensed, rage filling her with the urge to kill again.

Strength in serenity. Her amma's voice filled her head, quelling the anger.

Masterson could certainly try to kill her.

Or had he meant someone else's throat?

Discretion dictated a measured approach if Clementine were to learn the answers to these questions. Hildegard was correct. She must be more cautious from now on.

Masterson regained his composure, but his eyes stayed dark and narrowed. "Where did you get this?"

"They're not hard to come by these days."

He cursed and threw the ring against the back wall of the parlor. "Remember your purpose here."

She inspected another shiny blade in the light. "As I said, I will abide by the contract."

"I'm encouraged by your obedience." He tossed the iron poker on the floor next to the stove, narrowly missing Tinker's head. "Don't risk my anger in the future," he warned, and then marched out of the parlor, leaving the door open behind him.

Clementine closed and locked the door in his wake.

"Tinker." She turned back to the dog, who stared up at her with big eyes. "I may need to execute that bastard before this is done."

NINETEEN

The next day ...

Clementine's morning started with a farewell to Boone's and Jack's uncle. She officiated the service while the sun shone in a cloudless sky and warmed the moment for Boone and Jack, both clean-shaven and dressed in fine shirts and trousers.

For once, Ling and Gart had everything prepared. They'd even put together a first-rate casket of spruce and knotty pine. She'd like to think their diligence was due to her stressing the importance of this particular burial, but it probably had more to do with the bonus coins she promised them if they did a fine job.

Neither Boone nor Jack seemed to mind the references to Odin and Valhalla during her service. She was pretty sure that she even heard Boone humming when she sang the Norse funeral dirge to help Morton begin his new journey.

Through it all, the two orphans had stood close enough that their shoulders touched. Boone patted Jack's back occasionally, each of them sniffing in turn. Neither had spoken much at all, which was understandable.

Before they'd walked away from the grave to leave Ling and Gart to finish their part, Jack cleared his throat and said, "He's gone, Booney."

"But I'm right here," Boone responded.

She envied their lifelong bond. Did they have any idea how rare such a friendship was in these troubled times?

Clementine led the way back to The Pyre, unlocking the door and leaving it open behind her.

"Hank is taking the horses to the livery." Boone stomped the slushy snow from his boots outside the door and stepped in, shedding his coat. "Said he'd be back directly."

Jack followed Boone through the door, kicked it closed, and dumped an armload of wood in the crib next to the stove. "Sure is a purty day Uncle Morton gave us. Sunny and warm enough so's the snow is getting heavy and drippy."

Clementine noticed Jack staring toward the corner of the parlor near the door. Tinker was too. What were they looking at? The coat rack?

Jack shook his head, and then turned back to where Tinker sat, next to the stove. "Hey, Tink," he said in a soft voice. "I heard you howlin' through the door." He knelt beside the dog, whose tail thumped on the floor. He tugged playfully on her ear. "I got some good news." He pulled a length of oak wrapped in leather straps from under his coat and set it beside her blanket.

Clementine slid out of her coat, offering to take Jack's, and hung them both on the rack. Over at her parlor desk, she lifted a linen cloth that had been covering an array of food. The aroma of fresh bread and meat and more made her stomach growl.

"Hank set out some food for us this morning. Biscuits. Boiled eggs. Bacon. Hot coffee on the stove. Peach preserves." She smiled down at the jar, shaking her head. "Only Odin knows where he found peach preserves in Deadwood at this time of year. That man is a wonder, I swear." She blew her cold nose into her kerchief, seeing that Hank had also brought a chair from the other room so they could all sit while they ate.

"Almost got the makin's of a good San Francisco hangtown fry. Just need oysters." Jack played with Tinker's ears, glancing occasionally around the room with a frown.

"I'll never understand how you can eat oysters." Boone wrinkled his nose. "Slimy little buggers. Smell reminds me of those frog legs in Louisiana. I'll take a steak and a plate full of fried potatoes."

"That's fine, Booney. Don't fret. Food for sophisticates, that's me." Jack grinned. "Ain't meant to appeal to commoners like you."

"Bah." Boone eyed the food on the desk, reaching for the coffee. "Damn. Hank is a man I could ride with."

Jack stood and grabbed a piece of bacon. "Surely could. Way he handled himself in the mine. Always seems to know what and when. Helluva sailor."

Jack stuffed the piece of bacon in his mouth and took a bite of biscuit, then returned to the floor beside Tinker. "Okay, little Tink. Miss Clementine has you almost mended, so it's my job to get you movin'." He unwrapped the leather from the stick.

"Jack, is that ..." *a chair leg*, Clementine finished in her head. She watched as Jack pulled the blanket from Tinker's body.

"You're lookin' fine. What we have here is a new leg. Tooled the leather myself." He busied himself measuring, cutting, tying, and re-measuring, all the while talking to Tinker. "Uncle Mort always said, 'Anything happens to me, you take good care of Tink.' And that's what I mean to ..." He wiped his eyes with his sleeve. After a moment, he continued, "That leg is from the finest oak chair I could find. Course, the hotel ain't gonna be pleased about a three-legged chair, but ..."

Clementine approached Boone, who had just finished pouring two cups of coffee. He held out one to her and then sank into a chair.

"Thanks," she said, sitting down across from him. "Now that you're finished here, I imagine you two will be heading home to Santa Fe." She would miss them both. It wasn't only their companionship she'd come to enjoy, but the energy they infused into The Pyre and the life within it. Namely hers. Masterson was right. Her life had grown downright stale.

Boone leaned his elbow on the arm of the chair and looked

into her eyes for a long moment. "Uncle Morton has a man, Carlos. He knows the business. He's been taking care of things since we left. We," he said, pointing between Jack and himself, "haven't had the chance to talk about what comes next."

"Don't forget the contract Uncle Mort signed here in Deadwood." Jack said.

"We'll need to find out the details on that."

"There you go, Tink. Let's try that." Jack kneeled, clasping his hands under the dog's belly, and lifted her.

Tinker yipped excitedly and worked the stick in a circle on the wood floor. *Thunk-thunk-thunk.* While she hobbled, the leather tangled and the stick twisted up and back toward her tail.

"That's okay," Jack said, drawing Tinker back to him. "I see what's wrong. Let me fix it. Stop licking me," he said, laughing.

Clementine watched Jack with the dog for a moment, smiling at the two. "It's probably safe to assume we took care of your uncle's killer in that mine."

"I don't know. Maybe." Boone stared at his cup of coffee. "This feels unfinished to me."

"It isn't!" Jack looked up at Boone while adjusting the leather straps.

"What isn't what?" Clementine asked.

"We're not finished. The bastards in that mine might have done the killing, but I want to find the one who pulled the trigger. Sticks in my craw, Booney, and I mean to kill anyone—any *thing*—that had a part in Uncle Mort's death."

The determination in Jack's voice sent a shiver down Clementine's spine. No words from her would offer a measure of peace to ease his anger and grief. He would see his uncle avenged or die in the attempt.

Clementine sent Boone a raised brow. Was he of the same mindset under his seemingly calm exterior?

"It's not finished," he told Jack. "Probably best if we head home, though. Take care of a few things. Then we'll be back."

He nodded.

There it was, then. The decision had been made.

She sipped her coffee, regarding each man in turn. Both looked beaten down, worn like overworked oxen at the end of summer. Yet something shone through their weary exteriors. An inner quality. A resilience. A toughness. Pillars of granite. Their uncle would be proud.

Then again, he might call them foolish for not walking away from what could very easily end in death.

"There you go, Tink," Jack said. "Let's try that." He lifted the dog again, his face close to hers as he tightened his makeshift rig. Tinker snuck in a nose lick before trying her new leg again. He let her test her weight on it for a few steps. She stumbled and almost toppled, but he steadied her with gentle hands. "I got ya, girl." *Thunk thunk thunk.* "Looks like you're tryin' to kill a beetle! Ha! Look, Booney."

Boone sat forward, grinning at the two. "I believe that should work, Rabbit, soon as she learns to use it. Fine piece of work you've done."

"Thanks, Booney."

The three of them watched Tinker for several minutes as she stumbled and practiced, thunking around the parlor while her tail wagged.

Soon, Clementine felt Boone's gaze on her. When she looked his way, he glanced down to where her hands were wrapped around her coffee tin.

"What are you, Clementine Johanssen?"

His tone was curious, not insulting.

If she answered him with honesty, it would seal an unwritten deal between them. At this point, they could still walk away none the wiser beyond having a tall tale to share over a drink from time to time.

She looked at Jack, who was watching her as well. A grin crept up his face as she stared back. "Booney's havin' trouble believin' you're a new kinda Greek Amazon."

"Are you sure you want to know?" she asked Boone. She already knew where Jack stood on this. "The truth may not be palatable. Right now, you could leave and not look back, no harm done, no risks beyond perils of the trail."

"We both know it's too late for that," he answered.

She nodded. So be it. She set her coffee tin on the desk. "Follow me. I'd like to show you something."

Jack removed the peg leg, wrapped the blanket around Tinker, and grabbed another piece of bacon. "Here, Tink. Work on this and I'll be back for another lesson in a minute." He tossed the bacon to her and fell in line behind Boone.

Clementine led them down the hall to her quarters. "If I can't convince you to leave this fight, you need to have a better idea of what you're up against."

They hesitated in her doorway as she pulled the leather necklace with the key from her chemise. "Come closer." She unlocked the cabinet and swung the doors wide, standing aside.

They joined her in front of her wall of weapons. She watched their faces as they looked over each piece, not quite as lively as Hank during his first viewing of the collection, but still animated. Even Boone.

Their curiosity turned to wonder as she instructed them to explore the weapons with their hands. Each reached out to touch, Jack leaning toward the shiny metal of different blades, while Boone leaned toward the items with carefully worked wood and well-conditioned leather handles.

Periodically, Jack would shoot a frown toward her bed.

"This, I recognize." Boone gripped the bone handle of the black curved blade she had taken in victory from the white dog. "And this, too." He pointed the blade at the Eagle Claw she had finished cleaning and oiling and returned to its usual place the night before.

She smiled. "One of my favorites."

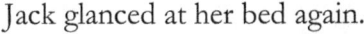

Jack glanced at her bed again.

"Is there something bothering you about my bed, Jack?"

"I, uh ... I don't ... no." He turned back to the weapons and made an effort to be particularly interested in one and then another.

Clementine looked at her bed. There was nothing out of the ordinary about it that she could see.

"What's this used for?" He pointed at a wooden rod about four feet long with a steel collar at one end. Inch-long spikes lined the inside of the collar, which was open enough for a man's neck to squeeze through.

She walked over to the cabinet. "That is called a *Mannfänger*, which translates to 'Man Catcher.' " She took it down. "You see, if the jaws are pushed against the neck, these springs allow the jaws to open. They snap shut once the victim's neck passes through. The spikes assure that the captured individual behaves." She grinned, leaning closer with it. "Would you like me to demonstrate?"

"Nope! I got it." Jack touched one of the spikes and grimaced. "Don't fuck with Miss Clementine, is what all of these weapons say to me."

Boone took the Man Catcher from her, turning it this way and that. "It looks downright evil." He ran his finger around the outside of the collar. "Used this on some poor devils, have ya?"

"Not devils, but yes. A few times. It's very effective."

He looked at her. "You're a killer?"

"I kill when necessary." She took the weapon from him and returned it to its hook. "I'm an Executioner."

He nodded slowly. "Things are going to turn sideways from here on out, aren't they?"

Clementine chuckled. "That's one way of saying it."

"I'll tell you what, Miss Clementine," Jack said, keeping his back to her bed. "What I would appreciate is a little schoolin' in some of this ..." he waved his hand back and forth at the cabinet, "this arsenal."

"I think that's probably a good idea." She closed the cabinet and locked it, leaning back against it. "If you two are set on seeing this through, you'll need to work on your close combat skills. We can decide later which best suits you."

Jack scowled toward her bed again, his head cocked.

"Rabbit!" Boone crossed his arms. "What in the hell are you looking at? You've been distracted since the committal."

Jack rubbed his chin, staring at Boone "I ..." He cringed.

"What?"

"I been seein' ... well, I been seein' this, uh ..." He pointed his thumb over his shoulder at the bed.

"WHAT?!"

"Ever since ... over by the bed." He ran his hands through his hair, glancing at the bed again. "Nope." He shook his head.

"Rabbit!"

"Dangnabbit! It's Uncle Mort. He's standin' over at the end of Miss Clementine's bed making faces at me."

Boone's jaw dropped.

Jack shook a finger at him. "Don't call me *loco*."

Clementine peered around Boone to the foot of her bed. "Your uncle is there now?"

Jack double-checked and then nodded, looking unhappy about it.

"You've been through a lot, Rab—" Boone started.

"Shut up, Boone."

"Since the funeral?" When he nodded, Clementine put her hand on his shoulder. "Does Morton speak to you? Do you hear him make any sounds?"

"He makes croakin' sounds. Babbles sometimes too, like a young'un learnin' to talk."

"Maybe if you get a little rest ..." Boone said, scratching his head as he stared at the end of her bed.

"Shut the hell up, Boone."

"I'm just trying to hel—"

Tap. Tap. Tap.

Someone was at the back door.

"Expecting company?" Boone asked her.

Clementine shook her head.

"I'll see who it is." He pointed at Jack. "Maybe you can help him."

"Be careful," Clementine called after him. She turned back to find Jack looking at the end of her bed again, shaking his head. "What is it?"

He blinked, his eyes watery. "It can't be Uncle Mort. Can it? I don't know what to do." His shoulders slumped.

She heard the back door open.

"It's all right." She squeezed his shoulder. "I believe you."

"Clementine!" Boone called, his voice higher than normal. "You need to see this!"

She stared Jack in the eyes. "I know what you are seeing."

"Holy shit," she heard Boone say and hurried to the back door in time to see him step outside.

She followed him out into the snow.

"Is it customary to receive deliveries this way?" Boone asked, kneeling beside a dead man left by the back of the building.

"No. Hank brings most through the front." Speaking of her assistant, where was he? Still grooming Fenrir and Fred the mule?

"There's a piece of paper pinned to his chest with a knife." Boone said.

That was a long way from ordinary as well. "Let me take a look."

She kneeled next to Boone, the cold snow soaking through her denim pants. The lapels of the man's coat and shirt had been torn aside, exposing his chest. The knife had been thrust through the piece of paper directly into the center of a large scar in the shape of a brand over his heart. His body had not begun to decay, the smell of death faint.

"That's the same symbol as what's on the rings," Boone said.

She nodded, frowning. "A brand instead of a ring," she said under her breath. "That suggests the possibility of a deeper commitment to the cult."

"Cult?"

"I'll tell you about it later." She looked closer at the knife. It was a slender blade. She thought back to the man who had passed through The Pyre earlier in the week. He'd been executed. His Achilles tendon sliced. *Disabled by the severing of his tendon. Then, a skillful thrust with a slender blade,* she'd written in her notes.

She shifted to his ankles. Both of his tendons had been sliced, probably with the same thin blade that was currently stuck in his chest. If she checked his side, did he have the same puncture that led to a slow, painful death?

"Why cut his ankles?" Boone asked, still down at the dead man's feet.

"To hobble him. That would allow the killer to take as much time as he wanted to finish him."

Boone blew out a whistle. "That's cold-hearted."

"Welcome to life at the coffin joint." She frowned at him. "You can still ride away from this."

He studied her for a moment. "No. I don't think I can."

"Let's see if this one still has all his teeth." She parted his stiff lips, pushing his lower jaw down. "Yep."

Boone had the same look as Tinker when she tried to understand English. "Teeth? What does that mean?"

"Someone in town has a fetish for canine teeth." Clementine pulled the knife from the body and held it up. "Huh. Part of the blade has snapped off inside the body."

"Ouch."

She picked up the note. "There's no blood on the paper. This man was dead before the note was pinned to him."

"Christ." Boone stood, wiping his hands on his coat.

She read the letter in silence:

Salutations, Clementine Johanssen,

I find myself once again in a position, as necessity dictates, to complete a task that has been delegated to you. I find this sort of work tedious and grow weary of accommodating your shortcomings. It is difficult to muster even a modicum of confidence in anyone so derelict in her duties.

And yet, it is my fervent hope that you find within yourself the ability to complete your duties autonomously and expeditiously.

In addition, I will expect recompense for my favored dagger. It was crafted in das Rheintal in Deutschland and I expect replacement in kind.

At the bottom, a *P* served as a signature.

She looked up to see Boone leaning against the doorframe, rubbing his shoulder as he scowled down at the dead man.

Jack joined them, standing in the doorway. "About what you said, Miss Clementine ..." He looked at the body and blinked. "Another one up the flume, huh? They usually get dropped at the back door like this?"

"Nope, this one is special," Boone answered for her. His gaze met hers. "What's the letter say?"

Clementine handed him the piece of paper. "Someone is attempting to communicate with me. Apparently, I haven't been performing my duties satisfactorily here in Deadwood."

"No shit?" Jack said, reading the letter over Boone's shoulder.

She ran her fingertips over the *caper-sus* scar on the corpse's cold chest. "But that's all about to change."

The End ... for now

If you enjoyed this episode of the Deadwood Undertaker Series, read on to learn about the Deadwood Mysteries, Ann's award-winning series that started it all, and the first chapter of Book 2, *A Long Way from Ordinary*.

More Books by Ann

Books in the Deadwood Mystery Series

WINNER of the 2010 Daphne du Maurier Award for Excellence in Mystery/Suspense

WINNER of the 2011 Romance Writers of America® Golden Heart Award for Best Novel with Strong Romantic Elements

Welcome to Deadwood—the Ann Charles version. The world I have created is a blend of present day and past, of fiction and non-fiction. What's real and what isn't is for you to determine as the series develops, the characters evolve, and I write the stories line by line. I will tell you one thing about the series—it's going to run on for quite a while, and Violet Parker will have to hang on and persevere through the crazy adventures I have planned for her. Poor, poor Violet. It's a good thing she has a lot of gumption to keep her going!

Shorts in the Deadwood Mystery Series

The Deadwood Shorts collection includes short stories featuring the characters of the Deadwood Mystery series. Each tale not only explains more of Violet's history, but also gives a little history of the other characters you know and love from the series. Rather than filling the main novels in the series with these short side stories, I've put them into a growing Deadwood Shorts collection for more reading fun.

About the Authors

Ann Charles is a *USA Today* bestselling author who writes award-winning mysteries that are splashed with humor, romance, paranormal, and whatever else she feels like throwing into the mix. When she is not dabbling in fiction, arm-wrestling with her children, attempting to seduce her husband, or arguing with her sassy cat, she is daydreaming of lounging poolside at a fancy resort with a blended margarita in one hand and a great book in the other.

Facebook (Personal Page):
http://www.facebook.com/ann.charles.author

Facebook (Author Page):
http://www.facebook.com/pages/Ann-Charles/37302789804?ref=share

Twitter (as Ann W. Charles):
http://twitter.com/AnnWCharles

Ann Charles Website:
http://www.anncharles.com

Sam Lucky likes to build things—from Jeep engines to Old West buildings to fun stories. When he is not writing, feeding his kids, attempting to seduce his wife, or tending the goldurn cats, he is planning food-based booksigning/road trips with his wife and working on one of his many home-improvement projects.

Sam Lucky's Website:
http://www.samlucky.com

Glossary

Adit —
A horizontal passage leading into a mine.

Bandoleer —
A belt of leather worn over the shoulder or strapped to a saddle. Small loops of leather laced around the length of the belt to hold firearm cartridges.
*"Always gotta be showin' off yer **bandoleer** to the ladies."*

Buckskin —
(Dime) Light tan, roughly the color of tanned deerskin, normally with dark brown to black mane, tail and legs.
*"That **buckskin** of yours eats as much as a piebald and a roan put together."*

Caboose —
Prison.
"Do that in front of the marshal and he'll put yer caboose in the calaboose."

Card Sharp —
A card player who can, by hook or by crook, through the course of a game of cards, relieve you of any moneys you may have thought yours, down to the lint balls stuck in the seams of your pockets.

Daisy —
Good or excellent.

Dirt Nap —
A state of permanent rest (dead).
*"All I did was shoot him. Now he's takin' a **dirt nap**."*

Flannel Mouth —
A smooth or fancy talker as in a salesman or politician.
*"Ever' time that **flannel mouth** flaps his lips I get itchin' to use my pig sticker."*

Gaited —
Get walking, go.

Groink —
Talented pigs, swine, or boar are capable of combining an oink and a grunt into one sound. (Less talented pigs tend to display characteristics of jealousy at the utterance.)
*"Oink oink oink. Oink, grunt, oink **groink**!"*

Hinny —
(Minny) Offspring of a male horse and a female donkey. (Mules are the reverse.) In comparison to a mule, they are known to be slightly smaller with smaller ears, a more horse-like head, and stout legs.
*"Ain't no secret that Minny the **hinny** is a **hinny** and a half."*

Jävla gris! —
Fucking pig!
*"Hvilken **jävla gris** til middag igjen?"*

Morgan —
(Fenrir) A horse breed dating to the late 1700s known for the ability and endurance to accomplish many tasks (pulling a plow or wagon, carrying a rider and racing, for example) efficiently. Incidentally, Rabbit's mother and father owned a pair of Morgans and used them to pull the family wagon west.

Pig Sticker —
A knife or bayonet, specifically in this series. Styled like a Bowie knife, a fixed blade knife made for Jim Bowie (1796–1863), with a blade usually 6"–10" long.
*"I'm the boss, ya squeekin' shave tail. This here **pig sticker** says so."*

Piebald —
(Nickel) Piebald horses have large, irregular patches of black and white on their coats. Boone takes every opportunity to mention that Nickel is above average size and intelligence for a Piebald.
*"That **piebald** eats like a roan."*

Potter's Field —
An area in a cemetery reserved for the unidentified or those of little means (poor).

Potzblitz —
Upon my soul.
"Er ist acht Meter groß? ***Potzblitz!****"*

Puddin' Foot —
An awkward horse or person.
"Listen, flannel mouth, if you don't get that ***puddin' foot*** *on the trail, he's gonna end up takin' a dirt nap next to that shave tail I done in with my pig sticker."*

Pyre —
A structure of wood constructed with the intent to burn a body as part of a funeral. For Norsemen, or Vikings, proper funerals where the body was burned helped lead the deceased into one of the nine realms in the afterlife. The most recognized realm is Valhalla, where fallen warriors ended up. The next most recognized realm is Helheim, where those who died in a state of disgrace traveled. For example, dying of old age was considered somewhat disgraceful.

It was also customary to send the deceased to Valhalla or Helheim with grave or burial goods, things that would be useful in the next realm. For example, a sword might be included with a warrior, or a thrall (slave) might be sent along with a nobleman. How a Norseman lived his or her life determined which realm was reached.

Clementine thought it fitting to name her undertaker business The Pyre.

Roan —
A pattern on a horse characterized by an even mixture of an off-white color and white over the body of the horse with the mane, head, and legs a solid color.
"That ***roan*** *eats more'n a Morgan."*

Shave Tail —
A "green" or inexperienced person or horse.
"You tell that ***shave tail*** *he's a gonna get the workin' end of my pig sticker if'n he don't shut his flappin' lips."*

A Long Way From Ordinary

Ann Charles
Sam Lucky

"Truth is stranger than fiction, but it is because Fiction is obliged to stick to possibilities; Truth isn't."
~Mark Twain

A Long Way from Ordinary

ONE

Late Fall 1876
Deadwood, Dakota Territory

The waves of death kept crashing into The Pyre, drowning Clementine Johanssen in corpses.

Today, for the first time in weeks, her undertaker exam tables were empty. Finally, she had a moment to sort through the signs of devilry she'd been finding on more and more bodies each day. These brandings and other strange markings made on the flesh of the dead, what did they all mean when it came to Deadwood's future? To her future? Not one to sit idle while she pondered, she grabbed a bucket and brush.

Who to hunt? Who to slay? Who to let live? Answers eluded her as she worked. There was too much death clouding her vision.

She was brushing the last of the whitewash on the back wall of the parlor when the front door banged open. An icy gust swirled around her legs, peppering her with snow, blowing away the smell of wet wood walls.

Hank Varney stomped across the threshold, as he tended to do, and knocked clumps of snow and mud from his boots. "Miss Clem, you ain't gonna believe what I seen!" He waved a rolled-up news sheet above his head, then frowned at the bucket of whitewash next to her. "What are you doin' that for? We just washed that not more'n two months ago."

"Hank, would you stoke the fire, please?" She winked at her assistant and nodded toward the door. "If we're going to heat all of Deadwood in the middle of winter, we'll need the stove good and hot."

"Huh? Oh." He kicked the door shut. "Street's a bustlin' this evenin'. Word is population is growin' by a few hunerd a day now in the Hills. Guess they don't know all the good placer claims is gone already."

Clementine could believe those numbers based on the increase in her "customers." The lure of gold in the Black Hills drew fortune seekers like locusts. In turn, opportunity filled the coffers of many who preyed on those new arrivals, tempting the gold-seekers' vices and profiting from their weaknesses.

Hank hung his coat and hat on the wall pegs and turned his attention to Tinker, the three-legged dog, who was working on a chunk of beef bone near the stove while she kept Clementine company.

"Hiyo, Tinker. I see you're 'bout done wrestlin' with the cow I brung you."

He plopped down beside her, crossed his legs, and set the paper next to him on the floor. The pup wormed into his lap and nuzzled and nipped at his hand as Tinker had done nearly every day since her *compadres*, Jack "Rabbit" Fields and Boone McCreery, had left for Santa Fe weeks earlier.

Make that three weeks and a day. Not that Clementine needed to count, because Hank was.

The two gunmen had made a friend in Hank. Clementine, too, for that matter, in spite of her reservations about emotional attachments. More than once over the last few weeks she'd found herself looking toward the south, wondering if the travelers would return as they'd promised Tinker. She tempered her hope with reality. There was a lot of trail between Deadwood and Santa Fe filled with all manner of trouble, including the perils of winter weather. They might have changed their minds about returning to this cold, lawless frontier. In Santa Fe, they had a freight business to run, a ranch to work, friends to help pass the time, and probably plenty of sunshine.

If common sense ruled their actions, she doubted they'd come back. The only thing waiting for them here besides Tinker and Hank was death. Clementine could feel a storm brewing over the northern Hills. A tempest not of wind or snow, but of malicious intent and foul deeds. She'd been bred and raised to fight. They hadn't.

Neither had Hank for that matter, but no amount of warnings had convinced him to find employment elsewhere. She couldn't have wished for a better assistant or friend. Watching him play with Tinker fueled a comforting warmth she'd not experienced since leaving her childhood home many, many years ago.

The dog squirmed around to face Hank and thumped the back of his hand with the peg leg Jack had rigged for her.

"Ow! Appears to me yer better at walkin' with that thing than you are sittin' in my lap."

Tinker wiggled her rump and yipped at him.

"She's healed up real good while the boys are away, Miss Clem."

She glanced at the paper on the floor next to him. "Hank."

His attention was focused entirely on Tinker. "You know I brought you somethin', don't ya. Course I did." He drew a piece of jerky from his coat pocket. "Uh oh," he said and stuck it in his mouth, his eyes wide.

The dog scolded him with a series of quick yips.

He pulled the jerky out. "Ho ho! Tinkerdoo. I'm just foolin' with ya." He held the jerky out and she grabbed it with her teeth, carefully avoiding his fingers.

"You're a good little girl, ain't ya? Just a good little girl." He scratched behind her ears and grabbed her front paw. "Next time I'll get ya—"

"Hank." Clementine balanced the brush on the rim of the

bucket.

He stopped mid-handshake and looked up, still holding Tinker's paw, waiting for Clementine to continue. His eyes creased in the corners; his brown, wavy hair curled over his collar. For a moment, he looked much younger than his forty-plus years. Just a boy and his dog.

She pointed at the sheet of paper. "What did you read that you came to tell me?"

"Oh!" He picked up the paper. "It's the *Trailblazer*."

"So I see." Deadwood's newspaper office was located several buildings down Main Street from The Pyre.

"You remember we blasted the Bloody Bones pretty good?"

"Of course."

The whole Bloody Bones mine incident was still fresh in Clementine's memory, from what Jack had found in the adit to the battle they'd all fought in the cavern shortly thereafter.

"You remember I said two kegs should do."

She nodded. Days after what Hank liked to call the "Battle of Bloody Bones," Clementine and he had hauled two full kegs of blasting powder into the adit and placed them near the entrance to the cavern. Their intent had been to seal off the mine further in, down deep in the preexisting tunnels past the cavern. To block the natural tunnels in the hillside that their foes had used in retreat. Where and to what they had retreated, Clementine didn't know.

But as it happened, the blasts from Jack's sawed-off shotgun during the battle had triggered cave-ins that efficiently collapsed those natural tunnels. With that task done, she and Hank had decided to use the powder to bring down the side of the hill, closing off the entrance to the mine. They hoped to keep gold seekers from meddling inside of Bloody Bones and once again freeing the troublemakers hidden deep within it rocky guts.

"And you recall the *Trailblazer* had somethin' to say about the blast." Hank frowned at the paper. "*The ground shook today,* it said."

It had shaken, knocking the snow off the pine trees all around them as they watched the hillside cover the mine's entrance. Hank's mule, Fred, had plopped his hind end down on the ground and let out a squeaky wail until the rumbling stopped.

"*Big doings apparent in Gayville*, it said," he continued. "All the way to Deadwood it shook, people talkin' ever'where about it."

Tinker wiggled off his lap, thumping over to her pile of blankets by the stove where she began to gnaw on the hunk of jerky held between her paws.

"It was quite impressive," Clementine said, grinning at the memory of Hank cursing and tugging on Fred the mule so they could hightail it out of the area and back to Deadwood before they were spotted by anyone.

"Prob'ly shouldn't have used quite so much powder, I s'pose." He rubbed the back of his neck.

"It should stay sealed. At least for a while."

He shook his head again. "I surely hope so." He held the paper up for her to read. "Look here what it says."

She read the first item aloud:

Winter reaches the Black Hills

The Hills are draped with increasingly mountainous drifts of snow and thrashed by icy winds. The resiliency of Deadwood's citizens is tested to breaking, and still unfriendlier times approach as we near the beginning of winter ..."

"Not that one, Miss Clem," Hank interrupted.

"Funny, I could swear winter arrived weeks ago."

This was Clementine's first taste of the snowy season in the Black Hills, but not her first experience with severely cold weather. Her childhood had been spent enduring long, dark, harsh Norse winters. Before the snow had started, she and Hank had prepared The Pyre for all the goddess of winter had in store for them. Thanks to her booming business, she had plenty of gold and coins tucked away to pay for food and more supplies.

In short, Clementine was ready for anything Deadwood could throw at her. Anything related to weather in any case. The *other* problem she might encounter might be another story. Time would tell.

Hank stood and brushed Tinker's fur from his trousers. "Down the page a ways."

She read another:

> ### *Icy death in the streets of Deadwood*
> *Hundreds of penniless and newly arrived citizens find adequate accommodation and nourishment woefully lacking in Deadwood. Exposure kills many and threatens more ...*

"Not that one either, Miss Clem. Down the page, toward the bottom. Goes onto the next."

She pointed at the article about icy deaths. "We certainly have seen more than a few souls dead from exposure come through The Pyre the last couple of weeks, especially with the temperature dropping lower every night."

"Yep." Hank snorted. "Fred the mule can't hardly keep up."

"I don't know what we'll do if this continues on like it is. Ling and Gart have bodies stacked like cordwood in the shed out back. Near full to the rafters." Her two-man, grave-digging crew had been scratching their heads lately about what to do with the corpses until they could put them in the ground. "Have those boys had any luck thawing the earth enough to dig at Ingleside?"

"Yup. But it's a slow, cold job. Can't keep up with the current business we're doin' here. 'Specially since extra fire fuel's hard to acquire presently, what with ever'body fightin' for wood and coal oil. Reminds me. Earp dumped his logs out front. I'll help the boys saw it up and stack it out back so's nobody gets the temptation to borrow it. Anyway, Ling sounds near to quit'n but Gart likes the pay, and if Gart don't quit, Ling won't neither."

"They're due some bonus. Maybe a few extra coins will keep

A Long Way From Ordinary

Ling happy."

Hank grunted in agreement. "I s'pose you still need to thaw the dead out, at least an itty bit, 'nough to see if they been stuck or not. And check teeth."

"More than ever."

Signs of trouble had been showing up more and more often in the last couple of weeks in the form of a symbol she'd found in one form or another on several corpses. The *caper-sus* emblem, which looked like a goat melting into a pig, seemed to be spreading. In addition, each victim with this branding or ring had been slain in a similar method—first a slicing of the tendon that Clementine figured was meant to hobble, and then a deep thrust of a blade through the lower jaw up into the brain or between the ribs to pierce the heart.

Quick, efficient deaths.

"The killer is back to work. But I haven't noticed any missing teeth since Big Joe." Weeks back, a few bodies had come through The Pyre missing a canine tooth.

"Don't comprehend takin' teeth from a dead man." Hank wrinkled his upper lip and poked at an exposed canine. He shuddered. "Downright revoltin'. Savage. Ain't enough to lay a man out, gotta violate his body, too."

Savage? Clementine considered that. There was something to this style of murder beyond desecration or defilement. In each instance, the tooth had been taken post mortem, and always the maxillary canine. Something else was at play here. Ritualistic perhaps, or possibly a trophy for a kill.

Hank was right. "It does seem savage, doesn't it?" Unlike the other execution-style killings.

"Yup. Causes me a little infirmity to think 'bout it." He leaned down and stroked Tinker's back, probably more to calm himself than Tinker.

In any case, there was an assassin out there responsible for some of the deaths. The slayings were precise, calculated.

Clementine wondered if she was being taunted?

Or was the killer like Clementine, an executioner hired to complete a job? If so, who was the beneficiary of these deaths? She had heard the words "rogue executioner" thrown about last month behind closed doors. Perhaps this slayer wasn't a rogue at a—

"Miss Clem, it's the next one down there, toward the bottom."

She focused on the sheet, scanning to the next item.

The rush is on! Again.

Recall, if you will, three weeks previous minus a day, the earth rumbled. The blast rattled glass and tin. Its origin, now established and confirmed, the abandoned, or rather previously abandoned, Golden Echo, in the area northwest of Gayville.

"Shouldn't a used so much blastin' powder," Hank said softly. "I knew better."

"What's done is done. After what we went through in that mine, we wanted it sealed. Both of us did." She squeezed his shoulder. "And I was glad to have you by my side, Hank."

He raised one side of his mouth into a lopsided smile and nodded at the paper for her to continue.

The subsequent search exposed neither the scoundrel responsible nor any victim of same, but the revelation of things more interesting indeed. Gold!

Prospector and city dandy alike commenced scouring the hills behind Gayville in hopes of becoming the next Comstock.

The claim was legally located, prospected and staked, but the owners, numbering and including three brothers, have been missing for slightly short of five months.

Reports indicate color varying from dust to nuggets as large in size as to fill a man's open hand are being taken from the

> *mine and it is said that veins run thick and deep into the mountain.*
>
> *The mine is generally considered abandoned, whether legally or otherwise, and as such, is claimed by an assembly of men of the opportunistic sort.*
>
> *Consequently, there is much discord and hostility in the area with four deaths and many fracases reported.*
>
> *We note that there has been neither demonstrable concern for the three brothers nor discernable intent to verify their well-being.*
>
> *Increasing numbers of men continue to occupy the area with equipment and a dismaying number of firearms.*
>
> *It is the opinion of the Trailblazer staff that the town of Gayville, possibly with the help of the miner court of Deadwood, rectify the growing problem without delay.*

"Damn it," Clementine muttered.

"That was my assessment."

"We're sitting on one massive powder keg here in the Black Hills, Hank. They'll open the Golden Echo mine again and follow that gold seam into the earth. To the very end. There's no stopping it. The gate will be opened again … eventually."

And then all hell would break loose.

Hank cocked his head and frowned at her. "We'll go right up that mountainside and seal it up again." He nodded once, apparently agreeing with himself.

"Maybe, but not yet. I think we have time until they remove all of that rock." The gold would keep luring them back, though. The avarice of men was so heightened by the prospect of striking it rich in these hills that Clementine didn't think sealing off the mine again was the final solution. She'd need to exterminate the vermin at the source. "Besides, that's not our biggest problem at the moment."

One of his eyebrows shot up. "It ain't?"

She didn't know if Hank was prepared to hear the extent of what she suspected was happening in the Black Hills.

Men and women were pouring into the gulches and filling them up with humanity. It was a virtually endless supply of *livestock*, as Clementine had heard them called. Humans arriving in the Hills with not a penny in a pocket, their last few dollars spent on the trip here, only to find that gold did not pave the streets. There were no fist-sized nuggets to pick from the streams as they had been told. Even worse, the prospects of anything regarding financial security did not materialize the moment they stepped from their horses or carriages. In short, they had arrived in the cold, icy realm of Hell, or whichever version of the Underworld they preferred.

All of these desperate souls offered a unique opportunity for the worst sort of evil to build armies. The increase in bodies bearing rings, burn scars, and even tattoos with the *caper-sus* emblem supported Clementine's suspicion that someone was recruiting these people for their nefarious plans.

But who was killing them? The rogue executioner? If so, to what end? Could Clementine's benefactor have summoned more than one slayer to do his bidding?

Aha! Maybe that was the answer. She looked at Hank. He stared back with both eyebrows raised, but she wasn't prepared to share her suspicion just yet.

She changed the subject. "Were you planning to stop by the Cricket this evening?"

He scrunched up one side of his face. "Don't cotton to that place. Swearengen likes them prizefights. Rowdy crowd there. That man sells a ruckus, that's what I say. Swearengen's a swindler, is what *they* say. Don't cotton."

"Where then? Belle Grande?"

"Prob'ly. Lose my money there, though. Card sharps. Good beer. Prob'ly go th—"

A series of thumps on the front door interrupted Hank.

A Long Way From Ordinary

"More business, maybe." He opened the door to a tall, lean man wearing a thick sheepskin coat.

"Jack Rabbit!"

"Ho there, Hank!" Jack Fields's grin lit up his face. "Damn, it's good to see you!"

Hank reached out and bear-hugged Jack, lifting the taller man off the ground. He shook him and then dropped him back onto his boots.

Another man stepped into the doorway behind Jack, his shoulders wider, his head a few inches taller, his black hat marred by a single bullet hole.

"Boone!" Hank grabbed Boone McCreery's hand in both of his and shook it vigorously. "It sure is mighty good to see the both of ya! Look Miss Clem, it's the Santa Fe Sidewinders." He stepped aside and pushed the pair into the room, closing the door behind them.

"Howdy, Miss Clementine. You're a sight for tired eyes." Jack grabbed the hat from his head, put it to his chest, and bowed toward Clementine.

"Hello, Jack." She crossed the room and hugged the blond traveler. He smelled fresh from the outside. The leather of his coat felt cool under her hands. "It's good to see you two here safe and sound," she said as she stepped back and turned to Boone, meeting his green eyes. "Welcome back, Boone."

Boone raised his hat to her and then whipped it against his leg, powdery snow swirling to the floor at his feet. "Rabbit's right, Clementine. You surely are a sight for some tired eyes."

She laughed, looking down at her old wool shirt and denim men's trousers. "I'm a sight, all right." Clementine hugged him. Boone was one of the few men she'd met who stood taller than she, besting her by a couple of inches. He smelled fresh from the outdoors, as well, his short beard tickling her cheek before she pulled away. When she stepped back, she feasted her gaze on the two men, far too happy to see them again. "You weren't due in for another couple of days according to Hank."

"That is correct, Miss Clementine," Jack said. "But Booney here kept pushin'. Nickel and Dime ain't none too happy about it either."

Boone glanced at her, the look on his face edging on sheepish. "A winter trail isn't a place to waste time, especially in Wyoming or the Dakota Territory."

"That's sure enough," Hank said. "You both got real clothes, looks like. Glad to see it. Winter's just gettin' started around here." Hank rubbed the sleeves of their thick sheepskin coats.

"So you know," Jack said to Boone, "I still didn't like the ride up here from Santa Fe any more than I did last time. Hey, Tink!" Jack dropped to his knees and began to ruffle the dog's fur. He smooshed his face against hers. Tinker mirrored his excitement with a swooshing rump and slobbery tongue, yipping and whining her excitement.

Clementine chuckled, glancing up to find Boone watching her with a hint of a smile. "You did a fine job taking care of Tink, Clementine. Thank you."

Her face warmed at his gratitude. "It was my pleasure. She's a sweetheart. Hank helped as well, bringing her bones and treats each morning."

Hank waved off her words, grinning as he watched Jack play with Tinker. "I'll get Keller to squeeze Nickel and Dime in at the livery. You boys got a place to sleep? Doesn't matter, you stay with me, up in Keller's hayloft above the stable. He charges me enough to cover you two along with me."

"With the line forming out front, I'm guessing business must be good." Boone pointed his thumb toward the window.

Line forming? "What do you mean?" Clementine asked.

"The body you're storing out front?"

Clementine exchanged frowns with Hank before striding to the door. She marched out onto the porch with Hank on her tail.

Out front were the four coffins Ling and Gart had propped

A Long Way From Ordinary

up against The Pyre's façade. "Advertising," Gart had said.

Three of the pine boxes were empty. She stood in front of the fourth, her hands on her hips. A body had been placed neatly in the tipped coffin. A man with his hands folded over his lower abdomen as if prepared for a parade of mourners to pass by and pay respects.

"Where'd this'n come from?" Hank muttered under his breath, scratching his jaw.

"What the hell is going on, Hank?" Clementine asked in a quiet voice. She glanced up and down the street, wondering who might have left this dead man on her doorstep.

"I surely don't know, Miss Clem. I'll take him in and put him on the table."

Jack stepped out to help Hank carry the body into the exam room. "It's a fine welcome back to Deadwood you arranged for us, Hank. Thank you kindly."

Hank snickered. "Happy to welcome you, Jack Rabbit."

After they'd settled the dead man on her exam table, she donned her leather work apron. "You boys can warm yourself by the fire if you'd like." She pointed toward the parlor. "There's coffee on the stove and some of those biscuits you like left over from breakfast. Hank has been doing his best to fatten Tinker and me up while you've been gone."

She followed the men into the parlor while tying her apron.

Boone slid out of his coat and carefully picked up Tinker. "You're looking like a young pup again, girl. I see Clementine and Hank have taken extra good care of you." He sat in one of the chairs by the fire with Tinker on his lap. Jack poured a cup of coffee and plopped into the chair beside Boone.

"I'll be just a few minutes." With that she left them to it and crossed into the exam room, where she prepared her instruments and grabbed her notebook.

Hank joined her shortly. "Who would have left him without informing us?" she asked.

He shook his head. "No rigor in him. Ain't frozen stiff. Wasn't there when I came in neither. Purt near fresh."

He fetched the measuring rule and they began the exercise they'd completed too many times to count since Clementine had hired him as an assistant at The Pyre a few short months ago. They measured the dead man's height and guessed his weight. Hank waited by the exam room stove while Clementine circled the table, scrutinizing him from head to toe.

The body was well-dressed, compared to most in Deadwood. Wool coat, hat, and pants. Stout leather boots.

She took up her notebook and wrote:

> *Adult male, approximately mid-twenties. Appropriate clothing for winter in Deadwood. Apparently well-nourished. No sign of exposure. Beard matted with blood but the injury is obscured.*

She'd explore that wound shortly. Setting down her notebook, she looked over at Hank. "Let's remove his clothes."

Hank grimaced, "Don't like this part."

"That makes two of us."

He started tugging on the dead man's boots while Clementine worked his arms free of the coat. Hank draped a muslin rag over the corpse's waist, muttering something about letting the man keep his "dignity."

Clementine stood over the body, staring at the brand on his chest. *Caper-sus* again.

"The placement of that brand reminds me of the man left at the back door shortly before Boone and Jack left for Santa Fe."

"If you say so, Miss Clem."

Oh, right. Hank hadn't been there to see that one. Boone and Jack had helped relocate the body to her table that day.

"Boone! Jack!" She called toward the parlor. "Will you come in here, please?"

She began checking the pockets of his coat as she waited,

A Long Way From Ordinary

looking for anything that might help identify who she had on her table. She found a piece of paper in one pocket, unfolded it and read:

Are you paying attention?

"Are you paying attention?" she repeated aloud.

"What's that, Clementine?" Boone joined her. He did a double-take at the corpse on the table. "He's been branded."

"Just like before," Jack said, leaning against the other exam table.

They confirmed her memory.

"Look at this." She handed Boone the note and began examining the man's body. She found no sign of any other injuries save the blood-soaked beard. He even had all his teeth. She felt around under his chin and found a small puncture.

"Jack, will you hand me that metal rod on the tray over there?" She pointed at the tray of instruments near her desk.

He obliged. "What's that for?"

She held the rod up between them. "You might want to look away," she said and then eased the rod into the hole under the dead man's chin. Listening, she leaned closer and slowly pushed it up until it clunked against the inside of his skull.

No familiar clink of metal.

"He wasn't shot." A glance up at her companions found each had turned a pale shade of gray, their faces a mixture of cringes and pained expressions.

She slowly moved the rod around in a small circle, exploring, trying to assess the damage done by … what? A blade? She pulled the rod back out. It came free with a sucking slurp.

All three men groaned.

"Miss Clem," Hank said, his whole face pinched tight. "That's revoltin'."

Boone turned away, saying over his shoulder, "Sounded like you were stirring porridge."

"I'm going to play with Tink." Jack hustled out of the room.

She wiped the rod clean with a strip of cloth. "I suspect this man was slain by the same individual who left the corpse at my back door before you headed for Santa Fe."

"Same brand too, isn't it?" Boone still had his back to her.

"Yes. But this one is different."

He turned, his gaze narrowed. "How so?"

"This man was well-dressed and fed. He's been taken care of or had the wherewithal to take care of himself."

Boone shot a quick look at the dead man. "The body left at the back door was extra lean," he said. "Hadn't been eating too well for a while. Clothes were threadbare. You're right. You make something of that?"

"Maybe." She crossed to her desk and pulled a piece of paper from her drawer, handing it to Boone, who had followed her. "This is the note from before you left. It's the same handwriting."

"Looks like it." He frowned down at the two notes. "Not signed with the letter P, though."

Clementine nodded, focusing on the corpse again. " 'Are you paying attention,' " she repeated the words on the paper. "If I were to guess, this man was higher up in rank. Possibly."

"Have you seen any rings or brandings with the *caper-sus* emblem since we left?"

"Yes, but not during the first week. Business has been up in general—namely due to exposure, accidents, and murders. But none of those who came through The Pyre during the first week after you left wore the sign. Then it started up again, slowly, one a day, sometimes two. But now we're seeing it more and more." She looked to Hank. "Right?"

"Yes, ma'am. Downright busy with 'em anymore."

"There's something else," she told Boone.

"Oh?"

"There seem to be two different forms of the *caper-sus* and no

A Long Way From Ordinary

discrimination in death." She opened a wooden box on her desk and pulled out two rings, handing them to Boone.

He studied each and then held one up. "This one has a curved horn, like a ram. And this one," he held up the other, "looks like some type of antelope horn on the goat. Is that the only difference?"

"That I can see."

"Do you think we're dealing with two different ... what was it you called them?"

"Cults." She nodded. "That would be my guess. It's possible that there are two rivals vying for some sort of control here in the Black Hills."

He lowered the rings, his gaze searching hers. "What aren't you telling me?"

"It's possible that one of them is led by the benefactor with whom I'm contracted to help."

Boone leaned against the desk. "It's becoming apparent there is a lot you know that Rabbit and I don't."

Clementine grimaced. "This reminds me of a quote from the saga of Hen-Thorir, an old Norse tale my amma used to tell me."

"Amma?" He handed her back the rings.

"My grandmother." She tucked them in her desk drawer.

"Is this a story about Vikings conquering insurmountable odds to win a battle?"

"Not quite. It's a tale about infighting that develops between neighbors and includes some people being burned alive and others beheaded. But it does end with a marriage, if that makes you feel better."

"What's the quote, Miss Clem?" Hank asked.

"That which has a bad beginning is likely to have a bad ending."

Boone frowned at Hank. "Has she always been this uplifting?"

"That's a question for later." Hank patted Boone on the shoulder. "I got just the place for you and Jack Rabbit. Good steaks and beer and maybe we can shuffle some cards. Then I'll take ya back to my roost for some shuteye. It might smell some, but it's comfortable and almost warm. Won't cost ya nothin' neither."

Look for the next book in the Deadwood Undertaker Series in late summer 2019.

Reader Questions for Ann & Sam

How long will we have to wait for book #2?
Aiming for late summer 2019.

What do you really think of Deadwood and how far out is the series going?
We love Deadwood! We go there at least once every year (Ann's mom lives in the northern Black Hills). The Deadwood and Lead area are loaded with character.
As for the series length, the story will tell itself. We are just the scribes writing it all down for you.

How do you cope with disagreements on subjects that come up on the writing?
We argue.

Who is your favorite character in the new series? Which one do you relate to?
Sam: I think Hank is probably the most fun to hang with, but Rabbit is fun too.
Ann: I like Clementine, but I relate best to Fred the mule.

Have you ever lived in Deadwood?
Not yet, but…

With all that's going on in your family with kids, pets, and now both of you writing, how do you find balance in your life (besides lots of tequila)?
We haven't seen balance since our first child was born. We are told by other parents that this is the new "norm."

What part of the author world do you like and dislike the most?
Sam: I enjoy sinking down into a story during the writing process. I don't enjoy an empty page with a blinking cursor.

Ann: I like creating scenes that make me laugh as I type. I dislike the bookkeeping part with a passion.

This one is for Sam: Have you ever written before, and if not, what finally inspired you to take the leap? How did you come up with the name Sam Lucky (almost like a character in a private detective novel)?
Sam: I've written a few things here and there over the years. As for my inspiration, it was time and this series is right up my alley. I love westerns and paranormal, so it seemed like a natural progression. In regards to the name "Sam Lucky," he answered the casting call and knocked our hats off with his performance.

Do you see dead people too? What is it about y'all's books that make a person not able to put them down til the last chapter has been finished?
Not yet, but we're always on the lookout for them. As for the books, it's a secret recipe we can't give out, but thank you for reading!

For Sam: How was it working with Ann, and what made you decide to do it?
Torture. Absolute torture. Wait ... is Ann going to read this? In that case, it was amazing. (LOL!)
It was time. There were stories to be told and I wanted to tell them with her.

Did you find it difficult to incorporate the Deadwood characters into the story?
No, it was actually fun to weave the story worlds together.

How do you research for your writing?
Books, books, books, internet, internet "rabbit holes," books.

Did Deadwood really have a female undertaker back in the day, or was that made up for the book?
There were female undertakers, but not in Deadwood (according to what we've read).

What do you like better, research or writing?
Sam: Research is a lot of fun. I've always enjoyed learning more about places and events, but it is fun to use that new knowledge to tell a tale.

Ann: Research! Especially when it involves seeing how many tequila shots are required to make one a little versus a LOT drunk.

Was the decision to write together in any way influenced by tequila?
Tequila started this …

        Tequila will end it.

CPSIA information can be obtained
at www.ICGtesting.com
Printed in the USA
LVHW050827160521
687567LV00001B/146